THE INFINITY BOX

THE
INFINITY
BOX

*A collection of
speculative fiction*

KATE
WILHELM

*HARPER & ROW
PUBLISHERS
New York, Evanston
San Francisco, London*

For Vicky, with love and appreciation

CONTENTS

THE INFINITY BOX

INTRODUCTION

Some of my happiest memories of growing up involve wandering between the stacks at the public library. I evolved a number of systems of selecting books, but the most successful was dividing the eight books (the limit then) between fiction and nonfiction in an orderly way. I picked two nonfiction books each trip, starting with A—anthropology—and working through; one book of short stories, and when they ran out, all too fast, I moved on to plays; and five novels. Again I started with A, and went through the alphabet. When I found an author I particularly liked, I read everything by him or her. If that wasn't enough, I selected by association, and in that way I read all the other Russian writers when I had finished with Tolstoi.

Meanwhile, changes were being made in the library. A new stack was added in one of the back corners to shelve the mysteries. I didn't care; I had my system, and I stuck to it, only now I added a mystery from time to time. Then another stack was tucked away back there, and it was for westerns. I recall the romantic, mythical world of Zane Grey with great affection, and I am glad that when I was twelve he had not yet been categorized, or I might have missed him. A new stack appeared much later—science fiction.

I think with sadness sometimes of the people who now go

directly to one of those stacks and take their limit; and of the others who avoid them altogether because they *know* they don't like those categories.

The problem with labels is that they all too quickly become eroded; they cannot cope with borderline cases at all. The books each label includes and excludes finally distort the label and render it meaningless. Science fiction came to mean almost everything that was not mundane, realistic fiction: aliens, galactic wars, robots, social satires, heroic fantasy. . . . No matter how expanded the label came to be, it was not comprehensive enough, and presently a new label was trundled out: speculative fiction. Quite likely most readers have their own ideas about what science fiction is or should be, and speculative fiction seldom fits neatly into the confines of those predetermined boundaries. Moreover, each writer who calls what he does speculative fiction, no doubt has his own definition of what his or her fiction actually is.

Speculative fiction as I define and use it involves the exploration of worlds that probably never will exist, that I don't believe in as real, that I don't expect the reader to accept as real, but that are realistically handled in order to investigate them, because for one reason or another they are the worlds we most dread or yearn for.

Who doesn't want to go back and change the past at certain vital points? Who doesn't want to write the script of his own daily life? In "The Time Piece" and "Man of Letters" I do both. In these two stories, in all my stories, I tried to be as honest as possible and answer What would it *really* be like?

What would it be like to live in the dream world, or the nightmare? What would it be like to be there when the wrong village and the wrong war meet? If you don't believe, you haven't been reading the papers for the past ten years.

The forms of corruption are many and varied; we are very skilled at recognizing it at the national level, but how corruptible is your neighbor, your spouse? You? Power and corruption, a pair of gloves that slide on so easily, that feel warm and comforting, until it is time to remove them. This was the genesis of the title story, "The Infinity Box." What kind of inner resources would a man need to resist a perversion that seemed irresistible and undiscoverable? I kept getting so many disparate images, scenes, actions that demanded to be part of this story that for a time I despaired of ever weaving them together, but then I discovered when I put them side by side, in an order of sorts, the edges of all those pieces seemed to flow together to make a whole. As soon as I knew I had the shape of a story I began to work on it, and no longer worried about too many parts. They were like pieces of a jigsaw puzzle that fill an entire table until they are put together.

The paranoia of pregnancy is caused by: (1) glandular secretions; (2) hormonal changes; (3) changes in the metabolism; (4) the presence of another person within one's body; (5) a latent instability; (6) the dehumanization of the patient by modern technology; . . . (N) Unknown. Choose one and only one, or all, or none. No matter which you chose, you are in good company. It has a ring, doesn't it? The paranoia of pregnancy. This phrase objectified, made concrete, rationalized, became "April Fools' Day Forever."

Some dreamers yearn for a return to an agrarian society, a return to a natural state where there are no polluting factories, where energy is something one's ancestors were obsessed with. I find this both tiresome and alarming, and I wonder if they have realized what the intermediate steps would be like. The breakdown of a civilization is not pretty, cannot be made pretty. If civilization crumbles, my story "The Red Canary" might be a prelude to an accelerating slide down the magic glass mountain.

Can a cataclysmic upheaval result in Utopia? Suppose you know exactly the society you wish to create; you have the methods to achieve it, and absolute control over the children and their education. Isn't this the ideal situation? When I thought about it at length, I knew that when the means are unworthy of the end, the end becomes ashes. Then I wrote "The Funeral."

If one could see into the future, would one be able to take that first step toward it? I mused about this, forgot it, and when it came back to me again, I saw that there wasn't one future, not for the protagonist in my story "Where Have You Been, Billy Boy, Billy Boy?", but rather several. Perhaps this is why we can see only backward in time.

This is how I work. I don't go out looking for story ideas, but now and then an article, sometimes no more than a phrase, will catch on something in my mind, a rough spot maybe, and it will stay there undergoing metamorphosis; accretions collect, and when the idea surfaces again, there may or may not be enough for a story, but at that time I always know a story is happening. If it is still more space than content, I try to forget it again, send it back where it can grow undisturbed, gather other bits that have also been examined, however briefly, and put away until later. Sooner or later the idea serves up images, scenes, a character. When that happens, I know I am ready to work with the material, mold it, add whatever I can to give it depth, other dimensions, actual people. The finished stories are often not realistic in the sense of the materialists—you won't find my worlds in your road atlases—but they are always very real psychically. And the psychic landscape has a more enduring reality than suburbia U.S.A. can ever achieve.

K. W.

THE
INFINITY
BOX

It was a bad day from beginning to end. Late in the afternoon, just when I was ready to light the fuse to blow up the lab, with Lenny in it, Janet called from the hospital.

"Honey, it's the little Bronson boy. We can't do anything with him, and he has his mother and father in a panic. He's sure that we're trying to electrocute him, and they half believe it. They're demanding that we take the cast off and remove the suit."

Lenny sat watching my face. He began to move things out of reach: the glass of pencils, coffee mugs, ashtray. . . .

"Can't Groppi do anything?" He was the staff psychologist.

"Not this time. He doesn't really understand the suit either. I think he's afraid of it. Can you come over here and talk to them?"

"Sure. Sure. We just blew up about five thousand dollars' worth of equipment with a faulty transformer. Lenny's quitting again. Some son of a bitch mislaid our order for wafer resisters. . . . I'll be over in half an hour."

"What?" Lenny asked. He looked like a dope, thick build, the biggest pair of hands you'd ever see outside a football field, shoulders that didn't need padding to look padded. Probably he was one of the best electronics men in the world. He was forty-six, and had brought up three sons alone. He never mentioned their mother and I didn't know if she was dead, or just gone. He was my partner in the firm of Laslow and Leonard Electronics.

"The Bronson kid's scared to death of the suit we put on him yesterday. First time they turned it on, he panicked. I'll run over and see. Where's that sleeve?" I rummaged futilely and Lenny moved stolidly toward a cabinet and pulled out the muslin sleeve and small control box. Once in a while he'd smile, but that was the only emotion that I'd ever seen on his face, a quiet smile, usually when something worked against the odds, or when his sons did something exceptionally nice—like get a full paid scholarship to MIT, or Harvard, as the third one had done that fall.

"Go on home after you see the kid," Lenny said. "I'll clean up in here and try to run down the wafers."

"Okay. See you tomorrow."

Children's Hospital was fifteen miles away, traffic was light at that time of day, and I made it under the half hour I'd promised. Janet met me in the downstairs foyer.

"Eddie, did you bring the sleeve? I thought maybe if you let Mr. Bronson feel it . . ."

I held it up and she grinned. Janet, suntanned, with red, sun-streaked hair, freckles, and lean to the point of thinness, was my idea of a beautiful woman. We had been married for twelve years.

"Where are the parents?"

"In Dr. Reisman's office. They were just upsetting Mike more than he was already."

"Okay, first Mike. Come on."

Mike Bronson was eight. Three months ago, the first day of school vacation, he had been run over and killed by a diesel truck. He had been listed DOA; someone had detected an echo of life, but they said he couldn't survive the night. They operated, and gave him a week, then a month, and six weeks ago they had done more surgery and said probably he'd make it. Crushed spine, crushed pelvis, multiple fractures in both legs. One of the problems was that the boy was eight, and growing. His hormonal system didn't seem to get the message that he was critically injured, and that things should stop for a year or so, and that meant that his body cast had to be changed frequently and it meant that while his bones grew together again, and lengthened, his muscles would slowly atrophy, and when he was removed from the cast finally, there'd be a bundle of bones held together by pale skin and not much else.

At Mike's door I motioned for Janet to stay outside. One more white uniform, I thought, he didn't need right now. They had him in a private room, temporarily, I assumed, because of his reaction to the suit. He couldn't move his head, but he heard me come in, and when I got near enough so he could see me, his eyes were wide with fear. He was a good-looking boy with big brown eyes that knew too much of pain and fear.

"You a cub scout?" I asked.

He could talk some, a throaty whisper, when he wanted to. He didn't seem to want to then. I waited a second or two, then said, "You know what a ham radio set is, I suppose. If you could learn the Morse code, I could fix a wire so that you could use the key." I was looking around his bed, as if to see if it could be done, talking to myself. "Put a screen with the code up there, where you could see it. Sort of a learning machine. Work the wire with your tongue at first, until they uncover your hands anyway. Course not everybody wants to talk to Australia or Russia or Brazil or ships at sea. All done with wires, some people are afraid of wires and things like that."

He was watching me intently now, his eyes following my gaze as I studied the space above his head. He was ready to deal in five minutes. "You stop bitching about the suit, and I start on the ham set. Right?" His eyes sparkled at that kind of language and he whispered, "Right."

"Now the parents," I told Janet in the hall. "He's okay."

Bronson was apelike, with great muscular, hairy forearms. I never did say who I was, or why I was there, anything at all. "Hold out your arm," I ordered. He looked from me to Dr. Reisman, who was in a sweat by then. The doctor nodded. I put the sleeve on his arm, then put an inflatable splint on it, inflating it slightly more than was necessary, but I was mad. "Move your fingers," I ordered. He tried. I attached the jack to the sleeve wire and plugged it in, and then I played his arm and hand muscles like a piano. He gaped. "That's what we're doing to your son. If we don't do it, when he comes out of that cast he'll be like a stick doll. His muscles will waste away to nothing. He'll weigh twenty-five pounds, maybe." That was a guess, but it made the point. "Every time they change the cast, we change the program, so that every muscle in his body will be stimulated under computer control, slightly at first, then stronger and stronger as he gets better." I started to undo the splint. The air came out with a teakettle hiss. "You wouldn't dream of telling Dr. Thorne how to operate on your boy. Don't tell me my business, unless you know it better than I do."

"But . . . Did it hurt?" Mrs. Bronson asked.

"No," Bronson said, flexing his fingers. "It just tingled a little bit. Felt sort of good."

I removed the sleeve and folded it carefully, and at the door I heard Mrs. Bronson's whisper, "Who is he?" and Janet's haughty answer, "That's Edward Laslow, the inventor of the Laslow Suit."

Enrico Groppi met me in the corridor. "I just came from Mike's room. Thanks. Want a drink?" Groppi was an eclectic—he took from here, there, anything that worked he was willing to incorporate into his system.

"That's an idea." I followed him to his office, left word for Janet to meet me there, and tried not to think about the possibility that the suit wouldn't work, that I'd built up false hopes, that Mike would come to hate me and everything I symbolized. . . .

I drove Janet home, leaving her car in the hospital lot overnight. That meant that I'd have to drive her to work in the morning, but it seemed too silly to play follow the leader back the county roads. To get home we took the interstate highway first, then a four-lane state road, then a two-lane county road, then a right turn off onto a dirt road, and that was ours. Sweet Brier Lane. Five one-acre lots, with woods all around, and a hill behind us, and a brook. If any of us prayed at all, it was only that the county engineers wouldn't discover the existence of Sweet Brier Lane and come in with their bulldozers and road-building equipment and turn us into a real development.

Our house was the third one on the narrow road. First on the left was Bill Glaser, a contractor, nice fellow if you didn't have to do more than wave and say hi from time to time. Then on the right came the Donlevy house that had been empty for almost three years while Peter Donlevy was engaged in an exchange program with teachers from England. He was at Cambridge, and from the Christmas cards that we got from them, they might never return. Then, again on the right, our house, set far back behind oak trees that made grass-growing almost impossible. Farther down and across the lane was Earl Klinger's house. He was with the math department of the university. And finally the lane dead-ended at the driveway of Lucas Malek and his wife. He was in his sixties, retired from the insurance business, and to be avoided if possible. An immigrant from East Europe, Hungary or some place like that, he was bored and talked endlessly if encouraged. We were on polite, speaking terms with everyone on the lane, but the Donlevys had been our friends; with them gone, we had drawn inward, and had very little to do with the neighbors. We could have borrowed sugar from any of them, or got a lift to town, or counted on them to call the fire department if our house started to burn down, but there was no close camaraderie there.

It was our fault. If we had wanted friends we certainly could have found them in that small group of talented and intelligent people. But we were busy. Janet with her work at the hospital where she was a physical therapist, and I at my laboratory that was just now after fourteen years starting to show a bit of profit. It could have got out of the red earlier, but Lenny and I both believed in updating the equipment whenever possible, so it had taken time.

It was a warm day, early in September, without a hint yet that summer had had it. I had the windows open, making talk impossible. Janet and I could talk or not. There were still times when we stayed up until morning, just talking, and then again weeks went by with nothing more than the sort of thing that has to take place between husband and wife. No strain either way, nothing but ease lay between us. We had a good thing, and we knew it.

We were both startled, and a little upset, when we saw a moving van and a dilapidated station wagon in the driveway of the Donlevy house.

"They wouldn't come back without letting us know," Janet said.

"Not a chance. Maybe they sold it."

"But without a sign, or any real-estate people coming around?"

"They could have been here day after day without our knowing."

"But not without Ruth Klinger knowing about it. She would have told us."

I drove past the house slowly, craning to see something that would give a hint. Only the station wagon, with a Connecticut plate. It was an eight-year-old model, in need of a paint job. It didn't look too hopeful.

Every afternoon a woman from a nearby subdivision came to stay with the children and to straighten up generally until we got home. Mrs. Durrell was as mystified as we about the van and the newcomer.

"Haven't seen a sign of anyone poking about over there. Rusty says that they're just moving boxes in, heavy boxes." Rusty, eleven, probably knew exactly how many boxes, and their approximate weight. "The kids are down at the brook watching them unload," Mrs. Durrell went on. "They're hoping for more kids, I guess. Rusty keeps coming up to report, and so far, only one woman, and a lot of boxes." She talked herself out of the kitchen, across the terrace, and down the drive to her car, her voice fading out gradually.

Neither Pete Donlevy nor I had any inclination for gardening, and our yards, separated by the brook, were heavily wooded, so that his house was not visible from ours, but down at the brook there was a clear view between the trees. While Janet changed into shorts and sandals, I wandered down to have a look along with Rusty and Laura. They were both Janet's kids. Redheads, with freckles, and vivid blue-green eyes, skinny arms and legs; sometimes I found myself studying one or the other of them intently for a hint of my genes there, without success. Laura was eight. I spotted her first, sitting on the bridge made of two fallen trees. We had lopped the branches off and the root mass and just left them there. Pete Donlevy and I had worked three weekends on those trees, cutting up the branches for our fireplaces, rolling the two trunks close together to make a footbridge. We had consumed approximately ten gallons of beer during those weekends.

"Hi, Dad," Rusty called from above me. I located him high on the right-angled branch of an oak tree. "We have a new neighbor."

I nodded and sat down next to Laura. "Any kids?"

"No. Just a lady so far."

"Young? Old? Fat?"

"Tiny. I don't know if young or old, can't tell. She runs around like young."

"With lots of books," Rusty said from his better vantage point.

"No furniture?"

"Nope. Just suitcases and a trunk full of clothes, and boxes of books. And cameras, and tripods."

"And a black-and-white dog," Laura added.

I tossed bits of bark into the brook and watched them bob and whirl their way downstream. Presently we went back to the house, and later we grilled hamburgers on the terrace, and had watermelon for dessert. I didn't get a glimpse of the tiny lady.

Sometime during the night I was brought straight up in bed by a wail that was animal-like, thin, high-pitched, inhuman. "Laura!"

Janet was already out of bed; in the pale light from the hall, she was a flash of white gown darting out the doorway. The wail was repeated, and by then I was on my way to Laura's room too.

She was standing in the middle of the floor, her short pajamas white, her eyes wide open, showing mostly white also. Her hands were partially extended before her, fingers widespread, stiff.

"Laura!" Janet said. It was a command, low-voiced, but imperative. The child didn't move. I put my arm about her shoulders, not wanting to frighten her more than she was by the nightmare. She was rigid and unmoving, as stiff as a catatonic.

"Pull back the sheet," I told Janet. "I'll carry her back to bed." It was like lifting a wooden dummy. No response, no flexibility, no life. My skin crawled, and fear made a sour taste in my mouth. Back in her bed, Laura suddenly sighed, and her eyelids fluttered once or twice, then closed and she was in a normal sleep. I lifted her hand, her wrist was limp, her fingers dangled loosely.

Janet stayed with her for a few minutes, but she didn't wake up, and finally Janet joined me in the kitchen, where I had poured a glass of milk and was sipping it.

"I never saw anything like that," Janet said. She was pale, and shaking.

"A nightmare, honey. Too much watermelon, or something. More than likely she won't remember anything about it. Just as well."

We didn't discuss it. There wasn't anything to say. Who knows anything about nightmares? But I had trouble getting back to sleep again, and when I did, I dreamed off and on the rest of the night, waking up time after time with the memory of a dream real enough to distort my thinking so that I couldn't know if I was sleeping in bed, or floating somewhere else and dreaming of the bed.

Laura didn't remember any of the dream, but she was fascinated, and wanted to talk about it: what had she been doing when we found her? how had she sounded when she shrieked? and so on. After about five minutes it got to be a bore and I refused to say another word. Mornings were always bad anyway; usually I was the last to leave the house, but that morning I had to drive Janet to work, so we all left at the same time, the kids to catch the schoolbus at the end of the lane, Janet to go to the hospital, and me to go to the lab eventually. At the end of the lane when I stopped to let the kids hop out, we saw our new neighbor. She was walking a Dalmatian, and she smiled and nodded. But Laura surprised us all by calling out to her, greeting her like a real friend. When I drove away I could see them standing there, the dog sniffing the kids interestedly, the woman and Laura talking.

"Well," was all I could think to say. Laura usually was the shy one, the last to make friends with people, the last to speak to company, the first to break away from a group of strangers.

"She seems all right," Janet said.

"Let's introduce ourselves tonight. Maybe she's someone from around here, someone from school." And I wondered where else Laura could have met her without our meeting her also.

We didn't meet her that day.

I got tied up, and it was after eight when I got home, tired and disgusted by a series of mishaps again at the lab. Janet didn't help by saying that maybe we had too many things going at once for just the two of us to keep track of. Knowing she was right didn't make the comment any easier to take. Lenny and I were jealous of our shop and lab. We didn't want to bring in an outsider, and secretly I knew that I didn't want to be bothered with the kind of bookkeeping that would be involved.

"You can't have it both ways," Janet said. Sometimes she didn't know when to drop it. "Either you remain at the level you were at a couple of years ago, patenting little things every so often, and leave the big jobs to the companies that have the manpower, or else you let your staff grow along with your ideas."

I ate warmed-over roast beef without tasting it, and drank two gin-and-tonics. The television sound was bad and that annoyed me, even though it was three rooms away with the doors between closed.

"Did you get started on Mike's ham set yet?" Janet asked, clearing the table.

"Christ!" I had forgotten. I took my coffee and headed for

the basement. "I'll get at it. I've got what I need. Don't wait up. If I don't do it tonight, I won't get to it for days." I had suits being tested at three different hospitals, Mike's, one at a geriatric clinic where an eighty-year-old man was recovering from a broken hip, and one in a veterans' hospital where a young man in a coma was guinea pig. I was certain the suit would be more effective than the daily massage that such patients usually received, when there was sufficient help to administer such massage to begin with. The suits were experimental and needed constant checking, the programs needed constant supervision for this first application. And it was my baby. So I worked that night on the slides for Mike Bronson, and it was nearly two when I returned to the kitchen, keyed up and tense from too much coffee and too many cigarettes.

I wandered outside and walked for several minutes back through the woods, ending up at the bridge, staring at the Donlevy house where there was a light on in Pete Donlevy's study. I wondered again about the little woman who had moved in, wondered if others had joined her, or if they would join her. It didn't seem practical for one woman to rent such a big house. I was leaning against the same tree that Rusty had perched in watching the unloading of boxes. I wasn't thinking of anything in particular, images were flitting through my mind, snaps, scraps of talk, bits and pieces of unfinished projects, disconnected words. I must have closed my eyes. It was dark under the giant oak and there was nothing to see anyway, except the light in Pete's study, and that was only a small oblong of yellow.

The meandering thoughts kept passing by my mind's eye, but very clearly there was also Pete's study. I was there, looking over the bookshelves, wishing I dared remove his books in order to put my own away neatly. Thinking of Laura and her nightmare. Wondering where Caesar was, had I left the basement light on, going to the door to whistle, imagining Janet asleep with her arm up over her head, if I slept like that my hands would go to sleep, whistling again for Caesar. Aware of the dog, although he was across the yard staring intently up a tree bole where a possum clung motionlessly. Everything a jumble, the bookshelves, the basement workshop, Janet, Caesar, driving down from Connecticut, pawing through drawers in the lab shop, looking for the sleeve controls, dots and dashes on slides . . .

I whistled once more and stepped down the first of the three steps to the yard, and fell. . . .

Falling forever, ice cold, tumbling over and over, with the knowledge that the fall would never end, would never change, stretching out for something, anything to grasp, to stop the tumbling. Nothing. Then a scream, and opening my eyes, or finding my eyes open. The light was no longer on.

Who screamed?

Everything was quiet, the gentle sound of the water on rocks, a rustling of a small creature in the grasses at the edge of the brook, an owl far back on the hill. There was a September chill in the air suddenly and I was shivering as I hurried back to my house.

I knew that I hadn't fallen asleep. Even if I had dozed momentarily, I couldn't have been so deeply asleep that I could have had a nightmare. Like Laura's, I thought, and froze. Is that what she had dreamed? Falling forever? There had been no time. During the fall I knew that I had been doing it for an eternity, that I would continue to fall for all the time to come.

Janet's body was warm as she snuggled up to me, and I clung to her almost like a child, grateful for this long-limbed, practical woman.

We met our new neighbor on Saturday. Janet made a point of going over to introduce herself and give her an invitation for a drink, or coffee. "She's so small," Janet said. "About thirty, or a little under. And handsome in a strange way. In spite of herself almost. You can see that she hasn't bothered to do anything much about her appearance, I mean she has gorgeous hair, or could have, but she keeps it cut about shoulder length and lets it go at that. I bet she hasn't set it in years. Same for her clothes. It's as if she never glanced in a mirror, or a fashion magazine, or store window. Anyway, you'll see for yourself. She'll be over at about four."

There was always work that needed doing immediately in the yard, and on the house or the car, and generally I tried to keep Saturday open to get some of it done. That day I had already torn up the television, looking for the source of the fuzzy sound, and I had replaced a tube and a speaker condenser, but it still wasn't the greatest. Rusty wanted us to be hooked up to the cable, and I was resisting. From stubbornness, I knew. I resented having to pay seventy-five dollars in order to bring in a picture that only three years ago had been clear and sharp. A new runway at the airport had changed all that. Their radar and the flight paths of rerouted planes distorted our reception. But I kept trying to fix it myself.

Janet was painting window shades for Laura's room. She had copied the design from some material that she was using for a bedspread and drapes. She had baked two pies, and a cake, and a loaf of whole-wheat bread. The house was clean and smelled good and we were busy. And happy. It always sounds hokey to say that you're a happy man. Why aren't you tearing out your hair over the foreign mess, or the tax problem, or some damn thing? But I was a happy man. We had a good thing, and knew it. Janet always baked on Saturday, froze the stuff and got it out during the week, so the kids hardly even knew that she was a working mother. They were happy kids.

Then Christine came along. That's the only way to put it. That afternoon she came up through the woods, dressed in brown jeans, with a sloppy plaid shirt that came down below her hips and was not terribly clean. Laura ran down to meet her, and she was almost as big as Christine.

"Hi," Janet said, coming out to the terrace. "Mrs. Rudeman, this is Eddie. And Rusty."

"Please, call me Christine," she said, and held out her hand.

But I knew her. It was like seeing your first lover again after years, the same shock low in the belly, the same tightening up of muscles, the fear that what's left of the affair will show, and there is always something left over. Hate, love, lust. Something. Virtually instantaneous with the shock of recognition came the denial. I had never seen her before in my life, except that one morning on the way to work, and certainly I hadn't felt any familiarity then. It would have been impossible to have known her without remembering, if only because of her size. You remember those who aren't in the range of normality. She was possibly five feet tall, and couldn't have weighed more than ninety pounds. It was impossible to tell what kind of a figure she had, but what was visible seemed perfectly normal, just scaled down, except her eyes, and they looked extraordinarily large in so tiny a face. Her eyes were very dark, black or so close to it as to make no difference, and her hair, as Janet had said, was beautiful, or could have been with just a little attention. It was glossy, lustrous black, thick and to her shoulders. But she shouldn't have worn it tied back with a ribbon as she had it then. Her face was too round, her eyebrows too straight. It gave her a childlike appearance.

All of that and more passed through my mind as she crossed the terrace smiling, with her hand outstretched. And I didn't want to touch her hand. I knew that Janet was speaking, but I didn't hear what she said. In the same distant way I knew that Laura and Rusty were there, Laura waiting impatiently for the introductions to be over so she could say something or other. I braced myself for the touch, and when our fingers met, I knew there had been no way I could have prepared myself for the electricity of that quick bringing together of flesh to flesh. For God's sake, I wanted to say, turn around and say something to Rusty, don't just stand there staring at me. Act normal. You've never seen me before in your life and you know it.

She turned quickly, withdrawing her hand abruptly, but I couldn't tell if she had felt anything, or suspected my agitation. Janet was oblivious of any currents.

"But you and Rusty and Laura have all met," she said. "I keep forgetting how great kids are at insinuating themselves into any scene."

"Where's Caesar?" Laura finally got to ask.

I had another shock with the name. My nightmare, my waking nightmare. Or had I heard her calling to the dog?

"I never take him with me unless he's been invited," Christine said. "You never know where you'll run into a dog-hater, or a pet cat, or another dog that's a bit jealous."

They talked about the dog we had had until late in the spring, a red setter that had been born all heart and no brain. He had been killed out on the county road. Again I was distantly aware of what they were saying, almost as if I were half asleep in a different room, with voices droning on and on beyond the walls. I was simply waiting for a chance to leave without being too rude.

The kids wandered away after a little while, and Janet and Christine talked easily. I began to listen when she mentioned Pete's name.

"Pete and Grace had been my husband's friends for a long time. Pete studied under him, and Grace and I were in classes together. So they invited me to stay in their house this year. Karl suggested Pete for the exchange program three years ago. He didn't believe there was a coherent American school of philosophy, and he thought that it would be good for Pete to study under the Cambridge system of Logical Positivism." She shrugged. "I take it that Pete didn't write to you and warn you that I'd be moving in. He said he would, but I guess I didn't really think he'd get around to it."

Karl Rudeman. Karl Rudeman. It was one of those vaguely familiar names that you feel you must know and can't associate with anything.

Janet had made a pitcher of gin and bitter lemon, and I refilled our glasses while I tried to find a tag to go with the name. Christine murmured thanks, then said, "It isn't fair that I should know so much about you both—from Pete—and that you know nothing about me. Karl was a psychologist at Harvard. He worked with Leary for several years, then they separated, violently, over the drugs. He died last May."

I felt like a fool then, and from the look on her face, I assumed that Janet did too. Karl Rudeman had won the Nobel for his work in physiological psychology, in the field of visual perception. There was something else nagging me about the name, some elusive memory that went with it, but it refused to come.

Christine stayed for another half hour, refused Janet's invitation to have dinner with us, and then went back home. Back through the woods, the way she had come.

"She's nice," Janet said. "I like her."

"You warn her about Glaser?"

"She's not interested. And it does take two. Anyway she said that Pete gave her the rundown on everyone on the lane. You heard her."

"Yeah," I lied. I hadn't heard much of anything anyone had said. "He must have been thirty years older than she is."

"I suppose. I always wonder how it is with a couple like that. I mean, was he losing interest? Or just one time a month? Did it bother her?" Since Janet and I always wondered about everyone's sex life, that wasn't a strange line for our talk to have taken, but I felt uncomfortable about it, felt as if this time we were peeking in bedroom-door keyholes.

"Well, since you seem so sure she wouldn't be interested in Bill Glaser, maybe she's as asexual as she looked in that outfit."

"Hah!" That's all, just one Hah! And I agreed. We let it drop then.

We had planned a movie for that night. "Get some hamburgers out for the kids and I'll take you around to Cunningham's for dinner," I said to Janet as she started in with the tray. She looked pleased.

We always had stuffed crab at Cunningham's, and Asti Spumante. It's a way of life. Our first date cost me almost a week's pay, and that's what we did, so I don't suggest it too often, just a couple of times a year when things have suddenly clicked, or when we've had a fight and made up to find everything a little better than it used to be. I don't know why I suggested it that night, but she liked the idea, and she got dressed up in her new green dress that she had been saving for a party.

When I made love to her late that night, she burst into tears, and I stroked her hair until she fell asleep. I remembered the first time she had done that, how frightened I'd been, and her convulsive clutching when I had tried to get up to bring her a drink of water or something. She hadn't been able to talk, she just sobbed and held me, and slowly I had come to realize that I had a very sexy wife whose response was so total that it overwhelmed her, and me. She sighed when I eased my numb arm out from under her. Pins-and-needles circulation began again and I rubbed my wrist trying to hurry it along.

Christine Warnecke Rudeman, I thought suddenly. Christine Warnecke. Of course. The photographer. There had been a display of her pictures at the library a year or two ago. She had an uncanny way of looking at things, as if she were at some point that you couldn't imagine, getting an angle that no one ever had seen before. I couldn't remember the details of the show, or any of the individual pieces, only the general impression of great art, or even greater fakery. I could almost visualize the item I had read about the death of her husband, but it kept sliding out of focus. Something about his death, though. Something never explained.

Tuesday I went home for lunch. I often did, the lab was less than a mile from the house. Sometimes I took Lenny with me, but that day he was too busy with a printed circuit that he had to finish by six and he nodded without speaking when I asked if he wanted a sandwich. The air felt crisp and cool after the hot smell of solder as I walked home.

I was thinking of the computer cutting tool that we were finishing up, wondering if Mike had mastered the Morse code yet, anticipating the look on his face when I installed the ham set. I was not thinking of Christine, had, in fact, forgotten about her, until I got even with the house and suddenly there she was, carrying a tripod out toward a small toolhouse at the rear of the lot.

I turned in the Donlevy drive. If it had been Ruth Klinger, or Grace Donlevy, or any of the other women who lived there, I would have offered a hand. But as soon as I got near her, I knew I'd made a mistake. It hit me again, not so violently, but still enough to shake me up. I know this woman, came the thought.

"Hi, Eddie." She put the tripod down and looked hot and slightly out of breath. "I always forget how heavy it can get. I had it made heavy purposely, so it could stay in place for months at a time, and then I forget."

I picked it up and it was heavy, but worse, awkward. The legs didn't lock closed, and no matter how I shifted it, one of them kept opening. "Where to?" I asked.

"Inside the toolshed. I left the door open. . . ."

I positioned it for her and she was as fussy as Lenny got over his circuits, or as I got over wiring one of the suits. It pleased me that she was that fussy about its position at an open window. I watched her mount a camera on the tripod and again she made adjustments that were too fine for me to see that anything was changed. Finally she was satisfied. All there was in front of the lens was a maple tree. "Want to take a look?" she asked.

The tree, framed by sky. I must have looked blank.

"I have a timer," she said. "A time-lapse study of the tree from now until spring, I hope. If nothing goes wrong."

"Oh." My disappointment must have shown.

"I won't show them side by side," she said, almost too quickly. "Sort of superimposed, so that you'll see the tree through time. . . ." She looked away suddenly and wiped her hands on her jeans. "Well, thanks again."

"What in hell do you mean, through time?"

"Oh . . . Sometime when you and Janet are free I'll show you some of the sort of thing I mean." She looked up, apologetically, and shrugged as she had that first time I met her. It was a strange gesture from one so small. It seemed that almost everything was too much for her, that when she felt cornered she might always simply shrug off everything with that abrupt movement.

"Well, I have to get," I said then, and turned toward the drive. "Do you have anything else to lug out here, before I leave?"

"No. The timer and film. But that's nothing. Thanks again." She took a step away, stopped and said, with that same shy apologetic tone, "I wish I could explain what I want to do, in words. But I can't."

I hurried away from her, to my own house, but I didn't want anything to eat after all. I paced the living room, into the kitchen, where the coffee I had poured was now cold, back to the living room, out to the terrace. I told myself asinine things like: I love Janet. We have a good life, good sex, good kids. I have a good business that I am completely involved in. I'm too young for the male climacteric. She isn't even pretty.

And I kept pacing until I was an hour later than I'd planned on. I still hadn't eaten, and couldn't, and I forgot to make the sandwich for Lenny and take it back to him.

I avoided Christine. I put in long hours at the lab, and stayed in the basement workshop almost every evening, and turned down invitations to join the girls for coffee, or talk. They were together a lot. Janet was charmed by her, and a strong friendship grew between them rapidly. Janet commented on it thoughtfully one night. "I've never had many woman friends at all. I can't stand most women after a few minutes. Talking about kids sends me right up the wall, and you know how I am about PTA and clubs and that sort of thing. But she's different. She's a person first, then a woman, and as a person she's one of the most interesting I've ever run into. And she has so much empathy and understanding. She's very shy, too. You never have to worry about her camping on your doorstep or anything like that."

She'd been there almost two months when Pete's letter finally arrived telling us about her. Janet read it aloud to me while I shaved.

" 'She's a good kid and probably will need a friend or two by the time she gets out of that madhouse in Connecticut. Rudeman was a genius, but not quite human. Cold, calculating, never did a thing by accident in his life. He wound her up every morning and gave her instructions for the day. God knows why she married him, why they stayed together, but they did. In his own way I think Rudeman was very much in love with her. He said once that if he could understand this one woman he'd understand the entire universe. May he rest in peace, he never made it. So be good to her.

" 'Grace sends love. She's been redoing our apartment. . . .' "

I stopped listening. The letter went on for three pages of single-spaced typing. The letter had left as many questions as it had answered. More in fact, since we already had found out the basic information he had supplied. I decided to go to the library and look up Rudeman and his death and get rid of that nagging feeling that had never gone away.

"Eddie, for heaven's sake!" Janet was staring at me, flushed, and angry.

"What? Sorry, honey. My mind was wandering."

"I noticed. What in the world is bothering you? You hear me maybe half the time, though I doubt it."

"I said I'm sorry, Janet. God damn it!" I blotted a nick and turned to look at her, but she was gone.

She snapped at Rusty and Laura, and ignored me when I asked if there was any more mail. Rusty looked at me with a What's-eating-her? expression.

I tried to bring up the subject again that night, and got no-where. "Nothing," she said. "Just forget it."

"Sure. That suits me fine." I didn't know what I was supposed to forget. I tried to remember if it was time for her period, but I never knew until it hit, so I just left her in the kitchen and went downstairs to the workroom and messed around for an hour. When I went back up, she was in bed, pretending to be asleep. Usually I'd keep at it until we had it out in the open, whatever it was, and we'd both explain our sides, maybe not convincing each other, but at least demonstrating that each thought he had a position to maintain. That time I simply left the bedroom and wandered about in the living room, picked up a book to read, put it down again. I found Pete's letter and saw that we'd been invited to visit them over Christmas. I seemed to remember that Janet had gone on about that, but I couldn't recall her words. Finally I pulled on a jacket and walked out to the terrace. I looked toward the Donlevy house, Christine's house now. Enough leaves had fallen by then so I could see the lights.

It's your fault, I thought at her. Why don't you beat it? Go somewhere else. Go home. Anywhere else. Just get out.

I was falling. Suddenly there was nothing beneath my feet, nothing at all, and I was falling straight down in a featureless grey vacuum. I groped wildly for something to hold on to, and I remembered the last time it had happened, and that it had happened to Laura. Falling straight down, now starting to tumble, my stomach lurching, nausea welling up inside me. Everything was gone, the house, terrace, the lights. . . . I thought hard of the lights that had been the last thing I had seen. Eyes open or closed, the field of vision didn't change, nothing was there. "Janet!" I tried to call, and had no way of knowing if I had been able to make the sound or not. I couldn't hear myself. A second sweep of nausea rose in me, and this time I tasted the bitterness. I knew that I would start crying. I couldn't help it; nausea, fear, the uncontrollable tumbling, unable to call anyone. Fury then displaced the helplessness that had overcome me, and I yelled, again without being able to hear anything, "You did this, didn't you, you bitch!"

Donlevy's study was warm, the colors were dull gold, russet, deep, dark green. There was a fire in the fireplace. The room was out of focus somehow, not exactly as I remembered it, the furniture too large and awkward-looking, the shelves built to the ceiling were too high, the titles on the topmost shelf a blur because of the strange angle from which I saw them. Before me was Donlevy's desk, cleaner than I'd ever seen it, bare with gleaming wood, a stand with pens, and several sheets of paper. No stacks of reports, journals, overflowing ashtrays . . . I looked at the papers curiously, a letter, in a neat legible handwriting. Two pages were turned face down, and the third was barely begun: ". . . nothing to do with you in any way. When I have finished going through the papers, then I'll box up those that you have a right to and mail them to you. It will take many weeks, however, so unti . . ." The last word ended with a streak of ink that slashed downward and across the page, and ran off onto the desktop.

Where was she, Christine? How had I got . . . I realized that I wasn't actually there. Even as the thought formed, I knew precisely where I was, on my own terrace, leaning against a post, staring at the lights through the bare trees.

I looked at the letter, and slowly raised my hand and stared at it, both on the terrace and in the study. And the one in the study was tiny, tanned, with oval nails, and a wide wedding band. . . .

"Eddie?"

Janet's voice jolted me, and for a moment the study dimmed, but I concentrated on it, and held it. "Yes."

"Are you all right?"

"Sure. I thought you were sleeping."

In the study . . . who the devil was in the study? Where was *she?* Then suddenly she screamed, and it was both inside my head and outside filling the night.

"My God!" Janet cried. "It's Christine! Someone must have . . ."

I started to run toward her house, the Donlevy house, and Janet was close behind me in her robe and slippers. In the split second before that scream had exploded into the night, I had been overcome by a wave of terror such as I had never known before. I fully expected to find Christine dead, with her throat cut, or a bullet in her brain, or something. Caesar met us and loped with us to the house, yelping excitedly. Why hadn't he barked at a stranger? I wanted to kick the beast. The back door was unlocked. We rushed in, and while Janet hesitated, I dashed toward the study.

Christine was on the floor near the desk, but she wasn't dead, or even injured as far as I could tell from a hurried examination. Janet had dropped to her knees also, and was feeling the pulse in Christine's wrist, and I saw again the small tanned hand that I had seen only a few minutes ago, even the wedding band. The terror that had flooded through me minutes ago surged again. How could I have dreamed of seeing that hand move as if it were my own hand? I looked about the study frantically, but it was back to normal, nothing distorted now. I had been dreaming, I thought, dreaming. I had dreamed of being this woman, of seeing through her eyes, feeling through her. A dream, no more complicated than any other dream, just strange to me. Maybe people dreamed of being other people all the time, and simply never mentioned it. Maybe everyone walked around terrified most of the time because of inexplicable dreams. Christine's eyelids fluttered, and I knew that I couldn't look at her yet, couldn't let her look at me. Not yet. I stood up abruptly. "I'll have a look around. Something scared her."

I whistled for Caesar to come with me, and we made a tour of the house, all quiet, with no signs of an intruder. The dog sniffed doors, and the floor, but in a disinterested manner, as if going through the motions because that was expected of him. The same was true of the yard about the house; he just couldn't find anything to get excited about. I cursed him for being a stupid brute, and returned to the study. Christine was seated on one of the dark green chairs, and Janet on one facing her. I moved casually toward the desk, enough to see the letter, to see the top lines, the long streak where the pen had gone out of control.

Janet said, "Something must have happened, but she can't remember a thing."

"Fall asleep? A nightmare?" I suggested, trying not to look at her.

"No. I'm sure not. I was writing a letter, in fact. Then suddenly there was something else in the room with me. I know it. It's happened before, the same kind of feeling, and I thought it was the farmhouse, the associations there. But maybe I am going crazy. Maybe Victor's right, I need care and treatment." She was very pale, her eyes so large that she looked almost doll-like, an idealized doll-like face.

"Who is Victor?" Janet asked.

"Eugenia's husband. She's . . . she was my husband's daughter." Christine sighed and stood up, a bit unsteadily. "If it starts again . . . I thought if I just got away from them all, and the house . . . But if it starts again here . . . ."

"Eddie, we can't leave her like this," Janet said in a low voice. "And we can't leave the kids alone. Let's take her home for the night."

Christine objected, but in the end came along through the woods with Janet and me. At our house Janet went to get some clothes on. Her gown and robe had been soaked with dew. While Janet was dressing, I poked up a fire in the fireplace, and then made some hot toddies. Christine didn't speak until Janet came back.

"I'm sorry this happened," she said then. "I mean involving you two in something as . . . as messy as this is."

Janet looked at me, waiting, and I said, "Christine, we heard from Pete and he seemed to think you might need friends. He seemed to think we might do. Is any of this something that you could talk to Pete about?"

She nodded. "Yes. I could tell Pete."

"Okay, then let us be the friends that he would be if he was here."

Again she nodded. "Lord knows I have to talk to someone, or I'll go as batty as Victor wants to believe I am."

"Why do you keep referring to him?" Janet asked. Then she shook her head firmly. "No. No questions. You just tell us what you want to for now."

"I met Karl when I was a student at Northwestern. He had a class in physiological psychology and I was one of his students and experimental subjects. He was doing his basic research then on perception. Three afternoons a week we would meet in his lab for tests that he had devised, visual-perception tests. He narrowed his subjects down to two others and me, and we are the ones he based much of his theory on. Anyway, as I got to know him and admire him more and more, he seemed to take a greater interest in me. He was a widower, with a child, Eugenia. She was twelve then." Her voice had grown fainter, and now stopped, and she looked at the drink in her hand that she had hardly touched. She took a sip, and another. We waited.

"The reason he was interested in me, particularly, at least in the beginning," she said haltingly, "was that I had been in and out of institutions for years." She didn't look up and her words were almost too low to catch. "He had developed the theory that the same mechanism that produces sight also produces images that are entirely mental constructs, and that the end results are the same. In fact, he believed and worked out the theory that all vision, whether or not there is an external object, is a construct. Vision doesn't copy anything in the real world, but instead involves the construction of a schematic, and so does visual imagination, or hallucination."

I refilled our glasses and added a log to the fire, and she talked on and on. Rudeman didn't believe in a psychological cause to explain schizophrenia, but believed it was a chemical imbalance with an organic cause that produced aberrated perception. This before the current wave of research that seemed to indicate that he had been right. His interest in Christine had started because she could furnish information on image projection, and because in some areas she had an eidetic memory, and this, too, was a theory that he was intensely interested in. *Eidetikers* had been discounted for almost a century in the serious literature, and he had reestablished the authenticity of the phenomena.

"During the year," she said, "he found out that there were certain anomalies in my vision that made my value to him questionable. Gradually he had to phase me out, but he became so fascinated in those other areas that he couldn't stand not starting another line of research immediately, using me extensively. That was to be his last year at Northwestern. He had an offer from Harvard, and he was eager to go there. Anyway, late in April that year I . . . I guess I flipped out. And he picked up the pieces and wouldn't let me go to a psychiatrist, but insisted on caring for me himself. Three months later we were married."

Janet's hand found mine, and we listened to Christine like that, hand in hand.

"He was very kind to me," Christine said slowly sometime during that long night. "I don't know if he loved me, but I think I would have died without him. I think—or thought—that he cured me. I was well and happy, and busy. I wanted to take up photography and he encouraged it and made it possible. All those years he pursued a line of research that he never explained to me, that he hadn't published up to the time of his death. I'm going through his work now, trying to decode it, separating personal material from the professional data."

She was leaving out most of it, I believed. Everything interesting, or pertinent, or less than flattering to her she was skipping over. Janet's hand squeezed mine; take it easy, she seemed to be saying. Christine was obviously exhausted, her enormous eyes were shadowed, and she was very pale. But, damn it, I argued with myself, why had she screamed and fainted? How had her husband died?

"Okay," Janet said then, cheerfully, and too briskly. "Time's up for now. We'll talk again tomorrow, or the next day, or whenever you're ready to, Christine. Let me show you your room." She was right, of course. We were all dead tired, and it was nearly three, but I resented stopping it then. How had her husband died?

She and Janet left and I kicked at the feeble fire and finished my last drink, gathered up glasses and emptied ashtrays. It was half an hour before Janet came back. She looked at the clock and groaned.

"Anything else?"

She went past me toward the bedroom, not speaking until we were behind the closed door. "It must have been gruesome," she said then, starting to undress. "Victor and Eugenia moved in with her. Karl's daughter and son-in-law. And Karl's parents live there, too. And right away Victor began to press for Karl's papers. They worked together at the university. Then he began to make passes, and that was too much. She packed up and left."

I had finished undressing first, and sat on the side of the bed watching her. The scattering of freckles across her shoulders was fading now, her deep red tan was turning softly golden. I especially loved the way her hip bones showed when she moved, and the taut skin over her ribs when she raised her arms to pull her jersey over her head. She caught my look and glanced at her watch pointedly. I sighed. "What happened to her tonight?"

"She said that before she finally had to leave the farm up in Connecticut, the last night there, Victor came into her third-floor room and began to make advances—her word, by the way. She backed away from him, across the room and out onto a balcony. She has acrophobia, and never usually goes out on that balcony. But she kept backing up, thinking of the scandal if she screamed. Her stepdaughter's husband, after all. In the house were Karl's mother and father, Eugenia. . . . Victor knew she would avoid a scene if possible. Then suddenly she was against the rail and he forced her backward, leaning out over it, and when she twisted away from him, she looked straight down, and then fainted. She said that tonight she somehow got that same feeling, she thinks that that memory flooded back in and that she lived that scene over again, although she can't remember anything except the feeling of looking down and falling. She screamed and fainted, just like that other night." Janet slipped into bed. "I think I reassured her a little bit anyway. If that's what happened, it certainly doesn't mean she's heading for another break. That's the sort of thing that can happen to anyone at any time, especially where one of those very strong phobias is concerned."

I turned off the light, and we lay together, her cheek on my shoulder, her left arm across my chest, her left leg over my leg. And I thought of Christine in the other room under the same roof. And I knew that I was afraid of her.

The next morning was worse than usual. Thank God it's Friday, we both said a number of times. I had no desire to see Christine that morning, and was relieved that she seemed to be sleeping late. I told Janet I'd leave a note and ask her to go out by the side door, which would latch after her. But when the kids left to catch their bus, she came out.

"I wasn't sure if you'd told them that I was here. I thought it would complicate things to put in an appearance before they were gone," she said apologetically. "I'll go home now. Thanks for last night. More than I can say."

"Coffee?"

She shook her head, but I was pouring it already and she sat down at the kitchen table and waited. "I must look like hell," she said. She hadn't brought her purse with her, her long hair was tangled, she had no makeup on, and her eyes were deeply shadowed with violet. I realized that she was prettier than I had thought at first. It was the appeal of a little girl, however, not the attraction of a grown woman.

She sipped the coffee and then put the cup down and said again, "I'll go home now. Thanks again."

"Want a lift to your house? I have to leave too."

"Oh, no. That would be silly. I'll just go back through the woods."

I watched her as far as I could make out the small figure, and then I turned off lights and unplugged the coffee pot and left. But I kept seeing that slight unkempt figure walking from me, toward the woods, tangled black hair, a knit shirt that was too big, jeans that clung to her buttocks like skin. Her buttocks were rounded, and moved ever so slightly when she walked, almost like a boy, but not quite; there was a telltale sway. And suddenly I wondered how she would be. Eager, actively seeking the contact, the thrust? Passive? I swerved the car, and tried to put the image out of mind, but by the time I had parked and greeted Lenny, I was in a foul mood.

Lenny always left the mail to me, including anything addressed to him that came in through the lab. In his name I had dictated three refusals of offers to join three separate very good firms. That morning there was the usual assortment of junk, several queries on prices and information, and an invitation to display our computer cutting tool and anything else of interest in the Chicago Exposition of Building Trades. Lenny smiled. We talked for an hour about what to show, how best to display it, and so on, and finally came down to the question we'd both been avoiding. Who would go? Neither of us wanted to. We finally flipped a coin and I lost.

I called Janet at the hospital and told her, and she suggested that we have some literature printed up, ready to hand out, or to leave stacked for prospective buyers to pick up.

"We should have literature," I called to Lenny, who nodded. "We can have a sketch of the machine, I guess," I said to Janet.

"Don't be silly. Let Christine take some pictures for you."

"Our neighbor, Christine Warnecke, would probably take pictures for us," I told Lenny. He nodded a bit more enthusiastically.

We scheduled the next two weeks as tightly as possible, planning for eighteen-hour days, trying to keep in mind the commitments we already had. We had to get a machine ready to take to Chicago, get it polished for photographs, get an assortment of programs for the computer, keep the running check on the wired suits in the hospital cases, finish installing a closed-circuit TV in a private school, and so on.

I was late for dinner, and when I got there Janet simply smiled when I muttered, "Sorry."

"I know," she said, putting a platter of fried chicken down. "I know exactly what it will be like for the next few weeks. I'll see you again for Thanksgiving, or thereabouts."

I kissed her. While I was eating, the telephone rang. Christine, wondering if we'd like to see some of the work she'd done in the past few years. I remembered her offer to show us, but I shook my head at Janet. "Can't. I've got to write up the fact sheet tonight and be ready for the printers. They can take it Thursday. Did you mention the picture to her?" I motioned to the phone. Janet shook her head. "I will.

"Hi, Christine. Sorry, but I've got things that I have to do tonight. Maybe Janet can. Listen, would you be willing to take a picture of a machine for us, Lenny and me? He's my partner." She said of course, and I told her that Janet would fill in the details and hung up. I shooed Janet out, and went downstairs. Hours later I heard her come back, heard the basement door open slightly as she listened to see if I was still there. I clicked my pen on my beer glass, and the door closed. For a couple of seconds I considered my wife, decided she was a good sort, and then forgot her as I made another stab at the information sheet.

By twelve thirty I had a workable draft. It would need some polish, and possibly some further condensation, but it seemed to be adequate. I went upstairs for a drink before going to bed. I didn't turn on the living-room lights, but sat in the darkened room and went over and over the plans we had made. Tomorrow I'd get Christine over to take the pictures. . . .

I suddenly saw her buttocks as she moved away from me, and

her enormous eyes as she sat at the table and sipped coffee, and the very small hand with its wide band of gold. I closed my eyes. And saw the hand again, this time it opened and closed before my face, turning over and over as I examined it. I saw the other hand, and it was as if it were my own hand. I could raise and lower it. I could touch the right one to the left one, lift one to . . . my face. I stared at the room, the guest room in the Donlevy house. I had slept there before. Janet and I had stayed there years ago while paint dried in our house. I knew I was seated in the darkened living room, with a rum collins in my hand, knew Janet was sleeping just down the hall, but still I was also in that other room, seeing with eyes that weren't my eyes.

I started to feel dizzy, but this time I rejected the thought of falling. *No!* The feeling passed. I lifted the hands again, and got up. I had been in a deep chair, with a book on my lap. It slipped off to the floor. I tried to look down, but my eyes were riveted, fixed in a straight-ahead stare. I ordered the head to move, and with a combination of orders and just doing it, I forced movement. I forced her-me to make a complete turn, so that I could examine the whole room. Outside, I ordered, and walked down the hall to the living room, to the study. There were other thoughts, and fear. The fear was like a distant surf, rising and falling, but not close enough to feel, or to hear actually. It grew stronger as the walk continued. Dizziness returned, and nausea. I rejected it also.

The nausea had to do with the way my eyes were focusing. Nothing looked normal, or familiar, if my gaze lingered on it. And there was movement where I expected none. I made her stop and looked at the study from the doorway. The desk was not the straight lines and straight edges that I had come to know, but rather a blur that suggested desk, that I knew meant desk, and that did mean desk if I closed my eyes, or turned from it. But while I looked at it, it was strange. It was as if I could look through the desk to another image, the same piece of furniture, but without the polish, without casters, the same desk at an earlier stage. And beyond that, a rough suggestion of the same desk. And further, wood not yet assembled. Logs. A tree on a forest floor. A tree in full leaf. As I looked at the tree, it dwindled and went through changes: leaves turned color and fell and grew again, but fewer; branches shortened and vanished and the tree shrank and vanished. . . .

I jerked away, and in the living room my heart was pounding and I couldn't catch my breath. I waited for the next few minutes, wondering if I were having a heart attack, if I had fallen asleep, wondering if I were going mad. When I could trust my hands to move without jerking, I lifted the drink and swallowed most of it before I put it down again. Then I paced the living room for several minutes. Nothing had happened, I knew. Overtired, imaginative, half asleep, with vivid near-dreams. I refused to believe it was anything more than that. And I was afraid to try it again to prove to myself that that was all there was to it. I finished the drink, brushed my teeth, and went to bed.

Christine turned up at the shop at four the next afternoon. She shook Lenny's hand, businesslike and brisk, and thoroughly professional. He could have eaten her for breakfast without making a bulge. Her greeting to me was friendly and open. She looked very tired, as if she wasn't sleeping well.

"If you don't mind, Eddie, maybe Mr. Leonard can help me with the machine. I find that I work better with strangers than with people I know."

That suited me fine and I left them alone in the far end of the lab. Now and again I could hear Lenny's rumbling voice protesting something or other, and her very quiet answers. I couldn't make out her words, but from his I knew that she insisted on positioning the machine on a black velvet hanging for a series of shots. I groaned. Glamour yet.

"It's the contrast that I was after," she said when she was through. "The cold and beautifully functional machine, all shiny metal and angles and copper and plastic, all so pragmatic and wholesome, and open. Contrasted by the mystery of black velvet. Like a sky away from the city lights. Or the bowels of a cave with the lights turned off. Or the deepest reaches of the mind where the machine was really born."

Right until the last I was ready to veto the velvet for background without even seeing it, but she got to me. It had been born in such a black bottomless void, by God. "Let's wait for proofs and then decide," I said. I wondered, had she looked at the machine, through it to the components, through them back to the idea as it emerged from the black? I tightened my hand on my mug and took a deep drink of the hot murky coffee. We probably had the world's worst coffee in the lab because Lenny insisted on making it and he never measured anything, or washed the pot. On the other hand, he seemed to think the stuff he turned out was good.

"I'll develop them later today and have proofs ready to show you tonight, if you want," Christine said to us.

"You want to pick them up and bring them in with you in the morning?" Lenny asked. I said sure, and Christine left. I didn't watch her walk away this time.

After dinner Janet and I both went over to her house to see the proofs. While I studied the pictures, Christine and Janet went to the kitchen to talk and make coffee. I finished and leaned back in my chair waiting for their return. Without any perceptible difference in my thoughts, my position, anything, I was seeing Janet through Christine's eyes. Janet looked shocked and unbelieving.

I stared at her and began to see other faces there, too. Younger, clearer eyes, and smoother-skinned, emptier-looking. I turned my head abruptly as something else started to emerge. I knew that if I had tried, I would have seen all the personality traits, including the ugliness, the pettiness, everything there was that went into her.

"What is it?" Janet asked, alarm in her voice.

I shook my head, *her* head. She tried to speak and I wouldn't let her. Without any warning I had crossed the threshold of belief. I knew I could enter her, could use her, could examine whatever was in her mind without her being able to do anything about it. I knew in that same flash that she didn't realize what was happening, that she felt haunted, or crazy, but that she had no idea that another personality was inside her. I pulled away so suddenly that I almost let her fall down.

From the other room I heard Janet's cry, followed by the sound of breaking glass. I hurried to the kitchen to find her standing over Christine, who was sitting on a stool looking dazed and bewildered and very frightened.

"What's wrong?" I asked.

Janet shook her head. "I dropped a glass," she said, daring me not to believe.

I wondered why she lied to me, but leaving them alone again, I knew why. I had always been the rationalist in the family. I refused to grant the existence of ghosts, souls, spirits, unseen influences, astrology, palmistry, ESP, anything that couldn't be controlled and explained. I marveled at my absolute acceptance of what had happened. It was like seeing a puzzle suddenly take form and have meaning, like a child's puzzle where animals are hidden in line drawings; once you locate them, you can't lose them again. You know. I knew now. It happens once, you don't believe it; twice, you still don't believe. Three times, it's something you've known all your life. I knew. My hands were shaking when I lighted a cigarette, but inwardly I felt calmer than I had felt before as I considered Christine. I wasn't afraid of her any longer, for one thing. It was something I was doing, not something being done to me. I could control it. And she didn't know.

I stubbed out the cigarette and sat down abruptly. Rudeman? Had he lived in her mind throughout their marriage? Is that what drew him to her, made him marry a girl twenty-five years younger than he'd been. Had he managed to keep her by this—

control? I couldn't use the word possession then. I wasn't thinking of it as possession. It was more like having someone else's mind open for inspection, a tour for the curious, nothing more.

If I talked to her now, made her see what had happened, quite inadvertently, she could probably get help, learn how to control it so that future intrusion would be impossible. If Rudeman had cared for her at all, hadn't wanted to use her, he would have cured her, or had it done somehow. Maybe he had known, maybe that's what those boxes of books were about, the years of experimentation. A little human guinea pig, I thought. Large-eyed, frightened, trusting. Completely ignorant of what was being done to it. And over the image of the frightened woman came the image of her slight figure as she walked away from me toward the woods, with her little fanny swinging gracefully, the rest of her body a mystery under concealing clothes.

The way she saw things, there wouldn't be any mystery about anything. Into and through and out the other side. No wonder Rudeman had been fascinated. How did she manage to live with so many conflicting images? Did that explain her schizophrenia? Just a name they applied to a condition that was abnormal, without knowing anything about what it was actually? The questions were coming faster and faster, and the thought of her, sitting out there in the kitchen, with answers locked up under that skull, was too much. I began to pace. Not again. Not now especially, with Janet there. *She'd* begin to suspect me of being responsible, just as I had suspected her of being responsible long before I had an inkling of what was happening. I thought of Christine as *her,* with special emphasis on it, separating *her* from all other hers in the world, but not able or willing to think of her by name.

I wondered what they were doing in the kitchen. What was she telling Janet? I started through the hall toward the kitchen, then stopped, and hurriedly returned to the living room. I couldn't look at her yet. I had to think, to try to understand. I needed time to accept all the way through what had happened between us. And I suddenly wondered what she saw when she looked at me, through me to all the things that I had always believed were invisible.

I couldn't stand being in that house any longer. I grabbed the proofs and stuffed them back into the envelope. In the hallway I yelled out to Janet, "I'm going back through the woods. I'll leave the car for you. Take your time."

She stuck her head out from the kitchen. I thought she looked at me with suspicion and coldness, but her words were innocuous, and I decided that I had imagined the expression. "I won't be much longer, honey. Be careful."

It was dark under the oak trees, with the tenacious leaves still clinging to the twigs, rustling in the wind. The ground was spongy and water came through my shoes quickly, ice cold, squishing with each step. A fine film of ice covered the two logs. I cursed as I slipped and slid across, thinking of the black frigid water below. At our side of the brook I paused and looked back at the glowing windows, and for just an instant I entered her. No transition now, just the sudden awareness of what she was seeing, what she was hearing, feeling, thinking. She moaned and fear throbbed in her temples. She shut her eyes hard. I got out as fast as I had entered, as shaken as she had been. I hadn't meant to do it. The thought and the act, if it could be called that, had been simultaneous. I rushed home, stumbling through the familiar woods, bumping into obstacles that seemed ominous: a log where yesterday the path had been clear, a hole covered with leaves, a trap to break an ankle in, a low branch that was meant to blind me, but only cut my cheek, a root that snaked out to lasso my foot, throwing me down face first into the ice-glazed leaves and dirt. I lay quietly for a minute. Finally I stood up and went on, making no attempt to brush off the muck. Muck and filth. It seemed fitting.

I still had a couple of hours of work to do that night. The following day Mike's body cast was being changed, and I had to be on hand. He had his ham operator's license, and Janet had said that the only problem now was that he didn't want to stop to sleep or eat or anything else. He was doing remarkably well in every way. She had kissed me with tears in her eyes when she reported. In the morning I had to drop the pictures off for Lenny, scoot over to the hospital, return for the pictures, take them back to her . . . I changed my mind. I'd let Lenny deliver the proofs. In fact, I wouldn't see *her* at all again. Ever.

I got in the tub and soaked for fifteen minutes, then put on pajamas and robe and went down to the basement to check out the program for Mike's computer. I didn't hear Janet come in, but when I went up at twelve thirty, she was in the living room waiting for me.

"I'm really concerned for her," she said. "I don't think she ought to be alone. And I don't think she's crazy, either."

"Okay. Tell." I headed for the kitchen and she followed. Janet had made coffee and it smelled good. I poured a cup and sat down.

"I don't know if I can or not," she said. "Christine has a gift of vision that I'm sure no one ever had before. She can see, or sense, the process of growth and change in things." I knew that I was supposed to register skepticism at that point, and I looked up at her with what I hoped was a prove-it expression. She became defensive. "Well, she can. She's trying to duplicate it with the camera, but she's very frustrated and disappointed in the results she's been able to get so far. She's got a new technique for developing time-lapse photographs. Whether or not it's what she is after, it's really remarkable. She prints a picture on a transparency, and shoots her next one through it, I think. When she prints that on another transparency, it gives the effect of being in layers, with each layer discernible, if you look hard enough. But she claims that for it to be successful, you should be able to see each stage, with all the others a blur, each one coming into focus with the change in attention you give to it. And that's how she sees."

I finished the coffee and got up to pour a second cup, without commenting. Standing at the stove, with my back to her, I said,

"I'm willing to believe that she's some kind of a genius. But, this other thing, the fainting, screams, whatever happened tonight. She needs a doctor."

"Yes. I know. I talked her into seeing Dr. Lessing. Lessing will be good to her." She made a short laughing sound, a snort of quickly killed mirth. "And he'll tell her to pick up a man somewhere and take him to bed. He thinks that widows and widowers shouldn't try to break the sex habit cold turkey." Again the tone of her voice suggested amusement when she added, "Knowing that she's coming to him through us, he'll probably recommend that she cultivate Lenny's company, two birds with one stone."

My hand was painfully tight on the cup handle. I remembered one night with Janet, saying, "Jesus, I wish I could be you just for once, just to see what happens to you when you cry like that, when you pass out, why that little smile finally comes through. . . ."

I knew my voice was too harsh then. I couldn't help it. I said, "I think she's a spook. I don't like being around her. I get the same feeling that I got when I was a kid around a great-uncle who had gone off the deep end. I was scared shitless of him, and I get the same feeling in the pit of my stomach when I'm near her."

"Eddie!" Janet moved toward me, but didn't make it all the way. She returned to her chair instead and sat down, and when she spoke again, her voice was resigned. Way back in Year One, we'd had an understanding that if ever either of us disliked someone, his feelings were to be respected without argument. It needed no rationalization: people liked or disliked other people without reason sometimes. And by throwing in a non-existent uncle I had made doubly sure that she wouldn't argue with me. Finis. "Well," Janet said, "she certainly isn't pushy. If you don't want to be around her, you won't find her in your path."

"Yeah. And maybe later, after I get out from under all this other stuff, maybe I'll feel different. Maybe I'm just afraid right now of entanglement, because I'm too pressed for time as it is."

"Sure," Janet said. I liked her a lot right then, for the way she was willing to let me drop Christine, whom she had grown very fond of, and was intrigued by. She was disappointed that she had been cut off at the water, that she wouldn't be able now to talk about Christine, speculate about her. God knows, I didn't want to think about her any more than I had to from then on.

The next few days blurred together. I knew that things got done, simply because they didn't need doing later, but the memory of seeing to them, of getting them done, was gone. The geriatric patient came out of his cast on Saturday practically as good as new. He was walking again the same day they removed it, with crutches, but for balance, and to give him reassurance. His leg and hip muscles were fine. Lenny and I laughed and pounded each other over the back, and hugged each other, and split a bottle of Scotch, starting at one in the morning and staying with it until it was gone. He had to walk me home because neither of us could find a car key. Lenny spent the night, what was left of it. On Sunday I slept off a hangover and Lenny, Janet, the kids, and Christine all went for a long ride in the country and came back with baskets of apples, cider, black walnuts, and butternuts. And Janet said that Christine had invited all of us over for a celebration supper later on.

"I didn't say we'd come," Janet said. "I can call and say you still are hungover. I sort of hinted that you might be."

"Honey, forget it. How's Lenny? You should have seen him last night. He laughed!"

"And today he smiled a couple of times," she said, grinning. "He's over at Christine's house now, helping with firewood, or something."

"Tell her that we'll be over," I said.

The kids grumbled a little, but we got Mrs. Durrell in to sit and we went over to Christine's. Lenny was in the living room mixing something red and steaming in a large bowl. "Oh, God," I prayed aloud, "please, not one of his concoctions." But it was, and it was very good. Hot cider, applejack, brandy, and a dry red wine. With cinnamon sticks in individual cups.

Steaks, salad, baked potatoes, spicy hot apple pie. "If I knew you was coming," Christine had murmured, serving us, but she hadn't belabored the point, and it was a happy party. She proposed a toast after pouring brandy for us. "To the good men of the earth. Eddie and Lenny, and others like them wherever they are."

I knew that I flushed, and Lenny looked embarrassed and frowned, but Janet said, "Hear, hear," and the girls touched the glasses to their lips. In a few moments we were back to the gaiety that was interrupted by the toast that lingered in my head for the rest of the evening.

Lenny was more talkative than I'd seen him in years. He even mentioned that he had been a physicist, something that not more than a dozen people knew. The girls were both looking pretty after a day in the cold air; their cheeks were flushed, and they looked happy. Janet's bright blue-green eyes sparkled and she laughed easily and often. Christine laughed too, more quietly, and never at anything she said herself. She still was shy, but at ease with us. And it seemed that her shyness and Lenny's introspective quiet were well matched, as if there had been a meeting of the selves there that few others ever got to know. I caught Lenny's contemplative gaze on her once, and when she noticed also, she seemed to consider his question gravely, then she turned away, and the flush on her cheeks was a bit deeper. The air had changed somehow, had become more charged, and Janet's touch on my hand to ask for a cigarette was a caress. I looked at her, acknowledging the invitation. Our hands lingered over the cigarette in the non-verbal communication that made living with her so nice.

I was very glad we had that evening together. Janet and I left at about twelve. Lenny was sitting in a deep chair before the fire when we said goodnight, and he made no motion to get up and leave then too. In our car Janet sighed and put her head on my shoulder.

Images flashed before my eyes: Christine's buttocks as she moved away from me; the tight skin across Janet's ribs when she raised her arms over her head; Christine's tiny, tiny waist, dressed as she had been that night, in a tailored shirt and black skirt, tightly belted with a wide leather belt; the pink nipples that puckered and stiffened at a touch; and darker nipples that I had never seen, but knew had to be like that, dark and large. And how black would her pubic hair be, and how hungry would she be after so long a time? Her head back, listening to a record, her eyes narrowed in concentration, her mouth open slightly. And the thought kept coming back: What would it be like to be her? What did Janet feel? What would *she* feel when Lenny entered her body? How different was it for a woman who was sexually responsive? She wouldn't even know, if I waited until she was thoroughly aroused. Sex had been in the air in the living room, we'd all felt it. After such a long period of deprivation, she'd crumble at Lenny's first touch. She'd never know, I repeated to myself.

When we got out of the car I said to Janet, "Get rid of Mrs. Durrell as fast as you can. Okay?" She pressed her body against mine and laughed a low, throaty laugh.

I was in a fever of anxiety then, trying to keep from going out into *her* too soon. Not yet. Not yet. Not until I had Janet in bed, not until I thought that *she* and Lenny had had time to be at ease with each other again after being left alone. Maybe even in bed. My excitement was contagious. Janet was in bed as soon as she could decently get rid of the sitter, and when my hand roamed down her body, she shivered. Very deliberately I played with her and when I was certain that she wouldn't notice a shift in my attention, I went out to the other one, and found her alone. My disappointment was so great that momentarily I forgot about Janet, until her sudden scream made me realize that I had hurt her. She muffled her face against my chest and gasped, and whether from pleasure or pain I couldn't tell, she didn't pull away.

She was fighting eroticism as hard as she could. Drawing up thoughts of plans, of work not yet finished, of the notebooks that were so much harder to decipher than she had suspected they would be, the time-lapse photos that were coming along. Trying to push out of her mind the ache that kept coming back deep in her belly, the awful awareness of her stimulation from too much wine, the nearness of Lenny and his maleness. She was hardly aware of the intrusion this time, and when I directed her thoughts toward the sensual and sexual, there was no way she could resist. I cursed her for allowing Lenny to leave, I threatened her, I forced her to unfold when she doubled up like a foetus, hugging herself into a tight ball. For an hour, more than an hour, I made love to Janet and tormented that other girl, and forced her to do those things that I had to experience for myself. And when Janet moaned and cried out, I knew the cause, and knew when to stop and when to continue, and when she finally went limp, I knew the total, final surrender that she knew. And I stared at the mirror image of the girl: large dark nipples, beautifully formed breasts, erect and rounded, deep navel, black shiny hair. And mad eyes, haunted, panic-stricken eyes in a face as white as milk, with two red spots on her cheeks. Her breath was coming in quick gasps. My control was too tight. Nothing that she thought was coming through to me, only what she felt with her body that had become so sensitive that when she lay back on the bed, she shuddered at the touch of the sheet on her back. I relaxed control without leaving and there was a chaotic blur of memories, of nights in Karl's arms, of giving up totally to him, being the complete houri that he demanded of her.

"Bitch!" I thought at her. "Slut." I went on and on, calling her names, despising her for letting me do it to her, for being so manipulable, for letting me do this to myself. And I brought her to orgasm again, this time not letting her stop, or ease up, but on and on, until suddenly she arched her back and screamed, and I knew. I don't know if she screamed alone, or if I screamed with her. She blacked out, and I was falling, spinning around and around, plummeting downward. I yanked away from her. Janet stirred lazily against me, not awake, hardly even aware of me. I didn't move, but stared at the ceiling and waited for the blood to stop pounding in my head, and for my heart to stop the wild fibrillation that her final convulsion had started.

Janet was bright-eyed and pink the next morning, but when she saw the full ashtrays in the living room and kitchen, she looked at me closely. "You couldn't sleep?"

"Too much to think of," I said, cursing the coffee pot for its slowness. "And just four days to do it."

"Oh, honey." She was always regretful when I was awake while she slept. She felt it was selfish of her.

I could hardly bring myself to look at Lenny, but he took my moods in stride, and he made himself inconspicuous. The machine was gleaming and beautiful, ready to crate up and put in the station wagon. We wouldn't trust it to anyone but one of us, and I would drive to Chicago on Friday, install it myself Saturday morning, hours before the doors of the exposition opened at four in the afternoon. Lenny, like Janet, took my jittery state to be nerves from the coming show. It was like having a show at the Metropolitan, or a recital at Carnegie Hall, or a Broadway opening. And I wasn't even able to concentrate on it for a period of two consecutive minutes. I went round and round with the problem I had forced on myself by not leaving Christine Warnecke Rudeman strictly alone, and I couldn't find a solution. I couldn't speak out now, not after last night. I couldn't advise her to seek help, or in any way suggest that I knew anything about her that she hadn't told us. And although the thoughts of the night before were a torture, I couldn't stop going over it all again and again, and feeling again the echo of the unbearable excitement and pleasures I had known. When Lenny left for lunch, I didn't even look up. And when he returned, I was still at the bench, pretending to be going over the installation plan we had agreed on for our space at the exposition. Lenny didn't go back to his own desk, or his work in progress on the bench. He dragged a stool across from me and sat down.

"Why don't you like Chris?" he asked bluntly.

"I like her fine," I said.

He shook his head. "No. You won't look at her, and you don't want her to look directly at you. I noticed last night. You find a place to sit where you're not in her line of sight. When she turns to speak to you, or in your direction, you get busy lighting a cigarette, or shift your position. Not consciously, Eddie. I'm not saying you do anything like that on purpose, but I was noticing." He leaned forward with both great hands flat on the bench. "Why, Eddie?"

I shrugged and caught myself reaching for my pack of cigarettes. "I don't know. I didn't realize I was doing any of those things. I haven't tried to put anything into words. I'm just not comfortable with her. Why? Are you interested?"

"Yes," he said. "She thinks she's going crazy. She is certain that you sense it and that's why you're uncomfortable around her. Your actions reinforce her feelings, giving you cause to be even more uncomfortable, and it goes on from there."

"I can keep the hell away from her. Is that what you're driving at?"

"I think so."

"Lenny," I said when he remained quiet, and seemed lost in his speculations, "is she? Going crazy again? You know she was once?"

"No. I doubt it. She is different, and difference is treated like mental illness. That's what I know. No more. From demonic possession to witchcraft to mental illness. We do make progress." His hands, that had been flat and unmoving on the benchtop, bunched up into fists.

"Okay, Lenny," I said. "I believe you. And I won't see her any more for the next couple of weeks, whatever happens. And, Lenny, if I'd known—I mean, I didn't realize that anything of my attitude was coming through. I didn't really think about it one way or the other. I wouldn't do anything to hurt her . . . or you."

He looked at me gravely and nodded. "I know that," he said. He stood up and his face softened a bit. "It's always people like you, the rationalists, that are most afraid of any kind of mental disorders, even benign ones. It shows."

I shook my head. "A contradiction in terms, isn't that? Mental disorders and benign?"

"Not necessarily." Then he moved his stool back down the bench and went back to work. And I stared at the sketches before me for a long time before they came back into focus. The rest of the afternoon I fought against going back to her and punishing her for complaining about me. I thought of the ways I could inflict punishment on her, and knew that the real ace that I would keep for an emergency was her fear of heights. I visualized strolling along the lip of the Grand Canyon with her, or taking her up the Empire State Building, the Eiffel Tower, or forcing her up the face of a cliff. And I kept a rigid control of my own thoughts so that I didn't go out to her at all. I didn't give in all week, but I had her nightmares.

On Wednesday Janet suggested that I should let Lenny go to Chicago and I snapped at her and called her a fool. On Thursday Lenny made the same suggestion, and I stalked from the lab and drove off in a white fury. When Janet came home I accused them of getting together and talking about me.

"Eddie, you know better than that. But look at you. You aren't sleeping well, and you've been as nervous as a cat. What's the matter with you?"

"Just leave me alone, okay? Tired, that's all. Just plain tired. And tired of cross-examinations and dark hints and suspicions."

They were getting together, the three of them, all the time. I knew that Lenny was spending his evenings with Christine, and that Janet was with them much of the time when I was busy down in the basement workshop or out at the hospital. They said, Janet and Lenny, that they were trying to decipher the code that Karl Rudeman had used in making his notes. I didn't believe them.

They were talking about me, speculating on whether or not I

was the one driving *her* crazy. I imagined the same conversation over and over, with Lenny insisting that I could have done *that* to her, and Janet, white-faced and frantic with indecision, denying it. Not while I had been with her, she would think. Not at a time like that.

Then I would snap awake, and either curse myself for being a fool, or become frightened by the paranoid drift of my thoughts. And I would know that none of it was true. Of course Janet wouldn't discuss what went on over there; I had practically forbidden her to do so. And Lenny wouldn't talk about it under the happiest circumstances, much less now.

Friday, driving to Chicago I began to relax, and after three hours on the road I was whistling and could almost forget the mess, could almost convince myself that I'd been having delusions, which was easier to take than the truth.

I slept deeply Friday night, and Saturday I was busy, getting our exhibit set up and getting acquainted with others who were also showing tools and machinery. From four until the doors closed at eleven, the hall got fuller and fuller, the noise level became excruciating, the smoke-laden air unbreathable. Our cutting tool drew a good, interested response, and I was busy. And too tired for the late dinner I had agreed to with two other exhibitors. We settled for hamburgers and beer in the hotel dining room, and soon afterward I tumbled into bed and again slept like a child. The crowds were just as thick on Sunday, but by Monday the idle curiosity-seekers were back at their jobs, and the ones who came through were businesslike and fewer in number. I had hired a business student to spell me, and I left him in charge from four until seven, the slack hours, so I could have an early dinner and get some rest. But I found myself wandering the streets instead, and finally I stopped in front of a library.

Karl Rudeman, I thought. How did he die? And I went in and looked up the clippings about him, and read the last three with absorption. When I went to dinner afterward, I was still trying to puzzle it out. He had had dinner with his family: his wife, parents, daughter, and son-in-law. After dinner they had played bridge for an hour or two. Sometime after that, after everyone else had gone to bed, he had left the house to roam through the fields that stretched out for a quarter of a mile, down to the river. He had collapsed and died of a heart attack at the edge of a field. Christine, awakening later and finding him gone, had first searched the house, then, when she realized that Karl was in his pajamas and barefooted, she had awakened her stepson-in-law and started a search of the grounds. Karl wasn't found until daylight, and then the tenant farmer had been the one to spot the figure in orange-and-black striped pajamas. There was no sign of violence, and it was assumed that he had been walking in his sleep when the fatal attack occurred.

Back to the exhibit, and the flow of evening viewers. Invitations, given and accepted, for drinks later, and a beaver flick. Lunch with a couple of other men the following day. A long talk with a manufacturer who was interested in procuring the order for the cutting tool, should there be enough interest to warrant it.

The obscene movie had been a mistake, I knew as soon as the girl jerked off her slip and opened her legs. Suddenly I was seeing *her,* open-legged on the edge of the bed before a mirror.

I pushed my way through a cluster of men at the back of the theater to get out into the cold November air again. I walked back to the hotel. A freezing mist was hanging head high, not falling, but just hanging there, and I gulped it in, thankful for the pain of the cold air in my throat. A prowl car slowed down as it passed me, it picked up speed again and moved on down the street. I had bought a stack of magazines and some paperbacks to read, but nothing in the room looked interesting when I took off my damp clothes and tried to persuade myself that I could fall asleep now.

I had room service send up a bottle of bourbon and ice, and tried to read a Nero Wolfe mystery. My attention kept wandering, and finally I lay back on the bed, balancing my drink on my stomach, and thought about *her*.

It was so easy, and gentle even. She didn't suspect this time, not at all. She was saying, ". . . because they're abstractions, you see. Emotions like fear, love, anger. First the physiological change in the brain, the electrochemical changes that take place stimulating those abstractions, and then the experience of the emotion."

"You mean to say he really believed that the feeling of anger comes after the chemical changes that take place?"

"Of course. That's how it is with a physiological psychologist. And you can see it operate; tranquilizers permit you to know intellectually but they don't let you react, so you don't experience the anger or fear, or whatever."

Lenny was sitting back in the green chair in the study, and she was behind the desk that was spread with snapshots and proofs.

"Okay. What triggers those changes in the first place?"

"Well, his specialty was sight, or vision, as he preferred to call it. Light entering the eye brings about a change in the chromophore in the first thousandth of a second, and after that the rest of the changes are automatic, a causal chain that results in the experiencing of a vision of some sort."

"I know," Lenny said gently. "But what about the vision that doesn't have an object in real space? The imaginary image? No light there to start the chain of events."

"A change brought about by electrochemical energy? The leakage of energy from cellular functioning? The first step is on a molecular level, not much energy is involved, after all. Lenny, it's happening . . ."

I got a jolt of fear then, along with the words spoken softly. Her hands clenched and a proof under her right hand buckled up and cracked. Before Lenny could respond, I pulled out and away.

I didn't know how she had found out, what I had done to give my presence away. But her knowledge had been as certain as mine, and the fear was named now, not the fear of insanity. It was a directed fear and hatred that I had felt, directed at me, not the aimless, directionless, more-powerful fear that my presence had stimulated before. She knew that something from outside had entered her. I sat up and finished my drink, then turned off the light. And I wondered what they had been finding in those notes. . . . Half a bottle and hours later I fell asleep.

I dreamed that I was being chased, that I kept calling back over my shoulder, "Stop, it's me! Look at me! It's me!" But it didn't stop, and steadily it gained ground, until I knew that I was going to be caught, and the thought paralyzed me. All I could do then was wait in rigid, motionless, soundless terror for it to reach out and get me.

The nightmare woke me up, and it was minutes before I could move. It was nearly daylight; I didn't try to sleep any more. I was too afraid of having *her* dreams again. At seven thirty I called Janet.

"Hey," she said happily. "I thought we'd never hear from you."

"I sent some cards."

"But you'll be here before they will. How's it going?"

"Fine. Boring after the first day. I went to a dirty movie last night."

"I hope you had bad dreams. Serve you right." Her voice was teasing and cheerful and happy, and I could see her smile and the light in her eyes.

"How's everything there?" I couldn't ask about Lenny and Christine. If they had found out anything, they hadn't told her. I'd know, if they had. We chatted for several minutes, then she had to run, and I kissed her over the wire and we both hung up at the same time, the way we always did. I was being stupid. Naturally they wouldn't tell her. Hey, did you know that your husband's been torturing this woman psychologically, that he raped her repeatedly, that he's contemplating killing her? I jerked from the bed, shaking.

I had a dull pain behind my right eye when I went down to breakfast. A wind was driving sleet through the streets like sheer white curtains, and I stopped at the doorway, shivering, and went back inside to the hotel dining room. I couldn't think, and I knew that I had to think now.

If Lenny deciphered the notebooks, and if Karl had known that she could be possessed—there, I thought with some satisfaction, I used the word. If he had known and put that in his notebooks, then Lenny was bright enough to know that the recurrence of her schizophrenia was more than likely due to a new invasion. I groaned. He wouldn't believe that. I couldn't even believe it. No one in his right mind would, unless he had done it and could prove it to himself. . . . I gripped my cup so hard that coffee splashed out and I had to use both hands to return the cup to the saucer. Had Lenny gone into her too?

The pain behind my eye was a knife blade now. Lenny! Of course. I tried to lift the coffee and couldn't. I flung down my napkin and got up and hurried back to my room, as fast as I could get out of there. I paced, but no matter how I came to it, I ended up thinking that the only way Lenny could have accepted the thing was through experience. First Rudeman, then me, and now Lenny.

He couldn't have her. She was mine now. And I would never give her up.

The pain was unbearable and I collapsed, sprawled across the bed, clutching my head. I hadn't had a migraine in years. It was not knowing. Not knowing how much they had found out, not knowing what they were doing, what they were planning, not knowing if there was a way they could learn about me.

I went to her abruptly, roughly. She dropped a pan of developer and moaned, and caught the sink in a dark room. "No!" she cried. "Please. No!"

I tried to make her remember everything Lenny had said to

her, tried to bring back his voice, but there was too much, it came too fast. She was too frightened, and intermixed were the revived thoughts of insanity, of Karl's voice, Lenny's words. Too much. She had to relax. I took her to the couch and made her lie down and stop thinking. I felt her fear, and hatred, and abhorrence, like a pulse beating erratically, with each beat the pressure increased, and then ebbed. She tried to break away, and we struggled, and I hurt her. I didn't know what I had done, how I had managed it, but she groaned and wept and fell down again, and now my pain was also her pain. "Karl," she whispered soundlessly, "please go. Please leave me alone. I'm sorry. I didn't know. Please."

I stayed with her for more than an hour, and then I tried to force her to forget. To know nothing about my presence. She struggled again, and this time she screamed piercingly, and for a moment the feeling of a plunge straight down was almost overwhelming, but everything stopped, and I could find nothing there to communicate with, nothing to probe. It was like being swallowed by a sea of feathers that stretched out in all directions, shifting when I touched them, but settling again immediately. She had fainted.

I fell asleep almost immediately and when I awakened it was nearly two, and my headache was gone. I went to the exposition.

That afternoon a man returned who had been at the stall for almost an hour on Saturday. He had a companion this time. "Hi, Mr. Laslow. Hendrickson, remember? Like you to meet Norbert Weill."

Of course, I knew who Norbert Weill was. If you had a home workshop, you had something of his in it. If you had a small commercial shop, you probably had something of his. If you had a hundred-man operation, you'd have something of his. He was about sixty, small and square, with muscles like a boxer's. He grunted at the introduction, his handshake was a no-nonsense test of strength. "Hendrickson says it'll cut through plastic, glass, aluminum, steel. Without changing nothing but the program. That right?"

"Yes. Would you like a demonstration?"

"Not here. In my shop. How much?"

"I can't discuss that without my partner, Mr. Weill."

"Get him, then. When can he make it?"

So it went. In the end I agreed to call Lenny, then get in touch with Weill again at his Chicago office. Lenny didn't sound very enthusiastic. "Let him have the machine in his own shop for a couple of weeks after you close down there. Then let him make an offer."

"I think he'll make the offer without all that, if we're both on hand to discuss it. Outright sale of this machine, an advance against royalties. Could come to quite a bundle."

"Christ! I just don't . . . Eddie, can you get away from that place for a couple of hours? I've got to have a talk with you. Not about this goddam machine, something else."

"Sure. Look, plan to fly up on Friday. It'll take an hour, no more. A couple of hours for the talk with Weill. A couple more with me, then fly back. Six hours is all. Or less maybe. You can afford to take one lousy day off."

"Okay. I'll call your hotel and let you know what time I'll get in." He sounded relieved.

"Hey, wait a minute. What the hell is going on? Is it one of the suits? The closed-circuit TV giving trouble? What?"

"Oh. Sorry, Eddie. I thought I said personal. Nothing at the shop. Everything's fine. It's . . . it's something with Chris. Anyway, see you Friday."

I didn't go back to the booth, but instead found a small coffee shop in the exposition building and sat there smoking and thinking about Lenny and Christine, and Janet and me, and Mr. Weill, and God knows what else. This was it, I thought, the break we'd been waiting for. I didn't doubt that. Money, enough for once to do the things we'd been wanting to do. A bigger shop, more equipment, maybe some help, even a secretary to run herd on books. And neither Lenny nor I cared. Neither of us gave a damn.

Sitting there, with coffee in front of me, a cigarette in my fingers, I probed Christine to see what was happening. She was talking in a low voice. Her eyes were closed. Going into her was like putting on distortion lenses, putting scrambling devices in my ears. Nothing was in clear focus, no thoughts were coherent all the way through. She was on something, I realized. Something that had toned down everything, taken off all the edges, all the sharpness.

"I used to walk on that same path, after . . . I saw the fields sown, the tractors like spiders, back and forth, back and forth, stringing a web of seeds. And the green shoots—they really do shoot out, like being released, a rubber band that is suddenly let go, but they do it in slow motion. It was a wheatfield. Pale green, then as high as my shoulders so that I was a head floating over the field, only a head. Magician's best trick. Float a head. Then the harvesters came and the snow fell. And it was the same walk. You see? And I couldn't tell which was the real one. They were all real. Are real. All of them are. The tranquilizers. He said I shouldn't take them. Have to learn how to find which one is now and concentrate on it. No tranquilizers."

She sighed, and the images blurred, fused, separated again. She turned off a tape recorder, but continued to lie still, with her eyes closed. Her thoughts were a chaotic jumble. If she suspected that I was there, she gave no indication. She was afraid to open her eyes. Trying to remember why she had walked along that path so many times after Karl died out there. In the beginning, the hours of training, hours and hours of testing. Then the experiments. Afraid of him. Terribly afraid. He had cleared the world for her, but he might scramble it again. So afraid of him. If she took the capsules and went to bed, it didn't matter, but now. Afraid to open her eyes. Lenny? Isn't it time yet? It's been so long—days, weeks. Snow has fallen, and the summer heat has come and gone. I know the couch is under me, and the room around me, and my finger on the switch to the recorder. I know that. I have to repeat it sometimes, but then I know it. Mustn't open my eyes now. Not yet. Not until Lenny comes back.

I smelled burning filter and put out the cigarette and drank coffee. What would she see if she opened her eyes now? Was that her madness? A visual distortion, a constant hallucination, a mixture of reality and fantasy that she couldn't tell apart? She turned her head, faced the back of the couch.

Very slowly I forced her to sit up, and then to open her eyes. It was much harder than making her respond had been before. She kept slipping away from me. It was as if there were so many other impulses that mine was just one of a number, no more powerful than any of the illusory ones that kept holding up images for her to scan and accept, or reject. Finally she opened her eyes, and the room began to move. There was no sequence, no before and after, or cause and effect. Everything was. Winter, with a fire in the fireplace, summer with fans in the windows, company talking gaily, the room empty, children playing with puzzles, a couple copulating on the couch, a man pacing talking angrily . . . They were all real. I knew we—I had to get out of there, and there was no place to go. I was afraid of the outside world even more than the inside one. I was afraid to move. The couch vanished from behind me. The room was moving again. And I knew it would vanish, and that I would fall, like I had fallen a thousand times, a million times.

"Help me!" I cried to the pacing man, and he continued to pace although the room was certainly fading. And the children played. And the couple made love. And the fans whirred. And the fire burned. And I fell and fell and fell and fell. . . .

I sat in the coffee shop and shook. I was in a sweat, and I couldn't stop the shaking in my hands. I didn't dare try to walk out yet. No more! No more. I shook my head and swore, no more. I'd kill her. She had learned what to do, what not to do, and through my stupidity and blundering, I'd kill her.

"Sir? Is anything wrong? Are you all right?"

The waitress. She touched my arm warily, ready to jump back. "Sir?"

"I . . . I'm sorry, Miss. Sleeping with my eyes open, I guess. I'm sorry." She didn't believe me. Behind her I saw another woman watching. She must have sent the waitress over. I picked up the check, but I was afraid to try to stand up. I waited until the girl turned and walked away, and then I held the top of the table until I knew my legs would hold me.

I had the boy I'd hired relieve me for the rest of the day, and I walked back to my hotel, slowly, feeling like an old man. I started the hour-long walk making myself promises. I would never touch her again, I'd help Lenny find out the truth about her and do whatever could be done to cure her, and to get her and Lenny together. They needed each other, and I had Janet and the children, and the shop. Everything I had driven for was either mine, or within sight by now. Everything. She was a danger to me, nothing else. By the time I got to the hotel I knew the promises were lies. That as long as I could get inside that woman's head, I would keep right on doing it. And now the thought had hit me that I wanted to be with her physically, just her and me, when I did it next time. It was a relief finally to admit to myself that I wanted to seize her body and mind. And I knew that I wanted everyone else out of her life altogether. Especially Lenny. Everyone who might be a threat, everyone who suspected that there was a mystery to be unraveled. The notebooks would have to be destroyed. If Karl had known, the knowledge must be destroyed. All of it. No one to know but me.

I looked on her then as a gift from God or the Devil, but my gift. From the instant of our first meeting, when the shock of seeing her had rattled me, right through that moment, everything had been driving me toward this realization. I hadn't wanted to see it before. I had ducked and avoided it. Pretending that she was abhorrent to me, making Janet and Lenny shield me from her, shield her from me. I walked faster and with more purpose. I had too much to do now to waste time. I had to learn exactly how to enter her without the panic she always felt as soon as she knew. And I had to find a way to make her rid herself of Lenny.

I bought a bottle of bourbon, and some cheese and crackers. I had to stay in to plan my campaign, make certain of all the details this time before I touched her. I knew I would have to be more careful than I had been in the past. I didn't want to destroy her, or to damage her in any way. I might have to hurt her at first, just to show her that she had to obey. That's what always hurt her, having to fight with her. And no more tranquilizers. Karl had been right. She shouldn't have drugs, not she. What else had he learned about her? How deep had his control been? The line from Pete's letter came back to me: "He wound her up each morning. . . ."

The bastard, I thought with hatred. Goddamned bastard.

It was almost five when I got to my room. There was a message from Lenny, to call him at *her* number. I crumpled up the note and flung it across the room. How much of the notebooks had he been able to get through? How much had he told her about what he had found there? I poured a generous drink and tried to think about Lenny and Karl, and all the time I kept seeing her, a tiny, perfectly formed figure, amazingly large dark eyes, doll-like hands. . . .

She would have called Lenny after my . . . visit. I cursed myself for clumsiness. I'd have her in an institution if I wasn't more careful. Had she been able to get back to present after I ran out this time? I realized that that's how I had always left her, in a panic, or in a faint. What if she, in desperation, jumped out a window, or took an overdose of something? I took a long drink and then placed the call. I was shaking again, this time with fear that she was hurt, really hurt.

Lenny answered. "Oh, Eddie. Can you get Weill tonight? I can get in by ten fifteen in the morning. Can you find out if he can see us then?"

I swallowed hard before I could answer. "Sure. He said to call anytime. Someone will be there. Is that all? I mean when I got the message to call you at . . . her house, I was afraid something had happened."

"No. It's all right. Chris has decided to feed me, that's all." There was a false note in his voice. Probably she was nearby, listening. I fought the impulse to go out to her to find out.

"Okay. If I don't call back, assume that it's set up."

"What's wrong with you? You sound hoarse."

"Out in the rain. A bug. I'm catching that mysterious 'it' that's always going around. See you tomorrow."

"Yeah. Take care of yourself. Get a bottle and go to bed."

"Sure, Lenny."

I stared at the phone after hanging up. He was suspicious. I could tell from his voice, from the way he hedged when I asked a direct question. Maybe not simply suspicious. Maybe they actually knew by now. Not that he could prove anything. To whom? Janet? A jury? I laughed and poured another drink, this time mixing it with water. "This man, ladies and gentlemen, entered the mind of this woman at will. . . ."

At breakfast the next morning I realized that I hadn't eaten anything for a couple of days, and still didn't want to then. I had coffee and toast, and left most of the soggy bread on the dish. Lenny met me at the hotel.

"God, Eddie, you'd better get home and go to bed. We can close up the display. You look like hell."

"A bug. I'll be all right. Maybe you could stay if I do decide to take off?"

"Let's close the whole thing. It's just three more days."

"I'll stay," I said. What an ideal set-up that would have been. Him here, me back home, Janet working.

I let Lenny do the talking at Weill's office, and we got a good offer, not as much as we had hoped, but probably more than Weill had planned to make. We ended up saying that our lawyer would go over the contract and be in touch.

"Let's go to your room where we can talk without interruption," Lenny said then, and neither of us mentioned Weill again. A few months ago, B.C., Before Christine, we'd have been arrested for disturbing the peace if we'd had this offer from someone like Weill, and now, we didn't even mention it again.

I lay down on my bed and let Lenny have the only chair in the room. My head was ringing and aching mildly, and my back and legs were stiff and sore. I didn't give a damn about Lenny's problems then.

Lenny paced. "God, I don't even know where or how to begin this," he said finally. "Back at the beginning of Christine and Karl. She was such a good subject for his experiments that he based much of his research on her alone, using the other two for controls mostly. Then he found out that she was too good, that what she could do was so abnormal that he couldn't base any conclusions on his findings on her. For instance, he trained her to see objects so small that they were too small to fall on the cones and rods in the retina. And he trained her to spot a deviation in a straight line so minute that it needs special equipment to measure. Same with a circle. She can tell the exact place that a circle deviates from sphericity, and again it needs sophisticated instruments to measure it. Stereo acuity. We lose it if the peripheral vision is flattened out, if we don't have the cues. She doesn't lose it. She can see things where there isn't enough light to see them. She can see things that are too far away to see. Same with her color perception. You need a spectrometer and a spectrophotometer to make the same differentiation she can do with a glance."

He stopped and threw himself down in the chair and lighted a cigarette before he continued. "I'm getting pretty well into the notebooks. It's tough going, very technical, in a field I know nothing about. And he knew nothing about physics, and used layman's language, and a sort of shade-tree mechanic's approach with some of the equipment he had to learn to use. Anyway, after a few years, he switched to a second code. He was paranoid about his secrets. A developing psychosis is written down there plain enough even for me to see. He was afraid of her." Lenny put out the cigarette and looked at me. I was watching him, and now I shook my head.

"What do you mean afraid? Her schizophrenia? Was she showing signs of it again?"

"Will you forget that! She's not a schizo! Pretend you look at this room and you see it as it's been all through its history, with everyone who was ever here still here. Suppose you can't stop yourself from straying in time, just the way you stray in space. If you were lost in a hotel like this one and had to knock on doors, or ask people the way to your room, that's being lost in space. Lost in time is worse because no one answers until you find your own time. But those who are in your time see the search, hear your end of it, and wham, you're in a hospital."

I swung my legs over the side of the bed and sat up, but the room was unsteady. I had to support my head on my hands, propped up on my knees. "So why isn't she locked up?"

"Because she learned how to control it most of the time. Maybe a lot of people are born able to see through time and learn as infants to control it, how to tell this present from all the other images that they see. Maybe only a few do it, and most of them never learn control. God knows something drives some children into autism that they never leave. She learned. But in periods of high stress she backslid. If she became overtired, or sick, or under a strain, she couldn't hold the present in sharp enough focus. So they had her in and out of hospitals. And Rudeman became fascinated by her, and began to do his own line of research, using her, and he realized that she was seeing layers of time. Can't you just see it? Him the famous physiological psychologist denying mind from the start, being forced finally to concede that there's something there besides the brain. He struggled. It's all there. He couldn't accept, then he looked for a reasonable cause for her aberrations, finally he knew that she was somehow existing partly in another dimension that opened time just as space is opened to the rest of us." Lenny's sudden laugh was bitter and harsh. "He preferred to think he was going mad, that she was mad. But the scientist in him wouldn't let it rest there. He devised one experiment after another to disprove her abilities, and only got in deeper and deeper. First understanding, then control. He taught her how to look at *now*. He forced her into photography as part of her therapy, a continuing practice in seeing what is now."

He couldn't see my face. If he had found out that much, he must have learned the rest, I kept thinking. I couldn't tell if he suspected me or not, but if he knew that someone was driving her back into that condition, he would go down the list of names, and sooner or later he would get to me. I knew he would stop there. Too many signs. Too much evidence of my guilt. He'd know. Janet would know. I remembered the toast that *she* had made that night in her house: to the good men. I wanted to laugh, or cry.

"Christ, Eddie, I'm sorry. Here you are as sick as a dog, and I'm going on like a hysterical grandmother."

"I'm not that sick," I said and raised my head to prove it. "It just seemed like as good a way as any to listen. It's a pretty incredible story, you have to admit."

"Yeah, but you ain't heard nothing yet. Chris thinks that Rudeman is haunting her. And why not? If you know you can see the past, where do you draw the line at what is or isn't possible? She's certain that he found a way to come back and enter her mind, and she's having a harder and harder time holding on to the present. She thinks he's having revenge. He always threatened her with a relapse if she didn't cooperate wholly with him in his research."

Lenny's big face registered despair and hopelessness. He spread his hands and said, "After you swallow half a dozen unbelievable details, why stop at one more? But, damn it, I can't take that, and I know something has driven her back to the wall."

I stood up then and looked through the drawer where I had put the bourbon. Then I remembered that it was in the bathroom. When I came back with it, Lenny took the bottle and said, "When did you eat last?"

"I don't remember. Yesterday maybe."

"Yeah, I thought so. I'll have something sent up, then a drink, or you'll pass out."

While we waited I said, "Look at it this way. She sees things that no one else sees. Most people would call that hallucinating. A psychiatrist would call it hallucinating. She thinks her dead husband is haunting her somehow. What in hell are you proposing to do, old buddy?"

Lenny nodded. "I know all that. Did you know that Eric is color blind?" I shook my head. Eric was his middle son. "I didn't know it either until he was tested for it at school. A very sophisticated test that's been devised in the past twenty-five years. Without that test no one would have suspected it ever. You see? I always assumed that he saw things pretty much the way I did. I assume that you see what I see. And there's no way on this earth to demonstrate one way or the other that you do or don't. The mental image you construct and call sight might duplicate mine, or it might not, and it doesn't matter as long as we agree that that thing you're sitting on is a bed. But do you see that as the same bed that I see? I don't know. Let me show you a couple of the easy tests that Karl Rudeman used." He held up a card and flashed it at me. "What color was it?"

I grinned. I had expected to be asked which one it was. "Red," I said. "Red Queen of Hearts."

He turned the card over and I looked at it and nodded, then looked at him. He simply pointed again to the card. It was black. A black Queen of Hearts. I picked it up and studied it. "I see what you mean," I said. I had "seen" it as red.

"Another one," he said. "How many windows are in your house?"

I thought a moment, then said, "Twenty-one."

"How do you know?"

"I just counted them." I was grinning at him and his simpleminded games. But then I started to think, how had I known, how had I counted them? I had visualized room after room, had counted the windows on the walls that I had drawn up before that inner eye. The bellboy rang and came in with a cart. I tipped him and we sat down to eat sandwiches and drink coffee. "So?" I asked, with my mouth full. "So I visualized the windows. So what does that mean?"

"It means that that's how you remember things. If you had an eidetic memory, you would have seen the walls exactly as they were when you memorized them, and you could have counted the books in your line of vision, read off the titles even. The question is: are you looking into the past? No answer yet. That's what Chris can do. And that's how she sees the past. That clearly. And she sees the anomalies. You see what you expect—a red Queen of Hearts. She sees what is. But, as you say, no psychiatrist would believe it. Rudeman didn't for years, not until he did a lot of checking."

I was wolfing down the sandwiches, while he was still working on the first one. I felt jubilant. He didn't know. She didn't know. Karl haunting her! That was as good a thing for her to think as anything else.

"Okay," I said, pouring more coffee. "I see that she'd have a problem with a psychiatrist. But what's the alternative, if she's as—sick—or bothered as she seems to be?"

"The answer's in the notebooks," Lenny said. "She knows it. She tried to find it at the farmhouse, but it was impossible to work there. And now she's afraid of Rudeman all over again. She believes that somehow she caused his death. Now she has to pay."

The strong waves of guilt I had got from her. But why had he wandered out in the fields barefoot and in pajamas?

"What scares me," Lenny said, "is the slowness of getting through those notes. Bad enough while he was sane, but immeasurably harder as his psychosis developed, for the last seven or eight years. It's like trying to swim in a tar pit. By the end it was bad enough that he was certifiable, I guess. He knew the contents of those notebooks would invalidate all the work he had done in the past. Chris doesn't want to talk about it, and all I know for sure is what I've been able to dig out of that code he used."

"Psychotic how?"

"Oh, God! I don't know what name they'd put on it. In the beginning he thought she was a puppet that he could manipulate as he chose. Then gradually he became afraid of her, Chris. Insanely jealous, mad with fear that she'd leave him, terrified that someone would find out about her capabilities and begin to suspect that there was more. Just batty."

"So what do you intend to do?"

"That's what I came up here to talk to you about. I'm going to marry her." I jerked my head around to stare at him in disbelief. He smiled fleetingly. "Yeah, it's like that. Not until next year sometime. But I'm taking her on a long, long trip, starting as soon as we can get the books we'll need ready. That's why I want to wrap up a deal with Weill as fast as we can. I'll need my share. We can handle the shop however you want—keep my bench waiting, or buy me out. Whatever."

I kept on staring at him, feeling very stupid. "What books?" I asked finally, not wanting to know, but to keep him talking long enough for me to try to understand what it would mean to me.

"Rudeman used his library shelves as keys throughout. Things like one — eleven — two ninety-eight — three — six. Top row, eleventh book, page two ninety-eight, line three, word six. First three letters correspond to ABC and so on. He'd use that for a while, then switch to another book. Chris memorized those shelves, so she can find the key books. Stumbled onto it a couple of years ago. That's why she dragged all of his books with her when she ducked out of that house. She just didn't have time to go through the notebooks to sort out the ones he had used."

"Lenny, are you sure? Isn't it just the sick-bird syndrome? I mean, my God, maybe she really *is* crazy! A lot of beautiful, charming, talented people are."

"No. She isn't. Rudeman would have known after all those years. He wanted her to be, but he couldn't convince himself in the slightest that she was." He stood up. "I didn't expect you to believe me. I would have been disappointed in you if you had. But I had to get it out, get some of this stuff said. Let you know you'll have the shop to yourself for a year or so."

"What are you going to do now?"

"Go home. Move in the Donlevy house. She's on tranquilizers, and they make it awfully hard to hold on to the present. She keeps wandering back and forth. It'll take a week to get things ready to leave." He mock-cuffed me and said, "Don't look so worried. I know what I'm doing."

When he was gone I wished that he had a real inkling of what he was doing, and I knew that he would never know. I thought about that line that everyone has that he can't cross, no matter what the evidence, unless there is an inner revelatory experience. Rudeman couldn't believe she looked into the past, until he experienced it through her. Then he drew the line at possession, until it was proven again, and with its proof he had come to doubt his own sanity. Lenny could accept the research that proved she could see the past, but no farther. Whatever Rudeman had said about possession he had written off as insanity. And I had blundered in and swallowed the whole thing without reservation, through experience, firsthand experience. I tried to think in what ways I was like Rudeman, making it possible for me to do what he had done, wondering why Lenny couldn't do it, why others hadn't. My gift. Like my fingerprints were mine alone. I gave Lenny ten minutes to make sure that he really was gone, then I looked in on her. I said it to myself that way, Think I'll look in on her now.

Met by a wave of hatred stronger than anything I'd ever experienced. Resistance. Determination not to be taken again. Thoughts: not going crazy. You're real and evil. Die! Damn you, die! I killed you once! How many times! *Die!*

I drew back, but not all the way. She thought she was winning. She conjured a vision of a man in pajamas, orange and black stripes, walking, a pain in the chest, harder and harder, gasping for air. . . . I clutched the arms of the chair and said, "No! Stop thinking. No more!" The pain returned, and this time I was falling, falling. . . . I had to get out. Get away from her. The witch, bitch, which witch bitch. Falling. Pain. I couldn't get loose. Falling. Out the window, over the rail, backward, seeing the ground . . . She screamed and let go.

I lay back in the chair, trying to catch my breath, trying to forget the pain in my chest, my shoulder, my left arm. I didn't have a heart condition. Perfectly all right. Medical exam just last year. Perfectly all right. I flexed the fingers in my hand, and slowly raised the arm, afraid the pain would return with movement.

Bitch, I thought. The goddam bitch. She hadn't taken the tranquilizer, she had been waiting, steeled against me, ready to attack. Treacherous bitch. I pushed myself from the chair and stood up, and saw myself in the mirror. Grey. Aged. Terrified. I closed my eyes and said again, "Bitch!"

Was she panting also, like a fighter between rounds? If I went again now, would she be able to attack again so soon? I knew I wouldn't try. The pain had been too real.

I looked at my watch then and nearly fell down again. An hour and a half? I held it to my ear, and shook it hard. An hour and a half! Shakily I called Weill's office and told Hendrickson that he could have the machine tool picked up any time. I was going home.

There wasn't much else there, nothing that I couldn't get to the car alone. And by five I was on the highway. An hour and a half, I kept thinking. Where? Doing what?

She would kill me, I thought over and over. Just like she killed her husband. The notebooks, I had to get them myself. I couldn't let Lenny take them away. Rudeman must have discovered too late that she had power too. But he must have suspected before the end. His psychosis. The new code, afraid she had learned the old one. He must have learned about this. He had kept her ten years before she killed him. It would be in the notebooks. I drove too fast, and got home in six hours. And not until the car squealed to a stop in the driveway did I even think about what I would tell Lenny or Janet. But I didn't have to tell her anything. She took one look at my face and cried, "Oh, my God!" And she pulled me from the car and got me inside and into bed somehow, without any help from me, but without hindrance either. And I fell asleep.

I woke up when Janet did to get the kids off to school. "Are you better? I called Dr. Lessing last night, and he said to bring you in this morning."

"I'm better," I said wearily. I felt like I was coming out of a long drugged sleep, with memories hazy and incomplete. "I need to sleep and have orange juice, and that's about it. No need for you to stay home." She said she'd see about that, and she went out to get Rusty up, and to find Laura's red scarf. I hadn't seen them for almost a week, hadn't even thought of them. They would expect presents. They always expected presents. When Janet came back in fifteen minutes, I convinced her that I really was all right, and finally she agreed to go on to work. She'd call at noon.

I had breakfast. I showered and dressed. And smoked three cigarettes. And convinced myself that I wasn't sick at all. And then I walked over to Christine's house.

Lenny met me at the door. "What the hell are you doing up and out? Janet said you came in sick as a dog last night." He gave me more coffee. At the kitchen table.

"I kept thinking about what you were saying about her." I indicated the rest of the house. "And I was sick, feverish, and decided I couldn't do anything else in Chicago. So I came home. Anything I can do to help?"

Lenny looked like he wanted to hug me, but he said merely, "Yeah, I can use some help."

"Tell me what to do."

"Just stick around until Chris wakes up. I gave her a sleeping pill last night. Should be wearing off soon. What I've been doing is going down the notebooks line by line and every time he used another book for his key, Chris visualizes the shelf and finds it there. Then we find that book in the boxes. And I go on to the next one. While she rests, or is busy with her work, I find the key words in the books and decode a line or two to make sure. Rather not lug that whole library with us if I can avoid it."

I was watching him as if he were a stranger. I was thinking of him as a stranger. I had no definite plan worked out, just a direction. *She* had to get rid of him. Before he learned any more from the notebooks.

And her. What did she know? I knew I had to find out without any more delay. I tried to reach her and found a cottony foggy world. The sleeping pill. I tried to jar her awake, and got glimpses of a nightmare world of grey concrete expanses. A hall, the grey of the floor exactly matched the grey of the walls and ceiling. The joints lost their squareness ahead of me, and the hallway became a tube that grew narrower and narrower and finally was only a point. I was running toward the point at a breakneck speed.

You're not Karl! Who are you? I pulled out. What if she brought the pain again? The pseudo heart attack? I was shaking.

"Jesus, Eddie, you should be in bed." Lenny put his hand on my forehead. "Come on, I'll take you home."

I shook my head. "I'm okay. Just get a chill now and then. How about the couch here? At least I'll be handy when she gets up."

He installed me in the study on the deep green couch, with an Indian throw over me. I drifted pleasantly for a while. Then, *Get out! Who are you?—I'll never get out again. Karl knew, didn't he? I'll finish what he started. You can't hurt me the way you hurt him. I'm too strong for you. We'll go away, you and me.* I laughed, and laughing pulled away. At the same instant I heard her scream.

I sat up and waited. Lenny brought her down in a few minutes. I didn't join them in the kitchen. I watched and listened through her, and she was so agitated now that she wasn't even aware of my presence. I was getting that good at it.

"Listen, Lenny, and then leave me alone. I thought it was Karl, but it isn't. I don't know who it is. He can get inside my mind. I don't know how. I know he's there, and he makes me do things, crazy things. He'll use me, just like Karl did all those years. I can't help myself. And night after night, day after day, whatever he wants me to do, wherever he wants me to go . . .'' She was weeping and her talk was beginning to break up into incoherent snatches of half-formed thoughts.

"Chris! Stop that! Your husband was crazy! He thought he could possess you. That's insane! And he half convinced you that he could do it. But God damn it, he's dead! No one else can touch you. I won't let anyone near you."

"He doesn't have to be near me. All these weeks . . . He's been in and out, watching, listening to us go over the notebooks. He knows what's in them now. I . . . He won't stop now. And if he says I have to go with him, I'll have to."

Her voice went curiously flat and lifeless. She was seeing again that tube that ended in a point, and suddenly she longed to be on it, heading toward that point. "I'd rather die now," she said.

Lenny's big face twisted with pain. "Chris, please, trust me. I won't let anyone near you. I promise. Let me help you, Chris. Please. Don't force me out now."

"It won't make any difference. You don't understand. If he makes me go with him, I can't fight it."

But she could. I didn't know if my thoughts reminded her of the heart attack, or if she would have thought of it herself. Karl sitting in her room, watching her with a smile on his face. "You will turn them down, of course, my dear. You can't travel to Africa alone."

"No, I won't turn them down! I want to take this assignment. . . ." Slipping, blurring images, fear of being alone, of not being able to keep the world in focus. Fear of falling through the universe, to a time where there was nothing, falling forever. . . . Staring at the rejection of the offer in her own handwriting. Karl's face, sad, but determined.

"You really don't want to travel without me, my dear. It wouldn't be safe for you, you know."

And later, waking up from dreamless sleep. Knowing she had to get up, to go down the hall to his room, where he was waiting for her. *No! It's over! Leave me alone.* Swinging her legs over the side of the bed, standing up, NO! I HATE YOU! *Your soft fat hands! You make me feel dirty! Why don't you die! Have a heart attack and die.*

Fighting it to the door, dragging herself unwillingly to the door, fighting against the impulse, despising him and even more herself. He was forcing her up flights of stairs, without rails, straight down for miles and miles, and he was at her side, forcing each step. She pushed him, and he screamed. Then he was there again, and she pushed again. And again. Then he was running, and she, clinging to the doorknob in her bedroom, she was running too, pushing him off the steps as fast as he managed to climb back on, and he stumbled and fell and now she knew he would fall forever, even as she fell sometimes. Swirling into darkness with pain and terror for company. She slipped to the floor, and awakened there much later knowing only that something was gone from her life. That she felt curiously free and empty and unafraid.

I lay back down and stared at the ceiling. I could hear her footsteps recede up the stairs, across the hall to her room. Lenny's heavy tread returned and there was the sound of measured pacing. Soon, I thought. Soon it would end. And after today, after she recovered from the next few hours . . . She would have to remain nearby, here in this house as long as possible. Above me she was starting to dress. I was there. She didn't doubt a presence haunting her. Nor did she question that he could force her to go away with him if he chose.

"Who?" she whispered, standing still with her eyes closed. She imagined the suppressed fury on Lenny's big face, the pulse in his temple that beat like a primitive drum summoning him from this time back to a time when he would have killed without a thought anyone who threatened his woman. I laughed and forced his face to dissolve and run like a painting on fire.

Suddenly I was jerked from my concentration by the sound of Janet's voice. "Where is he? How is he?"

"He's sleeping in the study. Feverish, but not bad." Lenny's reassuring voice.

Janet came into the study and sat on the couch and felt my face. "Honey, I was scared to death. I called and called and no answer. I was afraid you'd passed out or something. Let me take you over to Dr. Lessing."

"Get out," I said without opening my eyes. "Just get out and leave me alone." I tried to find *her,* and couldn't. I was afraid to give it too much attention with Janet right there.

"I can't just leave you like this. I've never seen you like this before. You need a doctor."

"Get out of here! When I need you or want you I'll be in touch. Just get the hell away from me now."

"Eddie!"

"For God's sake, Janet, can't you leave me alone? I've got a virus, a bug. I feel rotten, but not sick, not sick enough for a doctor. I just want to be left alone."

"No. It's more serious than that. Don't you think I know you better than that? It's been coming on for weeks. Little things, then bigger things, now this. You have to see a doctor, Eddie. Please."

Wearily I sat up and stared at her and wondered how I'd ever found her attractive or desirable. Freckled, thin, sharp features, razorlike bones . . . I turned away and said, "Get lost, Janet. Beat it. Yeah, it started a long time ago, but it takes a club over the head, doesn't it?"

"What do you mean?"

"Just what you think I mean. I'm sick. I'm tired. I want to be alone. For a long time. Tonight. Tomorrow night. Next week. Next month. Just get out of here and leave me alone. I'll pick up some things later on after you've gone to work."

"I'm going to call Dr. Lessing."

I looked at her and hoped I wouldn't have to hit her. I didn't want to hurt her, too. Her freckles stood out in relief against the dead white of her skin. I closed my eyes. "I won't see him. Or anyone else. Not now. Maybe tomorrow. Just leave me alone for now. I have to sleep."

She stood up and backed away. She had seen. She knew that I'd hit her if she didn't get out. At the door she stopped, and the helplessness in her voice made me want to throw something at her. "Eddie? Will you stay here for the next hour?"

So she could bring in her men in white. I laughed and sat up. "I had planned to, but I guess I'd better plan again. I'll be in touch."

She left then. I could hear her voice and Lenny's from the kitchen, but I didn't try to make out their words. A clock chimed twelve. I wanted to go out there and throw Janet out. I didn't want her around for the next half hour or so. I heard the back door, then the sound of a motor, and I sighed in relief.

I went to the kitchen and got coffee and stood at the window watching snow fall.

Lenny joined me. "Janet says you had a fight."

"Yeah. I was rough on her. Sickness brings out her mother-hen instincts, and I can't stand being fussed at. What was wrong with Christine?"

"A dream." He stared at the snow. "Supposed to get a couple of inches by night, I think. Won't stick long. Ground isn't cold enough yet."

"Lenny, for God's sake quit kidding yourself. She's sick. She needs professional help."

"She thinks—she's certain that he learned enough about her to put an end to this so-called illness. She's desperately afraid of a relapse. Hospitalization, shock therapy . . ."

"What if *you* are causing her present condition? Isn't it suggestive? Her husband, now you. It's a sexual fantasy. By making her reach a decision about you, you might push her off the deep end irreversibly."

He looked shocked. "That's crazy."

"Exactly. Lenny, these things are too dangerous for a well-meaning but non-professional man to toy with. You might destroy her. . . ."

"If she was crazy you'd be making good points," Lenny said distinctly. "She isn't."

I finished my coffee. *A doctor. Shots, pills, all yesterday and last years and decades ago. Questions. Lost forever and forever falling. Through all the yesterdays. Lenny wants to get a doctor for you. A psychiatrist. You have to get him out of here now. Immediately. Even if it kills him.*

She resisted the idea. She kept trying to visualize his face, and I wouldn't let it take shape. Instead I drew out of her memories of the institutions she'd been in.

Lenny's voice startled me, and I left her.

"I don't think it's such a good idea for you to be here when she comes down. She knows you think she's psycho."

I put down my cup. "Whatever you say."

She came into the kitchen then. She was deathly pale. She had a gun in her hand. I stared at it. "Where . . . ?"

She looked at it too, looked at it in a puzzled manner. "I had it in my car when I came here," she said. "I found it when I was unpacking and I put it upstairs in my room. I just remembered."

"Give it to me," Lenny said. He held out his hand and she put the small automatic in it.

I sighed my relief. That was the last thing I wanted her to do. She'd be locked up the rest of her life. Now if I could make her drive him out, maybe he'd use it himself.

Lenny kept his hand in his pocket, over the gun. "Why were you thinking of guns right now? Where was this?"

"In my train case. I told you . . ." She glanced at me and I turned my back to stare at the snow again. I was watching my own back then, and seeing Lenny's face and the kitchen that I was keeping in focus only through great effort. "I told you," she said again. "If he makes me go back with him, I'll have no choice." I made her add, "The only way I escaped from Karl was through his death."

She shuddered, and an image of Karl's face swam before her eyes. It was contorted with pain and fear. It was replaced by another face, Lenny's, also contorted by pain and fear. And the image of a hospital ward, and a doctor. And I watched his face change and become my own face. The image dimmed and blurred as I tried to force it away, and she fought to retain it. The concrete corridor was there. She forced the image of a man backward through the corridor, grey walls and ceiling and floor all one, no up and no down, just the cylinder that was growing smaller and smaller. I tried to pull away, and again there was a duel as she fought to keep the imagery. Cliffs, I thought. Crumbling edges, falling . . . Hospital, shots, electroshock . . .

"Chris, what is it?" Lenny's voice, as if from another world, faint, almost unrecognizable.

"I don't know. Just hold me. Please."

Cliffs . . . Exploding pain in my chest suddenly. Burning pain in my shoulder, my arm. Darkness. Losing her, finding her again. Losing . . .

"You!" Her voice coarse, harsh with disbelief.

I turned from the window clutching my chest. The room was spinning and there was nothing to hold on to. *Let go. They'll lock you up.* Pain.

"Eddie!"

"You!" she said again, incredulously.

Get the gun back! Lenny. No more pretense now. My hand found something to hold, and the room steadied. Feeling of falling, but knowledge of standing perfectly still, fighting against the nausea, the pain. *Get the gun. Reach in his pocket and take it out.* We, she and I, were in that other place where the grey corridor stretched endlessly. We had time because there was no time. She backed a step away from Lenny, and I forced her to move closer again, seeing the beads of sweat on her forehead, the trembling in her hands. From somewhere else I could hear Lenny's voice, but I couldn't hear the words now. GET THE GUN!

"Lenny, get out! Leave. Go away fast. He'll kill you!" Her voice came from that other place, but the words were echoed up and down the corridor.

You and I. I'll take care of you. I won't let anyone hurt you.

Lenny's hands on me, trying to force me to a chair. Seeing myself sprawled across the table unconscious. *"No!"* I tried to make her fall down an elevator shaft, and saw even clearer my own figure across the table. I tried to remember how it felt to fall in an uncontollable plunge, and nothing came. She had to faint. Something could be salvaged even now, if only she would faint, or have hysterics, or something, I couldn't break out, pull away. She was holding the back of a chair with both hands, holding so hard her muscles hurt. I saw her grasp tighten and felt the pain erupt again, this time blacking out everything momentarily. Lenny . . . I couldn't make her move. I slipped my hand into his pocket then and my fingers felt the metal, warm from the close pocket. I pulled it out and aimed it at Lenny. I was seeing his face from a strange angle, her angle. A cross-section of his face. A Dali painting of fear and shock. She was beating on me and I closed my other hand over her wrist, a child's wrist. Laura's wrist. Back in that timeless corridor. *Why didn't you look into the future too? Why just the past?*

He said I did. I repressed it. Too frightening. The image of the man sprawled across the table, clearer, detailed. Real.

Absolute terror then. Hers. Everything shifting, spinning away, resolving into strange shapes, displaced items of furniture, strange people moving about. Intolerable pain as she lashed out in desperation to find her way through the maze of time. And I was outside again.

I tried to go into her and couldn't. I could see her, wide-eyed, catatonic, and couldn't reach her at all. It was as if the wall that had been breached had been mended now, and once again kept me and all others outside. I didn't know how I had gone through it before. I didn't even know if I had.

I heard the gun hit the floor before I realized that I had dropped it. I felt the table under my cheek before I realized that I had collapsed and was lying across it. I heard their voices, and I knew that she had found her way back, but I couldn't see them. For the moment I was free of the pain. Almost uninterested in the figure slumped across the table.

"You'd better get an ambulance," she said. I marveled at the calm self-assurance in her voice. What had she seen while she had stood unmoving, rigid? She touched my forehead with fingers that were cool and steady.

"Was it real?" I whispered. "Any of it?"

"You'll never know, will you?" I didn't know if she said the words aloud or not. I listened to their voices drifting in and out of consciousness while we waited for the ambulance. Was it real? I kept coming back to that.

Was what real?

Anything.

THE TIME
PIECE

On a snowy December night in Manhattan, Richard Weiss was given a testimonial dinner, a solid gold watch, and told good-bye by his company. Following the official ceremonies there was a private party given jointly by the president of the company, Hanson Blakesley, and William Weiss, the firstborn son of the newly retired treasurer. William was the fastest-rising star of the company, the president said proudly with one arm about the younger Weiss's shoulders. A photographer duly snapped a shot, and the elder Weiss drank another glass of champagne.

"Rich, are you ready to go now?" his wife, Myrtle, asked later. "These parties just wear me out. Never can find a chair. All these people . . ."

"My last official party," he said. "Is my tie all right? Where'd the photographer go? We need pictures to go with the story in next month's magazine."

Myrtle sighed.

Rich posed with the president, with his fast-rising star-son, with the new treasurer, and at two in the morning he was ready to leave. The snow measured four inches. There were no taxis, and he no longer had use of the official company car.

"Hey, Dad, wait a sec! We'll drop you!" Jerry Lister, his daughter's husband, yelled from the doorway, not risking a snowflake on his tarnished-varnished hair. Rich sighed, as Myrtle did, and their sighs were harmonious.

"How the mighty . . . ," he said.

"It's a ride," Myrtle said.

Kathleen was in a pout at being dragged from the party so early. Sulkily she said, "So you are off tomorrow to the Bahamas, huh?"

"Forty-one years," her mother said. "Forty-one years in that company. And tonight, the last night, last official function. And we get no car."

"And then Florida. Boy, that's some life. Cruises, winter in Florida."

"Your father worked twelve hours a day, six days a week, in the beginning."

"You hear that, Jerry? Just listen to her. Are you ever going to be able to take *me* on a Bahama cruise? A winter in Florida?"

Jerry whistled and cut into fast-moving traffic, sliding on a layer of icy water over snow.

"Jerry, we've got time," Myrtle said. "Admire the snow. Like Christmas Eve."

"He always drives too fast," Kathleen said. "Ever since I bought that insurance. Thinks if he wrecks us, I'll be the one to get it, not him. Thinks that lucky star is all his. All his."

"Hey, let's see the watch," Jerry said, reaching over his shoulder. "How much is it worth?"

Rich clamped his right hand over the wrist watch as if afraid the groping fingers would somehow get it off his arm. "Tomorrow you can see, Jerry. Now you drive, okay? With two hands."

"Sure, Dad. Relax. Relax. Beats walking, doesn't it?"

"We'll let you know when, and if, we get there," Myrtle said. "The truck, Jerry. Watch the truck!"

"I don't know, Myrtle. I just don't know," Rich said later, peeling off his formal clothes. "William can't wait to usurp me. My only girl child married to a bum. Michael alienated, yes, alienated because his wife thinks we're poor white trash, or something. I can't figure out that girl. Never could. What does she expect? A strange woman Michael chose for his wife. Strange. And Eric. My poor little Eric. A hippie. What's it all about?" He turned to look at Myrtle but she was sleeping, with her mouth partly open.

"I just don't know," he said again. "My pretty little wife all blubber and open mouth and curlers," he said, even louder. Then he turned off the light and climbed into his own bed.

Myrtle started to write postcards as soon as they were shown to their cabin on the cruise ship. She wrote her way down the coast, across the ocean, through the islands, and on to Miami. What impressions she carried away from the cruise were formed by the postcards and curio shops. They sent tons of souvenirs home. She gained seven pounds on the trip.

They bought a three-bedroom house on the ocean, and every day for the first week they swam. Myrtle stepped on something that slithered under her foot, and she never went into the water again. Rich took up fishing and golf. He called his former associates once every three or four days, but the last call he made to Mr. Blakesley, he was told that the president was in conference and would call him back. He never did. Rich didn't call north again.

Myrtle joined several clubs and was happy with their activities. She went on a diet and bought new clothes in anticipation of the day she would be able to wear them. Rich canceled his golf appointments and bought a snorkel. He bought a small boat and sold it again when he learned that it was more trouble to launch and keep in repair than the pleasure he gained from it seemed worth. Kathleen left her husband and visited them for three weeks crying almost continuously. Jerry came to collect her and there was a noisy reunion and a reconciliation. They left together. Michael and Phyllis, his strange wife, visited them with their three children. Phyllis sniffed the ocean air through her long, straight nose and promptly started to sneeze and didn't stop again until they got to the airport to return to Denver, her home town. She pronounced the ocean too big and smelly.

"In New York she got claustrophobia, out here it's the sneezes.

I think she should see a head-shrinker," Rich said after seeing them off.

"Rich, what's the matter with you? You never used to brood and worry about the kids. Not when they were home and you could of been some help to me. Not when they were young and I was the one who sat up night after night, and you were always off somewhere, and they were out too late. Why didn't you worry then when it might have done some good?"

He paced. "Four times I gave Jerry Lister a job. Four times. Why does she always go back with him? You tell me, Myrtle. You're a woman, you know your daughter. Tell me, why?"

"When Michael broke his arm, where were you? Cleveland! You were in Cleveland."

"If I could only understand this one crazy girl. I think he even hits her."

"I'm going to the Women's Auxiliary. We're discussing the increase of filthy literature on newsstands this week, and what to do about it. What's the matter with you, you don't go to any of your clubs any more? For thirty years you were out three, four nights a week, this club, that club, this emergency. Now nothing. What's the matter?"

"We could go on a longer cruise. . . . You'd get writer's cramp." He lighted a cigar and said suddenly, "I'm going to get a job."

"Job? What do you mean get a job?"

"I mean work. Honest work."

"At your age? You're crazy. Who'd hire you now? For what? You just want to embarrass me."

"Got nothing to do with you. I need a job."

"Rich, have you been playing the market? You promised . . ."

"We are not in trouble. The only time I ever played the market we came out forty thousand dollars to the good."

"But I was scared silly all the time." She looked at her watch and picked up her purse and gloves. "Anyway, what kind of a job? Bank trustee? Adviser to a firm here?"

"God, I don't know. Just a job. After all, forty-five years of experience . . ."

A horn sounded from the driveway and Myrtle hurried to the door. "There's Lucille. I have to go, dear. Have a good evening. Back early."

" . . . shouldn't be allowed to go to waste," he finished to the empty room. His watch told him that it was March 14, 1970, 8:03 P.M.

On television there was a situation comedy, an action western, a game of some sort with people jumping up and down and hugging each other over a refrigerator that one or another of them had won, or had not won, but might. He turned it off. His watch told him that it was March 14, 1970, 8:13 P.M.

He walked on the beach for half an hour, then went to his library and picked up the volume of Mann that he was reading: *Joseph and His Brothers.* He was catching up on some of the things he hadn't had time for in the past. He read, and when he put the book down, his eyes tired, his watch told him it was March 14, 1970, 10:30 P.M. "Never did give Jerry a chance to examine it," he said aloud. "Never did tell him how much it was worth. Eight hundred thirty-nine dollars and ninety-eight cents. Retail. Cost four hundred fifty-nine dollars to manufacture." He rubbed a finger over the crystal, smearing it. He polished it to a gleaming surface with his handkerchief and then opened the case to look at the jeweled insides. "Preset at the factory," the advertisements read, "You need never do a thing but wear and admire it. Never wind, never set, never worry about the time again."

"Let time take care of itself," Rich said, repeating the first advertising slogan that had heralded the new watch. He found the screw that reset the watch during its annual cleaning, and he turned it.

He closed the case hurriedly when he heard Myrtle's voice from the other room. Finally. He got up and walked toward the door, and his steps faltered, then stopped.

"Rich, aren't you ready yet? Come on, it's getting late."

Myrtle was in front of him, climbing steps. She stopped, silhouetted against a closed door. Tall, statuesque, wide hips and narrow waist, full breasts. "For heaven's sake, Rich, come on. Let me look at you."

He backed down a step; she followed and touched his shoulder, brushing something from it. "You look fine, dear. Come on now. Don't be nervous. After all, Mr. Blakesley must like you or he wouldn't have invited us over, now would he?" She turned again toward the door saying, "It must be a promotion. Why else would he have us to tea?"

Rich looked down at himself: dressing gown, slippers. He felt his face, the heaviness at his jawline, the bushy eyebrows, and he turned to the glass door, using it as a mirror. White hair, lines, heavy glasses. He hadn't changed, was still Rich. But Myrtle?

"Myrtle," he said choking, "Look at me. What's happened?"

"I hear someone coming now. Don't forget, Rich, no language and don't eat as if you didn't get anything at home. . . . Here they come."

"Myrtle, look at me! I'm not who you think . . ."

"Mr. and Mrs. Weiss? This way, please."

He tried to hang back, but Myrtle's hand was firm on his arm. The maid closed the door and walked before them. Rich looked about desperately, searching for someplace to hide, someplace to run to. He remembered the old house. Blakesley's first house, a handsome brownstone that had long since been torn down to make room for high-rise apartments.

"Ah, Richard." Hanson Blakesley met them and took Rich's hand, squeezing it, pumping it vigorously. He was young, his hair dark, untouched by grey. "How pleasant this is, don't you think? Away from those musty offices. And the charming Mrs. Weiss. Come in, my dear. Here, this is a comfortable chair. You know Mrs. Blakesley, don't you."

Dianne Blakesley smiled at them wearily. She was pale and thin with great luminous eyes. Her hand that she held for Rich to kiss was limp.

He didn't touch the hand. She acted as if he had kissed it, and her eyes gazed into his with embarrassing candor.

"I don't know how to explain any of this," he said, pointing to his clothes. "Frankly . . ."

"I know you are surprised at this offer, but I've been watching you closely this past year that you've been with us. . . ."

"What I mean is that either I'm dreaming, or else something really wonky has happened. . . ."

"And now, no more business. You can let me know in a few days. . . . Mrs. Weiss, you are looking even more lovely than usual. It was a boy, wasn't it?"

"Yes. William."

"How nice. Is he a fat baby? Is he good?" Dianne Blakesley poured tea and smiled pleasantly.

"Look, you don't have to pretend that you don't notice anything. I mean that makes it even worse than it is. Myrtle, put down that cup and look at me. William is a grown man, older than Blakesley here even."

"Our two girls are in Newport with their grandparents. When they return we must let the children get together."

"God damn it! Look at me! I'm an old man. I retired from the company last winter. I'm sixty-five years old."

"I predict that we'll expand year after year. These are fine workmen who've come over as immigrants from Germany. Clockmakers, fine detail workers. . . ."

"Myrtle, let's get out of here. They're crazy. Both of them . . ."

"Mrs. Blakesley, they are beautiful children, both of them. Five and three? How wonderful . . ." Myrtle handed the photographs to Rich. He dropped them.

". . . and we'll be planning for new plants on the west coast in the next five or ten years. Diversify. That's the new word, Weiss. Spread out, cover the fields, as many of them as you can. . . ."

"Myrtle, I'm going. Right now. You can do as you please. I'm leaving." Backing toward the door, he waited for a sign of understanding. They continued to make small talk, to smile at each other.

Myrtle stood up. "Thank you so much for having us. We must be going. The baby, you know . . ."

"Of course, my dear." Dianne Blakesley didn't rise. She looked too frail to lift herself. Her eyes met Rich's again, and this time her eyelids drooped ever so slightly.

"No," he said. "You did that to me once and I was too young and green to know any better, but not again. Not with you."

She smiled at him gently. "Good-bye, Richard. I may call you Richard? I do hope that we'll all become very good friends."

"Oh, no, not this time. You'll not see me again, Mrs. Blakesley. I'm turning down the job. I know what'll happen to me. Stuck in that same office for the next forty years. Not this time."

Outside the house, waiting for a taxi, supplied by Blakesley, Myrtle squeezed his arm. "I can't stand it," she said. "I can't wait to get out of sight of the house and kiss you. What would they think if I kissed you here on the street? Treasurer's assistant at your age, with no more experience than you have. I knew you would be a success, Rich. I knew it. I told Papa that you would."

"God damn it, Myrtle! *Look at me!*"

"We'll move, of course. No more walk-ups. A first-floor apartment for now, and in a year or two, a house. Like this one. With an upstairs, and a maid to open the door . . ."

The watch. It was to blame. He fingered it, trying to shake her loose from his arm so he could open the back and get to the mechanism that would reset it.

". . . and a nurse for William."

"And grandparents in Newport?" He had it opened now.

"We'll have to buy new clothes. Did you notice the lace on her blouse? Handmade, of course . . ."

He turned the screw as far as it would go.

". . . and Lucille said that if I would be willing to serve on the board for the coming year, she is certain that we can clean up this whole area. . . ."

"Clean up?" He looked about quickly. The living room on the beach.

"Of course, I'm not at all certain that she's right. I mean, this has been going on for so many years that I'm afraid it will take more than just one year to drive them all out entirely, but . . ."

"Did you just get in?"

". . . at least we can make a stab at it. Did you watch the news? I heard that the blizzard has become worse."

"What? No. No, I was reading."

"Well. I guess there's always a blizzard somewhere or other. I hope Kathleen has enough sense not to get out in it."

Rich looked at the watch: 11:26. He opened it and turned the screw, very slowly and carefully, watching the hand until it was at 11:15. He looked up to see Myrtle coming through the doorway.

"It was such a good meeting, Rich. You wouldn't believe the stuff that's available on the stands right now, to say nothing of the films." She moved past him, taking off her gloves. She went into the bedroom and came out with her slippers on. "But the refreshments. Yii! German chocolate cake, at this time of night. I need something to settle my stomach. You want tea?"

"Kathleen called. She's pregnant."

"You'd think they'd take into consideration that some of us aren't as young as we used to be. You know. German chocolate cake at this time of night." Her voice faded as the kitchen door swung shut. She was back in a moment. "But the most exciting thing. Lucille is taking the bit in her own two hands. Forming a committee, a board of responsible women . . ." She moved toward the kitchen again.

"Jerry was killed in an automobile accident."

". . . and Lucille said that if I would be willing to serve on the board for the coming year, she is certain that we can clean up this whole area. . . ."

He turned the screw as far to the right as it would go.

"You'd think a woman who's almost forty would have enough sense not to get caught out in a blizzard, but I worry about her." The teakettle whistled and she left again.

Very cautiously he reset the watch for two minutes in the past.

". . . this time of night." Her voice faded as the kitchen door swung shut. She was back in a moment. "But the most exciting thing. Lucille is taking the bit in her own two hands. Forming a committee, a board of responsible women . . ." She moved toward the kitchen again. He followed her and caught the doorknob and held it. He felt the pressure from the other side as she tried to turn the knob. ". . . and Lucille said that if I would be willing to serve on the board for the coming year, she is certain that we can clean up this whole area. . . ." Her voice faded out, then sounded behind him stronger than before. She had gone out the other door, through the hallway and back into the living room.

"Of course, I'm not at all certain that she's right. . . ."

He turned the screw as far as it would go.

Rich heard her coming toward the door, and he moved to the living room and sat down. She followed with a tea tray.

"I thought you might change your mind," she said. "Honestly, I don't like to even think it, but I really believe that young snippet, Harry Lowenstein's wife, you know, the freckled girl all elbows and knees always uncovered almost up to her bottom, had the cake on purpose. At that age they can eat glass at midnight and sleep like angels." She sipped steaming tea, then belched.

"I can do it," Rich said. "I can do it! I can change the past."

"The way she smokes. And drinks, too, I hear, she'll get hers soon enough. Won't take another forty years either. . . ."

"I can go back and turn things around, undo things, do other things. . . ."

"You didn't hear *her* voting to clean the bookstores and the newsstands. Bet she reads every piece of trash that comes along. Wait until you see some of the stuff that's available. Lucille's bringing some of it over tomorrow."

"Myrtle, will you listen to me for just one minute? Please?"

"Oh, yes. I almost forgot. We had this film, too. I never believed in such things before. Never heard of such a thing. I always thought when they talked about blue films, that it had to do with color photography. But it doesn't, Rich. Did you know that?"

"Myrtle, just shut up a minute. Try to understand what I'm telling you. I can go back and change the past. Alter it. Make it different."

"We'll change things. You bet your little old shaving mug we will." She finished her tea and patted her stomach. "There. That's better. Are you coming now?"

"Myrtle! Look at me. Can't you hear what I'm saying to you? I can change things. I can change things for Eric, give him another chance . . ."

"Oh, Eric's all right, Rich. He wouldn't be mixed up with anything like this stuff. I mean, all young people aren't, you know, even if they don't work, and drop out of school, and play the guitar. He wouldn't do anything like this."

"Myrtle, not another word. Don't say another word. Just shut up and listen to me for one minute. Will you please?"

"Why, Rich, is something wrong?"

"Listen, Myrtle. I can make things different. I can change things. I made you go around through the hall, and the first time, two times, you came through the door to the living room. I made you do something different. The past can be changed."

She belched again. "I wish you would do something about that second piece of cake, then. She pressed it on me deliberately, I'm sure."

"Not your past. Just mine. I have to have been there."

"Oh, that's too bad." She went around him into the bedroom. "I almost forgot. Lucille's husband will talk to you about a position with the hospital. They need an advisor, or something. . . ."

He went back to the living room and her voice faded out. In a moment she looked through the open door and said, "Did you hear what I said?"

"I did change something. It can be done."

"I told her you'd give him a call. . . ." As she moved about getting ready for bed her voice rose and fell. ". . . no salary, naturally . . ."

"Naturally," he said, fingering the watch.

He walked around the living room, trying to think of another test. He stopped before the rogues' gallery: twenty or more pictures of the four children that covered one of the walls. Eric at twenty-one, handsome, laughing, a guitar on his legs. Kathleen in her sweet-sixteen party gown. Pretty, slim. William, forty, too much like his father to be handsome, but rugged-looking, capable. Michael. His hand stopped fingering the watch and he studied Michael's picture. He remembered exactly when and how Michael had met that strange girl. If he could change that . . . He turned away. None of his business. And besides they had three children, his grandchildren.

His gaze fell on snapshots on an end table. Jerry Lister and Kathleen had taken them after their boisterous reunion. Jerry Lister.

He sat down and closed his eyes, trying to remember. Finally he turned the watch hands backward.

He looked about the room and nodded. Okay so far. He was in his robe and slippers, and Jerry Lister was there, red-faced, almost frozen, no more than twenty. And Kathleen, a slip of a girl of seventeen.

She said, "Can we borrow your car? You know nothing will go wrong. . . ."

He turned the screw to the right. He had gone into it just about three minutes too late. He reset the watch and this time found himself seated, with the *Times* on his lap. He heard the record player from upstairs, and the television from the study, and he waited for the doorbell to ring. When it did he opened the door, admitting a frigid wind, barring a red-faced young man.

"Hi, I'm Jerry Lister. Is Kathleen home?"

"No. She is at her aunt's house. Good-bye." The boy pushed past him and was inside before he could brace himself. He turned the screw to the right. Again.

The doorbell rang. He answered it grimly. The wind rushed in and the boy tried to squeeze by Rich, who stood firmly in the way.

"Hi, I'm Jerry Lister. Is Kathleen home?"

"No. Get lost." He braced himself, but the wind blew stronger, and with it added to the weight of the boy who was also pushing now, he found that he couldn't shut the door.

"My car broke down. Water in the gas line froze, I think. Five or six blocks from here." The boy had won—he was stronger than he looked. He panted slightly and handed his coat to Rich and walked past him to the living room, where he held his hands out to the fire. "I heard on the radio that it's going down to twenty below tonight. Man, it's cold. . . ."

Rich turned the watch screw to the far right.

Another way. Meet him outside, before he got to the door. He reset the watch. In his robe and slippers he went out on the porch and met Jerry Lister coming up the walk.

"Just hold it right there, young man." Jerry kept walking. Rich grabbed his arm and Jerry tried to move toward the house, not looking at him. Rich pushed him from the sidewalk. The boy hesitated momentarily, then darted behind Rich and trotted through the frozen grass to the porch. "Like a goddam salmon," Rich muttered. He reached out toward the boy, running also now, and his hand closed on the doorknob. He looked about. He was in the hallway ready to open the door. He didn't turn the knob, but stood with it in his hand. It turned. Before he could shoot the bolt into place, the door was pushed open and Jerry Lister stood before him, half frozen, panting.

"Hi, I'm Jerry . . ."

"Oh, shut up!" Rich turned the screw.

He looked at the picture of Kathleen and Jerry taken here in his living room. Jerry was smiling broadly, and Kathleen was laughing. He had just told an obscene joke. "One more time," Rich said. "I'll try one more time."

He reset the watch.

The doorbell rang and he opened the door, and when the red-faced boy stepped inside, he swung at him with all his strength. The boy ducked.

"Hi, I'm Jerry Lister. . . ."

He swung again, and this time his fist glanced off Jerry's chin. Jerry hit Rich once, just above his robe belt. Rich staggered back and caught the wall to steady himself.

". . . Is Kathleen home?" The boy was taking off his coat. He held it out to Rich and walked past him to the living room. "My car broke down. . . ."

"You're a bum. You'll always be a bum. 'Water in the gas line froze, I think.' "

". . . Water in the gas line froze, I think."

Rich left him still talking and waited at the stairs. Kathleen came running down and past him into the living room. "You should see your face!"

"Kathleen, get back upstairs. You can't go out with this bum and he can't stay here and listen to records or watch television. . . ."

"Dad, have you met Jerry? My father, Mr. Weiss."

"I said, get back upstairs. And tell Eric to turn off that god-damned record player! Where is your mother?"

"Can we borrow your car? You know nothing will go wrong with it." Kathleen smiled prettily at him and he grabbed her shoulders and shook her.

"Will you listen to me! Tell him to go away."

"Hey, you got a television? Let's do that, Kathleen. . . ."

"All right! All right! I tried. So do whatever it is you do and next week tell me that you want to get married and see if I care. You'll be sorry. Both of you!" He turned the watch screw to the right.

"I tried," he said. "By God, I tried." He picked up the snap-

shot of the pair twenty years later, laughing, smiling, going nowhere, doing nothing, just laughing away their lives. Laughing,
fighting, separating, going back together. "I just don't know," he
said, and went to bed. Myrtle stirred restlessly throughout the night
and he wondered if it was the German chocolate cake, or the dirty
movies she'd seen.

"Have some more honey, dear. The biscuits are very good this
morning. I have to remember to tell Hannah. I think she forgets
to put in the soda sometimes. . . ."

"Myrtle, when was Eric home last time?"

"She never makes them the same way two days . . . What, dear?"

He repeated the question.

"Oh, two years ago, wasn't it? Right after the Chicago mess.
Do you like this tupelo honey, or do you like the wild honey
better? I can't make up my mind."

"Did you talk to him then?"

"Who?"

"Did you talk to Eric?"

"Of course." She opened another biscuit and considered the two
pitchers of honey.

"I don't mean just polite conversation, or mother-son fussing.
Did you really talk to him?"

"You know that Lucille is bringing over those pictures at eleven?
I told you, didn't I?" She looked up from the biscuit and said
then, "I'm sure we talked, dear."

"Don't you remember?"

"You know how upset I was with him. What do you want to
know?"

"I can't remember really talking to him. I wondered if you did."

She became thoughtful for five seconds, then shrugged and
said, "I'm sure we talked."

"Do you remember exactly when he came home, the day?"

"Let me think. He still had stitches, or were they out by then? It
was snowing. I remember that he was tracking snow on the Aubus-

son. It must have been a few days before Christmas. He wasn't there for Christmas, I know. But he drank a lot of eggnog. I remember that I told him he was drinking too much eggnog. . . ."

Rich stood up. "Okay, I thought you might know the exact day." He went to the study and closed the door. He had made a list earlier, a list of his children and what they talked about. He had written by William's name: business, inanities. Kathleen: Jerry. Michael: Denver real estate, or the grandchildren. And by Eric's name he had been able to write down nothing at all. When Myrtle had become pregnant at forty, people had predicted either a moron or a genius. Always one or the other, they had said, when the mother gets to that age. He'd been the other. But what did Eric talk about? How could he have forgotten? His fingers rested on the watch, but he didn't turn it yet. He wanted to remember first, then go back.

He thought a long time before he could remember when they'd had the very brief conversation. The night before Eric left again. He had given him a Christmas present, a check. Later it had come back endorsed over to . . . it was gone. Well, he could find the canceled check if he really wanted to know who Eric had given it to. That wasn't important now. Some charity, orphans, something like that. He tried several times before he got the time set for that night, and then when he returned to the present, he couldn't remember what they had talked about. He tried again.

"I will remember," he said. He had a notebook out and when Eric spoke, he made notes.

"Of course you're not bad, I didn't mean to imply that you were. Or the others like you."

Rich wrote: "I'm not bad."

"Have it your way, evil. But, you see what you do? You say if we're not evil, then we must be good. And I don't buy that."

Rich was busy writing and made no response. After a moment Eric continued.

"People have always done it. You hear what you want to hear, see what it pleases you to see, and let the rest go by the board. When America went pragmatic, it took most of the world with it, but now the excluded parts are pulling their way. Pragmatism just isn't good enough." He was talking too fast for Rich now. All he could do was make notes of key words and trust his memory to fill in. Or replay it over and over until he got it all.

"Dad, cut it out. You know I'm not a communist, or an anarchist. Not the way you mean that." Had he called his son a communist? He scribbled faster.

". . . keep right on playing. And we're not willing to any longer. But it won't just change. You have to do it yourself, scrap the part, create a new one and be ready to scrap it when it doesn't work, or doesn't mean anything any longer. And not just once a year, but every day, every minute, every second."

Myrtle entered, carrying a tray of eggnog and cookies. "Make him stay home, Rich. Tell him you'll give him a good job. How much would you want, Eric?"

"So long, Mother. Dad."

Rich turned the watch to the present. Most of the conversation was already gone. He looked at the notes and the scattered words meant nothing to him: communist . . . anarchy . . . roles, playing games. . . .

Roles? Games? He shook his head and put the notebook down. He didn't understand. He heard Myrtle's voice from the other room and the door opened. "Rich, Lucille's here. Did you want to see any of this material she brought along?"

"What? What material?"

"I told you. The stuff the club members picked up at various newsstands and bookstores."

"Not right now. Later maybe."

Had she told him? He couldn't remember. He supposed she must have. It was part of her role as the wife of a retired executive to take part now in citizens' groups for this or that cause. She would duly report to him anything of interest, and he would forget it, recognizing at some level that it was unimportant. When it was brought up, he would have to search for it, then remember vaguely, only to let it slip from consciousness as soon as she stopped talking about it. Dirty pictures. He laughed suddenly and went to the door and listened. They were in the next room. He could hear Myrtle's gasp, and a smothered scream. "They sell things like that?" He returned to his chair.

At lunchtime he went into the living room, where Myrtle and Lucille had the photographs and magazines opened on the coffee table and spread over the couch. Hurriedly they began to gather them together when he opened the door.

"Hannah says lunch is ready," he said.

"Don't look," Myrtle said, her face flame-colored. Lucille had turned her back, but her neck was scarlet.

"Why? If they're for sale they can't be all that bad."

"Just don't look now. I'll leave them for you," Lucille said.

He watched them scramble to pick up the offensive material. He said, "I don't think you ladies should spend hours poring over stuff like that."

"When you consider that children can just walk in and buy it . . ."

"I read that most of it's bought by men between twenty-three and thirty-five."

"Ten-year-olds, fourteen-year-olds. Getting their impression of the world from this . . . this . . . filth."

"And then going out and raping, torturing . . ."

"Ten-year-olds? Besides I read that these provide an outlet for repressed people. Psychiatrists say that it actually helps them."

"Spending lunch money on this filth, waiting to attack some lonely old woman who is helpless . . ."

Rich looked from his wife to her friend. Very slowly he said, "One, two, three, testing."

Myrtle looked up at him. "What did you say?"

"Nothing. Lunch is ready."

"Yes, we're coming."

He backed out and closed the door again.

He tried to turn the watch screw, but it was already as far as it would go to the right. He waited for them in the dining room, looking through the *Times*. He didn't read anything there.

Hannah came in and placed vichyssoise on the plates. Water beads formed on the iced bowls. Suddenly Rich became aware that she was talking to him.

". . . so I'll bring her on Friday, and then you can get acquainted and not have a complete stranger around."

"Who, Hannah? Who are you going to bring in?"

"My cousin. I told you, remember? She'll do for you and Mrs. Weiss while I'm gone."

"You're leaving?"

"Mr. Weiss, don't you remember? My daughter's getting married and I have to go to Arizona for the wedding, help her get ready and all. I told you last week."

"I guess I forgot. I'm sorry, Hannah."

Lucille swept into the room then, followed by Myrtle, who looked at Rich guiltily. When he met her gaze, she blushed. "I was thinking," he said, seating them, "what a curious thing memory is. Kids have such a different set of memories than their parents. We forget the unconnected things that to them were very important. Things they remember. We remember other things that were important to us and meant nothing to them."

There was an uneasy silence and the two women spooned soup. Rich tasted his and then put his spoon down. "So there are all those different sets of memories floating around, and no one to say which set is right, if any of them are. . . . Maybe there is no one single past."

"That's why we study history and keep diaries, records. I mean, you just can't trust your own memory even," Lucille said. She had been a history teacher in the thirties.

"I don't mean only big things that can be checked in books. I mean little things that you might forget within minutes, or seconds even."

"Like what?"

"Oh, like turning your back on someone and not knowing what he had on, or what color his eyes are. Little things. Like forgetting what someone said to you on a bus, or in an elevator; like forgetting who was in the elevator with you, although at the time you knew."

"But they don't mean anything to you. Why should you remember anything that has no meaning in your life? You are busy with your own thoughts at those times. You just answer people automatically."

"That's what I mean. And you live ninety percent of your life automatically, without remembering anything about it."

"Rich, what's got into you?" Myrtle glanced nervously at Lucille, then back to her husband. She touched the bell for Hannah. "Dear," she said to Lucille, "are you going to show those films to the Eastern Star committee on Friday night? Perhaps I could help you, if you need help. . . ."

"Fine. I really could use a hand. I'll pick you up. . . ."

Hannah brought in cheese soufflé and cleared away the soup bowls.

"I almost forgot," Rich said. "There's a call that I have to make. If you'll excuse me."

"Rich? Who to? Why now?"

"I'll be right back," he said and went into the study. He kicked at the door as he passed it, but he saw when he picked up the telephone that it hadn't closed. He shrugged.

"Operator, I want to call Eric Weiss at this number. If he isn't there, leave your operator's number for him to return the call, will you?"

"Rich, are you calling Eric? Why?" Myrtle stood in the open doorway.

"Go back to lunch, dear. I'll be with you in a minute."

She left the door and sat down again.

He could hear her say to Lucille, "Of course he isn't calling Eric. We haven't heard from him since he left the last time. Nothing in two years. You'd think he'd have a little more consideration for his mother, but not Eric. . . ."

"Hello. Eric? . . . Yeah, it's me. I remembered that you said you could be reached here if there was an emergency. Listen, Eric, I think I have found out something. I have this watch, the company gave it to me, and I can turn to the past. But nothing changes. Is that what you were trying to tell me? Today, suddenly, it was like living in the past. No matter what I said, they heard something else, just like the time you said I couldn't hear you. Is that what you meant?"

Myrtle smiled toward the door and had more soufflé. He could see her clearly, could hear her voice and Lucille's, but not the words.

"Hello? Eric . . . No. No, don't tell him. I'll call him back . . . sometime." He looked at the phone, puzzled, and slowly hung it up. "Eric wasn't in," he said, too low for the women to hear. "That was his roommate." He started to go back to his chair in the dining room.

"I think that's exactly right," Myrtle was saying. "Show all of it to as many organizations as we can, and then mobilize . . ."

"I could have sworn it was Eric," Rich said, picking up his napkin again.

"Probably a few PTAs at some point . . ."

"But wouldn't that be a mixed group? I mean . . ." Myrtle gulped some of her water.

"I just wanted to hear Eric's voice, so I did," Rich said.

"Well, sooner or later we'll have to. After all, it is the children we're concerned about."

"I know. I didn't mean . . . Yes, of course, PTA groups . . ."

Hannah brought in chocolate éclairs and coffee. Rich watched the women eating the pastries. "Six hundred calories at least," he said.

They didn't hear him. Lucille was talking about the plans she had made for the coming weeks. He looked past them, not listening to their words at all. "Ever since Eric was born," he said softly. "Twenty-seven years now. Never lost an ounce after he was born, just got fatter and fatter. Why?" Retaliation?

He left them still talking avidly, and he was certain that neither of them noticed when he left. He wandered to the yard and trimmed the roses. He talked to the bushes as he cut them back.

"We are making up our life stories as we go," he said. "That's why there's no future yet, why the watch turns to now and stops." He touched a tight green bud. Black spot. He'd have to spray. He pruned and the women came out and left in Lucille's car. He didn't know where they were going, although probably Myrtle had told him. She never went anywhere without telling him. He finished the roses and went back inside. They had left the magazines and pictures for him in his study. He pushed the heap to one side of the couch and sat down at the other end. Two old women poring over dirty pictures. He sighed.

Hannah brought in the mail and he looked through it, stopping at a letter from Kathleen. The envelope looked as if she had wiped a breakfast table with it. He ripped it open and took off his glasses to read the tiny, almost illegible script.

"Hold on to your hats. We're going to France, and God only knows where else after that. Jerry heard this fellow talking in a bar about the ship needing a bartender, and he went right down and got the job and got one for me to boot, in the nursery, so we're off next Tuesday." Rich put it down and lighted a cigar. "That bum," he said through the smoke. "That rotten bum. Bartender! By God, Myrtle will have a heart attack. . . ." He picked up the letter to finish reading it, but suddenly he started to laugh. "Bartender! Nursery helper!"

"What do you mean, you envy them?" Myrtle screamed at him that night. "Envy them! They're crazy, the both of them!"

"They're alive. They're keeping each other alive and conscious all the time."

"You're as crazy as they are."

"I'm waking up, after sixty-five years of dozing away my life. I'm waking up!"

"We just won't mention it to anyone. If anyone asks, we'll just say that they're abroad. That's all."

"It's a good feeling, Myrtle. Good. Going back to the past like I've been doing made me see it for the first time. How we always did what seemed expected. Not what we wanted, or what we should have done, only what was expected. Who did we think we were pleasing by acting all the time?"

"Lucille will know something's wrong. That bitch. She'll pry and pry."

"That's why we've hated him all these years. We knew he wasn't putting on an act. That scared us. We never knew what to expect out of him because he wasn't acting, wasn't even in the same play."

"I just won't mention Kathleen. She won't think to bring it up unless I give her a clue. . . ."

"Ninety percent of our lives gone. Just gone. Blanked out completely. High spots and low spots. Memories of high spots and low spots, and that's it."

"And William. Have they told him yet? Of course. Jerry never would keep his mouth shut about any of his nonsense. William won't talk. He knows about these things. . . ."

"Of course, I can have it all back now that I've got the watch. . . ."

"You and that watch! That's all you think about. What about this mess? What are we going to do? William could become vice-president within the next five years, but now . . . What a scandal for him to have to live down. His sister working in a nursery, his brother a bartender."

"Myrtle, shut up. Just shut up." She did, staring at him wide-eyed. "Now, just try not to react like this. Try a different set of reactions. Laugh, dammit. It's funny."

She shook her head and took a backward step. "You're crazy!"

"No, not that. That's standard reaction. Dance! Or . . . throw something. Break something nice, something that you like. The way Kathleen does when she gets mad. Try it. . . ."

She shook her head wordlessly. She looked frightened.

"Can you remember anything about yesterday? Say, at three in the afternoon, where were you, what were you doing?"

"I . . ." She shook her head again. "I don't know."

"And don't you see that your whole life is like that? A blank?"

"I'm going to bed. I have a terrible headache." She backed to the door and when he didn't try to stop her, she said, "You just don't know how hard this day has been, how busy I've been, and then to get news like that . . . You just don't understand. And tomorrow is going to be even busier, and then on Friday we have the films to show to the Eastern Star girls, and I have to help Lucille. . . ."

"And you will live in your world, and I'll live in mine, and now and then when something happens that rocks both of them we'll see each other, and maybe even hear each other, but most of the time we won't."

"And, Lucille's husband wants to know if you can come to his office next Wednesday. For the interview for the trustee's position, or whatever it was that he said he had."

"Someday, when Eric comes home for a visit, I'll talk to him about this. I think he might understand what I'm saying. Not about the watch. He'd say that it was a focus for my attention, that's all. A focal point to let me examine myself . . ."

"You didn't tell Hannah anything about Kathleen and Jerry, did you?" He didn't answer, and she continued as if he had. "That's good. I think Lucille's girl, Tully, pumps her without mercy. Nothing would be a secret long, once Hannah . . ."

THE RED
CANARY

Sometimes the baby played with old blocks that Tillich had found. The blocks were worn almost smooth, so that the letters and numbers were hard to read. You had to turn them this way and that, catch the light just right. The corners were rounded; there was no paint on them. Tillich remembered blocks like them. He thought the old worn ones were much nicer than the shiny sharp-cornered new ones had been. He never watched the baby play, actually. He would see it on the floor, with the blocks at hand, and he would busy himself somewhere else, because there was the possibility that the baby's movements with the blocks were completely random. In Tillich's mind was an image of the baby playing with blocks. He was afraid of shattering the image.

There had been another image. The baby sleeping peacefully, on its side after its morning bottle; its forefinger and index finger in its mouth. Tillich glanced at it each morning before leaving for work, in case it had wiggled out from its covers, or was under them completely. Always, in the dim dawn light the baby's sleep had been peaceful and Tillich had left quietly. One morning, for no reason, Tillich had entered the room, had gone to the other side of the bed to look at the infant. It wasn't asleep. It was staring, not moving, hardly even blinking, just staring at nothing at all, the two fingers in its mouth. It shifted its gaze to Tillich and stared up at him in an unfathomable look that was uncanny, eerie, inhuman, and somehow evil. Tillich backed away, out of its line of sight. At the partition that separated that end of the bedroom from the rest of it, he paused to look back. The baby looked asleep, unmoving, peacefully asleep.

"Tillich," he said at the dispensary. "Norma Tillich."
The dispensary nurse read the card he handed her.
"Any change? Does she need an appointment?"
"No. No change."
"Two a day, morning and night. Fourteen capsules. Please verify fourteen and sign at the bottom."
He hated the young woman on duty in the dispensary. If he could get there during his lunch break, she wouldn't be on duty. He never could make it until after work, however. She had a large, bony face. Her hands were large; strong fingers flicking out capsules, pills, moving deftly, sure of themselves. No need to verify the count when she was on duty. The computer card went back into the machine. He moved on. The line was always there, might always have been the same people in the same order. He hurried home. She would be hungry. The baby would be hungry and crying.

"Good morning, Mr. Rosenfeld."
"Good morning, Mr. Tillich. You are well, I trust?"
"Quite well, thanks." He poured boiling water over the soup powder, spread two large crackers with Pro-team and put them on the tray. He filled Mr. Rosenfeld's water pitcher and got some fresh cups out and put them on the bed stand. "Anything else, Mr. Rosenfeld?"
"No. No. That'll do me. Thank you kindly."
"You're welcome. I'll just drop in this evening."
"Not if you're busy, my friend."
"No trouble. Have a good day, Mr. Rosenfeld."

The old man nodded. He was eyeing his tray, impatient for his breakfast, too polite to begin until Tillich was gone.

The baby was always wet and usually soiled as well when he got home. Tillich changed it and put it in its bed with its bottle propped by it. Its color was greyed yellow.

"Norma, did he eat anything today?"

She looked vague. Then her face folded in somehow and collapsed in tears. "I don't know. I can't remember. You left the formula, didn't you? Did you forget its formula?"

"I didn't forget. The bottle's gone. You must have put it in the disposer. Did he take the milk?"

She wept for another minute or two, then jumped up, peeking at him between her fingers. She sang, *"I had a red canary. He couldn't sing. I left the window open and he flew away.* Would that be a bad thing to do? Let it fly away, I mean."

"No, that wouldn't be bad."

"Because I would. And I'd watch him fly away. Fly away. Fly away."

Sometimes she brought him her brush. "Would you like to do my hair?" It was long and silky when it was clean and brushed, alive with red-gold highlights in the dark blond. Her eyes were blue, sometimes green, her skin very pale and translucent. Blue veins made ragged ray patterns on her breasts, which were rounded, firm, exciting to him. She had nursed the baby for months. One day she hadn't, then another and another. It took days and days for her milk to stop, and all the while it seemed to puzzle her. She would come and show him her wet clothes, or drying milk on the bedding, on her belly. When he tried to put the baby to her breast again, she recoiled as if terrified. He awakened one night to find her kneeling over him trying to force the nipple between his lips. There was a taste of sweet milk on his mouth.

Mrs. de Vries lived on the same floor; he met her often. She usually had a child by the hand when they met. She was very thin and tired-looking. When he opened the door to an insistent knock, she was there.

"Mr. Tillich, will you please come? Please. I need someone."

He glanced back inside, Norma hadn't even looked up. She was watching the TV with a rapt expression. He hesitated a second, then stepped out into the hall, closing the door behind him. "What's wrong?"

"One of the kids. God, I don't know." She hurried him down the hall to her apartment. A girl about ten stood in the doorway. He had seen her before in the hall, down in the lobby. She had always seemed normal enough. She held the door open and moved aside as they came near.

Mrs. de Vries pushed Tillich past the girl, through the living room to a bedroom that had mattresses all over the floor. Two more children stared at him, then he saw the other child, alone on a mattress that was against the wall. The child, a boy, four, five, was having a convulsion. His back was arched, his tongue protruded between clamped jaws, blood and foam on his chin. He was already cyanotic.

Tillich turned to the woman. "Don't you have any medicine for him?"

"No. He never did this before. My God, what is it?"

"Call Pediatrics, Emergency." She stared. "Do you have a phone?"

"No."

"I'll go. What's his name? Symptoms?"

"Roald de Vries. Fever a hundred and four, all day."

He called Pediatrics, Emergency. "I'm sorry. We are already over capacity. Please leave patient's identification number, name, and reason for calling. Take patient to nearest hospital facility at eight A.M. Thank you. This is a recording."

He didn't have the number.

"I'll stay here," he told Mrs. de Vries. "Call them back and give his file number. Or they won't see him tomorrow."

The oldest child was the girl he had seen before. Waiting for her mother to return, he saw the welts on her arms, her neck. She seemed to have conjunctivitis. The next two children, boys about six and five, were very thin, and the larger of the two peed on the floor. The girl cleaned it up soundlessly. There were two bedrooms. A man slept in the other one. He had the dry, colorless skin of long illness; his sleep was unnatural. He was heavily sedated. Tillich looked at the ill child. His body was limp now and dripping sweat. The woman came back and he left. He saw her again a week later. Neither of them mentioned the child.

Tillich brought in the trains in section 3B. He picked them up fifty miles from the city, each one a brilliant speck of white or green light. His fingers knew the keys that opened and closed switches, that stopped one of the lights, hurried another. It was like weaving a complex spider web with luminous spiders.

He worked three hours, had a twenty-minute break, worked three more hours, had forty minutes for lunch, then the last three hours. He worked six days a week. He compared his work with a friend, Frank Jorgens, and both agreed it was harder than the air-traffic control job that Jorgens had.

"I have to have a raise," Tillich said to the union representative.

"You know better than that, Tillich. We don't ask for a raise for just one guy and his problems. Every sod has them."

He tried to apply directly to the personnel department; his application was rejected, accompanied by a notice that he could appeal through his union representative. He threw the application and the notice away.

"Tillich. Norma Tillich."

"Any change? Does she require an appointment?"

"Yes, we need to see her doctor."

"Please take your card and this form to one of the tables and fill it out. When you have completed it, return it to one of the attendants in Section Four-N. Thank you." The young woman looked at him directly, he frowned with disapproval.

Name. Age. Copy code from Line 3 of patient's identity card. Copy code from Lines 7, 8, 9. . . . Reasons for request to see physicians. Check one. If none apply, use back of application to state reason.

He rubbed his eyes. He should have written it out at home so he could simply copy it here. *She can't take care of the child. She neglects it. She doesn't eat or feed the baby, or keep it clean. It might injure itself. Or she might.* He read it dissatisfied. It was true, but not enough. He added only: *injure herself.*

"Thank you, Mr. Tillich. You will be notified next week when you come back. Report to this desk at that time. Fourteen capsules. Will you please verify the count and sign here."

His request was turned down. There was a typed message attached to her card. Tillick (they had misspelled the name), Norma. Non-aggressive. A series of dates and numbers followed. The times she had seen doctors, their diagnoses and instructions, all unintelligible to Tillich. Request denied on grounds of insufficient symptomatic variation from prognosis of 6-19-87-A-D-P/S-4298-Mc.

"Fourteen capsules. Verify count, please, and sign here."

The baby learned a new cry. It started high, wailed with increasing volume until it hit a note that made Tillich's head hurt. Then it cut it off abruptly and gasped a time or two and started over.

"You have to feed it while I'm gone," he said. "You can hold its bottle. Remember. Like this."

She wasn't watching. She was looking beyond him, past the baby, smiling at what she saw between herself and the streaked blue wall. He looked at the child, who was taking formula greedily, staring at him in its non-blinking way. Tillich closed his eyes.

After the baby was through, Tillich made their dinner. Tasti-meat, potatoes, soy-veg melange. She ate as greedily as the baby.

"Norma, while I'm at work you could eat some of the crackers I bought for you. The baby could chew on one. Remember them, Norma?"

She nodded brightly. The baby started to wail. She seemed not to hear it. While he cleaned up the dishes she watched TV. The baby wailed. Its next clinic appointment was in two months. He wondered if it would wail for the whole eight weeks, fifty-nine nights. He broke a plate, each hand gripping an edge painfully. He stared at the pieces. They were supposed to be unbreakable.

The baby wailed until twelve, when he fed it again. Gradually it quieted down after that, and by one it seemed to be sleeping. He didn't go past the partition to see.

Norma was waiting for him on their bed. Her cheeks were flushed, her nipples hard and dark red. He started to undress and she pulled at his clothes, laughing, stopping to nip his flesh on his stomach, his buttock when he turned around, his thigh. She crowed in delight at his erection, and he fell on her in savage coitus. She cried out, screamed, raked his back, bit his lip until it bled. She clung to him and tried to push him away. She called him names and cursed to him and whispered love words and gutter words. When it was over, she rolled from him, felt the edge of the bed and crept from it, staring at him in horror, or hatred. Or a combination. She backed to the door, crouching, ready to bolt. At the doorway she shrieked like a wild animal mortally wounded. Again and again she screamed. He buried his head in the bedding. Presently she became silent and he took a cover from the bed and put it over her on the couch, where she slept very deeply. He knew he could pick her up, carry her to bed, she wouldn't wake up. But all he did was cover her. He looked at the baby. It hadn't moved. He shivered and went to bed.

"Fourteen capsules. Verify fourteen, please, and sign. . . ."

"There are only thirteen."

The long capable fingers stopped. Tillich looked up. She returned his glance with no expression, then looked again at the pale green capsules. Her fingers moved deliberately as she counted, ". . . twelve. Thirteen." She pushed another one across the counter. "Fourteen. Please verify fourteen, Mr. Tillich." Again she met his gaze. Her eyes were grey, her eyelashes were very long and straight.

"Fourteen," he said and signed, and moved on.

The baby hated the park. It wailed and wouldn't be propped up. Tillich picked it up and for a time it was silent, staring at the bushes. Children were swinging, shouting, laughing, screaming. The spring sun was warm although the air still had a bite. Forsythias were in bloom, yellow arms waving. The baby stared at the long yellow branches. Soon it grew bored and started to cry again.

"I'm cold." Norma clung to his arm, her gaze shifting nervously, rapidly, very afraid. "I want to go home."

"You need some sun. So does the baby. Let's walk. You'll get warm."

He put the screaming child back in the baby carriage. The carriage was older than Tillich was; it squeaked, one wheel wobbled, the metal parts were all rusty, the plastic brittle and cracked. He knew they were very lucky to have it.

He wheeled the yelling baby and Norma clung to his arm. No one paid any attention to them. "I'm cold. I want to go home!" Soon she would be crying too. He walked a little faster.

"We'll go home now. This is the way." He didn't look at the people. The trees were leafing out, bushes in nearly full leaf, blooming. The grass was richly green. White clouds against the endless blue. He took a deep breath and closed his eyes a moment. For four weekends they hadn't been able to get out because of rain, or cold weather, or Norma's sniffles. Always something.

"I want to go home! I want to go home! I'm tired. I'm cold. *I want to go home!*" She was beginning to weep.

"We're going home now. See? There's the street. Just another block, then onto the street and a little more . . ." She wasn't listening. The baby screamed.

He saw the girl from the dispensary. She was wheeling a chair-bed, with a very old, frail-looking man on it. His face was petulant, half turned, tilted toward her, talking. She was walking slowly, looking at the trees, the flowering shrubs, the grass. A serene look was on her face.

Tillich turned the carriage to a path that led out of the park. The baby screamed. Norma wept and begged to be taken home.

Mrs. de Vries was in the hall outside his apartment. He thought she had been waiting for him.

"Mr. Tillich, is your wife better? Such a pretty girl."

"Yes, yes. She's coming along."

"I heard her screaming. Couple nights ago. Poor child."

He started to move on. She caught his arm. "Mr. Tillich, I'm only thirty-three. Would you believe that? Thirty-three." She looked fifty. Her fingers on his arm were red and coarse. "I . . . You need a woman, Mr. Tillich, I'm around. Wouldn't charge you much."

"No. Mrs. de Vries, I have to go in. No. I'm not interested."

"What am I to do, Mr. Tillich? What? They won't give us more money. I have two jobs and my kids are in rags. What'm I to do?"

"I don't know." He moved forward a step.

She motioned and her daughter approached. "She's a virgin, Mr. Tillich. Been having periods for six months now. All growed up inside. Five dollars, Mr. Tillich. Five dollars and you can keep her all night." She motioned the child closer. The girl pulled up her shift. Pale fuzz covered the mound. She turned around to show her round buttocks. They were covered with hives.

Tillich pushed Mrs. de Vries aside. "Bitch! Bitch! Your own daughter!"

"What'm I to do, you bastard? You tell me that. What'm I

to do?" He saw her yank the child to her and slap her hard. "Go get some pants on. Pull down your dress."

Tillich got his door open and slid inside. He was breathing hard. Norma didn't look up. She was watching TV. The baby was on the floor with the smooth blocks.

"Mr. Rosenfeld, don't you have any relatives?"

"None able. Brother's been in a house for twenty years."

"No children?"

"Son's dead. Cancer of the larynx. They didn't have a bed for him. He had to wait almost two years. By then it was Katie-bar-the-door." He looked thoughtful. "Two daughters, you know. Don't know where they are. Their husbands won't let them come around. First one shows up, state says I'm hers." He chuckled.

"Mr. Rosenfeld, don't you read the newspapers?"

"Watch it on TV."

"They miss some things, Mr. Rosenfeld. Starting next month there won't be any visiting-nurse service. Too expensive. Not enough nurses."

Mr. Rosenfeld looked frightened. After a moment he said, "Not the necessary visits."

"All of them, Mr. Rosenfeld."

"But . . . Look, son, I've got a tube in me that has to be changed every last day. Y'know? Every day. Takes someone who knows how. Good clean tubes. Dressings. Who's going to do all that except a nurse?" He picked at his sheet. "And change that? And give me a bath? Who?"

They stared at each other.

"Not you. Not you. I didn't mean that," Mr. Rosenfeld said. "You've been good to me. But you're not qualified for the tube job. Takes special training." He was paralyzed from the waist down.

"You'd better apply for a home," Tillich said finally.

"Did. Four years ago. I'm on the list."

"Well," Tillich said, "I have to go. I'll be by in the morning."

"Sure. Sure. Goodnight. Goodnight." Before Tillich got out he asked, "Your wife? I guess she wouldn't be able to have the training?"

"No. She's ill. Impossible."

"Oh, yes. Of course." He was staring fixedly at the ceiling when Tillich left.

"Do you walk here often?"

"When I can. That isn't very often." She looked at him. "How about you?"

"Not often enough. Not enough time."

"I've seen you a few times. Your wife is very pretty."

He didn't reply. There was nothing he could say. They were getting near the exit path that he would take. "Do you suppose you'll have time tomorrow to take a walk?"

She was silent so long he thought she hadn't heard. Then: "I think I will tomorrow."

"Maybe we'll see each other. I always come in at path number one-oh-two."

"That's near where I enter. Ninety-six."

"I'll wait for you at ninety-six."

She crouched in the doorway staring at him and shrieked. She didn't close her eyes while she screamed. He could see her stomach muscles tighten, her hands clench, then the shriek came. There was a glistening streak across her white thigh. Her legs were beautifully shaped. She shrieked. He pulled the cover over his head, pressing it against his ears. Twice or three times he had tried to comfort her, to quiet her, and it had been worse. He pressed harder on the covers. When she fell asleep on the couch, he covered her. She was thinner than she had been in the winter.

"Please verify fourteen . . ."

"You weren't in the park all week."

"Please sign. I was busy."

"When do you get off? I'll wait for you."

"Ten. Your wife and child. They need you. Who will make their dinner? Please, you must sign the forms and move on. Don't wait for me. I don't want to see you. I'm busy."

He signed and moved on.

The waiting room of the pediatrics center was an auditorium with all the sections filled to capacity. Tillich had to stand with the baby for half an hour before there was a vacant seat. The din in the hall was constant, very much like the sound of a high-powered motor. The loudspeaker was on steadily: "UN-3742-A-112." — "UN-2297-A / C-797." — "UN-1296-A / F-17." — "UN-3916-D-2000."

The smells of formula, vomit, urine, feces hung in the air, combining and recombining to make smells unnamed as yet, but much more repellent than any of them singly. The baby's screams were hardly noticeable here.

"Please refresh your memory regarding your child's identification number. You will be admitted to the doctors' examination rooms by number. Please refresh your memory regarding your child's identification number."—"UN-694-A/D-4921."—"UN-7129-A/F-1968."

He had to wait nine hours before he heard their number. He started; he had dozed; holding a screaming baby in the stinking auditorium amidst the bathroom and sickroom odors, he had dozed.

"Please strip the child and place it on the table. Keep on the far side of the table. Do not ask any questions, or give any medical details at this time. Thank you." It was a recording, activated by the closing of the door.

Tillich had barely finished undressing the baby when the second door opened and a woman came in. She was stooped, white-haired, with a death's-head face. The baby was screaming more feebly now, exhaustion finally weakening him. He was revived by her approach.

She held him with one hand and did a rapid and thorough eye, ears, nose, and throat examination. She went to his genitals, studied his feet. She pushed his legs up to his chest, then spread them apart. She sat him up and felt his back, then tried unsuccessfully to stand him up. Finally she made notations on his card. Only then did she glance at Tillich.

"We must make other tests. You will wait outside, please." She pressed a button. The door she had used was opened and an orderly motioned for Tillich to follow him.

"Why? What's wrong? What is it?"

The orderly touched his arm and wearily Tillich followed him. The baby wailed. This waiting room was even more crowded than the auditorium had been, but there was only a scattering of children; most of them were somewhere inside undergoing specialized diagnostic procedures. His head ached and he was very hungry. He didn't know how long he waited this time. Finally the orderly motioned for him to come.

"Please dress your child as quickly as possible and exit through the door marked B. An attendant on the other side will be happy to answer any questions. The time for your next appointment is indicated in the upper right-hand corner of your child's identification card. Thank you for your cooperation."

He carried the baby into the other room. The baby was listless now, no longer crying. Overhead a light sign flashed on and off: "If you have any questions, please be seated at one of the desks." He sat down.

"Yes, Mr. Tillich?" It was a young man, an orderly, or nurse, not a doctor.

"Why has his classification been changed? What does the new number and designation mean? Why is his next appointment a year from now instead of six months?"

"Hm. Out of infant category, you see. There will be medication. You can pick it up at Pediatrics dispensary, a month's supply at a time, starting tomorrow. Twenty-three allergens identified in his blood. Anemic. Nothing to be alarmed about, Mr. Tillich."

"What does the 'R/M.D. 19427' stand for? He's retarded, isn't he? How much?"

"Mr. Tillich, you'll have to discuss that with his doctor."

"Tell me this, would you expect a P/S 4298-MC to be able to care adequately for an R/M.D. 19427?"

"Of course not. But you're not . . ."

"His mother is."

"Why did you decide to come, after all?"

"I don't know. I guess because you look so miserable. Lonely, somehow." She stopped, looking straight ahead. A young couple walked hand in hand. "You do see people like that now and then," she said. "It gives me hope."

"It shouldn't. Norma was twenty-two before she . . . She was as normal as anyone at that age."

She started to walk again.

"What's your name?"

"Louisa. Yours?"

"David," he said. "Louisa is pretty. It's like a soft wind in high grass."

"You're a romantic." She thought a moment. "David goes back to the beginning of names, it seems. Bible name. Do you suppose people are still making new names?"

"Probably. Why?"

"I used to try to make up a name. They all sounded so ridiculous. So made up."

He laughed.

"You turn off here, don't you? Good-bye, David."

"Tomorrow?"

"Yes."

Norma slept. The baby lay quietly; he didn't know if it was asleep. He remembered laughing in the park. The sun shone. They walked not touching, talking fast, looking at each other often. And he had laughed out loud.

"No one came," Mr. Rosenfeld said. His voice rose. "No one came. They know I need a nurse. It's on my card. I signed over my pension so they'd take care of me. They agreed."

"Can I do something?"

"No!" he said shrilly. "Don't touch it. You know how long I'd last if an infection set in? Call them. Give them the numbers on my card. It's a mistake. A mistake."

Tillich copied the numbers, then went out to make the call. The first phone was out of order. He walked five blocks to the next one. Traffic was light. It was getting lighter all the time. He could remember when the streets had been packed solid, curb to curb, with automobiles, trucks, buses, motorbikes. Now there were half a dozen vehicles of all kinds in sight. He waited for the call to be completed, staring toward the west. One day he'd make up a little back pack, not much, a blanket, a cup, a pan maybe, a coat. He'd start walking westward. Across Ohio, across the prairies, across the mountains. To the sea. The Atlantic was less than five hundred miles east, but he never even considered starting in that direction.

"Please state patient's surname, given name, identification number, and purpose of this call."

He did. There was a pause, then the same voice said, "This data has been forwarded to the appropriate office. You will be notified. Thank you for your cooperation. This is a recording." So no one would argue, he knew. He stood staring westward for a long time, and when he got back to his building, he went directly to his own rooms.

"And so he died."

"He didn't just die. They killed him. *I* killed him. They were smart. They saw to it that he had a full week's supply of those pills. He took them all."

"I guess most of them had saved enough pills or capsules, same thing."

"So now they can claim truthfully that everyone who needs home nursing gets it." He kicked a stone hard.

She walked with her head bowed. "If they had known about you, your daily visits with the old man, probably they would have discontinued his nursing service sooner."

"But I'm not trained to insert a drainage tube."

"You learn or you lose whoever needs that kind of care."

He looked at her. She sounded bitter, the first time he had heard that tone from her. "You had something like that?"

"My husband. He needed constant attendance after surgery. On the sixth night I fell asleep and he hemorrhaged to death. I had learned how to change dressings, tubes, everything. And I fell asleep."

He caught her hand and held it for a moment between both of his. When they started to walk again, he kept holding her hand.

"When I get well, we'll have a vacation, won't we? We'll go to the shore and find pretty shells. Just us. You and me. Won't we?"

"Yes. That would be nice."

"Will they hurt me?"

"No. You remember. They'll look at your throat, listen to your heart. Weigh you. Take your blood pressure. It won't hurt." He held the baby because he hadn't dared leave it. They might be there all day. The baby cried very little now. It slept a lot more than it used to and when it was awake it didn't do anything except suck its fingers and stare fixedly at whatever its gaze happened to focus on. Tillich thought he should cut down on the medicine for it, but he liked it better like this. He didn't know what the medicine was for, if this effect was the expected one or not.

"You'll stay with me! Promise!"

"If I can."

"Let's go home now." She jumped up, smiling brightly at him.

"Sit down, Norma. We have to wait." The waiting room held over a hundred people. More were in the corridor. In this section few of the patients were alone. Many of them looked normal, able, healthy. Almost all had someone nearby who watched closely, who made an obvious effort to remain calm, tolerant, not to excite the patients.

"I'm hungry. I feel so sick. I really feel sick. We should go now." She stood up again. "I'll go alone."

He sighed, but didn't reply. The baby stared at his shirt. He shifted it. One eye had crossed that way. She went a few feet, walking sideways, through the chairs. She stopped and looked to see if he was coming.

"Don't shriek," he prayed silently. "Please don't shriek."

She took several more steps. Stopped. He could tell when the rush of panic hit her by the way she stiffened. She came back to him, terrified, her face a grey-white.

"I want to go. I want to . . ."

Over and over and over. Not loud, hardly more than a whisper. Until her number was called. They didn't admit him with her. He had known they wouldn't. She could undress and dress herself.

The trains came in from Chicago; from N.Y.; from Atlanta. Fruit from the south. Meat from the west. Clothing from the east. A virulent strain of influenza from the southwest. Tillich had guided it in.

"Cleanliness and rest, nature's best protection." The signs appeared overnight.

"If it gets worse," the superintendent said, "we'll have to quarantine our people here at work."

"But my wife is sick. And my child."

The superintendent nodded. "Then you damn well better stay well, don't you think?" He stomped off.

He thought of Louisa at the dispensary, in constant face-to-face contact with people. After work he was shaking by the time he reached Gate 96 and saw her standing there. He began to run toward her. She came forward to meet him. She looked frightened.

"Are you ill?" she asked.

"No. No. I'm all right. I got it in my head that you . . ." He took her face in his hands and examined her. Suddenly he pulled her to his chest and held her hard. Then he loosened his arms a bit, still without releasing her, and put his cheek on her hair, and they stayed that way for a long time, his cheek on her hair, her face against his chest, both with closed eyes.

He called the hospital about Norma. He told the recording about her shrieking fits after intercourse; about her sexuality that was as demanding as ever, about her neglect of self, of the baby. "Thank you for your cooperation. This is a recording." He called back and told the recording to go fuck itself. It thanked him.

"You should have reported an adverse reaction immediately," the nurse said. "Decrease the dosage from twenty drops to ten drops daily." She read the prescription from a computer print-out.

"And if that doesn't help?"

"There are several procedures, Mr. Tillich. These are doctor's orders. Report back in two weeks. You will be given a two-week supply of the medication."

"Can't someone just look at him?"

"I'm sorry, Mr. Tillich."

The baby wasn't eating. He moved very little and slept sixteen hours or more a day.

"You're killing him," he told the nurse. He got up. She would merely summon an orderly if he didn't leave. There was nothing she could do.

"Mr. Tillich, report to Room twelve-oh-nine before you leave the building." She was already looking past him at a woman with red eyes.

"My baby, she's been vomiting ever since she took that new medicine. And her bowels, God, nothing but water!"

Tillich moved away, back to the dispensary for the baby's medicine. He had been there for three hours already. The line was still as long as before. He took his place at the end.

Ninety minutes later he received the medicine. The dispensary nurse said, "Report to Room twelve-oh-nine, Mr. Tillich."

In 1209 there was a short line of people. It was a fast-moving line. When Tillich entered the room, a nurse asked his name. She checked it against a list, nodded, and told him to get in line. When he came to the head of the line, he was given a shot.

"What is it?" he asked.

The doctor looked at him in surprise. "Flu vaccine."

He saw the nurse at the door motioning to him. She put her forefinger to her lips and shook her head.

As he went out she whispered, "Louisa slipped your name in. For God's sake, keep your mouth shut."

A fast-moving freight from Detroit derailed when the locomotive's wheels locked as it slowed for a curve. Sixty-four cars left the track, tearing up a section a quarter of a mile long. It happened during the night, the specks of light were still motionless in that section when Tillich arrived.

"No more direct connection with Detroit," the superintendent said. "We're working on alternate routing now."

"Aren't they going to fix the tracks?"

"Can't. No steel's being allotted to any non-priority work. Just keep a hold on Sec. Seven until the computer gives us new routing. What a goddam mess."

Detroit was out. Jacksonville was out. Memphis was out. Cleveland. St. Paul.

Tillich wondered what a high priority was. Syringes, he

thought. Scalpels. Bone saws. He wondered if steel was still being produced.

"Can you get away at all?" he asked her desperately.

She shook her head. "No more than you can."

"I'll leave them. She isn't helpless. It's an act. If she got hungry enough, she'd get something."

She continued to shake her head. "I looked her up. She is very ill, David. She isn't malingering."

"What's wrong with her?"

"Primary schizophrenia. Acute depressions. Severe anemia, low blood sugar, renal dysfunction. There was more. I forget."

"Why don't they treat her? Try to cure her?"

She was silent.

"They know they can't. Or it would take too long to be worthwhile. Is that it? *Is that it?*"

"I don't know. They don't put reasons on the cards."

"Is there someplace we can go? Here, in the city?"

"I don't have any money. Do you?"

He laughed bitterly. "Your apartment?"

"Father, Mother, my brother Jason. He has tuberculosis, one lung collapsed. We have two rooms."

"I'll get some money. I'll get us a room somewhere."

He heard the baby wailing halfway down the hall. It was making up for the weeks of drugged silence. As he got nearer he could hear the TV also. Norma was watching it, singing, *"I had a red canary. It wouldn't fly."* She didn't look at him.

If it weren't for them, he thought clearly, he could take another job. Able-bodied men could work around the clock if they wanted to. All those hours in lines waiting for her medicine, waiting for the baby's medicine, waiting for her examination, the baby's examination. Shopping for them. Cleaning up after them. Cooking for them.

He shut his eyes, his back against the door. For a long time he didn't move. He felt a soft tug on his shirt and opened his eyes. She was there, holding out the hairbrush.

"Would you like to do my hair?"

He brushed her pale silky hair. "After I'm well, we'll have a vacation, won't we? Just the two of us. We'll go to the seashore and find pretty shells."

The baby wailed. The TV played. She sat with tears on her cheeks and he brushed her pale silky hair.

MAN OF
LETTERS

When their father didn't die after all, but rallied on his eighth day in Intensive Care (Terminal Section, they had both been certain), Mildred and her brother Hank stared at the doctor with almost moronic incomprehension. Prepared for death, they didn't know how to react to the new prognosis. Not that they disliked him, or wanted him dead (after all, both had more money than he would leave, and he was a nice man), but they had expected his demise long enough to go through the stages of unaccepting disbelief, to numbed no-think, to making unvoiced plans about the afterward. After the final announcement, after the public sorrow, after the smell of flowers faded and Mildred's collapse and subsequent week under a southern sun amidst rich foliage that, dying, knew nothing of death, so fast did the new replace the old. Hank had even visualized new letterheads, without the "Jr.," just plain Henry Sillitoe. Period. He had visualized his father's desk in his own office. The desk had a writing area marked off with heavy, deeply carved inlaid leather. He had done pencil rubbings of the ornate design as a child.

Warner put out the stub of a cigarette, lighted another one, put it down on the ashtray, and skimmed what he had written. With his fingers poised over the keyboard, he hesitated, then reread the opening of the new story. Nellie knocked on the door and he said, "Come on in."

"I just wanted to remind you that I have to go shopping, and Mrs. Olson might drop in with the curtains while I'm out. Give her the check on the table, will you?"

"Sure. Got a minute?"

Nellie nodded. She was dressed in sky-blue slacks and a sweater, her long black hair tied back with a blue-and-red polka-dot scarf. She looked sixteen, possibly eighteen, and was thirty. "I heard you clicking away," she said.

"Yeah. I'd like for you to read something." He handed her the page of typescript and she read it, then looked at him expectantly. "Just like Janice and Eugene, isn't it? Then what?"

"Janice and Eugene?"

"Yes, you know, Janice Murphy and her brother. Their father had a stroke or something and had to live with one or the other of them. Oh, it was awful. . . . Poor Janice."

"I don't know Janice Murphy."

"Really? She lives over at Pine Acres, and last year, or the year before that, I forget which, she was the chairman of the entertainment committee for the PTA. I told you. She's the one who planned that awful Halloween party where the parents had to dress up and you wouldn't go and Terry pretended that you had mumps or something. Anyway, she told me all about it when her father nearly died and they sold his house and everything because the doctors were so sure that he wouldn't live, and the house was jointly owned or something so that they could sell it, or else they got power of attorney because he was paralyzed or something like that, but then. Then, he got well. Just like that. And he had to move in with Janice. . . ."

Warner turned her off and stared at the page he had written. Again, he thought. He'd done it again. For three weeks he had been writing beginnings that were real, beginnings of life stories of people he knew, or that Nellie knew, or that he subsequently read about in the papers.

"But I don't even know Janice Murphy," he said again.

Nellie shrugged and returned the sheet of paper to him. "I guess there must be a lot of cases like that. It could happen to almost anyone. Well, I'm leaving. Don't forget Mrs. Olson. The check is on the table, all ready for her. Be back in a couple of hours."

At the door she said, "If I didn't have so darn far to drive, I wouldn't bother you about the check, you know. But thirteen miles to the underpass." She shrugged eloquently and left.

They lived five miles from Pine Acres, on the other side of the interstate highway. To get there they had to drive thirteen miles to the underpass, then twelve back down to the stores. Then twelve back up, and thirteen back down. "We could still sell this house and move," she said often, very often. But he wouldn't. He refused to live in a development. He couldn't stand the city any more. And they were within reach of New York, less than a two-hour drive. "But fifty miles just to shop!" That's what she always said. Always.

He heard the car starting. A two-year-old model with an insatiable thirst, a tendency to spring out of alignment if it even grazed a pebble, it had more recently developed a peculiar growl when the key was turned. It growled, gasped, choked, then started the more reassuring, mildly uneven hum.

Warner got out the folder of starts that he had discarded during the past three weeks and added the new one to the stack. He fanned them out on his desk and studied them. He wondered how different, if at all, they were from the stories he'd been doing for thirteen years. He was afraid that he wouldn't be able to find much difference if he went back to check through the others, the published stories.

He heard the back door slam. Terry and his friends after a snack, young teenagers, as insatiable as the car. He strained, listening, but he couldn't hear the refrigerator from his study. Presently the door slammed again.

A clock chimed, muffled by closed doors.

The car returned and the garage door clanged. It fell the last foot or so. He closed his eyes, concentrating. The radio came on. He was certain that the radio had come on, turned to low volume instantly. Nellie would be putting groceries away. And humming. He stood up, waiting for the squeak of leather, a spring rasping slightly with release. His shoes, leather-against-rug-scuffing sound, then leather on hardwood. At the door he tightened his lips, metal grated on metal from the hinge that he always forgot to oil. Down the hallway, carpeted, carpeting on stairs, the third and seventh steps loud, green wood that screamed when touched.

"Don't hum," he said under his breath to Nellie. "Don't be humming." At the door to the kitchen he stopped, trying to hear her over the cheerful radio voice. He opened the door gently, touching it with his fingertips only.

". . . drizzle and fog. Tomorrow, cloudy and cooler."

Nellie was humming.

Warner drew his hand back. His mouth twitched and suddenly he was laughing. He laughed almost silently, eyes tearing, his entire body shaking. He laughed until he ached, and felt weak, and had to lean against the wall for support. Finally finished, he pushed himself upright and went through the dining room to the entrance foyer, then out the front door.

He should go to the library, he thought as he walked. He should check it out for himself. A month ago he had listened with a sardonic grin as Hal Vronsky told about the story he had read. Story about a writer and wife and kid, living five miles from the nearest town, but having to drive nearly fifty miles to get to it and back. How the wife kept them just a little bit in debt, enough so that the guy never could break out of the kind of thing he was doing, hackwork of some sort. Hal had looked embarrassed suddenly. "Hell, not that part. But the rest of it—you know, the general situation—made me think of you right off."

"And you read it in a dentist's office, I suppose?"

"Yeah, as a matter of fact, I did. How'd you know that?"

And Warner had laughed. And again today he had laughed, but now, walking through fields that had turned brown with autumn, that would cover his legs and socks with sticktights, and fill his shoes with seeds and dust from dead grasses, now he was not laughing. He should go check it out at the library, just to satisfy his curiosity.

"So I'm cliché," he said. "And Nellie is a cliché wife. And Terry is a cliché son." He kicked a clump of mushrooms and watched the pieces scatter. And he finished the thought, "And I write cliché fiction."

He turned to his right, paralleling the highway that was half a mile away now. It was a river of many colors, with a swift current that now and then eddied. . . . Was that thought a cliché? He wondered. He was afraid that it was. There was old man Brunhild's barn ahead of him now, folding in on itself down to the ground practically. This quarter of his acreage had been cut off from the rest by the highway, and the old farmer was ignoring it. The barn had long needed repairs, but with the announcement four years ago of the highway's location, all thoughts of maintaining this part of the farm had vanished. On the roof of the barn, in letters that filled the available space, was the command: SEE ROCK CITY. Warner leaned against a fencepost and contemplated the sign moodily. He wondered if the paint that the old man had put in the barn was still there. As he drew nearer the decrepit building there was a scurrying sound. Rats, he thought with disgust, and hesitated, then started to whistle loudly, and scrape his feet, breaking dead grasses with audible snaps and rustlings. He found the paint and broke the end off his pocket knife opening the can. There were two broad brushes in the barn, and a homemade ladder that looked like it had a fifty-percent chance of holding his weight. Still whistling, he leaned it against the building, moved it when the roof edge crumbled, and then started to climb up, carrying the paint with him, and the brush in his teeth. He worked until it got so dark that he couldn't be certain that he had obliterated the T and Y in CITY, and then he went home.

"For God's sake, Warner, where have you been? Look at you!" Nellie, sweet in a white organdy pants suit, stared aghast, and he glanced down at himself. He was smeared with red paint from head down, his clothes spattered, smeared, caked with it. Both hands looked like he had been engaged in butchery. When he grinned he could feel the drying paint pulling his mouth and cheeks. "You've been painting!" Nellie exclaimed.

Warner shook his head hard. "I'll clean up," he said.

"You can't have a martini like that," she said, as if puzzled.

At the door to the garage he paused, wondering if she would improvise, or just wait until everything got back on the tracks that she was familiar with. She chose to wait. He scrubbed, first with turpentine, then in the shower with hot water and a bar of pink, engraved soap that looked edible, and still when he dressed and went to the living room, he had red paint deep in the pores of his hands and wrists, and his eyebrows were tinged with it, and when he smiled, the creases in his face were exaggerated, as if outlined with a red pencil. Nellie stared at him hard, then turned away with a sigh of patience tried and found not wanting.

"What in the world were you painting?" she asked, pouring his martini for him.

"Brunhild's barn."

She didn't know about Brunhild or his barn. She never had walked through the fields back that way. "Henry called twice," she said then, dismissing the paint. "He has something for you. An emergency, or something."

"Probably wants to know why the hell I haven't sent in a story for a month," Warner muttered. He sipped the martini, and shuddered. He looked at the drink and sniffed it cautiously, then tasted it again, more gingerly this time. Still bad. "How long till dinner?" he asked. "Do I have time to call him back first?"

Nellie nodded. "Half an hour. What's wrong with the martini?

It's the same mix that I always use." She picked it up and sniffed it, then put her tongue in it and finally drank it down. "What's wrong with it?" She sucked on the lemon slice. "You've just got paint-and-turpentine taste in your mouth."

Henry was his agent, and only once before had he wanted a call returned after office hours, and then it had been to talk Warner into doing a translation of an article a midwestern politician had written for one of the men's magazines. The trouble had been that it was in illiterate, phonetic, midwestern dialect, that it hadn't made any sense, that he had forgotten what his starting point was by the end of paragraph two and had rambled on for twenty pages. Warner was known to be reliable, with a readable style, and a knack for making sense out of incomprehensible sentences, even if he had to insert the sense.

He dialed Henry's number and he thought, The net will tighten now. I'm starting to wiggle a little bit, so they'll tighten the net, pull me back in. The thought was fleeting, and by the time Henry's voice was booming over the wires, he forgot it entirely.

"Warner, the ax has just fallen over at *The Woman's Home Advisor*. Adamski's out, and all the stuff he commissioned, right down to fillers. Stu Pryor is in, and he's desperate for material. He wants a four-parter, fifteen thousand words each installment, and he wants it by next Tuesday, the first part of it, anyway. I told him you'd do it for twelve thousand an installment."

Warner stared at the wall and tried not to think of twelve thousand dollars times four. "By Tuesday?" he said. "That's less than a week. . . ."

"Yeah, I know. They offered five thousand, and when I pointed out that the only man I knew who could do it that fast wouldn't consider it for anything less than fifteen . . ."

He went on at some length. By the time the conversation ended, Warner had agreed to start immediately and have the first installment ready to deliver by Tuesday. Over dinner he told Nellie about it. "Nothing far out. No drugs, no youth rebellion, no alienation. Just good wholesome women's fiction. A mystery maybe, with a put-upon heroine."

Nellie's eyes were shining and she leaned over the table to put her hand on his. "Thank God," she said. "I was afraid you'd turn it down. You've been acting so funny lately."

"Funny how?"

"Oh, not finishing anything. Sketching in incidents, then leaving them for new ones. Then today, going out to paint a barn, for heaven's sake! I mean, that's not your typical behavior, now, is it?"

They were alone, tall candles on the small table that she used when they dined together without Terry. Good heavy silver, crystal, china. Thick, thick carpet underfoot, ladderback chairs, a frostlike draperied wall for a background. Warner stared about with an air of discovery. They were a magazine illustration, he thought. Nellie, lovely in white, her husband, tall and distinguished-looking, even with a touch of red paint here and there. Wine on the table, a casserole in a silver stand . . . He stood up abruptly and dropped his napkin on his plate, with chicken and pea pods and saffron rice. Out of a gourmet magazine.

"I . . . excuse me, honey. I'll be in my study." He almost ran from the dining room. Nellie, he knew, would put the dishes in the dishwasher, leave the pans for Mrs. Wasserman to do in the morning, and spend the rest of the evening in front of the television, spending forty-three thousand two hundred dollars, what he would get after the ten percent taken out by his agent. He corrected himself. Nellie would know exactly how much to deduct for taxes too, and she would go over what was left by a couple of hundred dollars. A new car. Redecorate the kitchen. She'd been talking about a cooking island, with a copper hood, and a new ultrasonic oven. . . . And a second car for Terry, who would be sixteen in three months.

He sat at his desk and saw the fan of stories started and not finished. He picked up the latest one and put the page by his typewriter, then replaced the rest of them in the folder and returned it to his file, under INCOMPLETE.

Okay, he told himself, fifteen thousand words by Tuesday, or Monday night, actually, with delivery on Tuesday. Six days. Six into fifteen. All the time that he was doing his arithmetic, his fingers were busy, putting new paper into the typewriter, whipping it down to the midway point, titling the story: *The Day God Laughed.* Twenty-five hundred a' day, he thought, then stared at what he had written.

Slowly he pulled the paper out of the carriage and inserted another piece, this time working deliberately. Mildred, he thought, Mildred should get her father first. Not yet thirty, lawyer husband, two children. . . . He wrote, *Mildred is social climber, very eager for her husband to get into local politics, then work up through the ranks, and she feels that having her father on her hands will be a hindrance because there will be some traveling, and a good deal of entertaining to do. Janice can't bring herself to approach her brother Eugene outright, but she thinks that if she makes the old man so uncomfortable that he brings it up . . .* Warner stopped and shook his head. He scanned the page and crossed out the name Janice, and filled in with pencil above it, Mildred. He crossed out Eugene and wrote in Hank.

That would be the first part, he decided, and pulled the page from the machine. Part two. *The old man is shipped off to the son, but he never shows up there. Janice, Mildred, whoever the hell she is, is off with her husband on a speaking tour. . . .* He was jotting down the ideas now, sketching in the story. *End part two with confrontation between brother and sister, each accusing other of negligence. Eugene wants to notify police, etc., initiate a search, Janice-Mildred . . .* He couldn't remember which name he had chosen for her. It didn't matter. *She is afraid of what publicity will do to husband now at such a crucial stage in his career. End part two.*

Three. He stared at the paper filling up now with notes, and shook his head. No part three. He was tired, and sore from the unaccustomed painting, and his eyes were becoming blurry. He got up and went to the kitchen to make coffee, and while he waited for it, he checked on Terry, who was asleep, then looked in on . . . his wife. He couldn't think of her name for a moment and his hand on the doorknob tightened until it was painful. Nellie. Nellie was asleep.

Quietly he withdrew, tiptoeing away from the door, down the stairs again, hearing the scream of the third and seventh steps, and back to the kitchen, still trying to make no sound, as if afraid even down there he might awaken her, or the boy. Part three would have to be the search, he thought. And part four, reunion, and a subsequent search for a Good Home for the old man, a happy old folks' home where he could be of some use to others who were older and more helpless than he. . . .

Add a few subplots: Nellie's husband could misunderstand her. . . . Warner shook his head until it hurt. Nellie. His wife. The woman in the story was . . . What the hell difference did it make? He had given her the wrong name, so he couldn't remember it from one sentence to the next. He'd call her Gladys, or Mary. Good safe name. He sipped coffee, but the story wouldn't stay in focus now. He wondered how the real-life story of Janice and her brother ended. At two he went to bed.

The next morning he got up after Terry had gone to school. He had coffee and then went to find Nellie, who was sunning herself under the lamp in the bathroom, spread-eagled on a white fake-fur rug with nothing on but two cotton pads over her eyes. She looked exactly like a centerfold model.

"Honey, whatever happened to Janice? You know, the one the story reminded you of?"

She waved a greeting to him. "Oh, the poor thing. They finally had to put her father in a home, you know, one of those very pretty places for older people who aren't really sick or anything, but can't be expected to live alone either, and anyway he didn't have a home any more, and I guess he was sicker than they thought, because he died after a couple of months, but he was really happy there until the end. And Paul, her husband, you know, we voted for him last election and he's in the legislature now, a Representative from this district, and next national election he's going to run for Congress, I think. He seemed to think Janice did something terrible, but he was just under such a strain, too. Poor Janice has been going to a psychiatrist for months and months. He told her she has an identity problem, or something like that. I don't understand exactly, but it seems that sometimes she isn't really sure just who she is, or what she's up to, or anything at all. It couldn't be too serious because no one has even suggested that she be hospitalized. . . ."

Warner left her, closing the door gently. He pulled on an old hunting jacket and went outside. He walked through the fields until he came to the tilted barn whose roof he had painted. Nothing of the previous sign showed through. He continued to walk toward the highway; at that time of morning the traffic was scant, with bursts of automobiles, then nothing, then another flurry. He waited until he could cross, then went on to Pine Acres Shopping Center. He bought up all the slick magazines, all the pulps with any fiction, half a dozen paperback books, and six cans of white spray paint, and then started to walk back home. When he got to the barn again, he stopped to spray-paint on his own slogan:

GOD IS NOT DEAD
HE'S JUST A CLICHÉ

The letters were ten feet high.

Nellie nodded approvingly when she saw him with the magazines. "Research?"

"Something like that."

"Good. I'm off, dear. Historical Society meeting." She was bewitching in a pink cashmere suit, with a pink feathery thing on her head. Author's device, he thought, to get rid of wife in order to have protagonist alone for the next scene. He waved good-bye and went on into his study with his magazines.

He looked over the fiction quickly—three of the stories he had written, one under his own name, two with pseudonyms. They were all familiar, even the ones he hadn't done.

"Okay," he said then, and moved with a purposeful stride to his desk. "Now we negotiate." He put in a page of his best twenty-four-pound white bond with an embossed sun symbol on it, and began to type.

I quit. I resign. I want a better contract. Also, I am through with hackwork. I want to produce Art.

A blinding radiance filled the room, emanating from behind him. He didn't turn around. Crap. Cliché. Too many people saw God, or something that appeared with a blinding light. He studied the lines he had written, finding it hard to force his eyes to remain wide enough open to see them in the painful glare. He thought that God must be laughing although there was no sound. He examined the thought and shrugged. He didn't believe in God, and especially not a god that laughed. He wondered suddenly if that was a new idea, finally. The light dimmed and he was left with the idea of a laughing god. He gnawed on his thumb and tried to recall if he had ever read of such a thing in the Bible, where he seldom really read, but often browsed, for a title, or an appropriate quote for one of his characters to use at an opportune moment. He felt certain that God of the Bible never had laughed.

With the radiance gone, the room seemed dull and gloomy. He flicked on the lights, the desk lamp, the ceiling light, a floor lamp near the window where his armchair and end table were. The room still was cold and uncomfortable. He walked out to the hall, and thought he heard the sound of his typewriter, but when he stopped to listen, there was nothing. Mrs. Wasserman was in the kitchen cleaning the refrigerator, and she made him a chicken sandwich and talked endlessly about the failure of the walnut crop that year. Halfway through the sandwich Warner suddenly had to go back to his study to see what the typewriter had answered.

The lines he had written had been Xed out.

Warner laughed harshly. Even to his ears the laugh was ugly. "Okay," he said. "Proof. You need proof." He pulled the phone to him and as he was about to lift the receiver, the bell rang.

"Yeah," he said.

"Warner, Henry here. Listen, kid, relax. I got to thinking last night, and you know that long novella you sent me a couple of months back, the one about the blind girl who makes it with the pianist, turns out that she has perfect pitch or some damn thing. Well. What the hell, it's perfect for this four-parter. I got it out and reread it and it breaks up beautifully, suspense, pathos, everything. . . ."

Warner hung up. He drummed on the desktop, then looked up Hal Vronsky's number and dialed it. Mrs. Vronsky answered. "Our dentist? Hal's dentist?" There was a pause. Warner filled it in. "I've had this tooth bothering me off and on, and my dentist is sick. . . ."

With the name and address in his pocket he left the house again, after retyping his resignation and leaving it in the typewriter. In the driveway he hesitated, then returned to the house and gathered up all the magazines he had bought earlier.

He stopped again. Nellie was gone with the car. Angrily he yelled for Mrs. Wasserman.

"Leave that, will you?" he said brusquely. "I've got to get to the dentist over in Pine Acres. Can you run me over?"

She nodded and closed the refrigerator door and untied her apron. "I know what it's like to have a toothache, yessirree. I had one once that wouldn't give me no relief for weeks and weeks and this was when I was a little girl, you see, and we didn't have no dentist near at hand, not like today with a dentist on every corner, as you might say. And we had to wait until our regular day over to Middlebury, and then found out that the dentist was sick, and my ma had to end up pulling that tooth in spite of everything. Never grew back either."

She drove the thirteen miles to the underpass in half an hour, then twelve miles back to the shopping center in another half hour. "I'll wait if'n you want me to," she said kindly, jerking the car to a halt outside the medical building.

"No. I'll take a cab home," Warner said. "Thanks a lot, you were a big help."

"Yes," she agreed. "Always try to help. Now I'll just get me back and finish up that refrigerator." Still talking, she jerked away from the curb and rolled up the street in slow motion.

"Borgman, Borgman," he muttered, walking around the building examining the names on the brass door plates. Then he saw it, MELVIN S. BORGMAN, D.D.S. The office was closed. He shifted the slithery magazines, and considered. There had to be an office manager, or maintenance superintendent, someone in charge with a key. He made the circuit again and this time saw a small white placard that said simply SUPERINTENDENT. He knocked and after a wait of several minutes the door opened. A very old man eyed him suspiciously.

"Mr. uh . . ."

"Carmichael."

"Yes. Mr. Carmichael, I'm the new distributor's representative to service the office of Dr. Borgman. I'm supposed to collect the out-of-date magazines and leave him these new issues."

The old man didn't budge. "Never done that before."

"I know. It's a new, complimentary service. A trial run. I was due to arrive yesterday, but there was trouble with the shipment. . . ."

"Don't know. Never said nothing to me about letting you in."

"Mr. Carmichael, you can go with me. All I want to do is put these new magazines in the office and take out the old ones."

"I just don't know," he said stubbornly, but now he was moving as he muttered, and fishing on a long chain of keys for the right one.

Mr. Carmichael watched him closely as he selected the magazines that possibly could have fiction in them. Warner didn't dare examine tables of contents under the frankly unbelieving gaze of the old man. Warner picked up nine magazines and left fourteen in their place. He didn't bother with things like *Field and Stream*, or *Mechanics Illustrated*, or *Humpty Dumpty*.

"Whyn't you take them all?" the superintendent asked, his suspicions renewed.

"Dr. Borgman collects those. He told me himself that he collects them." Very slowly the old man nodded, as if his worst fears and doubts about the dentist had been confirmed. He never took his eyes off Warner until they were again outside the office and he had locked and tried the door three times. Then he turned and walked away without looking back.

Warner took a taxi home and beat Mrs. Wasserman by twenty minutes.

He skimmed through all the stories without finding one even vaguely reminiscent of himself and his life. Then he paused. You never recognize yourself in fiction, he knew. He had used any number of friends and acquaintances without their ever knowing. He began to comb through them again, and finally decided he had the one that Hal Vronsky must have meant. An artist, not a writer. A hack artist, an illustrator of the cheapest magazines, a penny-postcard sort of artist. With a wife and three children. But he did live in a location that suggested Warner's. He read the story carefully. The artist rebelled at doing hackwork after years of making a rather good living. His wife refused to believe he wanted to gamble on serious work, and spent all of the money they had, and some over, on a new house! Warner swallowed hard. She wouldn't dare.

That was the climactic scene. Her announcement of the purchase, conditional, of course, of the new house, on the other side of the country-club community that she wanted so much to be part of. Warner blinked. Incredible that such junk could have been written in the first place, bought and published in the second place, and read in the third place. He found the continuation. They fought, naturally, and she said that she'd buy the house with the money the courts awarded her from a divorce settlement. Warner shook his head. No motivation had been given to her, nothing but the scantiest sketch of her appearance, and here she was the pivotal character suddenly. Coming out of nowhere to change the course of his life . . . the character's life, that was.

He found the next continuation. She said that she'd be better off with him dead, his insurance would be sufficient, and he was a has-been anyway, hadn't done any real work for a month. . . .

The next continuation. The artist collapsed, and on awakening in a hospital realized that he had suffered from a temporary nervous disorder, that he had made life hell for everyone about him, that he was probably the best of his kind going, and looked forward with great anticipation to returning to his life's work, illustrating fourth-rate magazines that brought a touch of escapism to so many people, making their lives tolerable. End.

Warner flung the magazine from him and went to his desk, where his second ultimatum had been obliterated with h's and a's. *Hahahahaha.* He yanked it out and wrote.

Let x be the events of the world, all the events, all combinations and permutations of possible actions, places, things. New events can be added arithmetically only. One at a time. In the beginning when there were few events the addition of one was exciting and fun, but with the growing number, the addition of one is adding boredom to boredom. Ten million plus one. One is lost in the shuffle. Meaningless.

Let y equal the people of the world, growing geometrically, exponentially. Because already y is greater than x, there can only be constant repetition, and more boredom.

Let z equal processes, the combinations of x and y in all possible equations: x/x, x/y, y/y, y/x, $x \times y$, $x+y$, *etc. Because x is, prac-*

tically speaking, finite, the processes are again repetitive and boring after a short time. What can be has been, endlessly.

Let x', or y', or z', or any combination, be the goal and the endless search makes sense. An evolutionary leap, or a scientific breakthrough to a new kind of reality, or the disclosure of the ultimate secrets, whatever x' combined with y' could produce. Someone has to keep on searching, whether under a computer's guidance, or a god's, or a committee's. And the numbers make it imperative that the task be broken up into sections, and that there be people to run those sections, to keep mixing up the ingredients available and noting the results. And I quit!

I QUIT!

He felt better than he had in days when he left his study that afternoon. Terry had been home and was gone again, to band practice, or something. Nellie wasn't home yet. Dinner, she had said, would be late, and maybe they could go out. . . .

Echelons, he thought. There were regular echelons. The masses that acted like gas, predictable as a unit, but unpredictable molecule by molecule. Then slightly above them the ones who had escaped from the flask somehow, still more or less predictable, but capable now of new combinations. Janice, Nellie . . . all his characters in all his stories, he supposed. Then came those like him, capable of watching that level, but still watched by a level a bit higher. Henry? And so on. At the top? He stopped in the middle of mixing his martini, and wondered who, or what, was at the top, keeping an eye on the whole. He knew it was a fruitless speculation, but still he wondered. Was it someone, or something, capable of bargaining or willing to bargain? He put the shaker down and forgot about it. Suddenly he was thinking of the pulp magazines he had bought. Murders. Science fiction. Supernatural stories. If the scenarios were being written by real writers, why weren't those coming true also?

Why could he manipulate Janice, why could another writer determine his actions? Why didn't the Martians land? Or a tidal wave wipe out Los Angeles? Or a mad murderer chop off the hands of all spinsters over thirty and send them to lonelyhearts clubs? Or . . .

Nellie came home and he tried to forget the ideas for a while. She was adorable in a . . . No, actually, he thought, she looked a little tired, and she had a smudge on her chin, and a run in one stocking.

"Tired?" he asked.

"Um. We're getting ready for our annual dinner and dance." She looked in the martini shaker and glanced in surprise at the two empty glasses still on the tray, then filled them both. "Cheers," she said, upending hers. She poured another one and put it down on a table by the couch, where she sat down and took off her shoes. "All day I've been peeling apples. For dessert." She lighted a cigarette, and added, "Apple pies."

"What are you going to do with the money you raise?"

"Add to the kitchen facilities, enlarge the dining room of the club."

"So next year you can have a bigger dinner and dance?"

"Um." She sighed. "I saw Janice this afternoon. Funny, isn't it, when you bring up someone like that how often you see them in a day or two after not seeing them for months. Serendipity."

"Synchronicity," Warner said and she nodded.

"Something. Anyway, she's in such a bad way. I never did like her very much, such a shallow person, you know, nothing beneath the nice clothes and phony smile, but anyway, I hate to see her feeling so bad, and lost! You wouldn't believe how really lost she is. I never saw anything just like it. She was talking to Mrs. Loewenstein and when I joined them she just went right on, although I've never been close or anything. You'd think she wouldn't want to say such things in the presence of someone who's almost a stranger, but she doesn't seem to realize that I am. A stranger."

Warner watched her without listening closely. He had heard it said of someone who was acclaimed as a public speaker that his formula for success was to get before an audience, turn on his mouth, and when the time was over, to turn it off again. That was Nellie, he thought.

He wondered who was writing her.

He wondered who was writing him now. Not the same author as before, surely. He had got away from that creep. That slob wouldn't know what to do if he said jump and Warner laughed at him. Just like he didn't know exactly what to do about the character who laughed at his ultimatums. Wordlessly he left the living room, leaving Nellie talking on and on, with her eyes closed, wiggling her toes, holding her martini in one hand, a cigarette in the other.

His last message was gone altogether. He looked on the desk for it, and an accompanying message, but it wasn't there. When he turned to leave, he noticed scraps of paper on the floor and he picked up several and pieced them together enough to see that they were his last attempt to communicate. Torn into shreds.

Warner let the pieces float from his fingers. He sat down at his desk and thought for a moment, then put a fresh piece of paper in the typewriter. He wrote:

Janice, driven to despair by the continual absence of her husband, and the waves of guilt that washed her of all joy and happiness, drove faster and faster, as if she knew that ahead lay her final release from pain, that to achieve it all she had to do was concentrate on that point of light that lay ahead, as if that one red point was the gate to whatever heaven or hell awaited her ultimately. She felt peace for the first time in the two years since her father's death as she saw the point grow until she was lost in it.

He found the folder in the INCOMPLETE file, withdrew the story that he had started and outlined, and added the final page. He replaced the file, keeping out the finished story now. It would have to be titled and filed in the regular file, but tomorrow. He left it on his desk.

He took Nellie to dinner at an Italian restaurant that they were both fond of, and they drank too much Chianti, and Nellie's eyes sparkled, and she looked younger and more desirable than she had for a long time, so that when they got home he wanted to take her right off to bed. But they had to wait for Terry's arrival, and by the time they actually got to bed, it was after eleven, and the glow had faded somewhat. But it was still good, as always with Nellie. Afterward, she lay in the crook of his arm and with her face pressed against his ribs, she said in a low voice,

"I saw a beautiful house today. . . ." He grunted and pretended to be asleep.

The next morning he got out the INCOMPLETE folder and began finishing stories. At noon Nellie told him with a shocked expression that Janice had been killed on her way home last night. Driving too fast, possibly drinking, she had run into a traffic sign and had died instantly. Over the next few days it seemed that many of the people they knew were killed in sudden accidents.

Warner typed out his resignation and demands for a new contract every night before he closed his office. Along with the resignation one night he wrote: *Escape fiction is actually stimulus fiction. The writer doesn't believe in it; the reader doesn't believe in it. But now and again, someone is stimulated into new action by it, into a course that he might not have followed without it.* Sometimes the sheet vanished, sometimes it was Xed out, sometimes torn up. After he had gone through his files, finished every start of every story, he started a new story:

New York shivered under the icy blast of Arctic air that streamed out of the north. The very soul of the city seemed frozen, and it was as if the city had life, as if it was a living organism suffering now, shaken with death throes as its links with the rest of the country faltered and died, like the veins of a body fouled with calcium and other deposits that closed the vital passages. . . .

Warner paused, suddenly remembering the name of the writer who had written his, Warner's, story. Stephen Ashe. He was Henry's client too. Warner remembered seeing a manila envelope on

Henry's desk once with that name, asking about him. Another pulp hack. Reliable. Can turn them out to order, makes him valuable. He'll learn to write well enough someday. Nurse him along.

And another scene flashed before Warner's eyes. Henry's office, young Stephen Ashe in the leather chair across from Henry's cluttered desk, hardly room enough to move his legs. Eager, fresh-looking.

"I don't seem to be able to do much with this character, Henry. You know, the series I'm doing for Talbot."

"Yeah. Look, kid, I'll tell you. When you get a character that doesn't seem to come alive for you, or that doesn't seem to want to do the things that he has to to make the plot move along, get rid of him. Find someone else. God, the world's full of characters. Pick out someone new."

"Yeah," young fresh-faced Stephen Ashe said, relieved. "Yeah, that sounds right."

Warner pushed his chair back hard and stood up gripping his desk. *"No!"* I won't . . ." The room blurred slightly, seemed hazy around the edges of things, chairs merging with walls, walls and floor running together. He closed his eyes and when he opened them the room was gone, his desk gone, his chair, typewriter gone. And when he tried to open his mouth to scream, "No," again, his mouth was gone. They wouldn't deal, he thought sadly. Then that was gone too.

APRIL FOOLS'
DAY FOREVER

On the last day of March a blizzard swept across the lower Great Lakes, through western New York and Pennsylvania, and raced toward the city with winds of seventy miles an hour, and snow falling at the rate of one and a half inches an hour. Julia watched it from her wide windows overlooking the Hudson River forty miles from the edge of the city and she knew that Martie wouldn't be home that night. The blizzard turned the world white within minutes and the wind was so strong and so cold that the old house groaned under the impact. Julia patted the window sill, thinking, "There, there," at it. "It'll be over soon, and tomorrow's April, and in three or four weeks I'll bring you daffodils." The house groaned louder and the spot at the window became too cold for her to remain there without a sweater.

Julia checked the furnace by opening the basement door to listen. If she heard nothing, she was reassured. If she heard a wheezing and an occasional grunt, she would worry and call Mr. Lampert, and plead with him to come over before she was snowed in. She heard nothing. Next she looked over the supply of logs in the living room. Not enough by far. There were three good-sized oak logs, and two pine sticks. She struggled into her parka and boots and went to the woodpile by the old barn that had become a storage house, den, garage, studio. A sled was propped up against the grey stone-and-shingle building and she put it down and began to arrange logs on it. When she had as many as she could pull, she returned to the house, feeling her way with one hand along the barn wall, then along the basket-weave fence that she and Martie had built three summers ago, edging a small wild brook that divided the yard. The fence took her in a roundabout way, but it was safer than trying to go straight to the house in the blinding blizzard. By the time she had got back inside, she felt frozen. A sheltered thermometer would show no lower than thirty at that time, but with the wind blowing as it was, the chill degrees must be closer to ten or twenty below zero. She stood in the mud room and considered what else she should do. Her car was in the garage. Martie's was at the train station. Mail. Should she try to retrieve any mail that might be in the box? She decided not to. She didn't really think the mailman had been there yet, anyway. Usually Mr. Probst blew his whistle to let her know that he was leaving something and she hadn't heard it. She took off the heavy clothes then and went through the house checking windows, peering at the latches of the storm windows. There had been a false spring three weeks ago, and she had opened windows and even washed a few before the winds changed again. The house was secure.

What she wanted to do was call Martie, but she didn't. His boss didn't approve of personal phone calls during the working day. She breathed a curse at Hilary Boyle, and waited for Martie to call her. He would, as soon as he had a chance. When she was certain that there was nothing else she should do, she sat down in the living room, where one log was burning softly. There was no light on in the room and the storm had darkened the sky. The small fire glowed pleasingly in the enormous fireplace, and the radiance was picked up by pottery and brass mugs on a low table before the fireplace. The room was a long rectangle, wholly out of proportion, much too long for the width, and with an uncommonly high ceiling. Paneling the end walls had helped, as had making a separate room within the larger one, with its focal point the fireplace. A pair of chairs and a two-seater couch made a cozy grouping. The colors were autumn forest colors, brilliant and subdued at the same time: oranges and scarlets in the striped covering of the couch, picked up again by pillows; rust browns in the chairs; forest-green rug. The room would never make *House Beautiful*, Julia had thought when she brought in the last piece of brass for the table and surveyed the effect, but she loved it, and Martie loved it. And she'd seen people relax in that small room within a room who hadn't been able to relax for a long time. She heard it then.

When the wind blew in a particular way in the old house, it sounded like a baby crying in great pain. Only when the wind came from the northwest over thirty miles an hour. They had searched and searched for the minute crack that had to be responsible and they had calked and filled and patched until it seemed that there couldn't be any more holes, but it was still there, and now she could hear the baby cry.

Julia stared into the fire, trying to ignore the wail, willing herself not to think of it, not to remember the first time she had heard the baby. She gazed into the fire and couldn't stop the images that formed and became solid before her eyes. She awakened suddenly, as in the dreams she had had during the last month or so of pregnancy. Without thinking, she slipped from bed, feeling for her slippers in the dark, tossing her robe about her shoulders hurriedly. She ran down the hall to the baby's room, and at the door she stopped in confusion. She pressed one hand against her flat stomach, and the other fist against her mouth hard, biting her fingers until she tasted blood. The baby kept on crying. She shook her head and reached for the knob and turned it, easing the door open soundlessly. The room was dark. She stood at the doorway, afraid to enter. The baby cried again. Then she pushed the door wide open and the hall light flooded the empty room. She fainted.

When she woke up hours later, grey light shone coldly on the bare floor, from the yellow walls. She raised herself painfully, chilled and shivering. Sleepwalking? A vivid dream and sleepwalking? She listened; the house was quiet, except for its regular night noises. She went back to bed. Martie protested in his sleep when she snuggled against his warm body, but he turned to let her curve herself to fit, and he put his arm about her. She said nothing about the dream the next day.

Six months later she heard the baby again. Alone this time, in the late afternoon of a golden fall day that had been busy and almost happy. She had been gathering nuts with her friend Phyllis Govern. They'd had a late lunch, and then Phyllis had had to run because it was close to four. A wind had come up, threatening a storm before evening. Julia watched the clouds build for half an hour.

She was in her studio in the barn, on the second floor, where the odor of hay seemed to remain despite an absence of fifteen or twenty years. She knew it was her imagination, but she liked to think that she could smell the hay, could feel the warmth of the animals from below. She hadn't worked in her studio for almost a year, since late in her pregnancy, when it had become too hard to get up the narrow, steep ladder that led from the ground floor to the balcony that opened to the upstairs rooms. She didn't uncover anything in the large room, but it was nice to be there. She needed clay, she thought absently, watching clouds roll in from the northwest. It would be good to feel clay in her fingers again. She might make a few Christmas gifts. Little things, funny things, to let people know that she was all right, that she would be going back to work before long now. She glanced at the large blocks of granite that she had ordered before. Not yet. Nothing serious yet. Something funny and inconsequential to begin with.

Still thoughful, she left the studio and went to the telephone in the kitchen and placed a call to her supplier in the city. While waiting for the call to be completed, she heard it. The baby was in pain, she thought, and hung up. Not until she had started for the hall door did she realize what she was doing. She stopped, very cold suddenly. Like before, only this time she was wide awake. She felt for the door and pushed it open an inch or two. The sound was still there, no louder, but no softer either. Very slowly she followed the sound up the stairs, through the hall, into the empty room. She had been so certain that it originated here, but now it seemed to be coming from her room. She backed out into the hall and tried the room she shared with Martie. Now the crying seemed to be coming from the other bedroom. She stood at the head of the stairs for another minute, then she ran down and tried to dial Martie's number. Her hands were shaking too hard and she botched it twice before she got him.

Afterward she didn't know what she had said to him. He arrived an hour later to find her sitting at the kitchen table, ashen-faced, terrified.

"I'm having a breakdown," she said quietly. "I knew it happened to some women when they lost a child, but I thought I was past the worst part by now. I've heard it before, months ago." She stared straight ahead. "They probably will want me in a hospital for observation for a while. I should have packed, but . . . Martie, you will try to keep me out of an institution, won't you? What does it want, Martie?"

"Honey, shut up. Okay?" Martie was listening intently. His face was very pale. Slowly he opened the door and went into the hall, his face turned up toward the stairs.

"Do you hear it?"

"Yes. Stay there." He went upstairs, and when he came back down, he was still pale, but satisfied now. "Honey, I hear it, so that means there's something making the noise. You're not imagining it. It is a real noise, and by God it sounds like a baby crying."

Julia built up the fire and put a stack of records on the stereo and turned it too loud. She switched on lights through the house, and set the alarm clock for six twenty to be certain she didn't let the hour pass without remembering Hilary Boyle's news show. Not that she ever forgot it, but there might be a first time, especially on this sort of night, when she wouldn't be expecting Martie until very late, if at all. She wished he'd call. It was four-thirty. If he could get home, he should leave the office in an hour, be on the train at twenty-three minutes before six and at home by six forty-five. She made coffee and lifted the phone to see if it was working. It seemed to be all right. The stereo music filled the house, shook the floor and rattled the windows, but over it now and then she could hear the baby.

She tried to see outside, the wind-driven snow was impenetrable. She flicked on outside lights, the drive entrance, the light over the garage, the door to the barn, the back porch, front porch, the spotlight on the four pieces of granite that she had completed and placed in the yard, waiting for the rest of the series. The granite blocks stood out briefly during a lull. They looked like squat sentinels.

She took her coffee back to the living room, where the stereo was loudest, and sat on the floor by the big cherry table that they had cut down to fourteen inches. Her sketch pad lay here. She glanced at the top page without seeing it, then opened the pad to the middle and began to doodle aimlessly. The record changed; the wind howled through the yard; the baby wailed. When she looked at what she had been doing on the pad, she felt a chill begin deep inside. She had written over and over, MURDERERS. *You killed my babies.* MURDERERS.

Martie Sayre called the operator for the third time within the hour. "Are the lines still out?"

"I'll check again, Mr. Sayre." Phone static, silence, she was back. "Sorry, sir. Still out."

"Okay. Thanks." Martie chewed his pencil and spoke silently to the picture on his desk: Julia, blond, thin, intense eyes and a square chin. She was beautiful. Her thin body and face seemed to accentuate lovely delicate bones. He, thin also, was simply craggy and gaunt. "Honey, don't listen to it. Turn on music loud. You know I'd be there if I could." The phone rang and he answered.

"I have the material on blizzards for you, Mr. Sayre. Also, Mr. Boyle's interview with Dr. Hewlitt, A.M.S., and the one with Dr. Wycliffe, the NASA satellite weather expert. Anything else?"

"Not right now, Sandy. Keep close. Okay?"

"Sure thing."

He turned to the monitor on his desk and pushed the ON button. For the next half hour he made notes and edited the interviews and shaped a fifteen-minute segment for a special to be aired at ten that night. Boyle called for him to bring what he had ready at seven.

There was a four-man consultation. Martie, in charge of the science-news department; Dennis Kolchak, political-news expert; David Wedekind, the art director. Hilary Boyle paced as they discussed the hour special on the extraordinary weather conditions that had racked the entire earth during the winter. Boyle was a large man, over six feet, with a massive frame that let him carry almost three hundred pounds without appearing fat. He was a chain smoker, and prone to nervous collapses. He timed the collapses admirably: he never missed a show. His daily half hour, "Personalized News," was the most popular network show that year, as it had been for the past three years. The balloon would burst eventually, and the name Hilary Boyle wouldn't sound like God, but now it did, and no one could explain the X *factor* that had catapulted the talentless man into the firmament of stars.

The continuity writers had blocked in the six segments of the show already, two from other points—Washington and Los Angeles—plus the commercial time, plus the copter pictures that would be live, if possible.

"Looking good," Hilary Boyle said. "Half an hour Eddie will have the first film ready. . . ."

Martie wasn't listening. He watched Boyle and wondered if Boyle would stumble over any of the words Martie had used in his segment. He hoped not. Boyle always blamed him personally if he, Boyle, didn't know the words he had to parrot. "Look, Martie, I'm a reasonably intelligent man, and if I don't know it, you gotta figure that most of the viewers won't know it either. Get me? Keep it simple, but without sacrificing any of the facts. That's your job, kid. Now give me this in language I can understand."

Martie's gaze wandered to the window wall. The room was on the sixty-third floor; there were few other lights to be seen on this level, and only those that were very close. The storm had visibility down to two hundred yards. What lights he could see appeared ghostly, haloed, diffused, toned down to beautiful pearly luminescences. He thought of Boyle trying to say that, and then had to bite his cheek to keep from grinning. Boyle couldn't stand it when someone grinned in his presence, unless he had made a funny.

Martie's part of the special was ready for taping by eight, and he went to the coffee shop on the fourteenth floor for a sandwich. He wished he could get through to Julia, but telephone service from Ohio to Washington to Maine was a disaster area that night.

He closed his eyes and saw her, huddled before the fire in the living room glowing with soft warm light. Her pale hair hiding her paler face, hands over her ears, tight. She got up and went to the steps, looking up them, then ran back to the fire. The house shaking with music and the wind. The image was so strong that he opened his eyes wide and shook his head too hard, starting a mild headache at the back of his skull. He drank his coffee fast, and got a second cup, and when he sat down again, he was almost smiling. Sometimes he was convinced that she was right when she said that they had something so special between them, they never were actually far apart. Sometimes he knew she was right.

He finished his sandwich and coffee and wandered back to his office. Everything was still firm, ready to tape in twenty minutes. His part was holding fine.

He checked over various items that had come through in the last several hours, and put three of them aside for elaboration. One of them was about a renewal of the influenza epidemic that had raked England earlier in the year. It was making a comeback, more virulent than ever. New travel restrictions had been imposed.

Julia: "I don't care what they say, I don't believe it. Who ever heard of quarantine in the middle of the summer? I don't know why travel's being restricted all over the world, but I don't believe it's because of the flu." Accusingly, "You've got all that information at your fingertips. Why don't you look it up and see? They banned travel to France before the epidemic got so bad."

Martie rubbed his head, searched his desk for aspirin and didn't find any. Slowly he reached for the phone, then dialed Sandy, his information girl. "See what we have on tap about weather-related illnesses, honey. You know, flu, colds, pneumonia. Stuff like that. Hospital statistics, admittances, deaths. Closings of businesses, schools. Whatever you can find. Okay?" To the picture on his desk, he said, "Satisfied?"

Julia watched the Hilary Boyle show at six thirty and afterward had scrambled eggs and a glass of milk. The weather special at ten explained Martie's delay, but even if there hadn't been the special to whip into being, transportation had ground to a stop. Well, nothing new there, either. She had tried to call Martie finally, and got the recording: *Sorry, your call cannot be completed at this time.* So much for that. The baby cried and cried.

She tried to read for an hour or longer and had no idea of what she had been reading when she finally tossed the book down and turned to look at the fire. She added a log and poked the ashes until the flames shot up high, sparking blue and green, snapping crisply. As soon as she stopped forcing her mind to remain blank, the thoughts came rushing in.

Was it crazy of her to think they had killed her two babies? Why would they? Who were they? Weren't autopsies performed on newborn babies? Wouldn't the doctors and nurses be liable to murder charges, just like anyone else? These were the practical aspects, she decided. There were more. The fear of a leak. Too many people would have to be involved. It would be too dangerous, unless it was also assumed that everyone in the delivery room, in the OB ward, in fact, was part of a gigantic conspiracy. If only she could remember more of what had happened.

Everything had been normal right up to delivery time. Dr. Wymann had been pleased with her pregnancy from the start. Absolutely nothing untoward had happened. Nothing. But when she woke up, Martie had been at her side, very pale, red-eyed. *The baby is dead,* he'd said. And, *Honey, I love you so much. I'm so sorry. There wasn't a thing they could do.* And on and on. They had wept together. Someone had come in with a tray that held a needle. Sleep.

Wrong end of it. Start at the other end. Arriving at the hospital, four-minute pains. Excited, but calm. Nothing unexpected. Dr. Wymann had briefed her on procedure. Nothing out of the ordinary. Blood sample, urine. Weight. Blood pressure. Allergy test. Dr. Wymann: *Won't be long now, Julia. You're doing fine.* Sleep. Waking to see Martie, pale and red-eyed at her side.

Dr. Wymann? He would have known. He wouldn't have let them do anything to her baby!

At the foot of the stairs she listened to the baby crying. Please don't, she thought at it. Please don't cry. Please.

The baby wailed on and on.

That was the first pregnancy, four years ago. Then last year, a repeat performance, by popular demand. She put her hands over her ears and ran back to the fireplace. She thought of the other girl in the double room, a younger girl, no more than eighteen. Her baby had died too in the staph outbreak. Sleeping, waking up, no reason, no sound in the room, but wide awake with pounding heart, the chill of fear all through her. Seeing the girl then, short gown, long lovely leg climbing over the guard rail at the window. Pale yellow light in the room, almost too faint to make out details, only the silhouettes of objects. Screaming suddenly, and at the same moment becoming aware of figures at the door. An intern and a nurse. Not arriving, but standing there quietly. Not moving at all until she screamed. The ubiquitous needle to quiet her hysterical sobbing.

"Honey, they woke you up when they opened the hall door. They didn't say anything for fear of startling her, making her fall before they could get to her."

"Where is she?"

"Down the hall. I saw her myself. I looked through the observation window and saw her, sleeping now. She's a manic-depressive, and losing the baby put her in a tailspin. They're going to take care of her."

Julia shook her head. She had let him convince her, but it was a lie. They hadn't been moving at all. They had stood there waiting for the girl to jump. Watching her quietly, just waiting for the end. If Julia hadn't awakened and screamed, the girl would be dead now. She shivered and went to the kitchen to make coffee. The baby was howling louder.

She lighted a cigarette. Martie would be smoking continuously during the taping. She had sat through several tapings and knew the routine. The staff members watching, making notes, the director making notes. Hilary Boyle walked from the blue velvet hangings, waved at the camera, took his seat behind a massive desk, taking his time, getting comfortable. She liked Hilary Boyle, in spite of all the things about his life, about him personally, that she usually didn't like in people. His self-assurance that bordered on egomania, his women. She felt that he had assigned her a number and when it came up he would come to claim her as innocently as a child demanding his lollipop. She wondered if he would kick and scream when she said no. The cameras moved in close, he picked up his clipboard and glanced at the first sheet of paper, then looked into the camera. And the magic would work again, as it always worked for him. The X *factor.*

A TV personality, radiating over wires, through air, from emptiness, to people everywhere who saw him. How did it work? She didn't know, neither did anyone else. She stubbed out her cigarette.

She closed her eyes, seeing the scene, Hilary leaving the desk, turning to wave once, then going through the curtains. Another successful special. A huddle of three men, or four, comparing notes, a rough spot here, another there. They could be taken care of with scissors, Martie, his hands shoved deep into his pockets, mooching along to his desk.

"Martie, you going home tonight?" Boyle stood in his doorway, filling it.

"Doesn't look like it. Nothing's leaving the city now."

"Buy you a steak." An invitation or an order? Boyle grinned. Invitation. "Fifteen minutes. Okay?"

"Sure. Thanks."

Martie tried again to reach Julia. "I'll be in and out for a couple of hours. Try it now and then, will you, doll?"

The operator purred at him. He was starting to get the material he had asked Sandy for: hospital statistics, epidemics of flu and flu-like diseases, incidence of pneumonia outbreaks, and so on. As she had said, there was a stack of the stuff. He riffled quickly through the print-outs. Something was not quite right, but he couldn't put his finger on what it was. Boyle's door opened then, and he stacked the material and put it inside his desk.

"Ready? I had Doris reserve a table for us down in the Blue Light. I could use a double Scotch about now. How about you?"

Martie nodded and they walked to the elevators together. The Blue Light was one of Boyle's favorite hangouts. They entered the dim, noisy room, and were led to a back table where the ceiling was noise-absorbing and partitions separated one table from another, creating small oases of privacy. The floor show was visible, but almost all the noise of the restaurant was blocked.

"Look," Boyle said, motioning toward the blue spotlight. Three girls were dancing together. They wore midnight-blue body masks that covered them from crown to toe. Wigs that looked like green and blue threads of glass hung to their shoulders, flashing as they moved.

"I have a reputation," Boyle said, lighting a cigarette from his old one. "No one thinks anything of it if I show up in here three-four times a week."

He was watching the squirming girls, grinning, but there was an undertone in his voice that Martie hadn't heard before. Martie looked at him, then at the girls again, and waited.

"The music bugs the piss right out of me, but the girls, now that's different," Boyle said. A waitress moved into range. She wore a G-string, an apron whose straps miraculously covered both nipples and stayed in place somehow, and very high heels. "Double Scotch for me, honeypot, and what for you, Martie?"

"Bourbon and water."

"Double bourbon and water for Dr. Sayre." He squinted, studying the gyrating girls. "That one on the left. Bet she's a blonde. Watch the way she moves, you can almost see blondness in that wrist motion. . . ." Boyle glanced at the twitching hips of their waitress and said, in the same breath, same tone of voice, "I'm being watched. You will be too after tonight. You might look out for them."

"Who?"

"I don't know. Not government, I think. Private outfit maybe. Like FBI, same general type, same cool, but I'm almost positive not government."

"Okay, why?"

"Because I'm a newsman. I really am, you know, always was, always will be. I'm on to something big."

He stopped and the waitress appeared with their drinks. Boyle's gaze followed the twisting girls in the spotlight and he chuckled. He looked up at the waitress then. "Menus, please."

Martie watched him alternately with the floor show. They ordered, and when they were alone again Boyle said, "I think that immortality theory that popped up eight or ten years ago isn't dead at all. I think it works, just like what's-his-name said it would, and I think that some people are getting the treatments they need, and the others are being killed off, or allowed to die without interference."

Martie stared at him, then at his drink. He felt numb. As if to prove to himself that he could move, he made a whirlpool in the glass and it climbed higher and higher and finally spilled. Then he put it down. "That's crazy. They couldn't keep something like that quiet."

Boyle was continuing to watch the dancing girls. "I'm an intuitive man," Boyle said. "I don't know why I know that next week people will be interested in volcanoes, but if I get a hunch that it will make for a good show, we do it, and the response is tremendous. You know how that goes. I hit right smack on the button again and again. I get the ideas, you fellows do the work, and I get the credit. That's like it should be. You're all diggers, I'm the locator. I'm an ignorant man, but not stupid. Know what I mean? I learned to listen to my hunches. I learned to trust them. I learned to trust myself in front of the camera and on the mike. I don't know exactly what I'll say, or how I'll look. I don't practice anything. Something I'm in tune with . . . something. They know it, and I know it. You fellows call it the X *factor*. Let it go at that. We know what we mean when we talk about it even if we don't know what it is or how it works. Right. Couple of months ago, I woke up thinking that we should do a follow-up on the immortality thing. Don't look at me. Watch the show. I realized that I hadn't seen word one about it for three or four years. Nothing at all. What's his name, the guy that found the synthetic RNA?"

"Smithers. Aaron Smithers."

"Yeah. He's dead. They worked him over so thoroughly, blasted him and his results so convincingly, that he never got over it. Finis. Nothing else said about it. I woke up wondering why not. How could he have been that wrong? Got the Nobel for the same kind of discovery, RNA as a cure for some kind of arthritis. Why was he so far off this time?" Boyle had filled the ashtray by then. He didn't look at Martie as he spoke, but continued to watch the girls, and now and then grinned, or even chuckled.

The waitress returned, brought them a clean ashtray, new drinks, took their orders, and left again. Boyle turned then to look at Martie. "What, no comments yet? I thought by now you'd be telling me to see a head-shrinker."

Martie shook his head. "I don't believe it. There'd be a leak. They proved it wouldn't work years ago."

"Maybe." Boyle drank more slowly now. "Anyway, I couldn't get rid of this notion, so I began to try to find out if anyone was doing anything with the synthetic RNA, and that's when the doors began to close on me. Nobody knows nothing. And someone went through my office, both here at the studio and at home. I got Kolchak to go through some of his sources to look for appropriations for RNA research. Security's clamped down on all appropriations for research. Lobbied for by the AMA, of all people."

"That's something else. People were too loose with classified data," Martie said. "This isn't in the universities any more. They don't know any more than you do."

Boyle's eyes gleamed. "Yeah? So you had a bee, too?"

"No. But I know people. I left Harvard to take this job. I keep in touch. I know the people in the biochemical labs there. I'd know if they were going on with this. They're not. Are you going to try to develop this?" he asked, after a moment.

"Good Christ! What do you think!"

Julia woke up with a start. She was stiff from her position in the large chair, with her legs tucked under her, her head at an angle. She had fallen asleep over her sketch pad, and it lay undisturbed on her lap, so she couldn't have slept very long. The fire was still hot and bright. It was almost eleven thirty. Across the room the television flickered. The sound was turned off, music continued to play too loud in the house. She cocked her head, then nodded. It was still crying.

She looked at the faces she had drawn on her pad: nurses, interns, Dr. Wymann. All young. No one over thirty-five. She tried to recall others in the OB ward, but she was sure that she had them all. Night nurses, delivery nurses, nursery nurses, admittance nurse . . . She stared at the drawing of Dr. Wymann. They were the same age. He had teased her about it once. "I pulled out a grey hair this morning, and here you are as pretty and young as ever. How are you doing?"

But it had been a lie. He was the unchanged one. She had been going to him for six or seven years, and he hadn't changed at all in that time. They were both thirty-four now.

Sitting at the side of her bed, holding her hand, speaking earnestly. "Julia, there's nothing wrong with you. You can still have babies, several of them if you want. We can send men to the moon, to the bottom of the ocean, but we can't fight off staph when it hits in epidemic proportions in a nursery. I know you feel bitter now, that it's hopeless, but believe me, there wasn't anything that could be done either time. I can almost guarantee you that the next time everything will go perfectly."

"It was perfect this time. And the last time."

"You'll go home tomorrow. I'll want to see you in six weeks. We'll talk about it again a bit later. All right?"

Sure. Talk about it. And talk and talk. And it didn't change the fact that she'd had two babies and had lost two babies that had been alive and kicking right up till the time of birth.

Why had she gone so blank afterward? For almost a year she hadn't thought of it, except in the middle of the night, when it hadn't been thought but emotion that had ridden her. Now it seemed that the emotional response had been used up and for the first time she could think about the births, about the staff, about her own reactions. She put her sketch pad down and stood up, listening.

Two boys. They'd both been boys. Eight pounds two ounces, eight pounds four ounces. Big, beautifully formed, bald. The crying was louder, more insistent. At the foot of the stairs she stopped again, her face lifted.

It was a small hospital, a small private hospital. One that Dr. Wymann recommended highly. Because the city hospitals had been having such rotten luck trying to get rid of staph. Infant mortality had doubled, tripled? She had heard a fantastic figure given out, but hadn't been able to remember it. It had brought too sharp pains, and she had rejected knowing. She started up the stairs.

"Why are they giving me an allergy test? I thought you had to test for specific allergies, not a general test."

"If you test out positive, then they'll look for the specifics. They'll know they have to look. We're getting too many people with allergies that we knew nothing about, reacting to antibiotics, to sodium pentothal, to starch in sheets. You name it."

The red scratch on her arm. But they hadn't tested her for specifics. They had tested her for the general allergy symptoms and had found them, and then let it drop. At the top of the stairs she paused again, closing her eyes briefly this time. "I'm coming," she said softly. She opened the door.

His was the third crib. Unerringly she went to him and picked him up; he was screaming lustily, furiously. "There, there. It's all right, darling. I'm here." She rocked him, pressing him tightly to her body. He nuzzled her neck, gulping in air now, the sobs diminishing into hiccups. His hair was damp with perspiration, and he smelled of powder and oil. His ear was tight against his head, a lovely ear.

"You! What are you doing in here? How did you get in?"

She put the sleeping infant back down in the crib, not waking him. For a moment she stood looking down at him, then she turned and walked out the door.

The three blue girls were gone, replaced by two zebra-striped girls against a black drop, so that only the white stripes showed, making an eerie effect.

"Why did you bring this up with me?" Martie asked. Their steaks were before them, two inches thick, red in the middle, charred on the outside. The Blue Light was famous for steaks.

"A hunch. I have a standing order to be informed of any research anyone does on my time. I got the message that you were looking into illnesses, deaths, all that." Boyle waved aside the sudden flash of anger that swept through Martie. "Okay. Cool it. I can't help it. I'm paranoid. Didn't they warn you? Didn't I warn you myself when we talked five years ago? I can't stand for you to use the telephone. Can't stand not knowing what you're up to. I can't help it."

"But that's got nothing to do with your theory."

"Don't play dumb with me, Martie. What you're after is just the other side of the same thing."

"And what are you going to do now? Where from here?"

"That's the stinker. I'm not sure. I think we work on the angle of weather control, for openers. Senator Kern is pushing the bill to create an office of weather control. We can get all sorts of stuff under that general heading, I think, without raising this other issue at all. You gave me this idea yourself. Weather-connected sickness. Let's look at what we can dig out, see what they're hiding, what they're willing to tell, and go on from there."

"Does Kolchak know? Does anyone else?"

"No. Kolchak will go along with the political angle. He'll think it's a natural for another special. He'll cooperate."

Martie nodded. "Okay," he said. "I'll dig away. I think there's a story. Not the one you're after, but a story. And I'm curious about the clampdown on news at a time when we seem to be at peace."

Boyle grinned at him. "You've come a long way from the history-of-science teacher that I talked to about working for me five years ago. Boy, were you green then." He pushed his plate back. "What made you take it? This job? I never did understand."

"Money. What else? Julia was pregnant. We wanted a house in the country. She was working, but not making money yet. She was talking about taking a job teaching art, and I knew it would kill her. She's very talented, you know."

"Yeah. So you gave up tenure, everything that goes with it."

"There's nothing I wouldn't give up for her."

"To each his own. Me? I'm going to wade through that goddam snow the six blocks to my place. Prettiest little piece you ever saw waiting for me. See you tomorrow, Martie."

He waved to the waitress, who brought the check. He signed it without looking at it, pinched her bare bottom when she turned to leave, and stood up. He blew a kiss to the performing girls, stopped at three tables momentarily on his way out, and was gone. Martie finished his coffee slowly.

Everyone had left by the time he returned to his office. He sat down at his desk and looked at the material he had pushed into the drawer. He knew now what was wrong. Nothing more recent than four years ago was included in the material.

Julia slept deeply. She had the dream again. She wandered down hallways, into strange rooms, looking for Martie. She was curious about the building. It was so big. She thought it must be endless, that it wouldn't matter how long she had to search it, she would never finish. She would forever see another hall that she hadn't seen before, another series of rooms that she hadn't explored. It was strangely a happy dream, leaving her feeling contented and peaceful. She awakened at eight. The wind had died completely, and the sunlight coming through the sheer curtains was dazzling, brightened a hundredfold by the brilliant snow. Apparently it had continued to snow after the wind had stopped; branches, wires, bushes, everything was frosted with an inch of powder. She stared out the window, committing it to memory. At such times she almost wished that she was a painter instead of a sculptor. The thought passed. She would get it, the feeling of joy and serenity and purity, into a piece of stone, make it shine out for others to grasp, even though they'd never know why they felt just like that.

She heard the bell of the snowplow at work on the secondary road that skirted their property, and she knew that as soon as the road was open, Mr. Stopes would be by with his small plow and get their driveway. She hoped it all would be cleared by the time Martie left the office. She stared at the drifted snow in the back yard between the house and the barn and shook her head. Maybe Mr. Stopes could get that, too.

While she had breakfast she listened to the morning news. One disaster after another, she thought, turning it off after a few minutes. A nursing-home fire, eighty-two dead. A new outbreak of infantile diarrhea in half a dozen hospitals, leaving one hundred thirty-seven dead babies. The current flu-epidemic death rate increasing to one out of ten.

Martie called at nine. He'd be home by twelve. A few things to clear up for the evening show. Nothing much. She tried to ease his worries about her, but realized that the gaiety in her voice must seem forced to him, phony. He knew that when the wind howled as it had done the night before, the baby cried. She hung up regretfully, knowing she hadn't convinced him that she had slept well, that she was as gay as she sounded. She looked at the phone and knew that it would be even harder to convince him in person that she was all right, and, more important, that the baby was all right.

Martie shook her hard. "Honey, listen to me. Please, just listen to me. You had a dream. Or a hallucination. You know that. You know how you were the first time you heard it. You told me you were having a breakdown. You knew then that it wasn't the baby you heard, no matter what your ears told you. What's changed now?"

"I can't explain it," she said. She wished he'd let go. His hands were painful on her shoulders, and he wasn't aware of them. The fear in his eyes was real and desperate. "Martie, I know that it couldn't happen like that, but it did. I opened the door to somewhere else where our baby is alive and well. He has grown, and he has hair now, black hair, like yours, but curly, like mine. A nurse came in. I scared the hell out of her, Martie. She looked at me just like you are looking now. It was real, all of it."

"We're going to move. We'll go back to the city."

"All right. If you want to. It won't matter. This house has nothing to do with it."

"Christ!" Martie let her go suddenly, and she almost fell. He didn't notice. He paced back and forth a few minutes, rubbing his hand over his eyes, through his hair, over the stubble of his beard. She wished she could do something for him, but she didn't move. He turned to her again suddenly. "You can't stay alone again!"

Julia laughed gently. She took his hand and held it against her cheek. It was very cold. "Martie, look at me. Have I laughed spontaneously during this past year? I know how I've been, what I've been like. I knew all along, but I couldn't help myself. I was such a failure as a woman, don't you see? It didn't matter if I succeeded as an artist, or as a wife, anything. I couldn't bear a live child. That's all I could think about. It would come at the most awkward moments, with company here, during our lovemaking, when I had the mallet poised, or mixing a cake. Whammo, there it would be. And I'd just want to die. Now, after last night, I feel as if I'm alive again, after being awfully dead. It's all right, Martie. I had an experience that no one else could believe in. I don't care. It must be like conversion. You can't explain it to anyone who hasn't already experienced it, and you don't have to explain it to him. I shouldn't even have tried."

"God, Julia, why didn't you say what you were going through?

I didn't realize. I thought you were getting over it all." Martie pulled her to him and held her too tightly.

"You couldn't do anything for me," she said. Her voice was muffled. She sighed deeply.

"I know. That's what makes it such hell." He pushed her back enough to see her face. "And you think it's over now? You're okay now?" She nodded. "I don't know what happened. I don't care. If you're okay, that's enough. Now let's put it behind us. . . ."

"But it isn't over, Martie. It's just beginning. I know he's alive now. I have to find him."

"Can't get the tractor in the yard, Miz Sayre. Could of if you hadn't put them stones out there in the way." Mr. Stopes mopped his forehead with a red kerchief, although he certainly hadn't worked up a sweat, not seated on the compact red tractor, running it back and forth through the drive.

Julia refilled his coffee cup and shrugged. "All right. We'll get to it. The sun's warming it up so much. Maybe it'll just melt off."

"Nope. It'll melt some, then freeze. Be harder'n ever to get it out then."

Julia went to the door and called to Martie, "Honey, can you write Mr. Stopes a check for clearing the drive?"

Martie came in from the living room, taking his checkbook from his pocket. "Twenty?"

"Yep. Get yourself snowed in in town last night, Mr. Sayre?"

"Yep."

Mr. Stopes grinned and finished his coffee. "Some April Fools' Day, ain't it? Forsythia blooming in the snow. Don't know. Just don't know 'bout the weather any more. Remember my dad used to plant his ground crops on April Fools' Day, without fail." He waved the check back and forth a minute, then stuffed it inside his sheepskin coat. "Well, thanks for the coffee, Miz Sayre. You take care now that you don't work too hard and come down with something. You don't want to get taken sick now that Doc Hendricks is gone."

"I thought that new doctor was working out fine," Martie said.

"Yep. For some people. You don't want him to put you in the hospital, though. The treatment's worse than the sickness any more, it seems." He stood up and pulled on a flap-eared hat that matched his coat. "Not a gambling man myself, but even if I was, wouldn't want them odds. Half walks in gets taken out in a box. Not odds that I like at all."

Julia and Martie avoided looking at one another until he was gone. Then Julia said incredulously, "Half!"

"He must be jacking it way up."

"I don't think so. He exaggerates about some things, not things like that. That must be what they're saying."

"Have you met the doctor?"

"Yes, here and there. In the drugstore. At Dr. Saltzman's. He's young, but he seemed nice enough. Friendly. He asked me if we'd had our . . . flu shots." She finished very slowly, frowning slightly.

"And?"

"I don't know. I was just thinking that it was curious of him to ask. They were announcing at the time that there was such a shortage, that only vital people could get them. You know, teachers, doctors, hospital workers, that sort of thing. Why would he have asked if we'd had ours?"

"After the way they worked out, you should be glad that you didn't take him up on it."

"I know." She continued to look thoughtful, and puzzled. "Have you met an old doctor recently? Or even a middle-aged one?"

"Honey!"

"I'm serious. Dr. Saltzman is the only doctor I've seen in years who's over forty. And he doesn't count. He's a dentist."

"Oh, wow! Look, honey, I'm sorry I brought up any of this business with Boyle. I think something is going on, but not in such proportions, believe me. We're a community of what?—seven hundred in good weather? I don't think we've been infiltrated."

She wasn't listening. "Of course, they couldn't have got rid of all the doctors, probably just the ones who were too honest to go along with it. Well, that probably wasn't many. Old and crooked. Young and . . . immortal. Boy!"

"Let's go shovel snow. You need to have your brain aired out."

While he cleared the path to the barn, Julia cleaned off the granite sculptures. She studied them. They were rough-quarried blocks, four feet high, almost as wide. The first one seemed untouched, until the light fell on it in a certain way, the rays low, casting long shadows. There were tracings of fossils, broken, fragmented. Nothing else. The second piece had a few things emerging from the surface, clawing their way up and out, none of them freed from it, though. A snail, a trilobite-like crustacean, a winged insect. What could have been a bird's head was picking its way out. The third one had defined animals, warm-blooded animals, and the suggestion of forests. Next came man and his works. Still rising from stone, too closely identified with the stone to say for certain where he started and the stone ended, if there was a beginning and an end at all. The whole work was to be called *The Wheel*. These were the ends of the spokes, and at the hub of the wheel there was to be a solid granite seat, a pedestal-like seat. That would be the ideal place to sit and view the work, although she knew that few people would bother. But from the center, with the stones in a rough circle, the shadows should be right, the reliefs complementary to one another, suggesting heights that had been left out, suggesting depths that she hadn't shown. All suggestion. The wheel that would unlock the knowledge within the viewer, let him see what he usually was blind to. . . .

"Honey, move!" Martie nudged her arm. He was panting hard.

"Oh, dear. Look at you. You've been moving mountains!" Half the path was cleared. "Let's make a snowman, right to the barn door."

The snow was wet, and they cleared the rest of the path by rolling snowballs, laughing, throwing snowballs at each other, slipping and falling. Afterward they had soup and sandwiches, both of them too beat to think seriously about cooking.

"Nice day," Julia said lazily, lying on the living-room floor, her chin propped up by cupped hands, watching Martie work on the fire.

"Yeah. Tired?"

"Um. Martie, after you talked with Hilary, what did you do the rest of the night?"

"I looked up Smithers' work, what there was in the computer anyway. It's been a long time ago, I'd forgotten a lot of the arguments."

"And?"

"They refuted him thoroughly, with convincing data."

"Are you certain? Did you cross-check?"

"Honey, they were men like . . . like Whaite, and . . . Never mind. They're just names to you. They were the leaders at that time. Many of them are still the authorities. Men like that tried to replicate his experiments and failed. They looked for reasons for the failures and found methodological bungling on his part, erroneous conclusions, faulty data, mistakes in his formulae."

Julia rolled over, with her hands clasped under her head, and stared at the ceiling. "I half remember it all. Wasn't it almost a religious denunciation that took place? I don't remember the scientific details. I wasn't terribly interested in the background then, but I remember the hysteria."

"It got loud and nasty before it ended. Smithers was treated badly. Denounced from the pulpit, from the Vatican, from every scientific magazine . . . It got nasty. He died after a year of it, and they let the whole business die too. As they should have done."

"And his immortality serum will take its place along with the alchemist's stone, the universal solvent, a pinch of something in water to run the cars. . . ."

" 'Fraid so. There'll always be those who will think it was suppressed." He turned to build up the fire that had died down completely.

"Martie, you know that room I told you about? The nursery?

I would know it again if I saw it. How many nurseries do you suppose there are in the city?"

Martie stopped all motion, his back to her. "I don't know." His voice was too tight.

Julia laughed and tugged at his sweater. "Look at me, Martie. Do I look like a kook?"

He didn't turn around. He broke a stick and laid the pieces across each other. He topped them with another stick, slightly larger, then another.

"Martie, don't you think it's strange that suddenly you got the idea to look up these statistics, and Hilary approached you with different questions about the same thing? And at the same time I had this . . . this experience. Doesn't that strike you as too coincidental to dismiss? How many others do you suppose are asking questions too?"

"I had thought of it some, yes. But last night just seemed like a good time to get to things that have been bugging us. You know, for the first time in months no one was going anywhere in particular for hours."

She shook her head. "You can always rationalize coincidences if you are determined to. I was alone for the first time at night since I was in the hospital. I know. I've been over all that, too. But still . . ." She traced a geometrical pattern at the edge of the carpet. "Did you have a dream last night? Do you remember it?"

Martie nodded.

"Okay. Let's test this coincidence that stretches on and on. I did too. Let's both write down our dreams and compare them. For laughs," she added hurriedly when he seemed to stiffen again. "Relax, Martie. So you think I've spun out. Don't be frightened by it. I'm not. When I thought that was the case, six months ago, or whenever it was, I was petrified. Remember? This isn't like that. This is kooky in a different way. I feel that a door that's always been there has opened a crack. Before, I didn't know it was there, or wouldn't admit that it was anyway. And now it's there, and open. I won't let it close again."

Martie laughed suddenly and stopped breaking sticks. He lighted the fire and then sat back with a notebook and pen. "Okay."

Martie wrote his dream simply with few descriptions. Alone, searching for her in an immense building. A hospital? An endless series of corridors and rooms. He had forgotten much of it, he realized, trying to fill in blanks. Finally he looked up to see Julia watching him with a faint smile. She handed him her pad and he stared at the line drawings that could have been made to order to illustrate his dream. Neither said anything for a long time.

"Martie, I want another baby. Now."

"God! Honey, are you sure? You're so worked up right now. Let's not decide . . ."

"But I have decided already. And it is in my hands, you know."

"So why tell me at all? Why not just toss the bottle out the window and be done with it?"

"Oh, Martie. Not like that. I want us to be deliberate about it, to think during coitus that we are really making a baby, to love it then. . . ."

"Okay, honey. But why now? What made you say this now?"

"I don't know. Just a feeling."

"Dr. Wymann, is there anything I should do, or shouldn't do? I mean . . . I feel fine, but I felt fine the other times, too."

"Julia, you are in excellent health. There's no reason in the world for you not to have a fine baby. I'll make the reservation for you. . . ."

"Not . . . I don't want to go back to that same hospital. Someplace else."

"But, it's . . ."

"I won't!"

"I see. Well, I suppose I can understand that. Okay. There's a very good, rather small hospital in Queens, fully equipped. . . ."

"Dr. Wymann, this seems to be the only hang-up I have. I have to see the hospital first, before you make a reservation. I can't explain it. . . ." Julia got up and walked to the window high over

Fifth Avenue. "I blame the hospital, I guess. This time I want to pick it out myself. Can't you give me a list of the ones that you use, let me see them before I decide?" She laughed and shook her head. "I'm amazed at myself. What could I tell by looking? But there it is."

Dr. Wymann was watching her closely. "No, Julia. You'll have to trust me. It would be too tiring for you to run all over town to inspect hospitals. . . ."

"No! I . . . I'll just have to get another doctor," she said miserably. "I can't go in blind this time. Don't you understand?"

"Have you discussed this with your husband?"

"No. I didn't even know that I felt this way until right now. But I do."

Dr. Wymann studied her for a minute or two. He glanced at her report spread out before him, and finally he shrugged. "You'll just wear yourself out for nothing. But, on the other hand, walking's good for you. I'll have my nurse give you the list." He spoke into the intercom briefly, then smiled again at Julia. "Now sit down and relax. The only thing I want you to concentrate on is relaxing, throughout the nine months. Every pregnancy is totally unlike every other one. . . ."

She listened to him dreamily. So young-looking, smooth-faced, tanned, if overworked certainly not showing it at all. She nodded when he said to return in a month.

"And I hope you'll have decided at that time about the hospital. We do have to make reservations far in advance, you know."

Again she nodded. "I'll know by then."

"Are you working now?"

"Yes. In fact, I'm having a small showing in two weeks. Would you like to come?"

"Why don't you give me the date and I'll check with my wife and let you know?"

Julia walked from the building a few minutes later feeling as though she would burst if she didn't find a private place where she could examine the list of hospitals the nurse had provided. She hailed a taxi and as soon as she was seated she looked over the names of hospitals she never had heard of before.

Over lunch with Martie she said, "I'll be in town for the next few days, maybe we could come in together in the mornings and have lunch every day."

"What are you up to now?"

"Things I need. I'm looking into the use of plastics. I have an idea. . . ."

He grinned at her and squeezed her hand. "Okay, honey. I'm glad you went back to Wymann. I knew you were all right, but I'm glad you know it too."

She smiled back at him. If she found the nursery, or the nurse she had startled so, then she would tell him. Otherwise she wouldn't. She felt guilty about the smiles they exchanged, and she wished momentarily that he wouldn't make it so easy for her to lie to him.

"Where are you headed after lunch?" he asked.

"Oh, the library . . ." She ducked her head quickly and scraped her sherbet glass.

"Plastics?"

"Um." She smiled again, even more brightly. "And what about you? Tonight's show ready?"

"Yeah. This afternoon, in . . ." he glanced at his watch, ". . . exactly one hour and fifteen minutes I'm to sit in on a little talk between Senator George Kern and Hilary. Kern's backing out of his weather-control fight."

"You keep hitting blank walls, don't you?"

"Yes. Good and blank, and very solid. Well, we'd better finish up. I'll drop you at the library."

"Look at us," she said over the dinner table. "Two dismaler people you couldn't find. You first. And eat your hamburger. Awful, isn't it?"

"It's fine, honey." He cut a piece, speared it with his fork, then put it down. "Kern is out. Hilary thinks he got the treatment last month. And his wife too. They were both hospitalized for pneumonia at the same time."

"Do you know which hospital? In New York?"

"Hell, I don't know. What difference does . . . What are you getting at?"

"I . . . Was it one of these?" She got the list from her purse and handed it to him. "I got them from Dr. Wymann's nurse. I wouldn't go back to that one where . . . I made them give me a list so I could look them over first."

Martie reached for her hand and pressed it hard. "No plastics?" She shook her head.

"Honey, it's going to be all right this time. You can go anyplace you want to. I'll look these over. You'll just be . . ."

"It's all right, Martie. I already checked out three of them. Two in Manhattan, one in Yonkers. I . . . I'd rather do it myself. Did Senator Kern mention a hospital?"

"Someplace on Long Island. I don't remember . . ."

"There's a Brent Park Memorial Hospital on Long Island. Was that it?"

"Yes. No. Honey, I don't remember. If he did mention it, it passed right over my head. I don't know." He put the list down and took her other hand and pulled her down to his lap. "Now *you* give. Why do you want to know? What did you see in those hospitals that you visited? Why did you go to the library?"

"I went to three hospitals, all small, all private, all run by terribly young people. Young doctors, young nurses, young everybody. I didn't learn anything else about them. But, in the library I tried to borrow a book on obstetrics, and there aren't any."

"What do you mean, there aren't any? None on open shelves? None in at the time?"

"None. They looked, and they're all out, lost, not returned, gone. All of them. I tried midwifery, and the same thing. I had a young boy who was terribly embarrassed by it all searching for me, and he kept coming back with the same story. Nothing in. So I went to the branch library in Yonkers, since I wanted to see the hospital there anyway, and it was the same thing. They have open shelves there, and I did my own looking. Nothing."

"What in God's name did you plan to do with a book on obstetrics?"

"Isn't that beside the point? Why aren't there any?"

"It is directly to the point. What's going through your mind, Julia? Exactly what are you thinking?"

"The baby is due the end of December. What if we have another blizzard? Or an ice storm? Do you know anything about delivering a baby? Oh, something, I grant you. Everyone knows something. But what about an emergency? Could you handle an emergency? I thought if we had a book . . ."

"I must have wandered into a nut ward. I'm surrounded by maniacs. Do you hear what you're saying? Listen to me, sweetheart, and don't say a word until I'm finished. When that baby is due, I'll get you to a hospital. I don't care which one you choose, or where it is. You'll be there. If we have to take an apartment next door to it for three months to make certain, we'll do it. You have to have some trust and faith in me, in the doctor, in yourself. And if it eases your mind, I'll get you a book on obstetrics, but by God, I don't plan to deliver a baby!"

Meekly she said, "You just get me a book and I'll behave. I promise." She got up and began to gather up their dishes. "Maybe later on we'll want some scrambled eggs or something. Let's have coffee now."

They moved to the living room, where she sat on the floor with her cup on the low table. "Is Kern satisfied that no biological warfare agent got loose to start all this?"

Martie looked at her sharply. "You're a witch, aren't you? I never told you that's what I was afraid of."

She shrugged. "You must have."

"Kern's satisfied. I am too. It isn't that. His committee decided to drop it, at his suggestion, because of the really dangerous condition of the world right now. It's like a powder keg, just waiting for the real statistics to be released. That would blow it. Everyone suspects that the death rate has risen fantastically, but without official figures, it remains speculation, and the fuse just sits there. He's right. If Hilary does go on, he's taking a terrible risk." He sighed. "It's a mutated virus that changes faster than the vaccines that we come up with. It won't be any better until it mutates into something that isn't viable, then it will vanish. Only then will the governments start opening books again, and hospitals give out figures for admittances and deaths. We know that the medical profession has been hit probably harder than any other. Over-exposure. And the shortage of personnel makes everything that used to be minor very serious now."

Julia nodded, but her gaze didn't meet his. "Sooner or later," she said, "you'll have to turn that coin over to see what's on the other side. Soon now, I think."

Julia wore flowered pants and a short vest over a long-sleeved tailored blouse. With her pale hair about her shoulders, she looked like a very young girl, too young to be sipping champagne from the hollow-stemmed goblet that she held with both hands. Dwight Gregor was in the middle of the circle of stones, studying the effects from there. Gregor was the main critic, the one whose voice was heard if he whispered, although all others were shouting. Julia wished he'd come out of the circle and murmur something or other to her. She didn't expect him to let her off the hook that evening, but at least he could move, or something. She probably wouldn't know what his reactions had been until she read his column in the morning paper. She sipped again and turned despairingly to Martie.

"I think he fell asleep out there."

"Honey, relax. He's trying to puzzle it out. He knows that you're cleverer than he is, and more talented, and that you worked with the dark materials of your unconscious. He feels it and can't grasp the meaning. . . ."

"Who are you quoting?"

"Boyle. He's fascinated by the circle. He'll be in and out of it all evening. Watch and see. Haven't you caught him looking at you with awe all over his face?"

"Is that awe? I was going to suggest that you tell him I'm good and pregnant."

Martie laughed with her, and they separated to speak with the guests. It was a good show, impressive. The yard looked great, the lighting effects effective, the waterfall behind the basket-weave fence just right, the pool at the bottom of the cascading water just dark and mysterious enough. . . . Martie wandered about his yard proudly.

"Martie?" Boyle stopped by him. "Want to talk to you. Half an hour over by the fence. Okay?"

Gregor left the circle finally and went straight to Julia. He raised her hand to his lips and kissed it lightly, keeping his gaze on her face. "My dear. Very impressive. So nihilistic. Did you realize how nihilistic it is? But of course. And proud, also. Nihilistic but proud. Strange combination. You feel that man almost makes it, this time. Did you mean that? Only one toe restraining him. Sad. So sad."

"Or you can imagine that the circle starts with the devastation, the ruins, and the death of man. From that beginning to the final surge of life that lifts him from the origins in the dirt. . . . Isn't that what you really meant to say, my dear?" Frances Lefever moved in too close to Julia, overwhelming her with the sweet, sickening scent of marijuana heavy on her breath. "If that's where the circle begins, then it is a message of nothing but hope. Isn't that right, my dear?"

Gregor moved back a step, waving his hand in the air. "Of course, one can always search out the most romantic explanation of anything. . . ."

"Romantic? Realistic, my dear Dwight. Yours is the typical

male reaction. Look what I've done. I've destroyed all mankind, right back down to the primordial ooze. Mine says, Look, man is freeing himself, he is leaping from his feet-of-clay beginnings to achieve a higher existence. Did you really look at that one? There's no shadow, you know."

Dwight and Frances forgot about Julia. They argued their way back to the circle, and she leaned weakly against the redwood fence and drank deeply.

"Hey. Are you all right, Julia?"

"Dr. Wymann. Yes. Fine. Great."

"You looked as if you were ready to faint. . . ."

"Only with relief. They like it. They are fascinated by it. It's enigmatic enough to make them argue about meanings, so they'll both write up their own versions, different from each other's, and that will make other people curious enough to want to see for themselves. . . ."

Dr. Wymann laughed and watched the two critics as they moved about the large stones, pointing out to one another bits and pieces each was certain the other had missed.

"Congratulations, Julia."

"What did *you* think of it?"

"Oh, no. Not after real critics have expressed opinions."

"Really. I'd like to know."

Dr. Wymann looked again at the circle of stones and shrugged. "I'm a clod. An oaf. I had absolutely no art training whatever. I like things like Rodin. Things that are unequivocal. I guess I didn't know what you were up to with your work."

Julia nodded. "Fair enough."

"I'm revealed as an ass."

"Not at all, Dr. Wymann. I like Rodin too."

"One thing. I couldn't help overhearing what they were saying. Are you the optimist that the woman believes, or the pessimist that Gregor assumes?"

Julia finished off her champagne, looking at the goblet instead of the doctor. She sighed when it was all gone. "I do love champagne." She smiled at him then. "The stones will give you the answer. But you'll have to find it yourself. I won't tell."

He laughed and they moved apart. Julia drifted back inside the house to check the buffet and the bar. She spoke briefly with Margie Mellon, who was taking care of the food and drinks. Everything was holding up well. A good party. Successful unveiling. A flash-bulb went off outside, then another and another.

"Honey! It's really great, isn't it? They love it! And you! And me because I'm married to you!"

She never had seen Martie so pleased. He held her close for a minute, then kissed each eyelid. "Honey, I'm so proud of you I can't stand it. I want to strip you and take you to bed right now. That's how it's affected me."

"Me too. I know."

"Let's drive them all off early. . . ."

"We'll try anyway."

She was called to pose by the circle, and she left him. Martie watched her. "She is so talented," a woman said, close to his ear. He turned. He didn't know her.

"I'm Esther Wymann," she said huskily. She was very drunk. "I almost envy her. Even if it is for a short time. To know that you have that much talent, a genius, creative genius. I think it would be worth having, even if you knew that tomorrow you'd be gone. To have that for a short time. So creative and so pretty too."

She drained a glass that smelled like straight Scotch. She ran the tip of her tongue around the rim and turned vaguely toward the bar. "You too, sweetie? No drink? Where's our host? Why hasn't he taken care of you? That's all right. Esther will. Come on."

She tilted when she moved and he steadied her. "Thanks. Who're you, by the way?"

"I'm the host," he said coldly. "What did you mean by saying she has so little time? What's that supposed to mean?"

Esther staggered back from his hand. "Nothing. Didn't mean anything." She lurched away from him and almost ran the three steps that took her into a group of laughing guests. Martie saw

Wymann put an arm about her to help hold her upright. She said something to him and the doctor looked up quickly to see Martie watching them. He turned around, still holding his wife, and they moved toward the door to the dining room. Martie started after them, but Boyle appeared at the doorway and motioned for him to go outside.

The doctor would keep, Martie decided. He couldn't talk to him with that drunken woman on his arm anyway. He looked once more toward the dining-room doorway, then followed Boyle outside.

A picture or two, someone said. He stood by Julia, holding her hand, and the flashbulbs exploded. Someone opened a new bottle of champagne close by, and that exploded. Someone else began shrieking with laughter. He moved away from the center of the party again and sat down at a small table, waiting for Boyle to join him.

"This is as safe as any place we're likely to find," Boyle said. He was drinking beer, carrying a quart bottle with him. "What have you dug out?"

The waterfall splashed noisily behind them, and the party played noisily before them. Martie watched the party. He said, "The death rate, extrapolated only, you understand. Nothing's available on paper anywhere. But the figures we've come up with are: from one million eight hundred thousand five years ago, up to fourteen and a quarter million this year."

Boyle choked and covered his face with his handkerchief. He poured more beer and took a long swallow.

Martie waited until he finished, then said, "Birth rate down from three and a half million to one million two hundred thousand. That's live births. At these rates, with the figures we could find, we come up with a loss per thousand of sixty-three. A death rate of sixty-three per thousand."

Boyle glared at him. He turned to watch the party again, saying nothing.

Martie watched Julia talking with guests. She never had looked more beautiful. Pregnancy had softened her thin face, had added a glow. What had that bitch meant by saying she had so little time? He could hear Julia's words inside his head: *You'll have to turn it over sooner or later.* She didn't understand. Boyle didn't understand. Men like Whaite wouldn't have repudiated a theory so thoroughly if there had been any merit whatsoever in it. It was myth only that said the science community was a real community. There were rivalries, but no corruption of that sort. The whole scientific world wouldn't unite behind a lie. He rubbed his eyes. But how many of the scientists knew enough about biochemistry to form independent judgments? They had to take the word of the men who were considered authorities, and if they, fewer than a dozen, passed judgment, then that judgment was what the rest of the community accepted as final. Only the amateurs on the outside would question them, no one on the inside would think of doing so.

Martie tapped his fingers on the table impatiently. Fringe thinking. Nut thinking. They'd take away his badge and his white coat if he expressed such thoughts. But, damn it, they could! Six or eight, ten men could suppress a theory, for whatever reason they decided was valid, if only they all agreed. Over fourteen million deaths in the States in the past year. How many in the whole world? One hundred million, two hundred million? They'd probably never know.

"Hilary, I'm going up to Cambridge tomorrow, the next day, soon. I have to talk to Smithers' widow."

Hilary nodded. "At that death rate, how long to weed us out? Assuming Smithers was right, that forty percent can be treated."

"About twelve and a half years, starting two years ago." Martie spoke without stopping to consider his figures. He wasn't sure when he had done that figuring. He hadn't consciously thought of it.

He watched as Julia spoke with Dr. Wymann, holding his hand

several seconds. She nodded, and the doctor turned and walked away. What had Wymann's wife meant? Why had she said what she had? If "they" existed, she was one of them. As Wymann was. As Senator Kern was. Who else?

"I don't believe it!"

"I know."

"They couldn't keep such figures quiet! What about France? England? Russia?"

"Nothing. No statistics for the last four years. Files burned, mislaid, not properly completed. Nothing."

"Christ!" Boyle said.

Julia smoked too much, and paced until the phone rang. She snatched it up. "Martie! Are you all right?"

"Sure. What's wrong, honey?" His voice sounded ragged, he was out of breath.

"Darling, I'm sorry. I didn't want to alarm you, but I didn't know how else to reach you. Don't say anything now. Just come home, Martie, straight home. Will you?"

"But . . . Okay, honey. My flight is in fifteen minutes. I'll be home in a couple of hours. Sit tight. Are you all right?"

"Yes. Fine. I'm fine." She listened to the click at the other end of the line, and felt very alone again. She picked up the brief note that she had written and looked at it again. "Lester B. Hayes Memorial Hospital, ask for Dr. Conant."

"It's one on my list," she said to Martie when he read it. "Hilary collapsed at his desk and they took him there. Martie, they'll kill him, won't they?"

Martie crumpled the note and let it drop. He realized that Julia was trembling and he held her for several minutes without speaking. "I have to make some calls, honey. Will you be all right?"

"Yes. I'm fine now. Martie, you won't go, will you? You won't go to that hospital?"

"Sh. It's going to be all right, Julia. Sit down, honey. Try to relax."

Boyle's secretary knew only that she had found him sprawled across his desk and in the next few minutes, Kolchak, or someone, had called the ambulance and he was taken away to the hospital. The report they had was that he was not in serious condition. It had happened before, no one was unduly alarmed, but it was awkward. It never had happened before a show. This time . . . Her voice drifted away.

Martie slammed the receiver down. "It really *has* happened before. The hospital could be a coincidence."

Julia shook her head. "I don't believe it." She looked at her hands. "How old is he?"

"Fifty, fifty-five. I don't know. Why?"

"He's too old for the treatment, then. They'll kill him. He'll die of complications from flu, or a sudden heart attack. They'll say he suffered a heart attack at his desk. . . ."

"Maybe he did have a heart attack. He's been driving himself. . . . Overweight, living too fast, too hard, too many women and too much booze . . ."

"What about Smithers? Did you see Mrs. Smithers?"

"Yes. I saw her. I was with her all morning. . . ."

"And within an hour of your arrival there, Hilary collapses. You're getting too close, Martie. You're making them act now. Did you learn anything about Smithers, or his work?"

"It's a familiar kind of thing. He published prematurely, got clobbered, then tried to publish for over a year and had paper after paper returned. During that time he saw everything he'd done brought down around his ears. His wife believes he committed suicide, although she won't admit it even to herself. But it's there, in the way she talks about them, the ones who she says hounded him. . . ."

"And his papers?"

"Gone. Everything was gone when she was able to try to straighten things out. There wasn't anything left to straighten out. She thinks he destroyed them. I don't know. Maybe he did. Maybe they were stolen. It's too late now."

The phone shrilled, startling both of them. Martie answered. "Yes, speaking. . . ." He looked at Julia, then turned his back. His hand whitened on the phone. "I see. Of course: An hour, maybe less."

Julia was very pale when Martie hung up and turned toward her. "I heard," she said. "The hospital . . . it's one of theirs. Dr. Conant must be one of them."

Martie sat down and said dully, "Hilary's on the critical list. I didn't think they'd touch him. I didn't believe it. Not him."

"You won't go, will you? You know it's a trap."

"Yes, but for what? They can get to me any time they want. They don't have to do it this way. There's no place to hide."

"I don't know for what. Please don't go."

"You know what this is? The battle of the Cro-Magnon and the Neanderthal all over again. One has to eliminate the other. We can't both exist in the same ecological niche."

"Why can't they just go on living as long as they want and leave us alone? Time is on their side."

"They know they can't hide it much longer. In ten years it would be obvious, and they're outnumbered. They're fighting for survival, too. Hitting back first, that's all. A good strategy."

He stood up. Julia caught his arm and tried to pull him to her. Martie was rigid and remote. "If you go, they'll win. I know it. You're the only one now who knows anything about what is going on. Don't you see? You're more valuable than Boyle was. All he had was his own intuition and what you gave him. He didn't understand most of it even. But you . . . They must have a scheme that will eliminate you, or force you to help them. Something."

Martie kissed her. "I have to. If they just want to get rid of me, they wouldn't be this open. They want something else. Remember, I have a lot to come back for. You, the baby. I have a lot to hate them for, too. I'll be back."

Julia swayed and held on to the chair until he turned and left the house. She sat down slowly, staring straight ahead.

Martie looked at Dr. Wymann without surprise. "Hilary's dead?"

"Unfortunately. There was nothing that could be done. A fatal aneurism. . . ."

"How fortunate for you."

"A matter of opinion. Sit down, Dr. Sayre. We want to talk with you quite seriously. It might take a while." Wymann opened the door to an adjoining office and motioned. Two men in doctors' coats entered, nodded at Martie, and sat down. One carried a folder.

"Dr. Conant, and Dr. Fischer." Wymann closed the door and sat down in an easy chair. "Please do sit down, Sayre. You are free to leave at any time. Try the door if you doubt my word. You are not a prisoner."

Martie opened the door. The hallway was empty, gleaming black and white tiles in a zigzag pattern, distant noise of an elevator, sound of a door opening and closing. A nurse emerged from one of the rooms, went into another.

Martie closed the door again. "Okay, your show. I suppose you are in charge?"

"No. I'm not in charge. We thought that since you know me, and in light of certain circumstances, it might be easier if I talked to you. That's all. Either of these two . . . half a dozen others who are available. If you prefer, it doesn't have to be me."

Martie shook his head. "You wanted me. Now what?"

Wymann leaned forward. "We're not monsters, no more than any other human being, anyway. Smithers had exactly what he said he had. You know about that. He really died of a heart attack. So much for history. It works, Sayre. For forty percent of the people. What would you do with it? Should we have made it public? Held a lottery? It would have gone underground even more than it has now, but it would be different. We don't want to kill anyone. The others, the ones who couldn't use it, would search us out and exterminate us like vermin. You know that. In the beginning we needed time. We were too accessible, too vulnerable. A handful of people knew what it was, how to prepare it, how to test for results, how to administer it, what to watch for, all the rest. It's very complicated. We had to protect them and we had to add numbers."

Martie watched him, thinking, Julia knew. The babies. Both of them. The new pregnancy. She was afraid time was running out. This man, or another like him. Had they done anything, or simply failed to do something for the first two? Was there any difference really? His skin felt clammy and he opened his hands when he realized that his fingers were getting stiff.

"It's going on everywhere, more or less like here. Have you read . . . ? No, of course not. . . . I'll be frank with you, Sayre. The world's on a powder keg, has been for over a year. Martial law in Spain, Portugal, Israel, most of the Mid-East. Nothing at all out of China. Japan ripped wide open by strikes and riots, tighter than a drum right now. Nothing's coming out of there. It's like that everywhere. Clampdown on all news. No travel that isn't high-priority. France has been closed down for six months. More restrictions than when they were occupied. Same with England. Canada has closed her borders for the first time in history, as has Mexico. UNESCO recommended all this, in an effort to stop the epidemics, ostensibly. But really to maintain secrecy regarding the climbing death rate. And everyone's panic-stricken, terrified of being hit next. It must have been like this during the Plague outbreaks. Walled cities, fear. Your story coming now would ignite the whole world. There'd be no way to maintain any sort of order. You know I'm right. We couldn't let you and Boyle go on with it."

Martie stood up. "If you try to sell yourselves as humanitarians, I might kill you right now."

"It depends entirely on where you're standing. Most men with any kind of scientific training see almost immediately that what we've done, how we've done it, was the only way this could have been handled. Out in the open, with more than half the people simply not genetically equipped to tolerate the RNA, there would have been a global catastrophe that would have destroyed all of mankind. Governments are made up of old men, Sayre. Old men can't use it. Can you imagine the uprising against all the world governments that would have taken place! It would have been a holocaust that would have left nothing. We've prevented that."

"You've set yourselves up as final judges, eliminating those who can't take it. . . ."

"Eliminating? We upset the entire Darwinian framework for evolution by our introduction of drugs, our transplants, life-saving machines. We were perpetuating a planet of mental and physical degenerates, with each generation less prepared to live than the last. I know you think we're murderers, but is it murder to fail to prescribe insulin and let a diabetic die rather than pass on the genes to yet another generation?" Wymann started to pace, after glancing at his watch, checking it against the wall clock.

"There have been hard decisions, there'll be more even harder ones. Every one of us has lost someone he cared for. Every one! Conant lost his first wife. My sister . . . We aren't searching out people to kill, unless they threaten us. But if they come to us for treatment, and we know that they are terminal, we let them die."

Martie moistened his lips. "Terminal. You mean mortal, with a temporary sore throat, or a temporary appendix inflammation, things you could treat."

"They are terminal now, Sayre. Dying in stages. Dying from the day they are born. We don't prolong their lives."

"Newborn infants? Terminal?"

"Would you demand that newborn idiots be preserved in institutions for fifty or sixty years? If they are dying, we let them die."

Martie looked at the other doctors, who hadn't spoken. Neither of them had moved since arriving and sitting down. He turned again to Wymann. "You called me. What do you want?"

"Your help. We'll need people like you. Forty percent of the population, randomly chosen, means that there will be a shortage of qualified men to continue research, to translate that research into understandable language. The same sort of thing you're doing now. Or, if you prefer, a change of fields. But we will need you."

"You mean I won't suffer a thrombosis, or have a fatal wreck for the next twenty years, if I play along?"

"More than that, Martie. Much more than that. During your last physical examination for insurance you were tested, a routine test by the way. Not conclusive, but indicative. You showed no gross reactions to the synthetic RNA. You would have to be tested more exhaustively, of course, but we are confident that you can tolerate the treatments. . . ."

"What about Julia? What do you plan for her?"

"Martie, have you thought at all about what immortality means? Not just another ten years tacked on at the end, or a hundred, or a thousand. As far as we know now, from all the laboratory data, there is no end, unless through an accident. And with our transplant techniques even that is lessening every week. Forever, Martie. No, you can't imagine it. No one can. Maybe in a few hundred years we'll begin to grasp what it means, but not yet. . . ."

"What about Julia?"

"We won't harm her."

"You've tested her already. You know about her."

"Yes. She cannot tolerate the RNA."

"If anything goes wrong, you'll fold your hands and let her die. Won't you? *Won't you!"*

"Your wife is a terminal case! Can't you see that? If she were plugged into a kidney machine, a heart-and-lung machine, with brain damage, you'd want the plug pulled. You know you would. We could practice preventive medicine on her, others like her, for the next forty years or longer. But for what? For what, Dr. Sayre? As soon as they know, they'll turn on us. We can keep this secret only a few more years. We know we are pushing our luck even now. We took an oath that we would do nothing to prolong the lives of those who are dying. Do you think they would stop at that? If they knew today, we'd be hunted, killed, the process destroyed. Lepers would rather infect everyone with their disease than be eradicated. Your wife will be thirty-five when the child is born. A century ago she would have been doomed by such a late pregnancy. She would have been an old woman. Modern medicine has kept her youthful, but it's an artificial youthfulness. She is dying!"

Martie made a movement toward Wymann, who stepped behind his desk warily. Conant and Fischer were watching him very closely. He sank back down in the chair, covering his face. Later, he thought. Not now. Find out what you can now. Try to keep calm.

"Why did you tell me any of this?" he asked after a moment. "With Boyle gone my job is gone. I couldn't have hurt you."

"We don't want you to light that fuse. You're a scientist. You can divorce your emotions from your reason and grasp the implications. But aside from that, your baby, Martie. We want to save the baby. Julia has tried and tried to find a book on obstetrics, hasn't she? Has she been successful?"

Martie shook his head. The book. He had meant to ask about one at Harvard, and he'd forgotten. "The baby. You think it will be able to . . . The other two? Are they both . . . ?"

"The only concern we have now is for the successful delivery of the child that your wife is carrying. We suspect that it will be one of us. And we need it. That forty percent I mentioned runs through the population, young and old. Over forty, give or take a year or two, they can't stand the treatments. We don't know exactly why yet, but we will eventually. We just know that they die. So that brings us down to roughly twenty-five percent of the present population. We need the babies. We need a new generation of people who won't be afraid of death from the day they first grasp the meaning of the word. We don't know what they will be, how it will change them, but we need them."

"And if it isn't able to take the RNA?"

"Martie, we abort a pregnancy when it is known that the mother had German measles, or if there is a high probability of idiocy. You know that. Unfortunately, our technique for testing the foetus is too imperfect to be certain, and we have to permit the pregnancy to come to term. But that's the only difference. It would still be a therapeutic abortion."

Martie and Julia lay side by side, not touching, each wakeful, aware that the other was awake, pretending sleep. Julia had dried tears on her cheeks. Neither of them had moved for almost an hour.

"But goddam it, which one is Cro-Magnon and which Neanderthal?" Martie said, and sat upright.

Julia sat up too. "What?"

"Nothing. I'm sorry. Go back to sleep, honey. I'm getting up for a while."

Julia swung her legs off the bed. "Can we talk now, Martie? Will you talk to me about it now?"

Martie muttered a curse and left the room.

This was part of the plan, he knew. Drive them apart first, make it easier for him to join them later. He sat down in the kitchen with a glass half filled with bourbon and a dash of water.

"Martie? Are you all right?" Julia stood in the doorway. She was barely showing her pregnancy now, a small bulge was all. He turned away. She sat down opposite him. "Martie? Won't you tell me?"

"Christ, Julia, will you shove off! Get off my back for a while?"

She touched his arm. "Martie, they offered you the treatment, didn't they? They think you could take it. Are you going to?"

He jerked out of the chair, knocking it over, knocking his glass over. "What are you talking about?"

"That was the cruelest thing they could have done right now, wasn't it? After I'm gone, it would have been easier, but now . . ."

"Julia, cut it out. You're talking nonsense. . . ."

"I'll die this time, won't I? Isn't that what they're planning? Did they tell you that you could have the babies if you want them? Was that part of it too?"

"Has someone been here?" Martie grabbed her arm and pulled her from the chair.

She shook her head.

He stared at her for a long time, and suddenly he yanked her against him hard. "I must be out of my mind. I believed them. Julia, we're getting out of here, now. Tomorrow."

"Where?"

"I don't know. Somewhere. Anywhere. I don't know."

"Martie, we have to stop running. There are physical limits to how much I can run now. But besides that, there's really no place to run to. It's the same everywhere. You haven't found anyone who will listen to you. One check with your personal data file and that's it. We may never know what they put on your record, but it's enough to make every official pat you on the head and say, 'Don't worry, Dr. S. We'll take care of it.' We can't get out of the country, passport requests turned down for medical reasons. But even if we could . . . more of the same."

Julia was pale, with circles under her eyes. It was early in November, cold in Chicago, where the apartment overlooked Lake Michigan. A flurry of powdery snow blew in a whirlwind across the street.

Martie nodded. "They've covered everything, haven't they? Special maternity hospitals! For the safety and protection of the mother and child. To keep them from the filthy conditions that exist in most hospitals now. Keep them safe from pneumonia, flu, staph. . . . Oh, Christ!" He leaned his head against the glass and watched the dry dustlike snow.

"Martie . . ."

"Damn. I'm out of cigarettes, honey. I'll just run out and get some."

"Okay. Fine."

"Want anything?"

"No. Nothing." She watched him pull on his coat and leave, then stood at the window and watched until he emerged from the building and started to walk down the street. The baby kicked and she put her hand over her stomach. "It's all right, little one. It's all right."

Martie was only a speck among specks standing at the corner, waiting for the light to turn. She could no longer pick out his figure from those around him. "Martie," she whispered. Then she turned away from the window and sat down. She closed her eyes for a moment. They wanted her baby, this baby, not just another child who would become immortal. They were too aware of the population curve that rises slowly, slowly, then with abandon becomes an exponential curve. No, not just a child, but her particular child. She had to remember that always. The child would be safe. They wouldn't let it be harmed. But they wouldn't let her have it, and they knew that this time she wouldn't give it up. So she'd have to die. The child couldn't be tainted with her knowledge of death. Of course, if it too was unable to tolerate the RNA, there was no real problem. Mother and child. Too bad. No cures for . . . whatever they'd say killed them. Or would they keep her, let her try again? She shook her head. They wouldn't. By then Martie would be one of them, or dead. This was the last child for her.

"So what can I do?" she asked.

Her hands opened and closed convulsively. She shut her eyes hard. "What?" she whispered desperately. *"What?"*

She worked on the red sandstone on the ground floor of the barn. It was too big to get up to her studio, so she'd had her tools, bench, table, everything brought down. It was drafty, but she wore heavy wool slacks and a tentlike top, and was warm.

She whistled tunelessly as she worked. . . .

Julia stood up too fast, then clutched the chair for support. Have to remember, she told herself severely. Work. She had to go to work. She picked up her sketch pad, put it down again. Red sandstone, $10 \times 10 \times 8$. And red quartzite, $4 \times 3 \times 2$. She called her supplier on Long Island.

"Funny, Mrs. Sayre. Just got some in," he said. "Haven't had sandstone for . . . oh, years, I guess."

"Can you have it delivered tomorrow?"

"Mrs. Sayre, everyone who's ever touched rock is working. Had to put on an extra man. Still can't keep up."

"I know. And the painters, and composers, and poets . . ." They settled for the day after her arrival home.

She reserved seats on the six P.M. flight to New York, asked for their hotel bill within the hour, and started to pack. She paused once, a puzzled frown on her forehead. Every one of her friends in the arts was working furiously. They either didn't know or didn't care about the disastrous epidemics, the travel bans, any of it.

Martie walked slowly, his head bowed. He kept thinking of the bridge that he had stood on for an hour, watching filthy water move sluggishly with bits and pieces of junk floating on the surface: a piece of orange, a plastic bag, a child's doll with both arms gone, one eye gone. The doll had swirled in a circle for several minutes, caught in a branch, then moved on out of sight. Of no use to anyone, unwanted, unloved now. Imperfect, cast away.

The wind blew, whipping his coat open, and he shivered. On trial, before his judges. Martin Sayre, do you dare risk your immortal soul for this momentary fling? Confess, go to the flame willingly, with confession on your lips, accept the flame, that too is momentary, and rejoice forever in Paradise.

"Dr. Sayre, you're a reasonable man. You know that we can't do anything for your wife. She will be allowed to bear her child here. No other hospital would admit her, none of the city hospitals would dare. We won't harm her, Dr. Sayre. We won't do anything that is not for her own good. . . ."

Torquemada must have argued so.

And, somewhere else. He couldn't keep them apart, all the same, different faces, but the same. "Of course, the child will have to be taken from her, no matter what happens. The fear of death is a disease as dangerous almost as death itself. It drives man mad. These new children must not be infected with it. . . ."

And somewhere else. "Ah, yes, Dr. Sayre. Meant to call you

back, but got tied up. Appropriations Committee sessions, don't you know. Well now, Dr. Sayre, this little theory of yours about the serum. I've been doing some thinking on that, Dr. Sayre, and don't you know, I can't come up with anything to corroborate what you say. Now if you can furnish some hard proof, don't you know, well now, that would make a difference. Yes, sir, make a big difference."

And again, "Hello, Martie, I just don't know. You may be absolutely right. But there's no way to get to anything to make sure. I can't risk everything here on a wild-goose chase. I checked your data file, as you suggested, and they have a diagnosis made by a Dr. Fischer of Lester B. Hayes Memorial Hospital, who examined you extensively in four examinations from March through August of this year. He recommended treatment for schizophrenia; you refused. Face it, Martie, I have to ask myself, isn't this just a schizophrenic construct?"

He should have jumped, he decided. He really should have jumped. He opened the door to the apartment to find Julia surrounded by their luggage, her coat over a chair, and sketch pads strewn about her on the floor.

"Honey, what's the matter?"

"I want to go home. Now. We have seats for six o'clock. . . ."

"But, Julia, you know . . ."

"Martie, with you, or without you, I'm going home."

"Are you giving up, then? Is that it? You go slinking back licked now, let them take away your baby, do whatever they mean to do to you. . . ."

"Martie, I can't explain anything. I never can, you know. But I have to go back. I have work to do before the baby comes. I just have to. It's like this with every artist I know. Jacques Rémy, Jean Vance, Porter, Dee Richardson . . . I've been in touch with different ones here and there, and they're all driven to work now. Some of my best friends simply didn't have time to see me. None of them can explain it. There's a creative explosion taking place and we're helpless. Oh, if I could drink, I could probably resist it by getting dead drunk and staying that way. . . ."

"What are you going to do?" He picked up several sheets of her drawing paper, but there were only meaningless scribbles on it.

"I don't know. I can't get it on paper. I need my tools, the sandstone. My hands know, will know when they start. . . ."

"Julia, you're feverish. Let me get you a sleeping pill. We'll go home in a day or two, if you still feel like this. Please . . ."

She grabbed up her coat and swung it about her shoulders, jerking her arms through the sleeves, paying no attention to him. "What time is it?"

"Four. Sit down, honey. You're as pale as a ghost. . . ."

"We'll have to wait at the airport, but if we don't leave now, traffic will get so bad. Let's start now, Martie. We can have a sandwich and coffee while we wait."

At the airport she couldn't sit still. She walked the length of the corridors, rode the ramps to the upper levels, watched planes arriving and departing, walked to the lowest levels and prowled in and out of shops. Finally they boarded their plane and the strap forced her into a semblance of quietude.

"Martie, how do you, science, explain dreams? The content of dreams? Wait, there's more. And the flashes of intuition that almost everyone experiences from time to time? The jumps into new fields that scientists make, proposing new theories explaining the universe in a way that no one had ever thought of before? *Déjà vu* feelings? Oh, what else? Flashes of what seems to be telepathy? Clairvoyance? Hilary's X *factor?* All those things that scientists don't usually want to talk about?"

"I don't. I don't try. I don't know the answer. And no one else does either." The engines roared and they were silent until the mammoth jet was above the clouds. Clouds covered the earth from Chicago to Kennedy Airport.

Julia looked down sometime later and said, "That's like it is with us. There are clouds hiding something from us, and once in a while a strong light probes through for a minute. The clouds thin out, or the light is strong for a short time, whatever. It doesn't last. The cloud layer thickens, or the power source can't keep up the strength of the beam, and there are only the clouds. No one who wasn't there or didn't see through them at that moment would believe they could be penetrated. And trying to make a whole out of such glimpses is a futile thing. Now a bit of blue sky, now a star, now pitch-black sky, now the lights of a passing plane . . ."

"So we invent an infrared light that penetrates the clouds. . . ."

"What if there were something on the other side of the layer that was trying to get through to us, just as much as we were trying to get through from this side, and with as little success . . . ?"

She hadn't even heard him. Martie took her hand and held it, letting her talk on. Her hand was warm and relaxed now that they were actually heading for home.

"Suppose that it, whatever it is, gets through only now and then, but when it does it is effective because it knows what it's looking for, and we never do. Not infrared . . ." She had heard. "But the other direction. Inward. We send other kinds of probes. Psychoanalysis, EEG, drugs, hypnosis, dream analysis . . . We are trying to get through, but we don't know how, or what we're trying to reach, or how to know when we have reached it."

"God?" Martie turned to look at her. "You're talking about reaching God?"

"No. I think that man has always thought of it as God, or some such thing, but only because man has always sensed its presence and didn't know what it was or how it worked, but he knew that it was more powerful than anything else when it did work. So, he called it God."

"Honey, we've always been afraid of what we didn't understand. Magic, God, devils . . ."

"Martie, until you can explain why it is that more comes out of some minds than goes in, you haven't a leg to stand on, and you know it."

Like the new geometries, he thought. The sum can be greater than its parts. Or, parallel lines might meet in some remote distance. He was silent, considering it, and Julia dozed. "But, dammit," he breathed a few minutes later. . . .

"You're a Hull, Watson, Skinner man," Julia finished, not rousing from her light sleep. He stared at her. She hadn't studied psychology in her life. She didn't know Hull from Freud from Jung.

The polishing wheel screamed for hours each day as the carborundum paste cut into the quartzite. Martie dragged Julia from it for her meals, when it was time to rest, at bedtime.

"Honey, you'll hurt yourself. It might be hard on the baby. . . ."

She laughed. "Have I ever looked better or healthier?"

Thin, pale, but with a fiery intensity that made her more beautiful than he had seen her in their lives together. Her eyes were luminous. The tension that had racked her for months was gone. She carried the baby as if unaware of the extra burden, and when she slept, it was deep untroubled sleep that refreshed her wholly.

"You're the one who is suffering, darling," she said softly, fairy-touching his cheek. Her hands were very rough now, fingernails split and broken jaggedly. He caught her rough hand and pressed it hard against his cheek.

"Wymann has been calling, hasn't he?" Julia asked after a moment. She didn't pull her hand from his face. He turned it over and kissed the palm. "It's all right to talk about it, Martie. I know he's been calling. They want to see me as soon as possible, to make sure of the baby, to see if the delivery will be normal, or if a section is called for. It's all right."

"Have you talked to him?"

"No. No. But I know what they're thinking now. They're afraid of me, of people like me. You see, people who have high creativity don't usually have the right sort of genes to take their RNA. A few, but not enough. It worries them."

"Who've you been talking to?"

"Martie, you know where I've been spending my time." She laughed. "It is nice to be home, isn't it?" The fireplace half of the living room was cheerful and glowing, while shadows filled the rest of the long room. "Of course, when you consider that only about twenty-five percent of the people are getting the RNA it isn't surprising that there aren't many with creative abilities that have been developed to any extent. But, what is sad is that those few who were writers or painters, or whatever, don't seem to continue their work once they know they are immortal. Will women want to continue bearing children if they know they're immortal already?"

"I don't know. You think that the maternal instinct is just a drive to achieve immortality, although vicariously?"

"Why not? Is a true instinct stilled with one or two satisfying meals, or sex acts, or whatever? Women seem to be satisfied as soon as they have a child or two."

"If that's so, then, whatever happens, the race will be finished. If women don't want children, don't have to satisfy this drive, I should say, it's a matter of time. We have the means to prevent pregnancy, why would they keep on getting knocked up?"

"Because something else needs the children, the constantly shifting, renewing vision that is provided by children. Not us, not me. It. Something else. That thing that is behind us pushing, learning through us. You have the books. You've been reading everything you can find on psychology. The nearest we have been able to describe that something is by calling it the collective unconscious, I think."

"Jung's collective unconscious," Martie muttered. "You know, some scientists, philosophers, artists work right down the middle of a brightly illuminated strip, never go off it. Darwin, for instance. Skinner. Others work so close to the edge that half the time they are in the grey areas where the light doesn't follow, where you never knew if madness guided the pen or genius. Jung spent most of his time on the border, sometimes in the light, sometimes in the shadows. His collective unconscious, the fantasy of a man who couldn't stand mysteries not solved during his own lifetime."

Julia stood up and stretched. "God, I'm tired. Bath time." Martie wouldn't let her get into and out of the bathtub alone now. "Martie, if there is such a thing—and there is, there is—it's been threatened. It has to have the constantly shifting viewpoint of mankind in order to learn the universe. A billion experiences, a trillion, who knows how many it will need before it is finished? It was born with mankind, it has grown with mankind, as it matures so does man, and if mankind dies now, so will it. We are its sensory receptors. And what Wymann and the others propose is death to it, death to them eventually. It feeds the unconscious, nourishes it, gives it its dreams and its flashes of genius. Without it, man is just another animal, clever with his hands perhaps, but without the dream to work toward. All our probes into space, into the oceans, so few inward. We are so niggardly in exploring the greatest mystery of all, potentially the most rewarding of all."

She had her bath, and he helped her from the tub and dried her back and smoothed lotion over it. He tucked her into bed, and she smiled at him. "Come to bed, Martie. Please."

"Soon, honey. I'm . . . restless right now."

A few minutes later when he looked in on her, she was sound asleep. He smoked and drank and paced, as he did night after night. Julia was like one possessed. He grimaced at the choice of words. She worked from dawn until night, when he forced her to stop. He made their meals, or she wouldn't have eaten. He had to touch her before she knew he was there to collect her for a meal. He stood sometimes and watched her from the doorway, and he was frightened of her at those times. She was a stranger to him, her eyes almost closed, sometimes, he thought, and discarded the thought immediately, her eyes were all the way closed.

Her hands held life of their own, strong, white knuckled, thin hands grasping mallet and chisel. She couldn't wear gloves while she worked. She dressed in heavy wool pants, and a heavy sweater, covered by a tentlike poncho that she had made from an army blanket. She wore fleece-lined boots, but her hands had to be bare. He would touch her arm, shake her, and slowly recognition would return to her eyes, she would smile at him and put down her tools; without looking at the thing she was making, she would go with him. He would rub her freezing hands for her, help her out of the heavy garments that were much too warm for the house.

Sometimes after she had gone to bed, usually by nine, he would turn on the barn lights and stand and stare at her work. He wanted, at those times, to pull it down and smash it to a million pieces. He hated it for possessing her when he would have her sit on a velvet cushion and spend her last months and weeks with . . .

He threw his glass into the fireplace, then started to pick up the pieces and put them in an ashtray. Something wet sparkled on his hand, and he stared at it for a moment. Suddenly he put his head down on the floor and sobbed for her, for himself, for their child.

"Sayre, why haven't you brought her in for an examination?"

Martie watched Wymann prowl the living room. Wymann looked haggard, he thought suddenly. He laughed. Everyone was looking haggard except Julia.

Wymann turned toward him with a scowl. "I'm warning you, Sayre. If the child is orphaned at birth, the state won't quibble a bit about our taking it. With you or without you . . ."

Martie nodded. "I've considered that." He rubbed his hand over his face. A four- or five-day beard was heavy on his cheeks and chin. His hand was unsteady. "I've thought of everything," he said deliberately. "All of it. I lose if I take you up, lose if I don't."

"You won't lose with us. One woman. There are other women.

If she died in childbirth, in an accident, you'd be married again in less than five years. . . ."

Martie nodded. "I've been through all that, too. No such thing as the perfect love, lasting love. Why'd you come out here, Wymann? I thought you were too busy for just one patient to monopolize your time. Farthest damn housecall I've ever heard of. And not even called." He laughed again. "You're scared. What's going wrong?"

"Where's Julia?"

"Working. Out in the barn."

"Are you both insane? Working now? She's due in two weeks at the most!"

"She seems to think this is important. Something she has to finish before she becomes a mother and stops for a year or two."

Wymann looked at him sharply. "Is she taking that attitude?"

"You first. Why are you out here? What's wrong with the master plan for the emerging superman?"

"He's here because people aren't dying any more. Are they, Dr. Wymann?"

Julia stood in the doorway in her stocking feet, stripping off the poncho. "You have to do things now, don't you, Doctor? Really do things, not just sit back and watch."

"There is some sort of underground then, isn't there? That's why you two made the grand tour, organizing an underground."

Julia laughed and pulled off her sweater. "I'll make us all some coffee."

Martie watched her. "A final solution, Doctor. You have to come up with a new final solution, don't you? And you find it difficult."

"Difficult, yes. But not impossible."

Martie laughed. "Excuse me while I shave. Make yourself comfortable. Won't take five minutes."

He went through the kitchen and caught Julia from behind, holding her hard. "They'll have to change everything if that's true. They won't all go along with murder, wholesale murder.

This will bring it out into the open where we can decide. . . ."

Julia pulled away and turned to look at him squarely. "This isn't the end. Not yet. There's something else to come. . . ."

"What?"

"I don't know. I just know that this isn't the end, not yet. Not like this. Martie, have you decided? It's killing you. You have to decide."

He shrugged. "Maybe it will be decided for me. I'm going up to shave now."

She shook her head. "You'll have to make the decision. Within a week, I think."

"Dr. Wymann, why is it that proportionately more doctors than laymen are suicides?" Julia poured coffee and passed the sugar as she spoke. "And why are there more alcoholics and drug-users among the medical profession?"

Wymann shrugged. "I give up, why?"

"Oh, because doctors as a group are so much more afraid of death than anyone else. Don't you think?"

"Rather simplistic, isn't it?"

"Yes. Often the most unrelenting drives are very simplistic."

"Julia, you have to come in to be examined. You know that. There could be unsuspected complications that might endanger the baby."

"I'll come in, as soon as I finish what I'm doing. A few more days. I'll check in then if you like. But first I have to finish. It's Martie's Christmas present."

Martie stared at her. Christmas. He'd forgotten.

She smiled. "It's all right. The baby is my present. The sculpture is yours."

"What are you doing? Can I see?" Wymann asked. "Although, remember, I like understandable things. Nothing esoteric or ambiguous."

"This one is as simple . . . as a sunset. I'll go get my boots."

As soon as she had left them, Wymann stood up and paced

back and forth in quick nervous strides. "I bet it reeks of death. They're all doing it. A worldwide cultural explosion, that's what the Sunday *Times* called it. All reeking of death."

"Ready? You'll need warm clothes, Doctor."

Muffled in warm garments, they walked together to the barn. The work was ten feet high in places. The quartzite was gone, out of sight. Martie didn't know what she had done with it. What remained was rough sandstone, dull red, with yellow streaks. It looked very soft. She had chiseled and cut into it what looked like random lines. At first glance it seemed to be a medieval city, with steeples, flattened places, roofs. The illusion of a city faded, and it became a rough mountainous landscape, with stiletto-like peaks, unknowable chasms. Underwater mountains, maybe. Martie walked around it. He didn't know what it was supposed to be. He couldn't stop looking, and, strangely, there was a yearning deep within him. Dr. Wymann stood still, staring at it with a puzzled expression. He seemed to be asking silently, "This is it? Why bother?"

"Martie, hold my hand. Let me explain. . . ." Her hand was cold and rough in his. She led him around it and stopped at the side that the west light hit. "It has to be displayed outside. It should rest on a smooth black basalt base, gently curved, not polished, but naturally smooth. I know that they can be found like that, but I haven't been able to yet. And it should weather slowly. Rain, snow, sun, wind. It shouldn't be protected from anything. If people want to, they should be able to touch it. Sculpture should be touched, you know. It's a tactile art. Here, feel . . ." Martie put his hand where she directed and ran his fingers up one of the sharply rising peaks. "Close your eyes a minute," she said. "Just feel it." She reached out for Wymann's hand. He was standing a foot or slightly more to her left. He resisted momentarily, but she smiled and guided his hand to the work.

"You can see that there's order," she said, "even if you can't quite grasp it. Order covering something else . . ."

Martie didn't know when she stopped talking. He knew, his

hand knew, what she meant. Order over something wild and unordered, ungraspable. Something unpredictable. Something that began to emerge, that overcame the order with disorder, distorting the lines. The feeling was not visual. His hand seemed to feel the subliminally skewed order. Rain. Snow. Wind. The imperfections became greater, a deliberate deterioration of order, exposing the inexplicable, almost fearful inside. A nightmare quality now, changing, always changing, faster now. Grosser changes. A peak too thin to support itself, falling sideways, striking another lesser peak, cracking off the needle end of it. Lying at the base, weathering into sand, running away in a stream of red-yellow water, leaving a clean basalt base. Deeper channels being cut into the thing, halving it, dividing it into smaller and smaller bits, each isolated from the rest, each yielding to the elements, faster, faster. A glimpse of something hard and smooth, a gleam of the same red and yellow, but firm, not giving, not yielding. A section exposed, the quartzite, polished and gleaming. Larger segments of it now, a corner, squared, perfect, sharp. Even more unknowable than the shifting sandstone, untouched by the erosion.

But it would go, too. Eventually. Slowly, imperceptibly it would give. And ultimately there would be only the basalt, until in some distant future it would be gone too.

Martie opened his eyes, feeling as if he had been standing there for a very long time. Julia was watching him serenely. He blinked at her. "It's good," he said. Not enough, but he couldn't say anything more then.

Wymann pulled his hand from the stone and thrust it deep inside his pocket. "Why build something that you know will erode away? Isn't it like ice sculpture, only slower?"

"Exactly like it. But we will have a chance to look at it before it is gone. And feel it." She turned toward the door and waited for them to finish looking. "Next year, if you look at it, it will be different, and ten years from now, and twenty years from now. Each change means something, you know. Each change will tell you something about yourself, and your world, that you didn't know before." She laughed. "At least, I hope so."

They were silent as they returned to the house and the dancing fire. Martie made drinks for Wymann and himself, and Julia had a glass of milk. Wymann drank his Scotch quickly. He had opened his coat but hadn't taken it off. "It reeks of death," he said suddenly. "Death and decay and dissolution. All the things we are dedicated to eradicating."

"And mystery and wonder and awe," Martie said. "If you also kill those things, what's left? Will man be an animal again, clever with his hands and the tools he's made, but an animal without a dream. Inward that's what it means. Isn't that right, Julia? Inward is the only direction that matters."

"It itself is what it means," she said, helplessly almost. "I tried to explain what it means, but if I could say it, I wouldn't have had to do it. Inward. Yes. A particular way of looking, of experiencing the world, my life in it. When it doesn't apply any longer, it should be gone. Others will reinterpret the world, their lives. Always new interpretations, new ways of seeing. Letting new sensations pass into the unconscious, into the larger thing that uses these impressions and also learns." She drained her glass. "I'll see you in a week at the latest, Doctor. I promise. You personally will deliver my baby."

Why? Why? Why? Martie paced and watched the fire burn itself out and paced some more in the darkened, cooling room. Snow was falling softly, lazily, turning the back yard into an alien world. Why did she promise to go to them? Why to Wymann? What had he felt out there in the barn? Martie flung himself down in an easy chair, and eventually, toward dawn, fell asleep.

The hospital. The same dream, over and over, the same dream. He tried to wake up from it, but while he was aware of himself dreaming, he couldn't alter anything, could only wander through corridors, searching for her. Calling her. Endless corridors, strange rooms, an eternity of rooms to search . . .

"Julia is in good condition. Dilating already. Three or four days probably, but she could go into labor any time. I recommend that she stay here, Sayre. She is leaving it up to you."

Martie nodded. "I want to see her before we decide." He pulled a folded section of newspaper from his pocket and tossed it down on Wymann's desk. "Now you tell me something. Why did Dr. Fischer jump out of his window?"

"I don't know. There wasn't a note."

"Fischer was the doctor who, quote, examined me, unquote, wasn't he? The one who added that charming little note to my personal data record, that I'm schizophrenic? A psychiatrist."

"Yes. You met him here."

"I remember, Wymann. And you can't tell me why he jumped. Maybe I can tell you. He dried up, didn't he? A psychiatrist without intuition, without dreams, without an unconscious working for and with him. When he reached in, he closed on emptiness, didn't he? Don't all of you!"

"I don't know what you're talking about. Conant has scheduled you for testing starting tomorrow morning. If positive . . ."

"Go to hell, Wymann. You, Conant, the rest of you. Go to hell!"

"All right. Maybe that's rushing it. We'll wait until Julia has delivered. You'll want to be with your child. We'll wait. Julia's in room four-nineteen. You can go up whenever you want."

He tapped lightly on the door. Julia pulled it open, laughing, with tears on her cheeks. "I know. I know. You're going to be all right," she cried.

"Me? I came to tell you that *you'd* be all right."

"I've known that for a long time now. Martie, are you sure? Of course you are. You've seen. He, Wymann, doesn't realize yet. I don't think many of them do. . . ."

"Honey, stop. You're six jumps ahead of me. What are you talking about?"

"You'll catch up. It, the thing, the collective unconscious, whatever it is, has withdrawn from them. They're pariahs to it. Empty. They think that it's a reaction to the RNA, but it isn't. They want babies desperately, but already the reason for wanting the babies is getting dimmer. . . ." She stopped suddenly and pressed her hand against her stomach. A startled look crossed her face. "You'd better see if he's still in the building."

"She'll be all right. A few hours more." Dr. Wymann sat down in the waiting room with Martie. "Tell me something, Sayre. Why did she make that stone thing? Why do any of them make the things they do, write poetry, plays, paint? Why?"

Martie laughed.

"Funny," Wymann said, rubbing his eyes, "I feel that I should know. Maybe that I did know, once. Well, I should look in on her now and then." He stood up. "By the way, I found a memo on my desk, telling me to remind you of your appointment with Dr. Conant in the morning. Are you sick or something?"

"I'm fine, Doctor. Just fine."

"Good. Good. See you in a little while."

He walked down the hallways, glancing into rooms here and there, all equally strange. "Martie, down here. I'm down here." He turned toward the sound of her voice and followed it. "It's a boy, darling. Big, husky boy." He bowed his head and felt tears warm on his cheeks. When Wymann came out to tell him about his son, he found Martie sound asleep, smiling.

He stood over him for a minute, frowning. There was something else that he had to do. Something else. He couldn't remember what it was. Perfect delivery. No complications. Good baby. Good mother. No trouble at all. He shrugged and tiptoed from the room and went home, leaving Martie sleeping. The nurse would wake him as soon as Julia was ready to see him.

"Darling, you're beautiful. Very, very beautiful. I brought you a Christmas present after all." He held it out for her to take. A stuffed dog, one eye closed in a wink, a ridiculous grin on its face. "You knew how it would be just like I knew about our son, didn't you?"

"I just knew. It was threatened. Any other way of countering the threat would have endangered it even more. We have all those terrible things that we would have used on each other. No one would have survived the war that would have come. It left them. That awful vacuum in Wymann, in Conant, all of them. They do what they are trained to do, no more. They do it very well." She patted her newly flat stomach.

"You did it. You, others like you. The ones who could open to it, accept, and be possessed wholly. A two-way communication must take place during such times. That cultural explosion, all over the world. You at the one end of the spectrum, Wymann, them, at the other, from total possession to total absence."

"It will take some time to search the records, find our babies. . . ."

"They'll help us now. They need guidance. They'll have to be protected. . . ."

"Forever and ever."

WHERE HAVE YOU BEEN, BILLY BOY, BILLY BOY?

His building had fifty-nine floors. The outer walls were dark green marble with black trim; they had slit windows, not to aid visibility, but for aesthetic purposes. The slits reflected the evening sun and gleamed gold, they were silver in the morning, they sparkled and shone at times, then again they were merely black. The marble went up to about the third floor. It was very difficult to tell from the outside just how much of the building was faced with the polished marble, but surely not more than three floors. So wasteful to have carried it farther. From that point, not yet determined, but about the third floor, to the top the building was grey. They had done the slit windows all the way. Sometimes it looked like corduroy. Sometimes it looked like the building was dripping gold.

There were three very broad, shallow steps that led to the entrance of the building. Like the windows, the steps were ornamental. The building just as easily could have been level with the street. The step risers were less than six inches, possibly five, and were actually awkward, between steps and a level surface. There were brass planters in the steps, four feet wide, nine or ten feet long. One year the plants had been changed twenty-three times. They all died. Cigarette butts stuck out of the dirt, and gum wrappers, and drink cans, flattened or squashed into shapes that were topologically rather pleasing. They lay about the plants like fallen blossoms, colorful, not really hideous except that training said so.

The doors. Revolving doors, three. Two double doors with ten feet of air space between them. Four air walls. Bill never did understand how or why they worked; in the summer the air was cool, in the winter, hot. There was a definite line that separated the outside from the inside, even if it was invisible. The inside was different.

He walked alone, toward the elevators. No elevators went to all floors. There were banks that went from ground zero to eight, others that stopped first at nine and went up to fifteen, and so on. His first stop was thirty-four. He assumed that it continued after he left it at thirty-eight. The button lights indicated that it was prepared to rise another four floors.

Every morning from the time he left his spacious and empty apartment, got through the subway, across town on the bus, up the three low steps, and the elevators that went from the thirty-fourth floor to at least the thirty-eighth floor, he was quite alone.

"Let's take it again, something's wrong with the tempo. . . ." Rolly shook his long hair and fingered his beard.

"How about trying it with the drums?" Mole said. Lettered on the bass drum was: THE PICKLE DOOR.

Bill stood up, pushing his electric organ away from him. "Look, guys, let me set the stage. A guy alone, walking the streets. *Alone.* Dig? His girl's gone. Left him flat. No reason. Nothing. And there's not another one in the world for him." He shrugged at the skepticism. "Look, you want to hit the old crowd or not? You want to eat for a change? You want to get out of this stinking basement (no offense, Mole) with its rats that've evolved into five-foot-ten pink-skinned brown-suited squinty-eyed blood-sucking saber-toothed rodents, for chrissakes? No more fires, no more busts, no more gas attacks, just one winter of being warm and dry."

"No drums?"

"No drums! You asshole. Soft. Melancholic. Sad. Wistful. Now. *Go!*"

They took it from the top.

The apartment was clean. They had scraped the paint off down to bare wood and started over with it. Bill had had to put up wallboard here and there where the plaster crumbled when they had begun to scour the walls, but it had been worth it. He had divided the room with wallboard at the same time, and had not been forced to get a permit, with the pages of questions to be answered first. They called it a three-room apartment now. After the streets, in that section of the lower East Side, it was like entering another world. Clean walls, clean wood, bare, gleaming floors with small washable, and often washed, scatter rugs. And they had used their total debt limit for an air-conditioner so that they didn't have to worry about the daily pollution index, at least not after they got home from work. They both hated to leave their own rooms even to go down the hall to the bathroom. In the beginning they had tried to keep that clean, but they had given up.

She worked half days only. She would be eligible for a full-time job as soon as the baby was registered in a nursery at three. She met him at the door and kissed him, then drew back and said, "A few minutes ago Susan was looking at television with me, and as plain as day she said, 'NBC.' Can you imagine? And only two."

Susan started to cry and continued to cry through the newscast. She did it almost every night. It was her daily crying time, they agreed.

Billy was ten and his mother was thirty-five and didn't look it, his father was forty and did look it. He was a professor with Grave Responsibilities and Moral Convictions. It was almost Christmas. Every year Billy's mother took him to town to look at the windows and shop for Father and have a hot-fudge sundae and buy an early, not-secret gift for him. To ease the anticipation pains.

It was snowing lightly and the train was coming around the mountain in miniature America with flags on almost all the houses and an army standing at attention while a band of inches-high red-white-and-blue members played silent music. Tiny Christmas trees blinked and Santa Clauses swayed holding bulging stomachs. The train flashed around a hill out of sight and the skaters waltzed and the band played and the tree lights blinked and the snow fell gently. But now the store window's music was drowned by a roaring sound from the other end of the street and he felt his mother's hand tugging at him.

"Come on, Billy. Let's go inside. It looks like a demonstration."

He stared at the window, then down the street where the cars were suddenly obliterated by what looked like a black tidal wave.

Rolly twanged a discord. He looked at Bill helplessly. "I just don't dig it. I mean, it's going to put them to sleep. It's not like there's only one chick in the world."

"It ain't that," Mole said. "You know what it is. Crap. Shit. So he moons over a bird. So what?"

Bill ran his thumb over the keys, and then spun around. "Look, I listened to records at the library for three solid weeks, five-year-old records, ten-year-old records, twenty-year-old records. There hasn't been anything like this for ten years, fifteen years. So what's it going to cost to gamble on it now? We can do it under a moony name. Dreamers. Or, The Stardusters. Something corny. Or, The Sound. That's pretty good. Nostalgia, that's what we'll give them. For a time when a guy could just go out and walk up and down the streets if he wanted to."

On Monday, Wednesday, and Friday mornings they had meetings. And on Tuesday and Thursday afternoons they had meetings. The table was round. This month Henry Moreno was chairman. They discussed and planned for the next five years, so that no matter what the date, Bill's thoughts were supposed to be geared to five years in the future. Because We Plan Your Tomorrow—his department's motto.

"Say, who was it who came up with the idea of a self-rolling toothpaste tube?" Henry asked, during a pause in the proceedings.

He glanced at Walter Neery, who shrugged and looked blank. The inquiring gaze went around the table and no one suggested an answer. When it was Bill's turn to look blank, he did. He could have said, "Matt's idea." That would have singled out Matt for criticism. And next time he might be the one so named. So he looked blank, and Henry sighed and murmured, "Too bad. Wanted to put his name down for a bonus. But that's the way it goes. Joint efforts, joint decisions, joint benefits. Right, fellows?"

They nodded. Bill wondered if anyone else could turn off the world. He doubted it. They were all too preoccupied with Creating A Better World—the company's motto. "Like a phoenix," the small print went on, "we will rise again to fulfill the dreams of past generations. . . ."

"Anyway," Henry said, "market research has finished the survey. There will be a definite demand for the self-rolling tube. R and D is kicking it around now. And this department has earned another bonus point."

The eleven-o'clock newscast rehashed the same items that the baby had cried through earlier. Casualty figures remained stable. The Senate had finished all the legislation that the President had asked for in what was called the most efficient, most farsighted, most patriotic assembly ever gathered in Washington. The air inversion over London had claimed the ten-thousandth victim that morning. Washington announced the plans to recall the history books in all elementary and secondary schools to correct mistakes discovered by the Advisory Committee on Education.

"Are you certain that you won't mind if Dad comes here for a few weeks, just until he gets his bearings again?"

"You know I don't mind." She was applying a contact patch to his coveralls, and didn't look up.

"I'm sure that it won't be for long. He'll apply for a permit to move right away. He's pretty independent."

"Don't be so apologetic. I knew about him when we were married. It's all right. He made a mistake, and he's paid. I certainly don't hold that against him. Here, will this hold, do you think?"

He took the coveralls from her and put them down. "Let's turn off that blasted set and go to bed. We'll have our room to ourselves just five more nights before he gets here."

"With the curtain up we'll never know the baby's in there. Wait a minute. I'd better check the schedule. I forget if I turned it on when I first came home." He watched her check off the public-interest programs that had been on the air. She frowned over the schedule and he knew that she had forgotten. Rumor said that you could alter the meter, but he didn't know how, and he didn't know anyone who did.

"It's all right," he said. "Leave it alone. I'll turn it off later. Come on." So they made love in the bedroom, and in the other room the set talked on and on about the patience of the government and the intransigence of the enemy at the conference table, and about the rules and regulations regarding the recently passed Right to Inspect Bill.

Billy eavesdropped on his parents at every opportunity. It was a game with him, but a serious game. He had trouble imagining them without him, and was almost convinced that they discussed him exclusively when he was absent. They sat on the couch listening to a small tape recorder. And Billy became cramped and chilled from kneeling on the hall floor in his pajamas, also listening, thoroughly bored.

"Gentlemen, this is an executive session, you all understand. No word of what gets said in this room will be carried beyond those doors, nor will it appear in any report. Now, we have all heard the evidence of the experts. We have studied the charts, and the data. Gentlemen, unless we act immediately with every measure put forth by Dr. Gordon, our entire civilization is doomed."

"Now, Roger. Jest take it easy, son. Doctuh, do I understand you to say that unless each of those measures is enacted almost immediately and with absolute thoroughness, then there's no hope atall to save mankind?"

"No, sir. What I said, Senator, is that unless these things are done now, today, we'll all die. Our children will die. Their children won't be born. No 'almost,' Senator. No qualifications at all."

"I see, Doctuh. I see. You've heard of Malthews? Haven't you, suh?"

"Malthus? The Malthusian theory? Yes, sir, I have."

"Yes. You see, son, I jest read a little bit about this Malthews and it seems to me that he was saying a hundred years ago almost exactly what you're saying again today. Now, you see, son, how confusing this can get to an old non-scientist like me."

"Senator, I could recapitulate all the evidence you have heard and seen, but we have done that. We've been holding these meetings six months now. You know what the consensus of the participating scientists is. Not simply the population explosion, but the concomitant pollution, which was not foreseen by Malthus, sir. That is our concern. Not only here in the States, but around the world. The only real division we have had, sir, is in the timetable for the disaster that we all see. And about half of us think that even if we did initiate those steps immediately, it would still be too late. That the only way to save any part of mankind is through the decimation of our population now. Halve it. In order to save half. Not through war that would leave ruins and a weakened and irradiated billion people, but through a humane program that would leave the technology intact, and the survivors healthy and aware of the sacrifice of the dead. They would have to have leadership that would infuse them with a new sense of purpose."

"Doctuh, for weeks now something has been pestering at me. Jest won't go way, no, suh. Now in this here executive session, without anyone in here taking notes, and no tape recorders going, no stenographers. Jest between us here now, suh, I want to get this off my chest. You, suh, Doctuh Gordon, are looney."

One day they didn't come back when he entered the office. For the first time since discovery of the wondrous gift that he had, the gift was frightening. He stopped and stared at the empty office, the desks without girls, the files without clerks, the water fountains without two or three natty young men. Slowly, very carefully, he made his way past his secretary's empty chair, into his small office, where a memo reminded him that today the chairman from R&D would visit the regular Friday-morning conference. He went to the meeting and sat down in his customary chair, in an empty room. Once he felt compelled to speak, which he did, immediately forgetting what it was that he said. He left promptly at twelve and returned to his office, where he got his hat and coat. He stopped then. He was supposed to have lunch with Walter Neery and someone from Sales. He went through all the motions, arriving at the elevators where they were to meet at precisely twelve ten, taking the empty car down, walking alone around the corner to a French restaurant that they always used when it was on expense account.

He ate alone, but now and then made a comment to the air. He didn't know what happened to the bill. It came and went again, as food had done. Back in his office he clutched his head for a long time, and finally when he put his hands down again, he was smiling. It really was much better this way.

"Billy, don't let go of my hand! Whatever happens, don't let go!"

They weren't going to reach the door to the store. Too many people with the same idea, and the demonstrators were filling the street and the sidewalks, and the police were coming from the other direction with sirens blaring and there were popping noises not at all like guns or even windows breaking. And over it all the loudspeakers played "Silent Night" and when that was finished "The

Twelve Days of Christmas" and the train was coming over the mountain again.

"Honey, is it true that they have a way of telling if you're in the room with the TV or not?"

"No. Where'd you hear such a crazy thing?"

"Oh, some of the girls at work. You know. I mean it wouldn't do much good to turn it on and leave it on all the time if they know whether or not you're watching it too."

"Well, forget it. Another rumor."

"I wonder who starts such rumors. Haven't you ever wondered just where they come from, Bill?"

"Washington. What's to wonder? Is the room ready for him?"

"Yes. Do you think he'll be bitter?"

"About what? He made the speeches. He advocated genocide, or something. He never denied it. And they found him guilty of sedition. What's he got to be bitter about?"

"That sounds good. Keep it like that. Now let's try it again from the top. Exactly the same way. I'll get it on the recorder and then we'll decide if that's what we want to tape. Okay, guys."

They played it again, then listened to it. The Mole, whose basement room they used for practice, held his nose and made retching motions. But Rolly stared at Bill thoughtfully. "Yeah," he said. "Yeah. A guy alone, not in a compound or nothing, just alone, walking in the city at nighttime. The dumb bastards will eat their hearts out. They'll think it's romantic. Okay, let's make the master tape tomorrow." They broke up then.

Rolly and Bill stayed close together, and the handmade pipe gun in Bill's pocket was cool against his hand as they walked down the street. Rhonda joined them at The Joint and they stayed there until the crowds thinned out after three and then went to Bill's room. They skirted a bunch of blacks, twenty or twenty-five of them, conscious of the watchful eyes until they turned the corner. At his street Bill stopped again, briefly. An unmarked tank, with a uniformed skinhead visible through the observation bubble, was moving slowly down the street, sweeping for mines. They ducked into a doorway and waited for it to finish and rumble away. From the other end of the street a lone car appeared, headed for the tank. Bill looked up for the copter that he could hear faintly over the din of the city noise. He couldn't find its lights in the murky sky that seemed supported by the tops of the buildings.

"Christ!" he said in disgust. "Come on, let's go in the back way." He grabbed Rhonda's arm and nearly pulled her off her feet when she resisted.

"I want to watch."

"Come on. The copter will pick you off if you're on the street."

"What in hell's wrong with you guys tonight?" Rhonda asked furiously, inside the building. "Pussyfooting around like a couple of blows from Missouri or something."

"Wanta stay in one piece for just a little while, doll," Rolly said, panting. "Long enough to cash in and live it up for a change."

She marched into Bill's room and tossed a gas grenade down on a chair. Bill winced. One day when she did that, it would go. She hooked her thumbs under the tabs on her high pants and opened the twin zippers that let the pants fall down in two pieces around her knees. She kicked them off. The sounds of a pitched battle from the far end of the street erupted, and they all listened, identifying the equipment being used: gas bombs, homemade mines, automatic hand weapons, the whine of gas launchers. They relaxed.

"I can see it now," she said. "The Pickle Door, high as clouds on green stuff, living it up in a compound, manning the guns, taking guided tours of the city in armored buses. Funneeeee. They'll let you in the day it rains diamonds."

"You did what you could, darling. God knows you tried to make them understand."

"And what good will that do in ten years, or fifteen years?

Who's going to say, 'Oh, yes, Doctuh Gordon tried to make them see that the catastrophe was already on the way, a tiny snowball high on the slope'?''

"Sh, darling. I don't think Billy's asleep yet. He's all excited about going to town tomorrow. Christmas. Your coming home. It's all been too much for him too fast."

"You don't believe me, do you? Not even you."

"It isn't that. But what can I do? Except go on living. Try to keep us all alive and healthy and reasonably happy? What else can I do? What else can *you* do?"

"Write another book. Make more speeches. Find something that'll kill fifty percent of the population, without harming the other fifty percent."

"William!"

"Can you convince me that it's wrong? Isn't it better to lose half than to lose all? Isn't it?"

"And what about Billy?"

Billy, shivering on the floor outside the door, fell asleep waiting for the answer to the question.

They came back now and then. Not often, and they didn't stay. Someone would bob into his line of vision, then float out again before he could focus on the image. He realized that there was a mechanism working for him, something that warned him, or guided him, so that he never stumbled over any of them, or missed a cue, although he wasn't aware of them as they came. Occasionally he felt that he should say something or other, and when he did, the feeling of unease that had bothered him went away.

He hadn't seen a child for over a month. He walked through the park now without seeing the rows on rows of perambulators, the toddlers, the pre-schoolers, the elementary-school children, as numerous as ants. Breeding like cockroaches, they were trying to fill the gap with babies. No one stared at him wondering if he was William Gordon's son, wondering why he wasn't married yet, why he didn't have four, five, six children yet. He was certain that he was as hard for them to see as they were for him. He felt safe. He liked the silent world.

Bill stared at the ceiling and tried not to hear the television. He tried not to think about the evening, and could think of nothing else.

Her whisper: "He's so old. I thought he was younger."

"He always looked older than he was. He's only fifty-five."

Their bed touched the curtain that separated this half of the room from the baby's half. He could hear every snuffle that the baby made, every change in her breathing, every whimper and wheeze. And on the other side of the wallboard, *he* was listening to the television, chuckling at it, talking back. Bill's lips tightened. *He* had laughed a bit louder at a statement attributed to the President. He would get them all in trouble. He was a crazy, senile, babbling old man. They would have to take that into account, if he went on like that in front of anyone. They must know what they had done to him. . . . Bill heard his teeth grinding before he was aware of the movement of his jaw. What had they done to him? He was a prattling moron.

But why had he cried? What had he meant?

"I couldn't do it. I knew we should, that we could. I had the stuff. A last chance, that's what I told them. Just listen and do something now. A last chance. And when the time came, I couldn't do anything. They came and took away Billy and then they found it. We had it all. It would have been simple. I knew what to do. We had the stuff, all we needed. And they still trusted us enough. And I couldn't do it!" Then he had cried.

Why?

"Billy! Billy!" He couldn't see her at all. He was being pushed and he knew that he didn't dare fall. They'd walk on him. Boots cowboy boots snow boots police boots. He couldn't make out any of their faces they were all too close and he was too short. He couldn't tell the police from the marchers. The spectators from the demonstrators. He couldn't hear her screams any longer. There was one long scream in his ears and one long smear of red before his eyes. And a burning pain sharp burning pain of a cut or a lump or something that made him feel strange and lightheaded and not able to think. He couldn't breathe and his eyes were on fire and he was afraid to touch them because he might rub it in and he couldn't stop himself rubbing his eyes hearing the piercing scream that wouldn't end choking coughing being sick adding the smell of vomit to the scream and the red smear. Her face kept swimming before his burning eyes. White wide-eyed with a cut that started somewhere in her hair and went down her check down into her neck and blood on her lips like lipstick on Halloween coming down the corner of her mouth down her skin.

He wondered how long before someone noticed that he was acting strangely, or noticed that he wasn't really there much of the time. Promising young executive missing, without a clue. Would someone else move into his nice, airy apartment overlooking the Hudson? Would they put someone else in his office? Would he wander in one day and sit down in the new man's lap and never even realize it?

That night he burned all his father's notes, his diary, the newspaper clippings. He added them one page at a time, playing the "He loves me, loves me not" game. But he said, "He was right. He was wrong." Toward the end he dozed and lost track. And knew that there was no way he would ever know.

Billy couldn't tell which side was which. He was being swept along with people and when he tried to hold on to someone he was flung off and couldn't get his balance again and he fell and the boots did walk on him. And he couldn't tell whose boots they had been.

Bill found his father the next morning. He had hung himself from the water pipe in the kitchen half of his room. There was only an inch of space between his feet and the floor. If he had been an inch taller, he wouldn't have been able to do it.

Bill stared at him, hating him for doing it there, then. Before he touched the body he turned on the TV set. The meter would be waiting and there'd be enough questions without having them add any more about why they were avoiding the news. Then he went out to the corner phone and called the police, listening absently to the beep-beep that said the call was being recorded. A platoon of adolescents in grey uniforms marched by on their way to school. They didn't turn their heads to look at him in the booth.

Bill stiffened at the sound of a police tank starting the high-pitched wail of the tear-gas launcher. He relaxed again. It was at least a block away.

"Tell me how you got the scars, Bill," Rhonda said, tracing the one that started at his forehead and ended in his eyebrow. "Your old man?"

"No. I told you, he was killed during the Christmas riots. My old man and my mother, or so they said." He fingered the scars, then shook his head hard. "I told you I don't remember. An accident, or something. It doesn't signify." He sat up in the bed. "Listen, I've been thinking. We'd go out of our skulls in a compound. Right? How about a trailer, an armored trailer with a grenade launcher? We could take a trip. Maybe even make it out to the coast."

"Yeah, baby," Rhonda said, sitting up too, her eyes sparkling. "I heard that there are some small compounds out in the boonies that one guy with a launcher could take all by himself."

THE FUSION
BOMB

At dusk the barrier islands were like a string of jewels gleaming in the placid bay. The sea wasn't reflecting now, the only lights that showed were those of the islands and the shore lights that were from two to four miles westward. The islands looked like an afterthought, as if someone had decided to outline the coast with a faulty pen that skipped as it wrote in sparkles. Here and there dotted lines tethered the jewels, kept them from floating away, and lines joined them one to another in a series, connective tissue too frail to endure the fury of the sea. Then came a break, a dark spot with only a sprinkling of lights at one end, the rest of the island swallowed in blackness of tropical growth.

The few lights at the southern end seemed inconsequential, the twinkling of hovering fireflies, to be swept away with a brush of the hand. No lines joined this dark speck with the other, clearly more civilized, links of the chain that stretched to the north and angled off to the south. No string of incandescence tied it to the mainland. It was as if this dark presence had come from elsewhere to shoulder itself into the chain where it stood unrecognized and unacknowledged by its neighbors.

It was shaped like a primitive arrowhead. If the shaft had been added, the feathers would have touched land hundreds of miles to the south, at St. Augustine, possibly. The island was covered with loblolly pines, live oaks dripping with Spanish moss, cypress and magnolia trees. The thickened end was white sand, stucco houses, and masses of hewn stones, some in orderly piles and rows, others tossed about, buried in sand so that only corners showed, tumbled down the beach, into the water where the sea and bay joined. Philodendron, gone wild, had claimed many of the blocks, climbing them with stems as thick as wrists, split leaves hiding the worked surface of the granite and sandstone, as if nature were working hard to efface what man had done to her island. Those blocks that had been lost to the sea had long since been naturalized by barnacles, oysters, seaweeds; generations of sergeant majors and wrasses and blue crabs and stonefish had lived among them.

At low tide, as it was now, the water whispered gently to the rocks, secrets of the sea murmured in an unintelligible tongue that evoked memories and suggested understanding. Eliot listened hard, then answered: "So I'll tell the old bastard, take your effing island, and your effing job, and your effing money and stuff it all you know where." The sea mocked him and he took another drink. He sat on one of the stones, his back against another one, and he put a motor on the rocky end of the island and wound it up. It was a rubber-band motor. The arrowhead pointed due north and cut a clean swath, its motion steady and sure, like a giant carrier. And when he had circled the world, when he had docked at all the strange ports and sampled all the strange customs and strange foods, then he didn't know what to do with his mobile island, and he sank it, deep into the Marianas Trench where it could never be raised again, where it would vanish without a sign that it had existed. He drank again, this time emptying the glass. For a moment he hefted it, then he put it down on the rock next to him.

"Eliot! Where are you?"

He didn't answer, but he could see the white shape moving among the rocks. She knew damn well where he was.

"Pit, old man, I'm through. I quit. I'll leave by the mail boat in the morning, or swim over, or fly on the back of a cormorant."

"Eliot! For God's sake, don't be so childish! Stop playing games. Everyone's waiting for you."

"Ah, Beatrice, the unattainable, forever pure, forever fleeing, and fleet." But I had you once, twice, three times. Hot and sweaty in my arms.

"You're drunk! Why? Why tonight? Everyone's waiting for you."

She was very near now, not so near that he could make out her features, but near enough to know what she wore a white party dress, that she wore pearls at her throat, near enough so that the elusive whisper of the sea now became water swishing among rocks. He stood up. She was carrying her sandals.

"You'll bruise your feet. Stay there, or, better, go back and tell them that I do not wish to attend another bloody party, not another one for years and years."

"Eliot, the new girl's here. You'll want to meet her. And . . . it's a surprise, Eliot. Please come now. He'll be so disappointed."

"Why? He already hired her, didn't he? Tomorrow's time enough for me to meet her. And the only surprise around here is that we don't all die of boredom."

He picked up his glass and let a trickle of melted ice wet his lips. He should have brought the pitcher of gin and lemonade. Have to remember, he told himself sternly, no half measures from now on. Been too moderate around here. Moderation's no damn good for island living. He stood up. The sea tilted and the rock tried to slide him off into the water. He could hear vicious laughter, masked as waves rushed around stones.

Beatrice caught his hand and led him out of the jumbled rocks. "Come on, let's take a walk," she said.

But the drunkenness was passing, and he shook his head.

"I'm okay," he said. "Sitting too long, that's all. Let's go to the damn party and get it over with."

She half led, half pushed him along the cypress boardwalk toward the main house.

"The new girl. What's she like?"

"I'm not sure. You know she got over on the pretext that I had recommended her. Turns out that we lived in the same town back when we were growing up. So I should know her, except that I'm ten years older than she is. I dated her brother when I was sixteen, but I can't remember much about her. Or her brother either, for that matter. She was Gina's age when I saw her last. She's twenty now, a student, looking for summer work, perfect to spell Marianne while she has her baby, and so on. But you'll see."

Just what we need, he thought. A young single girl to liven things up around here. "Is she pretty?"

"No. Very plain actually. But do you think that will make any difference?" Beatrice sounded amused.

How well we know each other. She can follow my thought processes, come to my conclusions for me, without even thinking about it. A simple temporary dislocation of the ego.

The boardwalk led them around the ruins, and they approached the house from the back. Curiously old-fashioned and unglamorous, one floor that rambled, deep porch; there was a lot of ironwork, grilles, rails, scrolls, and curlicues that should have been offensive but were pleasing. They skirted a swimming pool that had been converted to a sunken garden and walked along the ornate porch to the front entrance. Wide windows, uncovered, with massive shutters at their sides. View of a room the width of the house, fireplace on one wall, bar and stools, low, gold-gleaming cypress furniture, red Spanish-tile floors that didn't show the scars of the constant polishing of the sand. Beyond the room there was a terrace, shielded from the sea wind by a louvered wall of glass. Moving figures broken into sections by the partly opened glass slats, the hum of voices, echo of Spanish guitars. All substantial and real, all but the fragmented people.

Eliot took a deep breath and entered the terrace. Beatrice paused a moment to speak to Mr. Bonner, who would go over to her place to baby-sit. Eliot was aware of their low conversation, as he was aware of the new girl, who stood out because she was new and very pale. Not pretty. Homely, actually. He nodded at Mr. Pitcock, whose eyes always seemed to see more than was visible. He was seventy; why weren't his eyes starting to dim? Pitcock knew that he'd been drinking, knew that he'd tried to forget the party, knew that if Beatrice hadn't been sent after him, he would have passed it up. So fire me, he thought at the old man, and knew that the old man was aware of that thought also. They shook hands and Pitcock introduced the new girl.

"Donna, this is the project director, Dr. Kalin. Eliot, Donna Bensinger."

"Hello, Eliot."

Too fast. Should have called him Dr. Kalin. He didn't like her pasty skin, or the limpness of her hand when he touched it, or the pale, myopic eyes, or the thin dun-colored hair that looked as if it needed a shampoo.

"I hope you won't find it too dull here, Miss Bensinger," he said, and looked past her at Ed Delizzio, who was standing at the bar. "Excuse me."

He thought he heard the dry chuckle of Thomas Pitcock as he left them, but he didn't turn back to see. "Christ," he said to Ed. "Just—Christ!"

"Yeah, I know what you mean." Ed poured a martini and put it in Eliot's hand. "Drink. That's all that's left." He refilled his own glass. "After this breaks up we're going to play some poker over at Lee's house. Want to sit in?"

"Sure."

"The buffet is ready in the dining room." Mrs. Bonner's voice was eerie over the intercom.

"Come on, let's eat." Pitcock led them across the patio, into the house, his hand on Donna's arm, talking cheerfully to her. He was tall, straight, bald, brown. Why didn't he stoop and falter?

Mary and Leland Moore beckoned to Eliot. Mary was small and tanned, hair sun-bleached almost white. She always seemed breathless. "Can you come over later? The boys are playing poker."

Eliot accepted again and they went into the dining room with the others. On the table was a glazed cold turkey, hot lobster in sherry sauce, biscuits, salads. There was an assortment of wines. He picked at the food and drank steadily, refusing to pretend an interest in the small talk and forced gaiety about him.

"I have no theory to forward as yet, sir," he said distinctly.

"Damn it, a hypothesis then."

"I don't have that much yet."

"A hunch. A wild guess. Don't couch it in formal terms. You must be thinking something by now. What?"

"Nothing. Can't you get it through your head that I won't be forced into a generalization?"

"You're afraid to."

He reached for the champagne and when he raised his gaze from the iced bottle, he caught the bright blue eyes on him. For a second he almost believed they had been speaking, but then he heard Marty's voice, and a giggle from Donna, and he knew that he had said nothing. The old man continued to watch him as he poured more champagne, spilling some of it, and replaced the bottle. "Fuck off," he said, raising his glass and returning the silent stare. Donna giggled louder and this time the others laughed also, and the old man's gaze shifted as he, too, chuckled at Marty's story.

After they ate, Mrs. Bonner appeared with a birthday cake, and they all sang to Eliot and toasted him with champagne. At eleven thirty Beatrice signaled that they should wrap it up. Eliot stood up and made his way to Pitcock.

"Thanks for the party," he said. He was very unsteady.

"Wait a second, will you? I have something for you, didn't want to bring it out before." The old man said good-bye to his guests and then left Eliot for a moment.

If he brings me a check, I'll rip it to shreds before his eyes. He thought longingly of another drink, but he didn't want to delay to mix it and drink it. The old man returned carrying a bulky package. He watched Eliot's face as he tore off the wrappings.

"I know how much you've admired my Escher works; thought

you might like one." It was a large, complicated drawing of builders who were destroying what they built, all in one process. Eliot stared at it: the figures seemed to be moving, toiling up stairs, stairs that flattened out and went down again somehow even as he watched. He blinked and the movement stopped. "Thanks," he said. "Just thanks."

Pitcock nodded. He turned to the window to look out at the beach. "It's a strange night, isn't it? Don't you feel the strangeness? If it were August I'd say a hurricane was on its way, but not so soon. Just strange, I guess."

Eliot waited a moment, wanting to force the talk to the futile project, the open-ended task that Pitcock had hired them to do, but he clamped his lips hard and remained silent.

"You accept the job then?" the old man had asked, in the plush office on the thirtieth floor of the glass-and-plastic building in New York. "Without questioning its merits? Promise to see it through?"

"I'll sign the three-year contract," Eliot said. "Seems fair enough to give it that much of a try."

"Good. And at the end of the three years we'll talk again, and between now and then, no matter how many doubts you raise, you'll carry on."

Eliot shrugged. I will do my best to uphold the honor of the project. He said, "I don't pretend to think that we'll be able to accomplish anything, except to add to the data, and to bring some order to a field that's in chaos. Maybe that's enough for now. I don't know."

The old man turned toward him, away from the window. "It's working out. I know you don't agree, but I can feel that it's taking shape. And now this feeling of strangeness. That's part of it. Undercurrents. Someone's projecting strong undercurrents, strong enough to affect others. You'll see. You'll see."

The others were loitering near the sunken garden, all except Beatrice, who had gone ahead to relieve Bonner of his baby-sitting chores. Eliot fell into step beside Mary.

Soon she'll say, You've been awfully quiet, something to that effect. And I'll say, Thinking. Been here two years and two months, for what? Doing what? Indulging a crazy old man in his obsession.

"Eliot, are you going to stay?"

"What?" He looked at the small woman, but could see only the pale top of her head.

"You've been acting like a man trying to come to a decision. We wondered if you are considering leaving here."

"I've been considering that for two years and two months," he said. "I'm no nearer a decision than I was when I first took it up." He indicated the house behind them. "He's crazy, you know."

"I don't know if he is or not. This whole project seems crazy to me, but then, it always did."

"Is Lee getting restless?"

"Isn't everyone?"

"Yeah, there is that."

The trouble was that there were only ten people on the island and they all spent nine tenths of their time on it. They were all tired of each other, tired of the island paradise, tired of Mrs. Bonner's turkeys and champagne parties, tired of the endless statistics and endless data that went nowhere.

We go through the motions of having fun at the parties, and each of us is there in body only, our minds busy with the data, busy trying to find an out without cutting off our connections with the old man. Each one of us afraid the goose will suddenly stop production, wondering if we have enough of the golden eggs to live on the rest of our lives, wondering if any of this is worth it. If anything out there in the real world would be any better, make any more sense. Twenty-five thousand a year, almost all clear, living quarters and most of the food thrown in, no need for cars or servants. Company plane to take us away for vacations, bring us back. Travel expenses, hotel expenses, everything paid for. Looking for ways to spend money. Endless project at twenty-five thousand a year, a raise to thirty, or forty? Keen eyes that see too much, files with too much in them, birthdays, childhood friends, illnesses, mistakes almost forgotten, but in the files.

Mary was talking again. "I almost wish we never had come here, you know? Lee would have been fine. He had a job at Berkeley all lined up. He would like to teach, I think. But probably not now. Not after this kind of freedom and so much money."

"He can always quit," Eliot said more brusquely than was called for. He liked Mary. Mary and Gina were the only ones that he did like. Neither was a threat to him in any way.

"At least we can always *say* that, can't we?"

They paused at his house and he remembered that he was supposed to bring some mixer. "I'll be over in a few minutes," he said, and left her as Lee and Ed drew near. He put the drawing down, but he didn't want to look at it again yet. Not until he was sober.

He stared at himself in the bathroom mirror and thought, Thirty. Good Christ! Back in April Beatrice had become thirty, and had cried. Then, furious with him for taking her, with herself for needing solace, she had run away from him, and since then had been cool and pleasant, and very distant. If he cried now, would she appear from nowhere to put her arm about his shoulders, to pat him awkwardly as she maneuvered him into bed and reassured him that he still had most of his life ahead? He laughed and turned away, not liking the mirror image. He was deeply suntanned, and his eyes were dark brown, his eyebrows straight and heavy, nearly touching, like a solid, permanent scowl.

"Just one thing more, Mr. Pitcock. Why me? Why did you select me for this project?" The contract was signed, the question made safe by the signatures.

"Because you're avaricious enough to do it. Because you're bright enough to see it through. Because you're cynical enough not to get involved personally, no matter what the data start to reveal."

That's me, he thought, searching his kitchen for mixer. Avaricious. Bright. Cynical.

Donna was seated at the round table, across from an empty chair, his chair. He put the mixer down and looked at them. Ed Delizzio, twenty-five, a statistician from Pitcock Enterprises. Dark, Catholic, observed all the holy days, went to mass each Sunday, had a crucifix over his bed, a picture of Mary and Jesus on his wall. Marty Tiomkin, atheist, twenty-four. Slavic type, tall, broad, serious, with a slow grin, a slower laugh, thick long fingers. Probably could swim to England, if the spirit ever moved him. Very powerful. He was the computer expert. He could program it, repair it, make it go when it was sick, talk it into revealing correlations or synchronicities where none seemed possible. He treated it like a wife who might fly to a distant lover at any time unless she received unswerving loyalty and devotion. Marty and Ed had been hired at the same time, almost two years ago. At first they had had separate houses, like the rest of the staff, but after a month they had decided to share one house. Inseparable now, they went off on weekend trips, during which they picked up girls from one of the northern islands, or made a tour of the houses of Charleston. Now and then they brought girls back to the island with them.

Donna was next to Marty, and on the other side of her was Leland Moore. He was tall and intense, probably the most honest one there, tortured by the futility of what he was doing, but also by the memory of a fatherless childhood in a leaky fifteen-foot trailer that his mother kept filled with other people's ironing. He wanted land, a farm or a ranch, with hills on it, and water. Slowly, month by month, he came nearer that goal, and he wouldn't leave, but he would suffer. Sitting by him was Mary, who worried about her husband too much. Who couldn't understand poverty as a spur because she never had experienced it, and thought only black people and poor southern dirt farmers ever did. Beatrice wasn't there.

"I can't stay," Eliot said. "Sorry. Too much booze too early tonight, and the champagne didn't help. See you tomorrow."

To sit across from Donna all night, to watch her peer at her cards, and watch those pale fat fingers fumble . . . He waved to them and shook his head at their entreaties to stay at least for a while.

"Will you show me the offices tomorrow, Eliot?" Her voice was like the rest of her, just wrong, too high-pitched, little-girl cute, with the suggestion of a lisp.

He shrugged. "Sure. Eleven?"

He walked up the beach. The tide was coming in fast now, the breakers were white-frosted and insistent. In the woods behind the dunes night life stirred, an owl beat the wind steadily, a deer snorted, the grasses rustled, reviving the legend of the Spaniards who walked by night, bemoaning the abandonment of the fort they had started and left. The air was pungent with the sea smells, and the life and death smells of the miniature jungle. He walked mechanically. Whatever thoughts he had were dreamlike in that he forgot them as quickly as they formed, so that by the time he turned at the end of the island and retraced his steps along the beach, it was as if he had spent the last hour or more sleepwalking. He stopped at the pier and then walked out on it to the end, where he was captain of a pirate ship braving the uncharted seas in search of unknown lands to conquer. It was flat and stupid and he let it go.

The pier was solid, a thousand feet out into the ocean; it seemed to move with the motion of the sea and the constant pressure of the wind. Eliot leaned against the end post where a brown pelican roosted every day to watch the sea and the land, alert for sub-versives, immorality, unseemly behavior, including littering of the beach. . . .

Lee Moore's house had a light; the others were all dark. Eliot wondered if they were still playing poker, if Donna Bensinger had won all their money, if Lee and Ed were singing dirty sea chanteys yet. He flicked his cigarette out into the water. Thirty, he thought, thirty. Forty thousand dollars in the bank, more every day, and no one to tell me to do this or that, to come in or stay out. Freedom and money. The dream of a sixteen-year-old washing dishes after school in a crummy diner. Buy a boat and go around the world after this is over. Or start traveling on tramps and never stop. Or—get a little place somewhere and let the money draw interest, live on the dividends forever. Or . . . He heard voices. Two pale figures running along the sand toward the waves. The tide had turned again. The urgency was gone. Proof, he thought, right here before our eyes day in and day out. Never changing, eternal cycles; he didn't know if he meant the tide or the couple. He looked at the nude figures. It had to be Donna, pale hair, white body. The man could have been any of them, too far up the beach to see him clearly. They ran into the surf and she shrieked, but softly, not for the world to hear. The man caught up with her and they fell together into the shallow water.

Eliot watched the laughing figures, rolling, grappling, and he felt only disgust for the girl, and the man, whoever he happened to be. Too quick. Everything about her was too quick. He started to move from the post, but there were others now coming from the dunes, running together so that it was impossible to say if there were two or three or even four of them. The light from a crescent moon was too feeble, he couldn't make them out. Now there was a tight knot in his middle, and he felt cold. He looked down at the swells of the sea, black and hard-looking here, but alive and moving, always moving. When he looked again at the beach he knew that there were six people, dancing together, running, playing. All naked, all carefree and happy now. They paired off and each couple became one being, and he turned away. Without looking again at the figures, he left the pier and hurried home. He was shivering from the constant wind on the pier.

Strange, fragmented dreams troubled his sleep. The night witch came to him and tormented his flesh while he lay unable to move, unable to respond, or refrain from responding when that pleased her. Then he was crawling up a cliff, barren and rocky, windswept and cold. He was lost and the wind carried his voice down into crevices when he tried to call for help. His hands hurt, and he knew his toes were bleeding, leaving strange trails, like the spoor of an unidentified animal. He was on a level plain, with a walking stick in his hand, weary and chattering with cold. The wind was relentless, tearing his clothes from him; the rock-strewn field that he traversed was like dry ice. He kept his eyes cast down, so he wouldn't lose the nebulous trail that he had to follow, strange reddish wavery lines, like blood from an unknown animal. He tried to use the walking stick, but each time he struck it on the boulder, he felt it attach itself, knew that it rooted and sprouted instantly, and he had to wrench it loose again.

Eliot sat on his porch drinking black coffee, a newspaper on the table ignored as he stared over the blue-green waters. The sun was hot already, the day calm, the water unruffled. Another perfect day in paradise. He frowned at the sound of light tapping on the screen door. Donna Bensinger opened it, called, "Hello, are you decent? Can I come in?"

"Sure. Around the corner on the porch." He didn't stand up She had on shorts, too short for her bulging pale legs, and a shirt that didn't conceal her stomach at all. Her hair was pulled back with a yellow ribbon; there were bright red spots on her cheeks, and her nose flamed, as did the tops of her bare feet and forearms. One morning and she was badly burned already. By the end of the day she'd be charred and by the next day probably in the hospital, or at least on her way home again. He motioned for her to sit down.

"Coffee?"

"Oh, no, thank you. This is all so fantastic, isn't it? I mean, the island, the houses for all of us, people to bring you groceries and anything you need, boats we can use. I never dreamed of a job like this. It's right out of a movie, isn't it?"

He turned from her to resume his contemplation of the quiet ocean. She continued to talk. He finished his coffee and stood up. "Let's go. I have a date at twelve. I can show you the offices and explain briefly what you're to do in half an hour or so."

Eliot was six feet tall, his stride was long and quick, and he made no pretense of slowing it for the girl. She trotted at his side. "Oh, I know that people have planted all this stuff, that it didn't just happen like this, I mean the orchids in the trees, and the jasmine and hibiscus and everything, but doesn't it look just like one of those dream islands where the heroine wears a grass skirt and sings and the hero dives for pearls, and there's a volcano that erupts in the end and they all get away in those funny boats with the things sticking out of the sides of them? Who started to build something here?"

"Spaniards. They brought in the rocks to build a fort, then abandoned it."

"Spaniards! Pirates!" She stopped abruptly, then had to run to catch up. "I can see the ships with all those sails, and slaves hauling the blocks all roped together, a Spaniard in black with a long whip . . ."

The pink stucco building that they were approaching was lavishly landscaped with tropical and semi-tropical plants imported from around the world: travelers' palms, fifteen-foot-high yucca plants, Philippine mahogany trees, a grouping of live oaks hung with grey-green Spanish moss that turned the light silver. A small lake before the building mirrored the trees, swans gliding through the water hardly distorted the images.

"The office builing used to be a guest house," Eliot said. "It has its own kitchen, a hurricane-proof basement. Come on." There was another of the wide porches; then they were inside, in the cooled air of the lobby. This had been converted into a lounge, with a coffee maker, tables and chairs, a color television, a fireplace. Eliot showed her through the building quickly. Her office was small but well furnished, and she nodded approval. The old dining room had been equipped with a computer, several desks and chairs, a typewriter desk, drawing table lighted by a pair of fluorescent lamps. Next door was the file room, cabinet after cabinet, with library tables in the center of the room, all covered with folders and loose papers. "Marianne usually kept it up to date, but these last weeks she really wasn't well enough."

She sounded put-upon. "I have to file all that stuff?"

"Beatrice will come over a couple of hours every day to show you the system, help you get caught up. She's Pitcock's private secretary, but she knows this work too."

He showed her the rest of the first floor, then they went downstairs to the recreation room, where he sat down and lighted a cigarette. "Any questions?"

"But you haven't told me anything about what I have to do, except the filing. And what you're doing here, all of you, I mean."

"Okay. I didn't know how much Pitcock told you. You'll handle correspondence, type up reports, keep the files up to date. We are studying the effects of cycles. First we establish the fact of cycles, correlate synchronous cycles, check them back as far as you can find records for, and predict their future appearance. We collect data from all over the world, Marty feeds it into his computer, and the monster spits out answers. The snowshoe hare and the lynx have the same cycle. There are business cycles of highs and lows that persist in spite of wars, technological discoveries, anything that happens. Weather cycles, excitability cycles in man. War and peace cycles. There are cycles of marriages in St. Louis, and cycles of migrations of squirrels in Tennessee." He stopped and stubbed out his cigarette hard, mashing it to shreds.

After the silence had lengthened long enough for him to light a new cigarette and for her to start fidgeting, she said, "But—why? I mean, who cares and why?"

Eliot laughed and stubbed out the new cigarette. "That's the best damn question anyone's asked around here for over two years."

At noon he picked up Gina to take her to Charleston. Beatrice was dressed, as if she too would go if he only asked again. He didn't look directly at her, nor did he ask. The day was not a success, although usually he enjoyed taking the child to town. He kept wondering what Beatrice was doing, what the others were doing, if they were all together. He returned to the island with Gina at six thirty. Pitcock and Bonner were talking on the dock when he brought the small boat in.

Pitcock reached for Gina's hand. "Have a good time, honey?'

"Eliot bought me a see-through raft. And a book about sea shells. And we went on rides at a carnival."

Eliot handed the parcels to Bonner, checked the boat again, then climbed out. The motor launch was gone. Pitcock stood up, still holding Gina's hand. "Come over to dinner later, Eliot? The others have gone out fishing. I'll see Gina home."

"Beatrice?"

"She's here. She'll be over later too."

"Okay. See you around eight?"

Donna was there. Eliot paused in the doorway when he saw her, shrugged, and entered. She smiled at him, dimpling both cheeks. Beatrice nodded, murmured thanks for Gina's gifts, then turned away. Pitcock handed him a martini, and Eliot sat down with it and studied an Escher drawing over the mantel. It reminded him of his dream, following his own trail that he was making so that he wouldn't get lost when he came along. He shook his head and tried to pick up the gist of the story Pitcock was telling. Donna was hanging on every word. She was no more burned than she had been that morning, must have spent the day inside somewhere. He wondered with whom, then concentrated on Pitcock.

"Selling you down the river was no idle threat, not just a little piece of slang that got started; what it was was a death sentence. It meant actually selling a slave to work in the bottom lands on the coast—downriver. Swamps, disease, floods, alligators, snakes. Sure death real quick. And the sands kept piling up on the islands, the rocks got buried deeper and deeper. In eighteen forty my great-granddaddy bought three of these islands, ten dollars an island, or some such amount. He was ashamed to put down the real figure he paid for them, just said they were cheap. Along about nineteen twenty-eight, twenty-nine, a hurricane came and stripped a lot of the sand away again, and by the time I got around to coming out to see the damage, hell, I found a pile of rocks and stones, the foundation of a fort, all that stuff. Decided to keep the island. But I sold off the other two. One island's enough for a man."

"Fifteen fifty," Donna said, her eyes wide. "Wow! I wonder what happened to them, the Spaniards."

Pitcock shrugged and glanced at the glasses the others were holding. He poured more martini into Eliot's, was waved away by Beatrice. Donna hadn't touched hers. "Malaria. Possibly a hurricane. They went ahead with St. Augustine, but they never came back up here."

"Well, I think they were crazy. It's the grooviest place I've ever seen. Last night the wind in the palm trees and the sound of the ocean, and the way the air smells here. I mean, I slept like a baby. I've never slept like that before in my life. And awake at dawn! I couldn't stand not going out right away! I just had to go out and jump into the water and swim "

Eliot laughed harshly and choked. "Nothing," he said when he finally could speak again. "Nothing. Just thinking how we all felt at first, then how the days began to melt into each other, and the weekends tended to blur and run together, and how you're always tearing off another page of the calendar, another month gone to hell."

Beatrice swept him with a sharp look, and he returned her gaze coldly. She was always so cool, so self-possessed, she didn't like scenes or emotional outbursts, and his voice had been thick with emotion. "Just don't go childish on me, okay? If you have something to say, say it, but don't pout or sulk or scream obscenities." And he said, "You can sweat and moan and cry, just like any other woman." "But not with you, not again. I don't like performing, even for an audience of only one."

"Dinner's ready." The goddam intercom.

"But the work's coming along," Pitcock said to Donna. Pitcock was laughing at him, Eliot knew, not on his face where it would show, or in his voice where it could be heard, but somewhere inside him there was laughter.

Pitcock told Donna about the hotel suite he maintained in the Windward Hotel, and the car there available at all times. "Bonner will run you over to the mainland or the other islands any time you want to go, pick you up again later, or you can just check in and spend the night. Nice shops, a movie or two. Don't want you getting lonesome, you know."

Donna's eyes grew larger and she ate without glancing at her food.

And later: "Supposing that you were an intelligent flea on a dog. Life's been pretty good, plenty to eat, no real drastic changes in your life, or that of your parents or grandparents. You can look forward to generations of the same existence for your children and theirs. But supposing that, because you are intelligent, you want to know more about this thing that is home to you, and when you start digging you find that it isn't the universe after all. What you thought was the whole world turns out to be a tiny bit of it, with masters ordering it, forces working on it that you never dreamed of. Things you thought were causes turn out to be effects, things that you thought were making you act in one way or another turn out not to be causing any such thing, they just happen to correspond to your actions. Take weather, for instance. Sunspots affect weather. Weather affects people, the way they feel, moody or elated. Right? Maybe. What if weather, sunspots, and moods are all the effects of something else that we haven't even begun to suspect yet? You see, they are synchronous, but not causal. What else has that same periodicity of eleven point three years? Some business cycles." Pitcock was warming up now. Eliot had forgotten how long it had been since there had been someone new to explain things to. He scowled at his wineglass and wished the old fool would finish. "A businessman was shown a chart of the ups and downs of his business, and he nodded and said yep, and he could explain each and every one of them. A strike, a lost shipment of parts, an unexpected government contract. Another man might compare the ups and downs to the excitability curve and claim that that explained it. Someone else might point to a weather chart and say that was the cause. Or the sunspot charts. Or God knows what else. But what if all those things are unrelated to each other, just happen to occur at the same time, all of them caused by something apart from any of them, something that happens that has all those effects? That's what we're after. Keep taking another step backward so you can get far enough away to see the whole pattern."

Or until you step off the end of the gangplank, Eliot added silently.

Donna was staring at Pitcock. "That's . . . that's kind of spooky, isn't it? Are you serious?"

"Let me tell you about one more cycle," Pitcock said, smiling benignly. "Ed will give you a chart tomorrow, your own personal information chart. Every day at the same time you will be required to X in a square that will roughly indicate your mental state for the day. Feeling very optimistic, happy. Moody, apprehensive. Actively worried. At the end of the month Ed will go over it with you and draw you a curve that will show you your high point and your low. It'll take about fifty days to finish it, probably. Most people seem to have a cycle of fifty to fifty-five days from one high to the next. Now, I'll warn you, nothing you do or don't do will change that chart. You're like a clock ticking away, when it's time to chime, there it is."

Donna made dimples, shaking her head. "I don't believe it. I mean, if I flunk a test, I feel low. Or if a boyfriend shows up with someone else. You know. And I feel good when I look nice and someone pays attention to me."

"Furthermore," Pitcock said, ignoring her, "statistics show that although the low points occupy only ten percent of the subject's life, during these periods more than forty percent of his accidents occur. This is the time that suicides jump, or take an overdose. It's the time that wives leave husbands, and vice versa. During the high points, roughly twelve percent of the time, twenty percent of the accidents take place, suggesting that there might be over-optimism. That other forty percent of all the accidents are spaced out in the rest of the time, sixty-eight percent of your life. It's the high and the low periods that you have to watch for."

"But why?" Donna said, looking from him to Beatrice to Eliot.

"That's one of the things we want to find out with this research," Pitcock said. He glanced at his watch. "May I suggest coffee on the terrace? It's always pleasant out there this time of the evening."

"Do you mind if I beg off?" Beatrice asked, rising. "I still have some packing to do. I want to get an early start with Gina in the morning." She added to Donna, "She's going to spend a couple of weeks with her grandparents in the mountains."

Donna nodded. "Could I come with you, help you pack or something?"

There was a quick exchange of glances between Beatrice and Pitcock; then she smiled and said of course. Eliot stood up also, but Pitcock said, "You won't rush off, too, will you? Something I wanted to bring up, if you aren't in a hurry."

Progress report? A dressing down? A boost in morale? Eliot shrugged and they watched the girls vanish among the magnolia trees. "Drambuie and coffee on the terrace. Right?" Pitcock moved ahead of him and sat down facing the sea. The breeze was warm and gentle, clouds drifted by the moon; a shift, and the moon was gliding among castles.

"What would you do if you left here tomorrow?" Pitcock asked after several minutes.

"I don't know. Hadn't thought about it. Not much, at least not very soon."

"Nothing so fascinating to you that you'd dash right off instantly to do it?"

" 'Fraid not."

"Listen." Pitcock leaned forward slightly. A loon cried out three times, then stopped abruptly, and once more there was only the sound of the waves and the wind in the palm trees.

Pitcock's voice was lower. "I have a suggestion then, Eliot. Not an order, merely a suggestion. How about starting a book on the data we've collected here?"

"Me? Write a book? About what?"

He listened to Pitcock's low voice, and his own articulated

thoughts, and those stirrings that never found words, and later he couldn't separate them. "If you knew you had to have surgery, would you permit it when your cycle is at its low point? You know you wouldn't. How about starting a business? You know the figures for failures and successes, the peaks and troughs. You'd be crazy to pick one of the low spots. An eagle doesn't have to understand updrafts and currents and jet streams in order to soar and ride the winds. . . ."

Something for everyone. Cycles on every side, ready to be used, causes unknown, but obviously there. Circadian cycles, menstrual cycles, creativity cycles, excitability cycles. War cycles, peace cycles. Constructive and destructive cycles. Determinism as conceived of in the past, so simplistic, like comparing checkers to chess. A reordering of life-styles, acceptance of the inevitable, using the inevitable instead of always bucking it, trying to circumvent it.

He walked on the beach and seemed to feel the earth stirring beneath his feet. Bits of the earth flowing down the river, into the bay, material to be used by the sea as it constructed the islands grain by grain, shaping them patiently, lovingly, as the very face of the earth was changed, subsiding here, growing there, swelling and ebbing. Eternal cycles of life and death.

He stumbled over the stones of the ruins and climbed the rough steps of the uncompleted tower, a sand-filled stone cylinder. There was lightning out over the ocean, a distant storm too far away to hear the thunder. He watched the flashing light move northward. I don't want to do your goddamned book, Pitcock. Hire yourself a nice obedient ghost writer and do it yourself. Where does it lead? What does it imply? Something I don't want to examine. Flea on the dog, ready to be scratched off, sprayed off, get swept off in the torrent of the river when the dog swims.

"Something happened last night. I don't know what it was, but it has everyone on the island uptight today. Do you know?"

"No." I don't know. I won't know. I dreamed a crazy dream. Or else they had a bacchanal, and I don't know which, and won't know.

"I thought I had time, five years, even more. But now . . . Don't tell me you won't do it, Eliot. Don't say anything about it for a while. Let it lie there. You'll come back to it now and again. See what happens if you don't worry it."

But I won't. I don't want to do it. I want to finish my three years and get the hell out. Chess and checkers. Not with humans, Pit. Not a game, even on a macrocosmic scale. Not fleas on a dog. Free agents, within the limits set down by our capabilities and the government.

He slept and dreamed, and rejected the dream on awakening. Although unremembered, it left an uneasy feeling in his stomach, and he felt as though he hadn't slept at all. Later he found himself at the ruins and he stood gazing at a mammoth oak tree. The Spaniards had built around it. They had laid a terrazzo floor between the tower and the fort, connected by a walkway that was to have been covered. The pillars were there. And they had built around the oak tree. Crazy pagans, he muttered. Hypocrites with your beads and crucifixes and inquisitions. He walked on the top layer of the stones that made up the fort. They hadn't closed the square. One tenth of it done, then abandoned.

That week Marty fell in love with Donna. Marty had been friendly to Eliot in the past, but now avoided him, refused to look directly at him, and managed to be gone with Donna every day when Mrs. Bonner announced lunch from the basement intercom at the office building.

Eliot kept to himself all week. He worked alone in his office, had a solitary dinner, then prowled about the island until early morning when fatigue drove him to bed and fitful sleep beset by dreams that vanished when he tried to examine them. He knew that the others were together much of the time. Sometimes late at night when the wind eased he could hear their voices, laughing, but he didn't see them again. He caught himself watching one or the other of them for an overt sign of conspiracy.

Friday afternoon Marty and Donna went to the northern islands for the weekend. Beatrice was gone, to the mountains to visit Gina.

Ed Delizzio and Eliot were invited to Lee's house for dinner on Friday night, and there was no graceful, or even possible, way for Eliot to refuse without hurting Mary's feelings.

"It's been a funny week, hasn't it?" Mary said. "Eliot . . ." She looked toward her husband, set her mouth, and continued quickly, "Last week, the night that *she* came, did you have a peculiar dream?"

Lee put his knife down too hard, and she said, "I have to find out. Has Marty spoken to you all week?" She had turned back to Eliot almost instantly.

"No. Why? What about a dream?"

"All right. We all dreamed of . . . an orgy. Either we dreamed it, or it happened. Lee and I talked about it right away, of course. We thought it was our dream, strange, but ours. Then something Marty said made me realize that he had dreamed it, too. Only he had the players mixed up. And Beatrice . . . Well, you can ask her what she dreamed sometime. So I asked Ed, and he said almost the same thing. You?"

Eliot nodded. "Yeah. Except I wasn't asleep. I saw it, down on the beach. I hadn't gone home yet."

No one moved or spoke. Mary paled, then she flushed crimson, and finally broke the silence with a sound that was meant to be a laugh but sounded more like a sob. She picked up her wineglass and choked on a swallow. Without looking at Eliot she said, "Well, if you saw what Lee and I dreamed, you must have had quite a show."

"It wasn't on the beach," Ed Delizzio said hoarsely. "It was back by the ruins, between the fort and the tower. We had a fire, and a ceremony. Rites of some kind." He stared ahead as if seeing it again. "I searched for ashes, for a scorched place. I got down on my knees the next morning and searched for a sign. . . . Nothing."

Eliot looked at him curiously, wondering how he had missed noting the haggard appearance of the younger man. Ed's eyes appeared sunken, haunted, as if there were only darkness before him that he was trying to pierce.

"It's her fault," Mary said softly. "I don't know how or why, what she has done, anything. But I know she's to blame. Night after night I wake up listening and I don't know what for."

"Hey, knock off talk like that," Lee said, and while his voice was light, his hand that closed over hers on the table made her wince.

Mary looked at Lee and there was certainty on her face.

Eliot stood up. "Is there coffee, Mary? I have an appointment with Pitcock later on. Can't dawdle here all night."

Lee looked relieved as Mary's face relaxed and she smiled a genuine smile and stood up. "Sorry, Eliot. Pie? Cherry pie and coffee coming up."

They all helped her clear the table and ate pie and drank coffee. Mary refilled the cups, then asked, "Are you quitting, Eliot? Is that why you have to see Mr. Pitcock?"

"Mary!" Lee looked at Eliot and shrugged eloquently.

Eliot laughed. "No, dear heart, I'm not quitting. In fact, I might write a book for the old goat."

Mary looked disappointed.

"She thinks that if you'd just quit then the whole thing will fold and I won't have to actually do anything," Lee said.

"You really want to go, don't you?" Eliot asked her.

"I was willing to stay, wasn't I, Lee? I never mentioned leaving, did I? But now, after this week, I'm afraid and I don't know why. I don't like that."

"Mary, relax. We were all together at dinner. Maybe the lobster was a little off. Or the wrong kind of mushroom in something or other. I mean, I was a lot more worried when I thought it was just me than I am now knowing that everyone experienced something like that."

She studied his face for a long time, then nodded. "You could be right, Eliot. I guess it must have been something like that."

Lee sighed, and even Ed seemed relieved. Soon after that Eliot left them and walked over to Pitcock's house.

"I decided to do the book," he said without preamble.

Pitcock was on the terrace alone. There was a touch of daylight remaining, enough to make the water look like flowing silver. "Would you mind telling me why you decided to do it?" Pitcock said after a moment.

"Mainly because I feel like there's something trying its damnedest to keep me from doing it." Eliot was surprised at his own words. He hadn't meant to say that, hadn't thought it consciously.

"I should warn you, Eliot, that it could be dangerous. Especially if you really feel that way."

"Dangerous how? Psychologically?"

"Sometimes I forget how bright you are. Sit down, Eliot. Sit down. Have you had dinner?"

Eliot refused another dinner and left the old man on his terrace. They would talk the next day. All my life, he thought, always drifting, everything too easy, too meaningless to become involved with any of it. Like a cork on the stream, this way and that, touching reality now and then, then bobbing away again. Never mattered if I got waterlogged and sank, or if I kept on floating along. Just didn't matter. Then that crazy old man pulled me into his madness, and now I don't feel like I'm floating with the current at all. I'm bucking it and I don't know why, or where I'm going, what I'll find when I get there. And I don't want to get out. I won't get out, and it, that mysterious it that I feel now, it will get in my way, and maybe even try to hurt me. . . . He laughed suddenly, but his laughter was not harsh, or cynical, but light with amusement and wonder.

Sunday afternoon. "Some things I should tell you, Eliot. There's a trust already set up, to continue this research. It's your baby."

"When did you do that?"

"Almost as soon as you came here I started making the arrangements. It doesn't have to be here, you understand. You can move the operations if you want to."

"And if I decide to quit, then what?"

"I would ask that you personally supervise finding the right man to carry on. I won't issue directives, anything like that, if that's what you mean. At your own discretion."

Eliot stared at him coldly. "No ties, of any sort. What I want goes. If I change the direction, whatever."

"Whatever."

They stopped to listen. Loud voices from the next house, Ed's house that he shared with Marty. Pitcock was staring toward the sound intently, not surprised, not startled.

Eliot left him and trotted along the boardwalk to Ed's house. Marty was backing Ed up against the screened porch. There was a cut on Ed's cheek. Marty's fists were hanging at his sides and at that moment neither was speaking. Off to one side Donna was pressed against the door of the house, holding her hands over her mouth hard.

"Knock it off, you two. What in Christ's name is going on?"

Neither of them paid any attention to Eliot. From nowhere a knife had appeared in Ed's hand. "Okay, Marty, baby. Come on in and get it. Come on, baby. Come on." Ed's voice was low.

Marty hesitated, his eyes on the knife. Before he could move again Eliot jumped him, knocking him to the ground. He brought his knee up sharply under Marty's chin, snapping his head back, then hit him hard just under the ribs. Marty gagged, doubled up gasping.

"Ed! Oh, Ed, he might have killed you! I thought he was going to kill you!" Donna ran to Ed and held him, sobbing.

Eliot watched, mystified. He helped Marty up, keeping a firm grasp on his arm. Marty had no fight left in him. He looked at Ed and Donna and from them to Eliot, his face twisted with contempt and hatred. Furiously he jerked loose from Eliot and turned away to go around the house, not speaking. A second later the front door slammed.

"Ed, come over to my house. You're hurt! You're bleeding. He was going to kill you!" Donna was tugging at Ed's arm.

"Is anyone going to fill me in? What was that all about?"

Donna looked blank. "I don't know. He went out of his mind. He started to scream and yell at me and I made him bring me back. Then he went at Ed. Over nothing. Nothing at all."

Ed shrugged. The knife was gone. Eliot wondered if he had even seen a knife. "Damned if I know," Ed said. He was breathing fast now, as if fighting off shock or fear. "He came at me calling me names like I haven't heard since I left the Bronx." Donna started to sob again and he put his arm about her shoulders. "It wasn't your fault," he said. "Hey. Don't do that. It wasn't your fault." He led her toward her house.

"So," Eliot told Pitcock later, "I tried to get something out of Marty. He was packing. He cursed me out and finished throwing his stuff into his suitcases, then left. Period."

Beatrice had returned, was waiting with Pitcock. Neither seemed at all surprised. "It was bound to happen," she said. "They were deadly rivals. That togetherness was too openly self-protective. Donna should have been twins." She shivered. "I didn't know Ed carried a knife out here. He's an expert, you know. It's in his file."

Eliot walked home with her later; at her door he said, "Something else, Beatrice. Something happened here last week, something inexplicable that has affected us all. A mass hallucination, a mass dream. That's all it was, a psychic event of some sort, not explained yet, but not real."

They had been standing close together; she drew away. "Are you certain, Eliot? Absolutely certain? Anything strong enough to touch every one of us, change us somehow, must have some reality of its own." Then she went inside.

They reorganized and rescheduled work on Monday. Without Marty at the computer there was much that would have to be postponed until they got a replacement. Donna and Ed smiled softly at each other and wandered off down the beach when it was lunchtime. Eliot watched and tried to see her as Marty must have seen her, as Ed obviously saw her. All he saw was the bulgy figure, sagging breasts in too-tight dresses, or halters. The thick legs and arms. Indentable flesh, skin that didn't tan but looked mottled, with red highlights. Thursday night he had dinner with Beatrice on her porch. She lived next to Mary and Lee Moore. They had no lights on yet when they heard Mary calling to Beatrice in a muffled but urgent voice.

"Damn," Beatrice said. She left Eliot. After a moment he followed her.

". . . your friend. Just do something. I won't have her crying on Lee's shoulder. Take her home, or something." Mary's voice was too controlled, too tight.

"For heaven's sake, Mary. Tell her to clear out. It's your house. Where's Ed?"

"He went for a walk, *she* said. I don't know. All I know is that she's in there crying on Lee's shoulder and they won't even hear me."

She broke then, suddenly and completely. Eliot couldn't see them, they were hidden by a fence of yellow oleanders, but he could hear her weeping and Beatrice's voice trying to soothe her. He circled them and approached the house.

Donna was in Lee's arms. He was holding her tightly, smoothing her dull hair. His eyes were closed. Their voices were too low to hear any of the words.

"Lee!" They didn't move apart. Lee opened his eyes and stared at Eliot blankly. "Lee! Snap out of it!"

"They used her," Lee said dully. "They both used her to get even with each other for some childish thing. They didn't care what happened to her at all."

Eliot took a step toward them, stopped again. "Lee, Mary's hurt. She needs you now. She's hurt, Lee."

Lee's face changed; slowly the life returned, then suddenly he looked like a man waking up. He dropped his arms from Donna and stepped around her without seeing her at all. "Mary? What's wrong with Mary?"

"She's out there. Beatrice found her. She needs you right now. By the oleanders."

Lee ran out of the house. Donna stared after him, her face tear-streaked and ugly. She turned to Eliot. "I was frightened. Ed had a knife, he began to talk crazy, saying if I would repent now and die before I sinned again, my soul would be saved. I was so frightened. He wants to kill me."

Eliot saw her hopelessness and despair, the overwhelming fear that had driven her to Lee for help. She was so agonizingly young and inexperienced, so susceptible. Her large eyes awash with tears that made eddies and shadows and revealed depths that he hadn't suspected before, her body hidden now by adolescent fat that would dissolve and reveal a woman with a firm slim figure, protected until she was ready to find union with . . . He blinked and laughed raucously. "God, you're good, doll!" He laughed again and now the tears were gone and her eyes were flat and hard, like a reflecting metal polished to a high sheen. Wordlessly she left the house.

He found Mary and Lee. Beatrice was nearby, her back to them. "All of you, come on in. I want to say something." Inside again he didn't know what he could say. Nothing that would make any sense.

"Mary, you have to forget this." Mary looked at the wall, her face composed and set. "I mean it, Mary, or else she will have won. You're giving her exactly what she came here for. She doesn't want Lee any more than she wanted Marty or Ed. She wants to drive wedges. To come between people. We all watched it happen. This is the very same thing. You're intelligent enough to see this, Mary. You too, Lee."

Lee had been watching him stonily. Now he said, "Hasn't it occurred to you that you're butting in on something you don't know a damn thing about? That girl was frightened. Mary acted like a bitch. Period."

Eliot sighed. "Oh, Christ."

"I'm leaving," Mary said furiously. "I won't stand by and see you make a fool of yourself. And when she throws you over, you'll know where to look for me."

"And you," Eliot said. "Right on cue. That's the scenario, all right. For God's sake, you two idiots, open your eyes and see what you're doing and why!" He jammed his hands into his pockets. They continued to avoid looking at one another. Finally Eliot shrugged. "Okay. If you really can't see it, then leave, Mary. It's the only thing to do. I'll take you over tonight."

"What are you talking about?" Lee demanded coldly.

"I mean that if you two are so caught up in this that you believe it's real, she has to go away, or one of you will kill the other one. Either snap out of it and convince me that you're aware of what's happened, or I'll take Mary to Charleston. I won't leave you together."

A new intentness came into Lee's face. Ignoring Mary, he took a step toward Eliot. "All this crazy talk. You're the one who started all this." His eyes narrowed and his hands clenched. "That night, down on the beach, I saw her with you. I let her convince me that it was a dream, but I saw you. I know what I saw. And I'm going to kill you, Kalin. I'm going to choke your lies right back down in your throat."

Suddenly the screen door was flung open and Ed Delizzio stepped into the room. Mary screamed. Ed had the same knife that he had threatened Marty with. This time he was holding it to throw. His quick look swept the room, stopped at Lee, and in the same instant that his arm rose, Mary moved toward Lee, her hands out. She pushed him hard; the knife flashed; she screamed again, this time in fear and pain. She staggered against Lee and fell. For a second Lee swayed, grey-faced; then he dropped to his knees at her side.

"It's nothing," she said shakily. "It touched my arm, that's all. Lee . . . Darling, please, don't. Please, Lee." He was rocking back and forth, holding her, weeping. When she tried to get up, he gathered her into his arms and lifted her and carried her into the bedroom. Beatrice followed them.

Eliot picked up the knife, closed it, and put it in his pocket.

"I guess we should call the police," Ed said emotionlessly.

"We'll call nobody," Eliot said. He studied Ed, who continued to stand in the doorway. Even his lips seemed bloodless. "Are you all right?"

"Yes. Spent. Used up. Everything's gone. I'm okay now. It's over." He looked like a shock victim: ashen-faced, blank, rigid.

They waited in silence until Beatrice returned. She was pale and avoided Ed's glance. "They're in there crying like babies. She's all right. Hardly even scratched. Mostly scared."

"Let's go," Eliot said. He motioned for Ed to leave with them. "We could use a drink."

Beatrice hesitated. "Can we leave them? You said . . ."

"Everything changes from moment to moment, honey. Everything's the same and everything keeps changing. They'll be all right now. Ed's going to keel over and I'm damned if I want to carry him across the island. Give us a drink, Beatrice. We all deserve it."

Beatrice kept close to him as they walked around the oleanders. "No lights," she said on her porch, then added quickly, "It makes us so visible." She left them. There was the sound of the refrigerator door, ice in glasses, liquor being poured. Then she was back and handed them both glasses, very strong bourbon and water. She pulled a chair closer to Eliot's. "How can she do this to us?"

"She's a witch," Ed said.

"No. She's not a witch. And she hasn't done a damn thing to any of us. Whatever we're doing, we're doing to ourselves." Eliot finished his drink and went inside to refill his glass. When he returned, Beatrice was alone.

"You upset him more than anything up to now. Eliot, is he likely to do anything like that again?"

"I don't think so. He sinned. Now he'll repent, in the good

traditional way. Prayers, good deeds, confession. Whatever he does to atone."

"Is it all over now? Who else is there to go berserk? Are you safe?"

"Nobody is safe from himself. Nobody that I know, anyway. Maybe Pitcock. I'm gambling on Pitcock, but I don't know." He drank deeply. The alcohol was numbing him now and he felt grateful.

The wind blew harder and the palm trees came to life. On the porch the silence deepened. Beatrice took Eliot's glass from his hand and went inside with it, bringing it back in a few moments without speaking. He put it down this time. There had been a need before, but the urgency was gone.

"I don't understand what's happening," Beatrice said quietly, "but whatever it is, it's changed you."

"Nobody understands, least of all me. I'm just groping for the right thing to do from one moment to the next, no plans, no overall theory to account for anything."

"It won't go on like this, will it? We couldn't stand this kind of turmoil day after day."

"No. It's building up to something. Can't you feel that? Each step is farther, each thrust more nearly mortal." Lassitude was creeping through his bones. Abruptly he stood up. "I have to go or I'll fall asleep here."

"Eliot . . . Do you have to go?"

"I think so. Are you afraid?"

"No. It isn't that. Yes, go now. I'll see you in the morning."

"No work tomorrow. I'm going by the office and post a sign, a declared holiday." He held her hand for a minute. Soon, he thought, soon. Then he left her and walked through the darkness of the shadows cast by the oak trees and the pines, around the ruins that rose abruptly, smelling the night-blooming cereus, and the sea, and the constant odor of decay that was present wherever there were tropical plants. The scents mingled, the drive toward life stronger than death, blossoms in decay, greenery erupting from the black. He didn't turn on a light when he got to the building, but walked through the dark lobby that echoed hollowly.

He sat at his desk for several minutes before he flicked the light switch. Then he typed the notice quickly and found Scotch tape to attach it to the door. His head was starting to throb and his weariness returned, making his legs ache and his back hurt. Outside the building, he hesitated at the lake. It was spring-fed, cool, clean water, without a ripple on its surface. The moon rode there as sedately as if painted. A whippoorwill cried poignantly.

Very slowly Eliot began to take off his clothes. He walked out into the water, and when it was up to his thighs, he dove straight out into it, down, down. The moon shattered and fled, the resting swams screamed alarm, and half a dozen ducks took flight. Eliot let out his air slowly, measuring it, and when it was gone he began to rise again, but suddenly he doubled in pain. He sank, struggling to loosen the knot in his stomach. The water was luminous now, pale green and silver, and where the bottom had been there was nothing. He sank lower, drifting downward like a snowflake. The broken moon was falling with him, flecks of silver, a streak of a heavier piece flashing by; the minuscule particles of it that touched him adhered, turning him into a radiant being, floating downward in the bottomless pool. From somewhere a thought came to him unwanted and obtrusive: The lake is only eight feet deep in the very center. He tried to push the thought away, but his body had heard, and the struggle began again, and now he tumbled and one leg stretched out until his toes felt the sandy bottom and pushed hard. He exploded in pain, as the moon had exploded. The water rushed in to fill his emptiness and he gasped and choked and coughed and the fire in his lungs was all there was.

He lay on the sand, raw and sore from retching, and he knew he couldn't move. His legs wouldn't hold him yet. Another spasm shook him and he heaved again.

He had little memory of getting to his house and into bed.

He dreamed that the Spaniards dragged themselves up from the shadows where they lived and toiled to complete the fort throughout the night. They were crude shadow figures themselves, silent, carrying impossibly heavy burdens on their backs, climbing the crude steps to lay the blocks, and the fort took shape and rose higher and higher. He woke to find it nearly noon.

There was a note on his table to see Pitcock as soon as convenient. He showered and made coffee, and after he had eaten he walked over to the main house. Pitcock was in his office.

"Ed came by to say he was leaving," Pitcock said. "He wouldn't tell me what happened. Will you?"

"Sure." His account was very brief, and when he got to his adventure in the lake, he summed it up in one sentence. "I went for a swim in the lake and nearly drowned."

"Part of the same thing?"

"I believe so."

"Yes. Well, we agreed that it would get dangerous."

"Yes."

"Have you seen Donna this morning?" Pitcock toyed with a pencil and when it fell, he jerked. He looked at his hands with curiosity. Before Eliot could answer his question, he said, "Maybe we should disband the project now. God knows we have to start over with a new staff."

"I haven't seen Donna. Do you really want to quit?"

"I feel like a man swimming the channel. I'm three quarters of the way there, but I want to turn around and go back. I feel like either way I'll lose something. I don't think I can make it all the way, Eliot."

"That's because we don't know exactly what's in the water for the last quarter of the trip. We keep finding out there are things that we weren't ready for. Ed's knife. I put it in my pocket, but it's not there now. Swimming in a lake that suddenly became bottomless. You can walk across that lake in the dry season. What's ahead? That's the question, isn't it?"

"Is it? I keep wondering, and if we found out that the earth is an illusion dreamed by a god, what harm have we done? Why are we being stopped? Who's meddling?"

Eliot stared at him, then shook his head. "I think you should go away for the weekend. Get away from here for a few days, see how you feel about it Monday. If you want to break it all up then, well, we can talk about it."

"You can't leave now, can you? You'll see it through, no matter what happens?"

"I can't leave now."

Pitcock looked shriveled and old, and for several minutes his bright blue eyes seemed clouded. Surprisingly, he laughed then. "You asked once why I picked you. Because I could see myself in you. The self that I could have been forty years ago. But instead I took the other path, extended an empire. Pitcock Enterprises. I thought there was time for it all, and I was wrong. I thought it was a kind of knowledge, that if I bypassed it, I could have it just the same if I forced someone else to seek it and let me see the results. Non-transferable. Not knowledge, then. Not in the accepted sense. I pushed you and prodded you and goaded you into going somewhere and I can't follow you. Leave me alone, Eliot. I have some work to do now."

Eliot stood up and started to leave, but stopped at the door. "Pit, I don't *know* anything. If I did, I would make you see it. But there's nothing."

Pitcock didn't look at him. He had picked up the pencil again and held it poised over a notebook as if impatient to resume an interrupted task. Eliot went out.

"Eliot, are you all right?" Beatrice was waiting for him. She held out his watch. "I found it by the lake."

Eliot took her in his arms and held her quietly for a long time. "I'm all right."

"The lake shore is a mess, as if you were fighting there. I went to your house and saw that you'd had breakfast. I knew it was all right, but still . . ."

They walked in the shade, toward the far end of the island. The trees, the dunes to the seaward side, all masked the sound of the ocean, and there were only bird songs and an occasional rustling in the undergrowth. There was a cool, mossy glen, where the air was tinted blue by a profusion of wild morning glories that never closed in the shadows. Very deliberately and gently Eliot made love to Beatrice in the glen.

She lay on her back with her eyes closed, a small smile on her face. "I feel like a wood nymph, doing what I have to do, without a thought in the world. My brain's on vacation."

He ran his finger over her cheek. She was humming. With a chill Eliot realized that she was humming "Ten Little Indians."

That afternoon Eliot made some preliminary notes:

Any eschatological system, whether religious, mathematical, physical, or simply theoretical for purposes of analogies, is counter to the world as it exists. Experimental bias, observer effect, by whatever name science would call it, the addition of life in a universe reverses the entropic nature of matter. Eschatology can validly be applied only to inert matter; the final dispersion of the atoms in a uniform, energyless universe is a reformulation of what others have called the death wish. Since man rose from the same inert matter, this pull or drive or simple tendency exerts its purpose in every cell of his being. But with the random chemical reaction that brought life to the lifeless, another, stronger drive was created. The double helix is the perfect symbol for this new, not-to-be-denied drive that manifests in rebirth, renewal, in an ever widening spiral of growth and change . . .

"Eliot!" Lee's voice jolted him awake. "Pitcock's missing. We can't find him anywhere."

"Where have you looked?" Eliot hurried out to join Lee. "Where's Bonner?"

"He went to check out the office building. We went through the house, then the ruins. He likes to prowl among them. I looked in on Beatrice. I thought he might be with you."

"Okay. Check out the other houses. I'll take the beach, work back through the stones toward his house."

Two hours until it would be dark, two hours, plenty of time to find him. Not in the woods, but among the dead rocks. A quarter of a mile of jumbled rocks, fan-shaped, narrowed at the ruins, spreading out at the water's edge, piled higher there with deeper cracks between them. Eliot zigzagged from the edge of the water to the ruins, back to the water. He called, and the whispering sea mocked him. From a distance he could hear Lee's voice calling. A catbird practiced Lee's shout, then gave it up and trilled sweetly. Eliot stopped abruptly. He strained to hear, then began working his way more slowly toward a high place where six of the massive stones had been piled up. "I'm coming, Pit." He couldn't be certain now if he had heard the old man or not. He searched frantically but carefully among the bases. Here the water lapped at the rocks with every third or fourth wave. The tide was turning.

"Eliot."

This time he knew he had heard. He found the old man lying in an unnatural position, his shoulders and his hips not in line. Pitcock was very pale, but conscious. His voice was a faint whisper.

"Can't move, Eliot. Back's hurt."

"Okay. Take it easy, Pit. We'll get you out of here." Eliot clambered back up the rocks and yelled for Lee. An answer came back faintly, and he waited until Lee was closer. "Bring a stretcher, a door, something to carry him on." Lee appeared at the head of the rocks and waved. "Tell Bonner to get the launch ready. Mrs. Bonner to call the hospital." Lee waved again and ran toward Pitcock's house. Eliot returned to the old man.

There was nothing he could do now. He found his handkerchief and wiped Pitcock's face gently. He was perspiring hard.

"Heard someone crying. Couldn't find her. Slipped . . ."

"Don't talk now, Pit. Save it. Your pulse is good. It's not serious, I'm sure. Rest."

"Eliot, don't send me over tonight. Isn't fair, not now. Get me back to the house. Help me up." His face was grey, cold, and moist. His eyes were glazed.

Damn Lee! Where was Bonner? "Take it easy, Pit. Soon now. Just take it easy." He yanked his shirt off and covered the old man with it. He mopped his face again.

"I didn't do it, Eliot. I didn't want to fall." He looked past Eliot and groaned. His eyes closed. Beads of sweat came together and a trickle ran across one eye, another down his temple. Eliot wiped his face again and the man shuddered. "She's up there," he mumbled. "Watching us."

Eliot looked over his shoulder, across the tumbled rocks. She was standing on the wall of the fort, not moving, a dark shape against the paling sky. "Don't worry about her, Pit," he said. "I'll take care of her." He caught a motion and turned to see Lee and Bonner picking their way among the blocks with a door. Beatrice darted before them, burdened with blankets and a beach mat.

"How bad?"

"I don't know. Shock." He glanced quickly toward the fort. She was gone.

"For God's sake, be careful!" he said moments later as they started to move Pitcock to the door, padded now with the beach mat. They covered him and fastened him down securely with the blankets, and then Lee and Eliot carried him to the motor launch. Mrs. Bonner met them at the dock.

"There'll be an ambulance waiting." She looked at Pitcock and turned white. "My God! Oh, my God!"

"Go with them," Eliot said to her. "You too," he told Beatrice. "Get out of here."

"No. I couldn't help him."

They got him on board and Lee worked with the mooring line. Eliot turned again to Beatrice. "Please go on. Stay with him. He might want you."

"Don't send me away, Eliot. Please don't send me away."

He nodded and the three of them stood on the dock and watched until the launch started to pick up speed in the smooth water of the bay. As the roar diminished, the silence of the island settled preternaturally. "Where's Mary?"

"In our house."

"Let's get her. We have to stay together tonight." They started across the island. Under the trees the light was a somber yellow, the air hot and still, thick and oppressive. Through the branches overhead the sky was dirty yellow, the color of Donna's hair. No bird stirred, no tree frogs sang, the palm fronds stood stiff and unmoving. Eliot set a fast pace and they hurried a bit more. When they came to the ruins, twilight had descended, and rounding the aborted building they involuntarily stopped. Before them was a concrete ocean, gray on gray, the sea and horizon an encapsulating solid that was closing the distance to them rapidly.

"Get Mary, fast. We'll go to the office building." Eliot's hand closed hard on Beatrice's arm. She was gazing about in wonder. She reached out to touch the granite block, then her hand swept through the air, her fingers spread apart, as if trying to feel for something not there. "It's an illusion, a trick of the light. A storm's coming fast."

She looked at him, touched his cheek as she had touched the rock. "But I can't tell the difference. This afternoon I dreamed, I thought, or hallucinated, something. Everything was like a flat illustration from a book. I . . . ." She shook herself and laughed self-consciously. "I found your watch. Here." She pulled it from her pocket and handed it to him. Eliot stared at it for a long time. Then Lee and Mary were with them and they turned to go to the office building.

Halfway there, the wind came. It came with a shriek that was too high-pitched, and it carried sand and dust that brought night. The island shook, and the trees ground their branches together. Eliot grasped Beatrice's hand and pulled her, blinded by flying matter and the driving wind that was tearing up rotted and rotting leaves and twigs and stripping leaves from the oaks and needles from the pines. It was a hot wind. When the noises ebbed they could hear the sea pounding. A tree shuddered and crashed down across the walk and they stopped, panting, then ran on, clambering over the trunk. Now they could see the office building and the lake dimly. The lake looked like a saucer of water rocking back and forth. There was no sign of the waterfowl. They began to run across the parklike setting and the water rocked higher on the far side of the lake.

"For the love of God, hurry!" Eliot cried, and nearly yanked Beatrice off her feet. The water was swinging back now, and at the same time the wind increased, pushing the water up and out of its banks. Lee and Mary had reached the building, but Beatrice stumbled. Eliot knocked her to the ground and wrapped his arms around her, and the water hit them.

They rolled with the wall of water, tumbled over and over, grinding against the walk, against the sand and bushes. Beatrice went limp and Eliot held her head tight against him and let himself roll. He closed his hand over her mouth and nose so she wouldn't breathe in the roiling water and dirt. When he knew he could hold his breath no longer, that Beatrice would die if she didn't get air, the water abruptly fell. Everything stopped, even the wind paused. There were hands on him, Lee, trying to help him up. Eliot resisted feebly, the hands persisted, and the weight that was Beatrice was removed.

"Can you get up, Eliot? Can you move? I'll carry her inside and come back for you." Again the peace returned, but after an infinitely long time he opened his eyes and knew that he had to get up, had to get inside the shelter of the building. The wind was starting to build again and he struggled to his knees, then pulled himself upright and, staggering uncertainly, stumbled to the entrance as Lee was coming out for him.

He was hardly aware of being led inside, of anything that happened for the next few minutes. Beatrice smiled wanly at him, then lay back on the couch where Lee had put her. Outside, the storm built to a new intensity.

"How long has it been?" Mary asked much later. There was no light in the building, the electricity had long since failed. They could hear the howling wind, now and again punctuated by explosive noises as if a wrecking crew were hard at work destroying the island and everything on it.

Eliot looked at his watch; it had stopped. He shrugged. Something crashed into the building and the whole structure shuddered.

"What is it?" Lee asked later. "A tornado would have gone long ago. There wasn't any report of a hurricane. What is it?"

Eliot stood up. The building shuddered again with a new blast of wind. "I have to go find her," he said.

"No!" Beatrice, pale and torn and cut and filthy, and very beautiful. He touched her cheek lightly. She backed away from him and sat down. Very frightened. Tears standing in her eyes. No one else said anything.

No matter which way he went, the wind was in his face. The rain drove against him horizontally, blinding him, and he was buffeted with debris of the storm. There were trees downed everywhere, and he stumbled and fell over them and crawled and dragged himself to his feet again and again. He lost his sandals and knew that his feet were bleeding. His bare chest was hatchmarked by cuts and scrapes. Then he felt the smooth terrazzo underfoot and he knew that soon he would find her. He fell again, hard against a roughly worked block that was cold and wet. The pounding rain dissolved him; he flowed through the rock where there was silence and peace and no more pain. He rested. Very slowly, after a long time, he found himself withdrawing from the nothingness of rest; the rock was cutting into his chest, and where it had scraped his cheek raw there was pain. He pulled away. Lightning burned the air, sizzling so close that he was blinded. The thunder that was almost simultaneous with it deepened and he vibrated with the roar. Blinded and deafened, he pushed himself away from the rock, reeled backward, and clung to the great oak tree until his vision cleared again. Then he lurched away from the place, toward the water's edge and the jumbled rocks there. Behind him lightning flashed again, the tree exploded, showering a geyser of splinters over him. He didn't look back. The tree crashed to the ground, one of the branch ends brushing him as it fell.

The thunder of the sea contested the thunder of the air, overcame it as he drew nearer until there was only the roar of the ocean. The waves were mountainous, crashing over the highest of the rocks now, grinding rocks against rocks, smashing all to a powdery sand that it would fling away to rest in a watery grave. Eliot saw her then.

I've come for you.

You can't touch me.

Yes. I can. I know you.

She laughed and was gone. He waited, bracing himself against the wind, and lightning illuminated her again, closer.

Don't run any more. I'll still be here, no matter how far you run. Always closer.

A wave broke over his feet, and again she laughed and the moment was over. He didn't move.

Eliot, go back to them. Or they'll all die. And death is real, Eliot. No matter what else isn't, death is real.

He had only to reach out to touch her now. Her flesh was as alive as his own, the arm that he caught twisted and pulled reassuringly.

You'll kill them all, Eliot. Beatrice. Lee. Mary. They'll die. Look at the water. It's going to cover the island.

Another wave broke, higher on his leg this time. The water was rushing among the blocks, reaching out for the fort now.

She struggled to free herself, she clawed his face and bit and tried to bring her knee up. Eliot twisted her around and they slipped and fell together, his grasp on her arm broken. He brought his hands up her body and fastened them on her throat, and the waves were over his head as he choked her and beat her head against the rocks and knew that he was drowning, being swept out to sea by the furious undertow, but still he held her. Her struggles became feebler.

God! Help me!

He can't! He brings destruction and plagues and wars and death. No help.

She was hardly moving, and they were both swept up together and dashed against the piled-up blocks. Eliot blacked out, but his hands didn't let go, and when the pain released him, he knew that he still held her although he could no longer feel her.

God, please! Please.

He brings the floods and the winds and devastates the land and kills mankind. He is death and I'm sending you back to him.

You're crazy. You can't kill. They'll punish you. They'll hang you. Put you in an institution for the rest of your life.

And the spark of life that is stronger than all the powers of death commands the waters to be stilled, and they are quiet.

There was only silence now.

"Help me pull him out of there." Lee's voice. "Can you unlock his hands?"

"Is he dead? For God's sake, Lee, is he dead?"

"No. Beatrice, get out of the way. He's . . ."

Eliot opened his eyes to a tranquil night. He was between two stone blocks, waves breaking over his legs. His hands and arms ached and he looked at them; his fingers were locked together. There was no sign of her. Beatrice reached down to touch him and he felt his muscles relax, and took her hand.

"It's over then?"

"Yes. How? What happened?" Beatrice shook her head violently. "Never mind. Not now. Let's get you inside. You're hurt."

They walked around the toppled oak tree, but in the wet black ground there were sprouts already, palely green, tenacious. There would be a grove there one day.

"The oak tree is the only casualty," Lee said in wonder. "You'd think with all that wind, the thunder and lightning, the whole island would be gone. One tree."

Eliot felt Beatrice's hand tighten in his, but he didn't say anything. She knows. A temporary displacement of the ego and she comes up with what I'm thinking, just like that. He didn't find it at all curious that no one asked what had happened to Donna. They were on the spiral, safely now, and they would continue to search for patterns that would prove to be elusive, but maybe, now, not too elusive after all.

THE VILLAGE

Mildred Carey decided to walk to the post office early, before the sun turned the two blocks into a furnace. "They've done something to the weather," she said to her husband, packing his three sandwiches and thermos of lemonade. "Never used to be this hot this early."

"It'll get cooler again. Always does."

She followed him to the door and waved as he backed out of the drive. The tomato plants she had set out the day before were wilted. She watered them, then started to walk slowly to town. With a feeling of satisfaction she noticed that Mrs. Mareno's roses had black spot. Forcing the blooms with too much fertilizer just wasn't good for them.

Mike Donatti dozed as he awaited orders to regroup and start the search-and-clear maneuver. Stilwell nudged him. "Hey, Mike, you been over here before?"

"Nope. One fucken village is just like the others. Mud or dust. That's the only fucken difference."

Stilwell was so new that he was sunburned red. Everyone else in the company was burned black. "Man, could we pass," they liked to say to Latimore, who couldn't.

Mr. Peters was sweeping the sidewalk before the market. "Got some good fresh salami," he said. "Ed made it over the weekend."

"You sure Ed made it, not Buz? When Buz makes it, he uses too much garlic. What's he covering up is what I want to know."

"Now, Miz Carey, you know he's not covering up. Some folks like it hot and strong."

"I'll stop back by after I get the mail."

The four Henry children were already out in the street, filthy, chasing each other randomly. Their mother was not in sight. Mildred Carey pursed her lips. Her Mark never had played in the street in his life.

She dropped in the five-and-dime, not to buy anything but to look over the flats of annuals, petunias, marigolds, nasturtiums. "They sure don't look healthy," she said to Doris Offinger.

"They're fine, Miz Carey. Brother bought them fresh this morning from Connor's down at Midbury. You know Connor's has good stock."

"How's Larry getting along? Still in the veterans' hospital at Lakeview?"

"Yes. He'll be out in a couple of weeks, I guess." Doris' pretty face remained untroubled. "They've got such good doctors down there, I hate to see him get so far from them all, but he wants to come home."

"How can these people stand this heat all the time?" Stilwell said after a moment. The sun wasn't up yet, but it was eighty-six degrees, humidity near one hundred percent.

"People, he says. Boy, ain't you even been briefed? People can't stand it, that's the first clue." Mike sighed and sat up. He lighted a cigarette. "Boy, back home in August. You know the hills where I come from are cold, even in August?"

"Where's that?"

"Vermont. I can remember plenty of times it snowed in August. Nights under a blanket."

"Well, he can help out here in the store. With his pension and the store and all, the two of you are set, aren't you? Isn't that Tessie Hetherton going in Peters' market?"

"I didn't notice her. Did you want one of those flats, Miz Carey?"

"No. They aren't healthy. Connor's must have culled the runts and set *them* out." She stood in the doorway squinting to see across the way to Peters' market. "I'm sure it was. And she told me she's too arthritic to do any more housework. I'll just go talk to her."

"I don't think she will, though. Miz Avery wanted her on Wednesdays and she said no. You know Mr. Hetherton's got a job? With the paper mill."

"Shtt. That won't last. They'll pay off a few of last winter's bills and then he'll start to complain about his liver or something and she'll be hustling for work, I know that man." She left the store without looking back, certain that Doris would be eyeing the price tags of the flats. "You take care of yourself, Doris. You're looking peaked. You should get out in the sun.

"Mrs. Hetherton, you're looking fit again," Mildred Carey said, cornering the woman as she emerged from the store.

"Warm weather's helped some."

"Look, can you possibly come over Thursday morning? You know the Garden Club meets this week, and I can't possibly get ready without some help."

"Well, I just don't know . . . Danny's dead set against my going out to work again."

"But they're going to have to close down the mill. And then where will he be?"

"Close it down? Why? Who says?"

"It's been in the papers for weeks now. All those dead fish, and the stink. You know that committee came up and took samples and said they're the ones responsible. And they can't afford to change over the whole process. They're going to move instead."

"Oh, that. Danny said don't hold your breath. They're making a study, and then they'll have to come up with a plan and have it studied, and all in all it's going to take five years or even more before it all comes to a head."

"Hm. Another big kill and the Department of Health . . ."

Mrs. Hetherton laughed and Mildred Carey had to smile too. "Well, anyway, can you come over just this time? For this one meeting?"

"Sure, Miz Carey. Thursday morning? But only half a day."

The schoolbus turned the corner and rolled noisily down the broad new street. The two women watched it out of sight. "Have you seen the Tomkins boys lately?" Mildred Carey asked. "Hair down to here."

"Winona says they're having someone in to talk about drugs. I asked her point blank if there are drugs around here and she said no, but you never can tell. The kids won't tell you nothing."

"Well, I just thank God that Mark is grown up and out of it all."

"He's due home soon now, isn't he?"

"Seven weeks. Then off to college in the fall. I told him that he's probably safer over there than at one of the universities right now." They laughed and moved apart. "See you Thursday."

"Listen, Mike, when you get back, you'll go through New York, won't you? Give my mother a call, will you? Just tell her . . ."

"What? That you got jungle rot the first time out and it's gone to your brain?"

"Just call her. Say I'm fine. That's all. She'll want to have you over for dinner, or take you to a good restaurant, something. Say you don't have time. But it'd mean a lot to her to have you call."

"Sure. Sure. Come on, we're moving."

They walked for two hours without making contact. The men were straggling along in two uneven columns at the sides of the road. The dirt road was covered with recent growth, no mines. The temperature was going to hit one hundred any second. Sweat and dirt mixed on faces, arms, muddy sweat trickled down shirts.

The concrete street was a glare now. Heat rose in patterns that shifted and vanished and rose again. Mildred Carey wondered if it hadn't been a mistake to rebuild the street, take out the maples and make it wide enough for the traffic that they predicted would be here in another year or two. She shrugged and walked more briskly toward the post office. That wasn't her affair. Her husband, who should know, said it was necessary for the town to grow. After being in road construction for twenty-five years, he should know. Fran Marple and Dodie Wilson waved to her from outside the coffee shop. Fran looked overdue and miserable. Last thing she needed was to go in the coffee shop and have pastry. Mildred Carey smiled at them and went on.

Claud Emerson was weighing a box for Bill Stokes. Bill leaned against the counter smoking, flicking ashes on the floor. "Don't like it here, get out, that's what I say. Goddam kids with their filthy clothes and dirty feet. Bet they had marijuana up there. Should have called the troopers, that's what I should have done."

"They was on state land, Bill. You had no call to run them off."

"They didn't know that. You think I'm going to let them plop themselves down right outside my front door? Let 'em find somewhere else to muck about."

Claud Emerson stamped the box. "One seventy-two."

Stilwell and Mike were following Laski, Berat, and Humboldt. Berat was talking.

"You let it stick out, see, and come at them with your M16 and you know what they watch! Man, they never seen nothing like it! Scared shitless by it. Tight! Whooee! Tight and hot!"

Stilwell looked as if he saw a green monster. Mike laughed and lit another cigarette. The sun was almost straight up when the lieutenant called for a break. He and Sergeant Durkins consulted a map and Humboldt swore at great length. "They've got us lost, the bastards. This fucken road ain't even on their fucken map."

Mildred Carey looked through the bills and advertising in her box, saving the letter from Mark for last. She always read them twice, once very quickly to be sure that he was all right, then again, word for word, pausing to pronounce the strange syllables aloud. She scanned the scrawled page, then replaced it in its envelope to be reread at home with coffee.

Bill Stokes's jeep roared outside the door, down the street to screech to a halt outside the feed store.

Mildred shook her head. "He's a mean man."

"Yep," Claud Emerson said. "Always was, always will be, I reckon. Wonder where them kids spent the night after he chased them."

Durkins sent out two scouts and the rest of them waited, cursing and sweating. A helicopter throbbed over them, drowned out their voices, vanished. The scouts returned.

Durkins stood up. "Okay. About four miles. The gooks are there, all right. Or will be again tonight. It's a free-fire zone, and our orders are to clean it out. Let's go."

Loud voices drifted across the street and they both looked toward the sound. "Old Dave's at it again," Claud Emerson said, frowning. "He'll have himself another heart attack, that's what."

"What good does arguing do anyway? Everybody around here knows what everybody else thinks and nobody ever changes. Just what good does it do?" She stuffed her mail into her purse. "Just have to do the best you can. Do what's right and hope for the best." She waved good-bye.

She still had to pick up cottage cheese and milk. "Maybe I'll try that new salami," she said to Peters. "Just six slices. Don't like to keep it more than a day. Just look at those tomatoes! Sixty-nine a pound! Mr. Peters, that's a disgrace!"

"Field-grown, Miz Carey. Up from Georgia. Shipping costs go up and up, you know." He sliced the salami carefully, medium thick.

A new tension was in them now and the minesweepers walked gingerly on the road carpeted with green sprouts. Stilwell coughed again and again, a meaningless bark of nervousness. Durkins sent him to the rear, then sent Mike back with him. "Keep an eye on the fucken bastard," he said. Mike nodded and waited for the rear to catch up with him. The two brothers from Alabama looked at him expressionlessly as they passed. They didn't mind the heat either, he thought, then spat. Stilwell looked sick.

"Is it a trap?" he asked later.

"Who the fuck knows?"

"Company C walked into an ambush, didn't they?"

"They fucked up."

Mildred Carey put her milk on the checkout counter alongside the cottage cheese. Her blue housedress was wet with perspiration under her arms and she could feel a spot of wetness on her back when her dress touched her skin. That Janice Samuels, she thought, catching a glimpse of the girl across the street, with those shorts and no bra, pretending she was dressing to be comfortable. Always asking about Mark. And him, asking about her in his letters.

"That's a dollar five," Peters said.

They halted again less than a mile from the village. The lieutenant called for the helicopters to give cover and to close off the area. Durkins sent men around the village to cover the road leading from it. There was no more they could do until the helicopters arrived. There were fields under cultivation off to the left.

"What if they're still there?" Stilwell asked, waiting.

"You heard Durkins. This is a free-fire zone. They'll be gone."

"But what if they haven't?"

"We clear the area."

Stilwell wasn't satisfied, but he didn't want to ask the questions. He didn't want to hear the answers. Mike looked at him with hatred. Stilwell turned away and stared into the bushes at the side of the road.

"Let's go."

There was a deafening beating roar overhead and Mildred Carey and Peters went to the door to look. A green-and-brown helicopter hovered over the street, then moved down toward the post office, casting a grotesque shadow on the white concrete. Two more of the monstrous machines came over, making talk impossible. There was another helicopter to the north; their throb was everywhere, as if the clear blue sky had loosened a rain of them.

From the feed-store entrance Bill Stokes shouted something lost in the din. He raced to his jeep and fumbled for something under the seat. He straightened up holding binoculars and started to move to the center of the street, looking through them down the highway. One of the helicopters dipped, banked, and turned, and there was a spray of gunfire. Bill Stokes fell, jerked several times, then lay still. Now others began to run in the street, pointing and shouting and screaming. O'Neal and his hired hand ran to Bill Stokes and tried to lift him. Fran Marple and Dodie Wilson had left the coffee shop, were standing outside the door; they turned and ran back inside. A truck rounded the corner at the far end of the street and again the helicopter fired; the truck careened out of control into cars parked outside the bank. One of the cars was propelled through the bank windows. The thunder of the helicopters swallowed the sound of the crash and the breaking glass and the screams of the people who ran from the bank, some of them bleeding, clutching their heads or arms. Katharine Ormsby got to the side of the street, collapsed there. She crawled several more feet, then sprawled out and was still.

Mildred Carey backed into the store, her hands over her mouth. Suddenly she vomited. Peters was still on the sidewalk. She tried to close the door, but he flung it open, pushing her toward the rear of the store.

"Soldiers!" Peters yelled. "Soldiers coming!"

They went in low, on the sides of the road, ready for the explosion of gunfire, or the sudden eruption of a claymore. The helicopters' noise filled the world as they took up positions. The village was small, a hamlet. It had not been evacuated. The word passed through the company: slopes. They were there. A man ran into the street holding what could have been a grenade, or a bomb, or anything. One of the helicopters fired on him. There was a second burst of fire down the road and a vehicle burned. Now the company was entering the village warily. Mike cursed the slopes for their stupidity in staying.

Home was all Mildred Carey could think of. She had to get home. She ran to the back of the store and out to the alley that the delivery trucks used. She ran all the way home and, panting, with a pain in her chest, she rushed frantically through the house pulling down shades, locking doors. Then she went upstairs where she could see the entire town. The soldiers were coming in crouched over, on both sides of the road, with their rifles out before them. She began to laugh suddenly; tears streaming, she ran downstairs again to fling open the door and shout.

"They're ours," she screamed toward the townspeople, laughing and crying all at once. "You fools, they're ours!"

Two of the khaki-clad GIs approached her, still pointing their guns at her. One of them said something, but she couldn't understand his words. "What are you doing here?" she cried. "You're American soldiers! What are you doing?"

The larger of the two grabbed her arm and twisted it behind her. She screamed and he pushed her toward the street. He spoke again, but the words were foreign to her. "I'm an American! For God's sake, this is America! What are you doing?" He hit her in the back with the rifle and she staggered and caught the fence to keep her balance. All down the street the people were being herded to the center of the highway. The soldier who had entered her house came out carrying her husband's hunting rifle, the shotgun, Mark's old .22. "Stop!" she shrieked at him. "Those are legal!" She was knocked down by the soldier behind her. He shouted at her and she opened her eyes to see him aiming the rifle at her head.

She scrambled to her feet and lurched forward to join the others in the street. She could taste blood and there was a stabbing pain in her jaw where teeth had been broken by her fall. A sergeant with a notebook was standing to one side. He kept making notations in it as more of the townspeople were forced from their houses and stores into the street.

Mike Donatti and Stilwell herded a raving old woman to the street; when she tried to grab a gun, Mike Donatti knocked her down and would have killed her then, but she was crying, obviously praying, and he simply motioned for her to join the others being rounded up.

The sun was high now, the heat relentless as the people were crowded closer together by each new addition. Some of the small children could be heard screaming even over the noise of the helicopters. Dodie Wilson ran past the crowd, naked from the waist down, naked and bleeding. A soldier caught her and he and another one carried her jerking and fighting into O'Neal's feed store. Her mouth was wide open in one long unheard scream. Old Dave ran toward the lieutenant, clutching at him, yelling at him in a high-pitched voice that it was the wrong town, damn fools, and other things that were lost. A smooth-faced boy hit him in the mouth, then again in the stomach, and when he fell moaning, he kicked him several times about the head. Then he shot him. Mildred Carey saw Janice Samuels being dragged by her wrists and she threw herself at the soldiers, who fought with her, their bodies hiding her from sight. They moved on, and she lay in a shining red pool that spread and spread. They tied Janice Samuels to the porch rail of Gordon's real-estate office, spread her legs open, and half a dozen men alternately raped and beat her. The sergeant yelled in the gibberish they spoke and the soldiers started to move the people as a lump toward the end of town.

Mike Donatti took up a post at the growing heap of weapons and watched the terrorized people. When the order came to move them out, he prodded and nudged, and when he had to, he clubbed them to make sure they moved as a unit. Some of them stumbled and fell, and if they didn't move again, they were shot where they lay.

The filthy Henry children were screaming for their mother. The biggest one, a girl with blond hair stringing down her back, darted away and ran down the empty street. The lieutenant motioned to the troops behind the group and after an appreciable pause there was a volley of shots and the child was lifted and for a moment flew. She rolled when she hit the ground again. Marjory Loomis threw herself down on top of her baby, and shots stilled both figures.

The people were driven to the edge of town, where the highway department had dug the ditch for a culvert that hadn't been laid yet. The sergeant closed his notebook and turned away. The firing started.

The men counted the weapons then, and searched the buildings methodically. Someone cut down a girl who had been tied to a rail. She fell in a heap. Fires were started. The lieutenant called for the helicopters to return to take them back to base camp.

Berat walked with his arm about Stilwell's shoulders, and they laughed a lot. Smoke from the fires began to spread horizontally, head high. Mike lighted another cigarette and thought about the cool green hills of Vermont and they waited to be picked up.

THE FUNERAL

No one could say exactly how old Madam Westfall was when she finally died. At least one hundred twenty, it was estimated. At the very least. For twenty years Madam Westfall had been a shell containing the very latest products of advances made in gerontology, and now she was dead. What lay on the viewing dais was merely a painted, funereally garbed husk.

"She isn't real," Carla said to herself. "It's a doll, or something. It isn't really Madam Westfall." She kept her head bowed, and didn't move her lips, but she said the words over and over. She was afraid to look at a dead person. *The second time they slaughtered all those who bore arms, unguided, mindless now, but lethal with the arms caches that they used indiscriminately.* Carla felt goose bumps along her arms and legs. She wondered if anyone else had been hearing the old Teacher's words.

The line moved slowly, all the girls in their long grey skirts had their heads bowed, their hands clasped. The only sound down the corridor was the sush-sush of slippers on plastic floor-ing, the occasional rustle of a skirt.

The viewing room had a pale green plastic floor, frosted-green plastic walls, and floor-to-ceiling windows that were now slits of brilliant light from a westering sun. All the furniture had been taken from the room, all the ornamentation. There were no flowers, nothing but the dais, and the bedlike box covered by a transparent shield. And the Teachers. Two at the dais, others between the light strips, at the doors. Their white hands clasped against black garb, heads bowed, hair slicked against each head, straight parts emphasizing bilateral symmetry. The Teachers didn't move, didn't look at the dais, at the girls parading past it.

Carla kept her head bowed, her chin tucked almost inside the V of her collarbone. The serpentine line moved steadily, very slowly. "She isn't real," Carla said to herself, desperately now.

She crossed the line that was the cue to raise her head; it felt too heavy to lift, her neck seemed paralyzed. When she did move, she heard a joint crack, and although her jaws suddenly ached, she couldn't relax.

The second green line. She turned her eyes to the right and looked at the incredibly shrunken, hardly human mummy. She felt her stomach lurch and for a moment she thought she was going to vomit. "She isn't real. It's a doll. She isn't real!" The third line. She bowed her head, pressed her chin hard against her collarbone, making it hurt. She couldn't swallow now, could hardly breathe. The line proceeded to the South Door and through it into the corridor.

She turned left at the South Door and, with her eyes downcast, started the walk back to her genetics class. She looked neither right nor left, but she could hear others moving in the same direction, slippers on plastic, the swish of a skirt, and when she passed by the door to the garden she heard laughter of some Ladies who had come to observe the viewing. She slowed down.

She felt the late sun hot on her skin at the open door and with a sideways glance, not moving her head, she looked quickly into the glaring greenery, but could not see them. Their laughter sounded like music as she went past the opening.

"That one, the one with the blue eyes and straw-colored hair. Stand up, girl."

Carla didn't move, didn't realize she was being addressed until a Teacher pulled her from her seat.

"Don't hurt her! Turn around, girl. Raise your skirts, higher. Look at me, child. Look up, let me see your face. . . ."

"She's too young for choosing," said the Teacher, examining Carla's bracelet. "Another year, Lady."

"A pity. She'll coarsen in a year's time. The fuzz is so soft right now, the flesh so tender. Oh, well . . ." She moved away, flicking a red skirt about her thighs, her red-clad legs narrowing to tiny ankles, flashing silver slippers with heels that were like icicles. She smelled . . . Carla didn't know any words to describe how she smelled. She drank in the fragrance hungrily.

"Look at me, child. Look up, let me see your face. . . ." The words sang through her mind over and over. At night, falling asleep, she thought of the face, drawing it up from the deep black, trying to hold it in focus: white skin, pink cheek ridges, silver eyelids, black lashes longer than she had known lashes could be, silver-pink lips, three silver spots—one at the corner of her left eye, another at the corner of her mouth, the third like a dimple in the satiny cheek. Silver hair that was loose, in waves about her face, that rippled with life of its own when she moved. If only she had been allowed to touch the hair, to run her finger over that cheek . . . The dream that began with the music of the Lady's laughter ended with the nightmare of her other words: "She'll coarsen in a year's time. . . ."

After that Carla had watched the changes take place on and within her body, and she understood what the Lady had meant. Her once smooth legs began to develop hair; it grew under her arms, and, most shameful, it sprouted as a dark, coarse bush under her belly. She wept. She tried to pull the hairs out, but it hurt too much, and made her skin sore and raw. Then she started to bleed, and she lay down and waited to die, and was happy that she would die. Instead, she was ordered to the infirmary and was forced to attend a lecture on feminine hygiene. She watched in stony-faced silence while the Doctor added the new information to her bracelet. The Doctor's face was smooth and pink, her eyebrows pale, her lashes so colorless and stubby that they were almost invisible. On her chin was a brown mole with two long hairs. She wore a straight blue-grey gown that hung from her shoulders to the floor. Her drab hair was pulled back tightly from her face, fastened in a hard bun at the back of her neck. Carla hated her. She hated the Teachers. Most of all she hated herself. She yearned for maturity.

Madam Westfall had written: "Maturity brings grace, beauty, wisdom, happiness. Immaturity means ugliness, unfinished beings with potential only, wholly dependent upon and subservient to the mature citizens."

There was a True-False quiz on the master screen in front of the classroom. Carla took her place quickly and touch-typed her ID number on the small screen of her machine.

She scanned the questions, and saw that they were all simple declarative statements of truth. Her stylus ran down the True column of her answer screen and it was done. She wondered why they were killing time like this, what they were waiting for. Madam Westfall's death had thrown everything off schedule.

Paperlike brown skin, wrinkled and hard, with lines crossing lines, vertical, horizontal, diagonal, leaving little islands of flesh, hardly enough to coat the bones. Cracked voice, incomprehensible: *they took away the music from the air . . . voices from the skies . . . erased pictures that move . . . boxes that sing and sob . . .* Crazy talk. And, . . . *only one left that knows. Only one.*

Madam Trudeau entered the classroom and Carla understood why the class had been personalized that period. The Teacher had been waiting for Madam Trudeau's appearance. The girls rose hurriedly. Madam Trudeau motioned for them to be seated once more.

"The following girls attended Madam Westfall during the past five years." She read a list. Carla's name was included on her list.

On finishing it, she asked, "Is there anyone who attended Madam Westfall whose name I did not read?"

There was a rustle from behind Carla. She kept her gaze fastened on Madam Trudeau. "Name?" the Teacher asked.

"Luella, Madam."

"You attended Madam Westfall? When?"

"Two years ago, Madam. I was a relief for Sonya, who became ill suddenly."

"Very well." Madam Trudeau added Luella's name to her list. "You will all report to my office at eight A.M. tomorrow morning. You will be excused from classes and duties at that time. Dismissed." With a bow she excused herself to the class Teacher and left the room.

Carla's legs twitched and ached. Her swim class was at eight each morning and she had missed it, had been sitting on the straight chair for almost two hours, when finally she was told to go into Madam Trudeau's office. None of the other waiting girls looked up when she rose and followed the attendant from the anteroom. Madam Trudeau was seated at an oversized desk that was completely bare, with a mirrorlike finish. Carla stood before it with her eyes downcast, and she could see Madam Trudeau's face reflected from the surface of the desk. Madam Trudeau was looking at a point over Carla's head, unaware that the girl was examining her features.

"You attended Madam Westfall altogether seven times during the past four years, is that correct?"

"I think it is, Madam."

"You aren't certain?"

"I . . . I don't remember, Madam."

"I see. Do you recall if Madam Westfall spoke to you during any of those times?"

"Yes, Madam."

"Carla, you are shaking. Are you frightened?"

"No, Madam."

"Look at me, Carla."

Carla's hands tightened, and she could feel her fingernails cutting into her hands. She thought of the pain, and stopped shaking. Madam Trudeau had pasty white skin, with peaked black eyebrows, sharp black eyes, black hair. Her mouth was wide and full, her nose long and narrow. As she studied the girl before her, it seemed to Carla that something changed in her expression, but she couldn't say what it was, or how it now differed from what it had been a moment earlier. A new intensity perhaps, a new interest.

"Carla, I've been looking over your records. Now that you are fourteen it is time to decide on your future. I shall propose your name for the Teachers' Academy on the completion of your current courses. As my protégée, you will quit the quarters you now occupy and attend me in my chambers. . . ." She narrowed her eyes, "What is the matter with you, girl? Are you ill?"

"No, Madam. I . . . I had hoped. I mean, I designated my choice last month. I thought . . ."

Madam Trudeau looked to the side of her desk where a records screen was lighted. She scanned the report, and her lips curled derisively. "A Lady. You would be a Lady!" Carla felt a blush fire her face, and suddenly her palms were wet with sweat. Madam Trudeau laughed, a sharp barking sound. She said, "The girls who attended Madam Westfall in life shall attend her in death. You will be on duty in the Viewing Room for two hours each day, and when the procession starts for the burial services in Scranton, you will be part of the entourage. Meanwhile, each day for an additional two hours immediately following your attendance in the Viewing Room you will meditate on the words of wisdom you have heard from Madam Westfall, and you will write down every word she ever spoke in your presence. For this purpose there will be placed a notebook and a pen in your cubicle, which you will use for no other reason. You will discuss this with no one except me. You, Carla, will prepare to move to my quarters immediately, where a learning cubicle will be awaiting you. Dismissed."

Her voice became sharper as she spoke, and when she finished the words were staccato. Carla bowed and turned to leave.

"Carla, you will find that there are certain rewards in being chosen as a Teacher."

Carla didn't know if she should turn and bow again, or stop where she was, or continue. When she hesitated, the voice came again, shorter, raspish. "Go. Return to your cubicle."

The first time, they slaughtered only the leaders, the rousers, . . . would be enough to defuse the bomb, leave the rest silent and powerless and malleable. . . .

Carla looked at the floor before her, trying to control the trembling in her legs. Madam Westfall hadn't moved, hadn't spoken. She was dead, gone. The only sound was the sush, sush of slippers. The green plastic floor was a glare that hurt her eyes. The air was heavy and smelled of death. Smelled the Lady, drank in the fragrance, longed to touch her. Pale, silvery-pink lips, soft, shiny, with two high peaks on the upper lip. The Lady stroked her face with fingers that were soft and cool and gentle. *. . . when their eyes become soft with unspeakable desires and their bodies show signs of womanhood, then let them have their duties chosen for them, some to bear the young for the society, some to become Teachers, some Nurses, Doctors, some to be taken as Lovers by the citizens, some to be . . .*

Carla couldn't control the sudden start that turned her head to look at the mummy. The room seemed to waver, then steadied again. The tremor in her legs became stronger, harder to stop. She pressed her knees together hard, hurting them where bone dug into flesh and skin. Fingers plucking at the coverlet. Plucking bones, brown bones with horny nails.

Water. Girl, give me water. Pretty pretty. You would have

been killed, you would have. Pretty. The last time they left no one over ten. No one at all. Ten to twenty-five.

Pretty. Carla said it to herself. Pretty. She visualized it as p-r-i-t-y. Pity with an r. Scanning the dictionary for p-r-i-t-y. Nothing. Pretty. *Afraid of shiny, pretty faces. Young, pretty faces.*

The trembling was all through Carla. Two hours. Eternity. She had stood here forever, would die here, unmoving, trembling, aching. A sigh and the sound of a body falling softly to the floor. Soft body crumbling so easily. Carla didn't turn her head. It must be Luella. So frightened of the mummy. She'd had nightmares every night since Madam Westfall's death. What made a body stay upright, when it fell so easily? Take it out, the thing that held it together, and down, down. Just to let go, to know what to take out and allow the body to fall like that into sleep. Teachers moved across her field of vision, two of them in their black gowns. Sush-sush. Returned with Luella, or someone, between them. No sound. Sush-sush.

The new learning cubicle was an exact duplicate of the old one. Cot, learning machine, chair, partitioned-off commode and washbasin. And new, the notebook and pen. Carla never had had a notebook and pen before. There was the stylus that was attached to the learning machine, and the lighted square in which to write, that then vanished into the machine. She turned the blank pages of the notebook, felt the paper between her fingers, tore a tiny corner off one of the back pages, examined it closely, the jagged edge, the texture of the fragment; she tasted it. She studied the pen just as minutely; it had a pointed, smooth end, and it wrote black. She made a line, stopped to admire it, and crossed it with another line. She wrote very slowly, "Carla," started to put down her number, the one on her bracelet, then stopped in confusion. She never had considered it before, but she had no last name, none that she knew. She drew three heavy lines over the two digits she had put down.

At the end of the two hours of meditation she had written her name a number of times, had filled three pages with it, in fact, and had written one of the things that she could remember hearing from the grey lips of Madam Westfall: "Non-citizens are the property of the state."

The next day the citizens started to file past the dais. Carla breathed deeply, trying to sniff the fragrance of the passing Ladies, but they were too distant. She watched their feet, clad in shoes of rainbow colors: pointed toes, stiletto heels; rounded toes, carved heels; satin, sequined slippers. . . . And just before her duty ended for the day, the Males started to enter the room.

She heard a gasp, Luella again. She didn't faint this time, merely gasped once. Carla saw the feet and legs at the same time and she looked up to see a male citizen. He was very tall and thick, and was dressed in the blue-and-white clothing of a Doctor of Law. He moved into the sunlight and there was a glitter from gold at his wrists and his neck, and the gleam of a smooth polished head. He turned past the dais and his eyes met Carla's. She felt herself go lightheaded and hurriedly she ducked her head and clenched her hands. She thought he was standing still, looking at her, and she could feel her heart thumping hard. Her relief arrived then and she crossed the room as fast as she could without appearing indecorous.

Carla wrote: "Why did he scare me so much? Why have I never seen a Male before? Why does everyone else wear colors while the girls and the Teachers wear black and grey?"

She drew a wavering line figure of a man, and stared at it, and then Xed it out. Then she looked at the sheet of paper with dismay. Now she had four ruined sheets of paper to dispose of.

Had she angered him by staring? Nervously she tapped on the paper and tried to remember what his face had been like. Had he been frowning? She couldn't remember. Why couldn't she think of anything to write for Madam Trudeau? She bit the end of the pen and then wrote slowly, very carefully: *"Society may dispose of its property as it chooses, following discussion with at least three members, and following permission which is not to be arbitrarily denied."*

Had Madam Westfall ever said that? She didn't know, but she had to write something, and that was the sort of thing that Madam Westfall had quoted at great length. She threw herself down on the cot and stared at the ceiling. For three days she had kept hearing the Madam's dead voice, but now when she needed to hear her again, nothing.

Sitting in the straight chair, alert for any change in the position of the ancient one, watchful, afraid of the old Teacher. Cramped, tired and sleepy. Half listening to mutterings, murmurings of exhaled and inhaled breaths that sounded like words that made no sense. . . . *Mama said hide child, hide don't move and Stevie wanted a razor for his birthday and Mama said you're too young, you're only nine and he said no Mama I'm thirteen don't you remember and Mama said hide child hide don't move at all and they came in hating pretty faces. . . .*

Carla sat up and picked up the pen again, then stopped. When she heard the words, they were so clear in her head, but as soon as they ended, they faded away. She wrote: "hating pretty faces . . . hide child . . . only nine." She stared at the words and drew a line through them.

Pretty faces. Madam Westfall had called her pretty, pretty.

The chimes for social hour were repeated three times and finally Carla opened the door of her cubicle and took a step into the anteroom, where the other protégées already had gathered. There were five. Carla didn't know any of them, but she had seen all of them from time to time in and around the school grounds. Madam Trudeau was sitting on a high-backed chair that was covered with black. She blended into it, so that only her hands and her face seemed apart from the chair, dead-white hands and face. Carla bowed to her and stood uncertainly at her own door.

"Come in, Carla. It is social hour. Relax. This is Wanda, Louise,

Stephanie, Mary, Dorothy." Each girl inclined her head slightly as her name was mentioned. Carla couldn't tell afterward which name went with which girl. Two of them wore the black-striped overskirt that meant they were in the Teachers' Academy. The other three still wore the grey of the lower school, as did Carla, with black bordering the hems.

"Carla doesn't want to be a Teacher," Madam Trudeau said dryly. "She prefers the paint box of a Lady." She smiled with her mouth only. One of the academy girls laughed. "Carla, you are not the first to envy the paint box and the bright clothes of the Ladies. I have something to show you. Wanda, the film."

The girl who had laughed touched a button on a small table, and on one of the walls a picture was projected. Carla caught her breath. It was a Lady, all gold and white, gold hair, gold eyelids, filmy white gown that ended just above her knees. She turned and smiled, holding out both hands, flashing jeweled fingers, long, gleaming nails that came to points. Then she reached up and took off her hair.

Carla felt that she would faint when the golden hair came off in the Lady's hands, leaving short, straight brown hair. She placed the gold hair on a ball, and then, one by one, stripped off the long gleaming nails, leaving her hands just hands, bony and ugly. The Lady peeled off her eyelashes and brows, and then patted a brown, thick coating of something on her face, and, with its removal, revealed pale skin with wrinkles about her eyes, with hard, deep lines beside her nose down to her mouth that had also changed, had become small and mean. Carla wanted to shut her eyes, turn away, and go back to her cubicle, but she didn't dare move. She could feel Madam Trudeau's stare, and the gaze seemed to burn.

The Lady took off the swirling gown, and under it was a garment Carla never had seen before that covered her from her breasts to her thighs. The stubby fingers worked at fasteners, and finally got the garment off, and there was her stomach, bigger, bulging, with cruel red lines where the garment had pinched and squeezed her. Her breasts drooped almost to her waist. Carla couldn't stop her eyes, couldn't make them not see, couldn't make herself not look at the rest of the repulsive body.

Madam Trudeau stood up and went to her door. "Show Carla the other two films." She looked at Carla then and said, "I order you to watch. I shall quiz you on the contents." She left the room.

The other two films showed the same Lady at work. First with a protégée, then with a male citizen. When they were over Carla stumbled back to her cubicle and vomited repeatedly until she was exhausted. She had nightmares that night.

How many days, she wondered, have I been here now? She no longer trembled, but became detached almost as soon as she took her place between two of the tall windows. She didn't try to catch a whiff of the fragrance of the Ladies, or try to get a glimpse of the Males. She had chosen one particular spot in the floor on which to concentrate, and she didn't shift her gaze from it.

They were old and full of hate, and they said, let us remake them in our image, and they did.

Madam Trudeau hated her, despised her. Old and full of hate . . .

"Why were you not chosen to become a Woman to bear young?"

"I am not fit, Madam. I am weak and timid."

"Look at your hips, thin, like a Male's hips. And your breasts, small and hard." Madam Trudeau turned away in disgust. "Why were you not chosen to become a Professional, a Doctor, or a Technician?"

"I am not intelligent enough, Madam. I require many hours of study to grasp the mathematics."

"So. Weak, frail, not too bright. Why do you weep?"

"I don't know, Madam. I am sorry."

"Go to your cubicle. You disgust me."

Staring at a flaw in the floor, a place where an indentation distorted the light, creating one very small oval shadow, wondering when the ordeal would end, wondering why she couldn't fill the notebok with the many things that Madam Westfall had said, things that she could remember here, and could not remember when she was in her cubicle with pen poised over the notebook.

Sometimes Carla forgot where she was, found herself in the chamber of Madam Westfall, watching the ancient one struggle to stay alive, forcing breaths in and out, refusing to admit death. Watching the incomprehensible dials and tubes and bottles of fluids with lowering levels, watching needles that vanished into flesh, tubes that disappeared under the bedclothes, that seemed to writhe now and again with a secret life, listening to the mumbling voice, the groans and sighs, the meaningless words.

Three times they rose against the children and three times slew them until there were none left none at all because the contagion had spread and all over ten were infected and carried radios. . . .

Radios? A disease? Infected with radios, spreading it among young people?

And Mama said hide child hide and don't move and put this in the cave too and don't touch it.

Carla's relief came and numbly she walked from the Viewing Room. She watched the movement of the black border of her skirt as she walked and it seemed that the blackness crept up her legs, enveloped her middle, climbed her front until it reached her neck, and then it strangled her. She clamped her jaws hard and continued to walk her measured pace.

The girls who had attended Madam Westfall in life were on duty throughout the school ceremonies after the viewing. They were required to stand in a line behind the dais. There were eulogies to the patience and firmness of the first Teacher. Eulogies to her wisdom in setting up the rules of the school. Carla tried to keep her attention on the speakers, but she was so tired and drowsy that she heard only snatches. Then she was jolted into awareness. Madam Trudeau was talking.

". . . a book that will be the guide to all future Teachers, showing them the way through personal tribulations and trials to achieve the serenity that was Madam Westfall's. I am honored by this privilege, in choosing me and my apprentices to accomplish this end. . . ."

Carla thought of the gibberish that she had been putting down in her notebook and she blinked back tears of shame. Madam Trudeau should have told them why she wanted the information. She would have to go back over it and destroy all the nonsense that she had written down.

Late that afternoon the entourage formed that would accompany Madam Westfall to her final ceremony in Scranton, her native city, where her burial would return her to her family.

Madam Trudeau had an interview with Carla before departure. "You will be in charge of the other girls," she said. "I expect you to maintain order. You will report any disturbance, or any infringement of rules, immediately, and if that is not possible, if I am occupied, you will personally impose order in my name."

"Yes, Madam."

"Very well. During the journey the girls will travel together in a compartment of the tube. Talking will be permitted, but no laughter, no childish play. When we arrive at the Scranton home, you will be given rooms with cots. Again you will all comport yourselves with the dignity of the office which you are ordered to fulfill at this time."

Carla felt excitement mount within her as the girls lined up to take their places along the sides of the casket. They went with it to a closed limousine, where they sat knee to knee, unspeaking, hot, to be taken over smooth highways for an hour to the tube. Madam Westfall had refused to fly in life, and was granted the same rights in death, so her body was to be transported from

Wilmington to Scranton by the rocket tube. As soon as the girls had accompanied the casket to its car, and were directed to their own compartment, their voices raised in a babble. It was the first time any of them had left the school grounds since entering them at the age of five.

Ruthie was going to work in the infants' wards, and she turned faintly pink and soft-looking when she talked about it. Luella was a music apprentice already, having shown skill on the piano at an early age. Lorette preened herself slightly and announced that she had been chosen as a Lover by a gentleman. She would become a Lady one day. Carla stared at her curiously, wondering at her pleased look, wondering if she had not been shown the films yet. Lorette was blue-eyed, with pale hair, much the same build as Carla. Looking at her, Carla could imagine her in soft dresses, with her mouth painted, her hair covered by the other hair that was cloud-soft and shiny. . . . She looked at the girl's cheeks flushed with excitement at the thought of her future, and she knew that with or without the paint box, Lorette would be a Lady whose skin would be smooth, whose mouth would be soft. . . .

"The fuzz is so soft now, the flesh so tender." She remembered the scent, the softness of the Lady's hands, the way her skirt moved about her red-clad thighs.

She bit her lip. But she didn't want to be a Lady. She couldn't ever think of them again without loathing and disgust. She was chosen to be a Teacher.

They said it is the duty of society to prepare its non-citizens for citzenship but it is recognized that there are those who will not meet the requirements and society itself is not to be blamed for those occasional failures that must accrue.

She took out her notebook and wrote the words in it.

"Did you just remember something else she said?" Lisa asked. She was the youngest of the girls, only ten, and had attended Madam Westfall one time. She seemed to be very tired.

Carla looked over what she had written, and then read it aloud.

"It's from the school rules book," she said. "Maybe changed a little, but the same meaning. You'll study it in a year or two."

Lisa nodded. "You know what she said to me? She said I should go hide in the cave, and never lose my birth certificate. She said I should never tell anyone where the radio is." She frowned. "Do you know what a cave is? And a radio?"

"You wrote it down, didn't you? In the notebook?"

Lisa ducked her head. "I forgot again. I remembered it once and then forgot again until now." She searched through her cloth travel bag for her notebook and when she didn't find it, she dumped the contents on the floor to search more carefully. The notebook was not there.

"Lisa, when did you have it last?"

"I don't know. A few days ago. I don't remember."

"When Madam Trudeau talked to you the last time, did you have it then?"

"No. I couldn't find it. She said if I didn't have it the next time I was called for an interview, she'd whip me. But I can't find it!" She broke into tears and threw herself down on her small heap of belongings. She beat her fists on them and sobbed. "She's going to whip me and I can't find it. I can't. It's gone."

Carla stared at her. She shook her head. "Lisa, stop that crying. You couldn't have lost it. Where? There's no place to lose it. You didn't take it from your cubicle, did you?"

The girl sobbed louder. "No. No. No. I don't know where it is."

Carla knelt by her and pulled the child up from the floor to a squatting position. "Lisa, what did you put in the notebook? Did you play with it?"

Lisa turned chalky white and her eyes became very large, then she closed them, no longer weeping.

"So you used it for other things? Is that it? What sort of things?"

Lisa shook her head. "I don't know. Just things."

"All of it? The whole notebook?"

"I couldn't help it. I didn't know what to write down. Madam Westfall said too much. I couldn't write it all. She wanted to touch me and I was afraid of her and I hid under the chair and she kept calling me, 'Child, come here, don't hide, I'm not one of them. Go to the cave and take it with you.' And she kept reaching for me with her hands. I . . . They were like chicken claws. She would have ripped me apart with them. She hated me. She said she hated me. She said I should have been killed with the others, why wasn't I killed with the others."

Carla, her hands hard on the child's shoulders, turned away from the fear and despair she saw on the girl's face.

Ruthie pushed past her and hugged the child. "Hush, hush, Lisa. Don't cry now. Hush. There, there."

Carla stood up and backed away. "Lisa, what sort of things did you put in the notebook?"

"Just things that I like. Snowflakes and flowers and designs."

"All right. Pick up your belongings and sit down. We must be nearly there. It seems like the tube is stopping."

Again they were shown from a closed compartment to a closed limousine and whisked over countryside that remained invisible to them. There was a drizzly rain falling when they stopped and got out of the car.

The Westfall house was a three-storied, pseudo-Victorian wooden building, with balconies and cupolas, and many chimneys. There was scaffolding about it, and one of the three porches had been torn away and was being replaced as restoration of the house, turning it into a national monument, progressed. The girls accompanied the casket to a gloomy, large room where the air was chilly and damp, and scant lighting cast deep shadows. After the casket had been positioned on the dais which also had accompanied it, the girls followed Madam Trudeau through narrow corridors, up narrow steps, to the third floor where two large rooms had been prepared for them, each containing seven cots.

Madam Trudeau showed them the bathroom that would serve their needs, told them goodnight, and motioned Carla to follow her. They descended the stairs to a second-floor room that had black, massive furniture: a desk, two straight chairs, a bureau with a wavery mirror over it, and a large canopied bed.

Madam Trudeau paced the black floor silently for several minutes without speaking, then she swung around and said, "Carla, I heard every word that silly little girl said this afternoon. She drew pictures in her notebook! This is the third time the word cave has come up in reports of Madam Westfall's mutterings. Did she speak to you of caves?"

Carla's mind was whirling. How had she heard what they had said? Did maturity also bestow magical abilities? She said, "Yes, Madam, she spoke of hiding in a cave."

"Where is the cave, Carla? Where is it?"

"I don't know, Madam. She didn't say."

Madam Trudeau started to pace once more. Her pale face was drawn in lines of concentration that carved deeply into her flesh, two furrows straight up from the inner brows, other lines at the sides of her nose, straight to her chin, her mouth tight and hard. Suddenly she sat down and leaned back in the chair. "Carla, in the last four or five years Madam Westfall became childishly senile; she was no longer living in the present most of the time, but was reliving incidents in her past. Do you understand what I mean?"

Carla nodded, then said hastily, "Yes, Madam."

"Yes. Well, it doesn't matter. You know that I have been commissioned to write the biography of Madam Westfall, to immortalize her writings and her utterances. But there is a gap, Carla. A large gap in our knowledge, and until recently it seemed that the gap never would be filled in. When Madam Westfall was found as a child, wandering in a dazed condition, undernourished, almost dead from exposure, she did not know who she was, where she was from, anything about her past at all.

Someone had put an identification bracelet on her arm, a steel bracelet that she could not remove, and that was the only clue there was about her origins. For ten years she received the best medical care and education available, and her intellect sparkled brilliantly, but she never regained her memory."

Madam Trudeau shifted to look at Carla. A trick of the lighting made her eyes glitter like jewels. "You have studied how she started her first school with eight students, and over the next century developed her teaching methods to the point of perfection that we now employ throughout the nation, in the Males' school as well as the Females'. Through her efforts Teachers have become the most respected of all citizens and the schools the most powerful of all institutions." A mirthless smile crossed her face, gone almost as quickly as it formed, leaving the deep shadows, lines, and the glittering eyes. "I honored you more than you yet realize when I chose you for my protégée."

The air in the room was too close and dank, smelled of moldering wood and unopened places. Carla continued to watch Madam Trudeau, but she was feeling lightheaded and exhausted and the words seemed interminable to her. The glittering eyes held her gaze and she said nothing. The thought occurred to her that Madam Trudeau would take Madam Westfall's place as head of the school now.

"Encourage the girls to talk, Carla. Let them go on as much as they want about what Madam Westfall said, lead them into it if they stray from the point. Written reports have been sadly deficient." She stopped and looked questioningly at the girl. "Yes? What is it?"

"Then . . . I mean after they talk, are they to write . . . ? Or should I try to remember and write it all down?"

"There will be no need for that," Madam Trudeau said. "Simply let them talk as much as they want."

"Yes, Madam."

"Very well. Here is a schedule for the coming days. Two girls on duty in the Viewing Room at all times from dawn until dark, yard exercise in the enclosed garden behind the building if the weather permits, kitchen duty, and so on. Study it, and direct the girls to their duties. On Saturday afternoon everyone will attend the burial, and on Sunday we return to the school. Now go."

Carla bowed, and turned to leave. Madam Trudeau's voice stopped her once more. "Wait, Carla. Come here. You may brush my hair before you leave."

Carla took the brush in numb fingers and walked obediently behind Madam Trudeau, who was loosening hair clasps that restrained her heavy black hair. It fell down her back like a dead snake, uncoiling slowly. Carla started to brush it.

"Harder, girl. Are you so weak that you can't brush hair?"

She plied the brush harder until her arm became heavy and then Madam Trudeau said, "Enough. You are a clumsy girl, awkward and stupid. Must I teach you everything, even how to brush one's hair properly?" She yanked the brush from Carla's hand and now there were two spots of color on her cheeks and her eyes were flashing. "Get out. Go! Leave me! On Saturday immediately following the funeral you will administer punishment to Lisa for scribbling in her notebook. Afterward report to me. And now get out of here!"

Carla snatched up the schedule and backed across the room, terrified of the Teacher who seemed demoniacal suddenly. She bumped into the other chair and nearly fell down. Madam Trudeau laughed shortly and cried, "Clumsy, awkward! You would be a Lady! You?"

Carla groped behind her for the doorknob and finally escaped into the hallway, where she leaned against the wall, trembling too hard to move on. Something crashed into the door behind her and she stifled a scream and ran. The brush. Madam had thrown the brush against the door.

Madam Westfall's ghost roamed all night, chasing shadows in and out of rooms, making the floors creak with her passage, echoes of her voice drifting in and out of the dorm where Carla tossed restlessly. Twice she sat upright in fear, listening intently, not knowing why. Once Lisa cried out and she went to her and held her hand until the child quieted again. When dawn lighted the room Carla was awake and standing at the windows looking at the ring of mountains that encircled the city. Black shadows against the lesser black of the sky, they darkened, and suddenly caught fire from the sun striking their tips. The fire spread downward, went out, and became merely light on the leaves that were turning red and gold. Carla turned from the view, unable to explain the pain that filled her. She awakened the first two girls who were to be on duty with Madam Westfall and after their quiet departure, returned to the window. The sun was all the way up now, but its morning light was soft; there were no hard outlines anywhere. The trees were a blend of colors with no individual boundaries, and rocks and earth melted together and were one. Birds were singing with the desperation of summer's end and winter's approach.

"Carla?" Lisa touched her arm and looked up at her with wide, fearful eyes. "Is she going to whip me?"

"You will be punished after the funeral," Carla said, stiffly. "And I should report you for touching me, you know."

The child drew back, looking down at the black border on Carla's skirt. "I forgot." She hung her head. "I'm . . . I'm so scared."

"It's time for breakfast, and after that we'll have a walk in the gardens. You'll feel better after you get out in the sunshine and fresh air."

"Chrysanthemums, dahlias, marigolds. No, the small ones there, with the brown fringes . . ." Luella pointed out the various flowers to the other girls. Carla walked in the rear, hardly listening, trying to keep her eye on Lisa, who also trailed behind. She was worried about the child. Lisa had not slept well, had eaten no breakfast, and was so pale and wan that she didn't look strong enough to take the short garden walk with them.

Eminent personages came and went in the gloomy old house and huddled together to speak in lowered voices. Carla paid little attention to them. "I can change it after I have some authority," she said to a still inner self who listened and made no reply. "What can I do now? I'm property. I belong to the state, to Madam Trudeau and the school. What good if I disobey and am also whipped? Would that help any? I won't hit her hard." The inner self said nothing, but she thought she could hear a mocking laugh come from the mummy that was being honored.

They had all those empty schools, miles and miles of school halls where no feet walked, desks where no students sat, books that no students scribbled up, and they put the children in them and they could see immediately who couldn't keep up, couldn't learn the new ways, and they got rid of them. Smart. Smart of them. They were smart and had the goods and the money and the hatred. My God, they hated. That's who wins, who hates most. And is more afraid. Every time.

Carla forced her arms not to move, her hands to remain locked before her, forced her head to stay bowed. The voice now went on and on and she couldn't get away from it.

. . . rained every day, cold freezing rain and Daddy didn't come back and Mama said, hide child, hide in the cave where it's warm, and don't move no matter what happens, don't move. Let me put it on your arm, don't take it off, never take it off show it to them if they find you show them make them look. . . .

Her relief came and Carla left. In the wide hallway that led to the back steps she was stopped by a rough hand on her arm. "Damme, here's a likely one. Come here, girl. Let's have a look at you." She was spun around and the hand grasped her chin and lifted her head. "Did I say it! I could spot her all the way down the hall, now couldn't I? Can't hide what she's got with long skirts and that skinny hairdo, now can you? Didn't I spot her!" He laughed and turned Carla's head to the side and looked at her in profile, then laughed even louder.

She could see only that he was red-faced, with bushy eyebrows and thick grey hair. His hand holding her chin hurt, digging into her jaws at each side of her neck.

"Victor, turn her loose," the cool voice of a female said then. "She's been chosen already. An apprentice Teacher."

He pushed Carla from him, still holding her chin, and he looked down at the skirts with the broad black band at the bottom. He gave her a shove that sent her into the opposite wall. She clutched at it for support.

"Whose pet is she?" he said darkly.

"Trudeau's."

He turned and stamped away, not looking at Carla again. He wore the blue and white of a Doctor of Law. The female was a Lady in pink and black.

"Carla. Go upstairs." Madam Trudeau moved from an open doorway and stood before Carla. She looked up and down the shaking girl. "Now do you understand why I apprenticed you before this trip? For your own protection."

They walked to the cemetery on Saturday, a bright, warm day with golden light and the odor of burning leaves. Speeches were made, Madam Westfall's favorite music was played, and the services ended. Carla dreaded returning to the dormitory. She kept a close watch on Lisa, who seemed but a shadow of herself. Three times during the night she had held the girl until her nightmares subsided, and each time she had stroked her fine hair and soft cheeks and murmured to her quieting words, and she knew it was only her own cowardice that prevented her saying that it was she who would administer the whipping. The first shovelful of earth was thrown on top of the casket and everyone turned to leave the place, when suddenly the air was filled with raucous laughter, obscene chants, and wild music. It ended almost as quickly as it started, but the group was frozen until the mountain air became unnaturally still. Not even the birds were making a sound following the maniacal outburst.

Carla had been unable to stop the involuntary look that she

cast about her at the woods that circled the cemetery. Who? Who would dare? Only a leaf or two stirred, floating downward on the gentle air effortlessly. Far in the distance a bird began to sing again, as if the evil spirits that had flown past were now gone.

"Madam Trudeau sent this up for you," Luella said nervously, handing Carla the rod. It was plastic, three feet long, thin, flexible. Carla looked at it and turned slowly to Lisa. The girl seemed to be swaying back and forth.

"I am to administer the whipping," Carla said. "You will undress now."

Lisa stared at her in disbelief, and then suddenly she ran across the room and threw herself on Carla, hugging her hard, sobbing. "Thank you, Carla. Thank you so much. I was so afraid, you don't know how afraid. Thank you. How did you make her let you do it? Will you be punished too? I love you so much, Carla." She was incoherent in her relief and she flung off her gown and underwear and turned around.

Her skin was pale and soft, rounded buttocks, dimpled just above the fullness. She had no waist yet, no breasts, no hair on her baby body. Like a baby she had whimpered in the night, clinging tightly to Carla, burying her head in the curve of Carla's breasts.

Carla raised the rod and brought it down, as easily as she could. Anything was too hard. There was a red welt. The girl bowed her head lower, but didn't whimper. She was holding the back of a chair and it jerked when the rod struck.

It would be worse if Madam Trudeau was doing it, Carla thought. She would try to hurt, would draw blood. Why? Why? The rod was hanging limply, and she knew it would be harder on both of them if she didn't finish it quickly. She raised it and again felt the rod bite into flesh, sending the vibration into her arm, through her body.

Again. The girl cried out, and a spot of blood appeared on her back. Carla stared at it in fascination and despair. She couldn't help it. Her arm wielded the rod too hard, and she couldn't help it. She closed her eyes a moment, raised the rod and struck again. Better. But the vibrations that had begun with the first blow increased, and she felt dizzy, and couldn't keep her eyes off the spot of blood that was trailing down the girl's back. Lisa was weeping now, her body was shaking. Carla felt a responsive tremor start within her.

Eight, nine. The excitement that stirred her was unnameable, unknowable, never before felt like this. Suddenly she thought of the Lady who had chosen her once, and scenes of the film she had been forced to watch flashed through her mind. . . . *remake them in our image.* She looked about in that moment frozen in time, and she saw the excitement on some of the faces, on others fear, disgust and revulsion. Her gaze stopped on Helga, who had her eyes closed, whose body was moving rhythmically. She raised the rod and brought it down as hard as she could, hitting the chair with a noise that brought everyone out of his own kind of trance. A sharp, cracking noise that was a finish.

"Ten!" she cried and threw the rod across the room.

Lisa turned and through brimming eyes, red, swollen, ugly with crying, said, "Thank you, Carla. It wasn't so bad."

Looking at her, Carla knew hatred. It burned through her, distorted the image of what she saw. Inside her body the excitement found no outlet, and it flushed her face, made her hands numb, and filled her with hatred. She turned and fled.

Before Madam Trudeau's door, she stopped a moment, took a deep breath, and knocked. After several moments the door opened and Madam Trudeau came out. Her eyes were glittering more than ever, and there were two spots of color on her pasty cheeks.

"It is done? Let me look at you." Her fingers were cold and moist when she lifted Carla's chin. "Yes, I see. I see. I am busy now. Come back in half an hour. You will tell me all about it. Half an hour." Carla never had seen a genuine smile on the

Teacher's face before, and now when it came, it was more frightening than her frown was. Carla didn't move, but she felt as if every cell in her body had tried to pull back.

She bowed and turned to leave. Madam Trudeau followed her a step and said in a low vibrant voice, "You felt it, didn't you? You know now, don't you?"

"Madam Trudeau, are you coming back?" The door behind her opened, and one of the Doctors of Law appeared there.

"Yes, of course." She turned and went back to the room.

Carla let herself into the small enclosed area between the second and third floors, then stopped. She could hear the voices of girls coming down the stairs, going on duty in the kitchen, or outside for evening exercises. She stopped to wait for them to pass, and she leaned against the wall tiredly. This space was two and a half feet square perhaps. It was very dank and hot. From here she could hear every sound made by the girls on the stairs. Probably that was why the second door had been added, to muffle the noise of those going up and down. The girls had stopped on the steps and were discussing the laughter and obscenities they had heard in the cemetery.

Carla knew that it was her duty to confront them, to order them to their duties, to impose proper silence on them in public places, but she closed her eyes and pressed her hand hard on the wood behind her for support and wished they would finish their childish prattle and go on. The wood behind her started to slide.

She jerked away. A sliding door? She felt it and ran her finger along the smooth paneling to the edge where there was now a six-inch opening as high as she could reach and down to the floor. She pushed the door again and it slid easily, going between the two walls. When the opening was wide enough she stepped through it. The cave! She knew it was the cave that Madam Westfall had talked about incessantly.

The space was no more than two feet wide, and very dark. She felt the inside door and there was a knob on it, low enough for children to reach. The door slid as smoothly from the inside as it had from the outside. She slid it almost closed and the voices were cut off, but she could hear other voices, from the room on the other side of the passage. They were not clear. She felt her way farther, and almost fell over a box. She held her breath as she realized that she was hearing Madam Trudeau's voice:

". . . be there. Too many independent reports of the old fool's babbling about it for there not to be something to it. Your men are incompetent."

"Trudeau, shut up. You scare the living hell out of the kids, but you don't scare me. Just shut up and accept the report. We've been over every inch of the hills for miles, and there's no cave. It was over a hundred years ago. Maybe there was one that the kids played in, but it's gone now. Probably collapsed."

"We have to be certain, absolutely certain."

"What's so important about it anyway? Maybe if you would give us more to go on we could make more progress."

"The reports state that when the militia came here, they found only Martha Westfall. They executed her on the spot without questioning her first. Fools! When they searched the house, they discovered that it was stripped. No jewels, no silver, diaries, papers. Nothing. Steve Westfall was dead. Dr. Westfall dead. Martha. No one has ever found the articles that were hidden, and when the child again appeared, she had true amnesia that never yielded to attempts to penetrate it."

"So, a few records, diaries. What are they to you?" There was silence, then he laughed. "The money! He took all his money out of the bank, didn't he?"

"Don't be ridiculous. I want records, that's all. There's a complete ham radio, complete. Dr. Westfall was an electronics engineer as well as a teacher. No one could begin to guess how much equipment he hid before he was killed."

Carla ran her hand over the box, felt behind it. More boxes.

"Yeah yeah. I read the reports, too. All the more reason to

keep the search nearby. For a year before the end a close watch was kept on the house. They had to walk to wherever they hid the stuff. And I can just say again that there's no cave around here. It fell in."

"I hope so," Madam Trudeau said.

Someone knocked on the door, and Madam Trudeau called, "Come in."

"Yes, what is it? Speak up, girl."

"It is my duty to report, Madam, that Carla did not administer the full punishment ordered by you."

Carla's fists clenched hard. Helga.

"Explain," Madam Trudeau said sharply.

"She only struck Lisa nine times, Madam. The last time she hit the chair."

"I see. Return to your room."

The man laughed when the girl closed the door once more. "Carla is the golden one, Trudeau? The one who wears a single black band?"

"The one you manhandled earlier, yes."

"Insubordination in the ranks, Trudeau? Tut, tut. And your reports all state that you never have any rebellion. Never."

Very slowly Madam Trudeau said, "I have never had a student who didn't abandon any thoughts of rebellion under my guidance. Carla will be obedient. And one day she will be an excellent Teacher. I know the signs."

Carla stood before the Teacher with her head bowed and her hands clasped together. Madam Trudeau walked around her without touching her, then sat down and said, "You will whip Lisa every day for a week, beginning tomorrow."

Carla didn't reply.

"Don't stand mute before me, Carla. Signify your obedience immediately."

"I . . . I can't, Madam."

"Carla, any day that you do not whip Lisa, I will. And I will also whip you double her allotment. Do you understand?"

"Yes, Madam."

"You will inform Lisa that she is to be whipped every day, by one or the other of us. Immediately."

"Madam, please . . ."

"You speak out of turn, Carla!"

"I . . . Madam, please don't do this. Don't make me do this. She is too weak. . . ."

"She will beg you to do it, won't she, Carla? Beg you with tears flowing to be the one, not me. And you will feel the excitement and the hate and every day you will feel it grow strong. You will want to hurt her, want to see blood spot her bare back. And your hate will grow until you won't be able to look at her without being blinded by your own hatred. You see, I know, Carla. I know all of it."

Carla stared at her in horror. "I won't do it. I won't."

"I will."

They were old and full of hatred for the shiny young faces, the bright hair, the straight backs and strong legs and arms. They said: let us remake them in our image and they did.

Carla repeated Madam Trudeau's words to the girls gathered in the two sleeping rooms on the third floor. Lisa swayed and was supported by Ruthie. Helga smiled.

That evening Ruthie tried to run away and was caught by two of the blue-clad Males. The girls were lined up and watched as Ruthie was stoned. They buried her without a service on the hill where she had been caught.

After dark, lying on the cot open-eyed, tense, Carla heard Lisa's whisper close to her ear. "I don't care if you hit me, Carla. It won't hurt like it does when she hits me."

"Go to bed, Lisa. Go to sleep."

"I can't sleep. I keep seeing Ruthie. I should have gone with her. I wanted to, but she wouldn't let me. She was afraid there would be Males on the hill watching. She said if she didn't get caught, then I should try to follow her at night." The child's voice was flat, as if shock had dulled her sensibilities.

Carla kept seeing Ruthie too. Over and over she repeated to herself: I should have tried it. I'm cleverer than she was. I might have escaped. I should have been the one. She knew it was too late now. They would be watching too closely.

An eternity later she crept from her bed and dressed quietly. Soundlessly she gathered her own belongings, and then collected the notebooks of the other girls, and the pens, and she left the room. There were dim lights on throughout the house as she made her way silently down stairs and through corridors. She left a pen by one of the outside doors, and very cautiously made her way back to the tiny space between the floors. She slid the door open and deposited everything else she carried inside the cave. She tried to get to the kitchen for food, but stopped when she saw one of the Officers of Law. She returned soundlessly to the attic rooms and tiptoed among the beds to Lisa's cot. She placed one hand over the girl's mouth and shook her awake with the other.

Lisa bolted upright, terrified, her body stiffened convulsively. With her mouth against the girl's ear Carla whispered, "Don't make a sound. Come on." She half led, half carried the girl to the doorway, down the stairs, and into the cave and closed the door.

"You can't talk here, either," she whispered. "They can hear." She spread out the extra garments she had collected and they lay down together, her arms tight about the girl's shoulders. "Try to sleep," she whispered. "I don't think they'll find us here. And after they leave, we'll creep out and live in the woods. We'll eat nuts and berries. . . ."

The first day they were jubilant at their success and they giggled and muffled the noise with their skirts. They could hear all the orders being issued by Madam Trudeau: guards in all the halls, on the stairs, at the door to the dorm to keep other girls from trying to escape also. They could hear all the interrogations, of the girls, the guards who had not seen the escapees. They heard the mocking voice of the Doctor of Law deriding Madam Trudeau's boasts of absolute control.

The second day Carla tried to steal food for them, and, more important, water. There were blue-clad Males everywhere. She returned emptyhanded. During the night Lisa whimpered in her sleep and Carla had to stay awake to quiet the child, who was slightly feverish.

"You won't let her get me, will you?" she begged over and over.

The third day Lisa became too quiet. She didn't want Carla to move from her side at all. She held Carla's hand in her hot, dry hand and now and then tried to raise it to her face, but she was too weak now. Carla stroked her forehead.

When the child slept Carla wrote in the notebooks, in the dark, not knowing if she wrote over other words or on blank pages. She wrote her life story, and then made up other things to say. She wrote her name over and over, and wept because she had no last name. She wrote nonsense words and rhymed them with other nonsense words. She wrote of the savages who had laughed at the funeral and she hoped they wouldn't all die over the winter months. She thought that probably they would. She wrote of the golden light through green-black pine trees and of birds' songs and moss underfoot. She wrote of Lisa lying peacefully now at the far end of the cave amidst riches that neither of them could ever have comprehended. When she could no longer write, she drifted in and out of the golden light in the forest, listening to the birds' songs, hearing the raucous laughter that now sounded so beautiful.